Acclaim for Denise Nicholas a

"A first-time novelist best known as a television actress . . . Nicholas rises to [the challenge of writing about the civil rights movement] better than most literary veterans. While she comes to the book with her [own] memories . . . she has delivered something infinitely richer and more artistically satisfying than a veiled memoir. She has found the human complexity within the over-arching passion play. . . . It is impossible to praise *Freshwater Road* too much."

— *Washington Post*

"This magnificent work . . . was unconsciously overlooked by many book-review sections. It deserves not only accolades, but a large, avid readership."

— *Newsday,* Best of 2005 Roundup

"Denise Nicholas brings alive all the colors and emotions of the civil rights movement during the perilous adventure that was Freedom Summer."

— Janet Fitch, author of *White Oleander*

"A sensitive and absorbing story of a young woman coming of age emotionally and racially."

— *Booklist*

"A finely realized and written novel."

— *Detroit Free Press*

"Extraordinary. . . . Impassioned prose, full-blooded characters, and rich feeling."

— *PAGES*

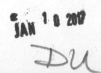

"Accomplished. . . . Nicholas appears poised to have an equally successful second career as a novelist."

— *Chicago Reader*

"Vivid, intricate and powerful; a book that will make you squirm with discomfort and dread, breathe with relief, then gasp with outrage. The characters in this book are so real and the events of that Mississippi summer are so well-described that I almost felt like I was reading a history book instead of a novel. Pick up a copy of this incredible book. If you ask me what one novel to read this winter, 'Freshwater Road' gets my vote."

—Terri Schlichenmeyer, syndicated columnist

Freshwater Road

Freshwater Road

DENISE NICHOLAS

BOLDEN

AN AGATE IMPRINT

CHICAGO

Freshwater Road
ISBN 13: 978-1-57284-195-6
ISBN 10: 1-57284-195-8
Bolden Books trade paperback printing: April, 2016

The Library of Congress has cataloged the hard cover edition of this book as follows:

Library of Congress Cataloging-in-Publication Data

Nicholas, Denise
    Freshwater road / by Denise Nicholas.
        p.   cm.
    Original hardcover edition ISBN: 1-932841-10-5;
    ISBN-13: 978-1-932841-10-7 (hardcover)
        1. African American women—Fiction. 2. Civil rights movements—
    Fiction. 3. Southern States—Fiction. 4. Young women—Fiction. I. Title.
    PS3614.I337F74 2005
    813'.6—dc22

                                                                2005007607

10 9 8 7 6 5 4 3 2 1

Agate books are available in bulk at discount prices.
Single copies are available prepaid direct from the publisher.

agatepublishing.com

In Memoriam

Otto Nicholas, Sr.
and Michele Burgen

"History claims everybody,
whether they know it or not,
and whether they like it or not."

PHILLIP ROTH
New York Times, September 2004

1

Out of Memphis with night drawing up thick to the windows, Celeste felt the air pressing down. She'd dressed in a gabardine jumper and a long-sleeved blouse against the lingering cool of a June Ann Arbor morning. Now, her clothes weighed on her like a damp blanket. She closed her eyes. Before sunset, the trees had segued to a double-dyed richness of color and the loamy soil had turned blood-rust. Soft-talking voices of the train passengers mutated from the flat singsong of the midwest to the sloping drawls of the deep south. She shuddered, remembering a life she'd never lived, then laughed at the irony. Every Negro in America had a nightmare of Mississippi, of dying in the clutches of a hatred so deep it spoke in tongues.

The conductor, a tall square-jawed dark-skinned man, his upper body leaning into the car as if primed to run in the other direction, called out, "Senatobia." He clanged the metal door closed. Earlier, he'd walked the aisle swaying with the train, announcing the names of towns, his resonant voice a clarion call to freedom. He nodded to her quiet self, scrunched in her corner, a map of the southern states spread on the seat next to her. The mimeographed sheets from One Man, One Vote blared out in bold type, "How to Stay Alive in Mississippi." He knew why she was on this train.

She peered through the dirty window when he poked his head into the car and called out, "Sardis." Not a soul on the platform. They barely stopped. The train lurched forward, slow-waddling south.

Sardis. Senatobia. Idyllic names. She checked her map.

"Grenada." What's he saying? An island paradise in the Caribbean with long, sun-drenched beaches and fountains splashing cool water on lush flowers? A quick glance to her. Why does he duck his head in and out like he's hiding in a closet? His eyes are like black marbles in the murky train light.

Saliva had pooled in the corner of her mouth by the time he called out, "Vaughan." At the soft edge of sleep, Celeste dreamed of Negroes darting their ghostly selves like wild children playing hide and go seek. The conductor peeked from behind a tree. She forgot completely where she was going and why. When he called out "Canton," her stomach growled in yearning for Chinese food at one of Shuck's stops in Detroit. Egg foo yung, shrimp in oyster sauce, sweet and sour pork. Shuck's diamond pinkie ring sparkled against his brown skin in the neon light as he held the white carryout bags away from his camel hair coat.

In the foggy back hollow of her surface doze, a new voice calls out, "Jack-son, Miss'sippi." *Miss Sippi lives down the street.* She longs to sleep past her ticketed stop, but can't escape the appalling pictures of hunted people scattering behind her eyes. "Jack-son." When the train braked with a low howl and a long screech, she woke fully, gagging on the oily aftertaste of a Memphis ham sandwich, remembering Momma Bessie's warning that pork dreams were always nightmares.

By the time The City of New Orleans Limited rolled into the Jackson station, Celeste had been slouching upright on a worn-down seat for more than twelve hours. Counting the night trip from Ann Arbor to Chicago and the hard wait at the station there, it was closer to twenty-four. No sign of that conductor. Maybe he'd never been there at all. She hoisted her green canvas book-bag onto her shoulder by the strap, wrestled her suitcase from behind the last row of seats, and stepped down to the platform. She took off toward the lobby, her suitcase banging her side, her book-bag bouncing against her back.

When a rich low voice called out, "Suh, lemme git dat fa ya, suh." Then, "Ma'am, I got dat, ma'am," Celeste turned to see a Negro porter bowing, grinning, and grabbing suitcases in one fluid intonation of the past. The porter caught her gape-mouthed stare, rolled his eyes, then flashed his pearly whites at the white passengers and continued his work. Ah, she thought, this was the real deal. Mississippi had to be the birthplace of the grovel, handmaiden to the blues, the crown jewel in the system of slavery, the kick-down place.

Celeste walked faster, her thighs chafing in the swollen heat, blessing her gym shoes with every step she took. She whizzed by lacquer-haired women wearing outdated sundresses and cigar chomping men. Out of the corners of their eyes came slices of stares, sharp as razor blades, which seemed to say, "I know why you're here, and you better go on home where you belong." The cigar smoke irritated her nose. At the end of her train, the dark well of soot-covered tracks disappeared into a pitch-black tunnel. She hurried on.

Under the yellowish glare of bare fluorescent tubes, just off the central waiting lobby of the station, Celeste came face to face with the first *Whites Only* sign she had ever seen in her life. She stared at the sign tacked to the ladies' room door, its letters hand printed and uneven. She needed to go to the bathroom. A blush warmed her ears and acids grumbled her stomach. She surveyed the nearly deserted lobby, the stragglers from her train passing through to the street and a few bag-toting travelers loitering about, smoking. No signs pointing the way to the Negro restrooms. Anger tightened her jaws. The pressure in her bladder grew. It had been a long time since the rest stop in Memphis. Just then, another Negro woman, colorful scarf over a head of rollers, suitcase and bags beating her body, pushed herself, back first, into the ladies' room as if that sign was not there. Celeste followed her in, afraid to turn around to see if anyone noticed.

The woman moved fast, shoving her things under a washbowl and then ducking into a stall. Celeste did the same. Squatted over the dirty toilet, panties down, she imagined being grabbed by the ankles from under the door. Her mind snapped to the television news film she'd seen of young people, Negro and white, yanked off buses and beaten until blood flowed down their faces. *Whites Only* signs flashed like backdrops to a bloodletting. Two minutes off the train and here she was already breaking the law. Her imagination ran on full. But this was real. Her father, Shuck, used to say she had good book sense and not too much of the other. She heard the woman flush and exit the stall. She took deep breaths, pulled the flush chain and came out into the glass-hard light of the bathroom.

Celeste eyed the ladies' room door, anxious to wash her hands and be on her way. "Is it okay to be in here?" She and the hair-rolled woman were co-conspirators. There was comfort in the assumed comradeship. At least she wasn't alone. They were *in* the *Whites Only* bathroom, had already *used* it. She had a story to tell, and she hadn't even gotten to the One Man, One Vote office.

The woman glanced at her sideways, digging in one of her bags, standing in front of the scum-pocked mirror. "Okay by *who*?" Her round eyes protruded slightly just above full cinnamon-brown cheeks. "Where *you* from?" Her head lurched back then settled as she worked on herself, her bag heaving up a comb and brush, toothpaste, a box of powder, a frayed puff, lipstick, rouge.

"Detroit." Negro people from the south favored the city of Detroit, that mystical blue-collar heaven of jobs. Shuck and Momma Bessie both did a lot of fussing about Negroes *still* coming up from the deep south searching for jobs that no longer existed, running the city services down the drain simply by the press of their numbers and needs. Celeste plunged soap containers along the line of washbowls. They were all empty. Still, she rejoiced at rolling up her long sleeves to the elbows and getting that fabric off her damp skin.

"Detroit, uh?" The woman smiled a knowing smile, as if honoring Celeste with a good check mark. "Chile, nobody pays that sign no mind no more. Course now, *white* ladies stopped coming in here." She indicated the overflowing trash receptacle, the dirty mirror and basins. "The law says we *can* come in here, it don't say they *have* to come in here." She squinted in the mirror.

Celeste took it in, trying to grasp the logic. "Where do *they* go?" She saw long corridors of bathrooms with color-coded signs, some white, some Negro, some integrated, and some unmarked. Wrong door, bad news. Maybe they gave their old ladies' rooms to Negroes and built spanking brand-new ones for themselves, left the signs up to confuse everyone. How long could they do that?

"I don't give a damn *where* they go." The woman applied her makeup as she talked, manicured nails glowing fuchsia. Then her deft hands quickly removed hair rollers. She brushed her hair, then applied rouge and powder to her face. "Those signs were down 'til the white folks got word about this Freedom Summer thing." She glanced at Celeste with a suspicious narrowing of her eyes, then coughed. She took a plug of toothpaste on her finger, rubbed it on her teeth, bent to get a swig of water from the faucet, gargled, then spat the residue in the bowl.

Celeste, remembering the instruction from One Man, One Vote about announcing to strangers her reasons for being in the south, rinsed her hands under the warm water, splashed some on her face, and volunteered nothing. No way to know who might run straight to the local police, the Klan, or some other enemy. Too late she discovered the paper towel dispenser was empty, too. "You from Jackson?"

"Mound Bayou." The woman paused. "Ever hear of it?"

"No." Celeste stood there dripping.

"It's a all-colored town, north of here. Bolivar County. Ain't nothin' up there but a post office and a lot of mud. But it's ours."

Wouldn't be long before Detroit was an all-colored town, too, if you listened to Shuck and Momma Bessie. Shuck always had a story about some white business or another moving to the suburbs. Still, she thought, she might like to go to Mound Bayou, see it for herself. She'd never realized how Negro Detroit was until she arrived in nearly all-white Ann Arbor. She'd missed Detroit in her bones that first semester and ran home every weekend—until she met J.D. That ended the trips home; Shuck didn't take to her dating a white guy, and he let her know it in no uncertain terms.

"You can't stay in Mound Bayou too long. Sure to lose your mind." The woman laughed. "Somebody like you, from way up there in Detroit and all, you sure to God would forfeit your mind."

The woman made Detroit sound like it was all the way to Hudson Bay, Canada.

Celeste chuckled and got a good look at her own tired face in the mirror.

"They got other ones. Different places in the south." The woman packed her things, took off her flats and slipped on pink pumps, shoved the flats into one of her bags. "Don't want to miss my train. Going to New Orleans for a few days. Get out of Miss'sippi for a minute. Catch my breath." She headed for the door, high heels clicking on the dirty tile floor. "Always wanted to go to Detroit. Get me one of them jobs at Ford's Motor Car Company."

Celeste might have told her that those jobs were now as rare as gold nuggets in a well-panned stream. She took one last glance at her sallow, travel-weary face in the mirror. Her shoulder length hair had risen to its peak of fullness and become a frizzled helmet of curls, waves, and flyaway strands. Her gray-green eyes had receded under heavy dark brows, sunk in pits of fatigue. Her lips needed color. She needed color. Whatever make-up she'd had on when she began her journey lived now on the small train pillow she'd left on her seat. She grabbed her suitcase and book-bag and followed the woman to the door. Didn't want to be in that *Whites Only* ladies' room alone, whether anybody paid the sign any attention or not. It was still up there.

The woman bumped half way out then turned back, her face primed and ready. "What's your name, girl?"

"Celeste Tyree."

"I'm Mary Evans. Pleased to meet you. You ever been in Miss'sippi be-fore?" She had a dubious look on her face as she appraised Celeste.

"No. First time. First time in the south." Even in her fatigue, Celeste's face pressed forward with expectation and fear.

"Well, let me tell you something. You be careful, girl, you hear. Miss'sippi ain't nothin' to play with." She lowered her voice for the last of it, eyes doing a fast flit around the lobby. "You have a nice stay, now, you hear?"

"Thank you." Celeste angled out the door checking for any hard-eyed men in uniform with billy clubs, cattle prods, snarling dogs. "Have a good time in New Orleans."

"Sure to do that. It's a good-time place." The woman sang the words as she fast-walked away, her pink pumps gleaming in the dingy, yellow-lit station.

Celeste figured the woman had guessed why she was there by the way she'd looked at her, sizing her up. But she'd said nothing. Knew better than to venture into that conversation. She checked again for enemies in uniform then bounded across the emptying lobby, through the double glass doors into the dank air of a June Mississippi night.

A sparse parade of cars moved slowly up and down the street. In her rising confusion, she considered trying to hitch a ride. How far could it be? *Not here.* Across the way were closed stores, a darkened coffee shop. She waited under the hooded overhang of the station, the dim yellow lights throwing shadows on the pavement, the late night air heavy as a stack of Momma Bessie's Kentucky-made patchwork quilts. She pulled the paper out of her book bag with the phone number and the address of the One Man, One Vote office, but she didn't want to call before she'd exhausted her options.

Anxious to be on her way, she stepped to the curb and reached for the door handle of the only empty cab. The cab jerked forward, then stopped a few yards beyond her reach. An embarrassment flushed her warm body, followed by a flash of chills. She took a sneaky look around and locked eyes with the grinning porter, who had just clanked his metal-wheeled cart onto the pavement trailed by a small pack of white people who seemed to snicker at her obvious ineptitude at things southern. The porter gave her a tit-for-tat glance as he loaded his passengers into the waiting cab. *Her cab.* He rolled his cart back into the station, eyes glued to the air in front of him. Celeste stood alone on the pavement, Mississippi like a stain spreading through her body.

"Wharsomevers y'all goin', ah can fetchu."

The voice sounded like liquid, the words humbled and broken. She turned to see a dark, bent-over man standing in the yellow hue of the station lights. He had the blues all over him and not a note of music played. He doffed his black cabby hat when he spoke.

"Ah say, wharsomevers y'all goin', ah can fetchu. I's a caib."

A reminder this time, as if her confusion and fear had mounted on her face and he'd seen it. Relieved, Celeste showed him the mimeographed paper with the address, not saying a word. The cabby nodded with a hint of a smile and directed her toward his cab. Only now did she see the other taxi stand, the Negro one, down the block, a good hike from the station entrance. She followed him, the front of her head tightening into a mask of fake nonchalance as she stepped into the back seat holding her book-bag in her lap like it was a child. The cab was black with light writing on the side. She needed to remember that. Easy. It was black. The cabby hefted her suitcase into the trunk then hunched himself into the driver's seat. They inched away from the station, Celeste having no idea where she was going or if she'd ever get there. She wanted to mark the place she was leaving but her neck wouldn't turn.

The slow-moving car and the heavy heat made her head loll back, though she didn't quite close her eyes; instead, she stared into the cab's dark ceiling, wondering what Shuck would think when he got her letter. He more than likely would blame her white boyfriend—now ex-boyfriend—for this decision to go south. Shuck's gaze charred the air in front of the student union when he first laid eyes on J.D. He'd ordered her into his sleek Cadillac and drove around in circles, telling her that a Negro woman with a white man

8 DENISE NICHOLAS

would always be lonely. She'd never seen Shuck like that. "It has to do with history," he said. "And no one woman is strong enough to buck it."

Shuck's words never left her head—even though she and J.D. kept doing what they'd always done, like going to Blues Night at Glinty's Bar and taking long rides on his motorcycle over two-lane country roads. But she and J.D. started arguing, about the blues of all things. J.D. claimed immense knowledge; he could produce long lists of blues singers he'd seen and heard, and swore he understood the blues as well as anyone. Celeste roared back, hands flying to her hips like someone she'd seen on a Detroit street, that unless he'd been shackled nude before the world, sold like a head of cattle, and hated like the plague, he didn't know a damned thing about the blues. When J.D. argued that Celeste didn't even look particularly Negro, that she'd grown up in circumstances as comfortable as he had (proving that she had no more claim on the blues than he), her fury erupted, spewed, and blistered until he'd walked out the door. She tried to flick off the implications of the deeper truth he'd touched upon—the truth of her own privilege—but in the end, it was Shuck's belief that she clung to, that race in America lived outside the purview of class or privilege, out there in a world all its own, not tethered to anything except hatred. That belief of Shuck's went deeper than any other, and J.D. helped her know it.

A floral sweetness floated on the midnight air. Shadows behind trees and hedges, white faces staring at the Negro cab prowling the lonely streets. In Ann Arbor right now, small groups of students roamed the campus, lingered in the clubs, made out in each available hallway, alcove, doorway, grove of trees. At Shuck's Royal Gardens Bar in Detroit, music and jolly repartee mingled with clinking ice cubes in every sort of glass. Laughter rang in the dim blue light. Bluesy jazz swore in the pauses. But here in Jackson, Mississippi, nothing moved that you could see except the police cars that patrolled the streets in droves, parked at intersections as if expecting an army of gun-toting gangsters or armed revolutionaries.

Away from Shuck, she began to lose ground, his sheltered world losing dimension, unable to project out to the galaxy beyond the West Side of Detroit, where things hadn't changed much in two generations. In Ann Arbor, she'd tested herself on the wrong seas. By the time the Movement speakers appeared on campus looking for recruits and money, she volunteered, gladly. There was always Shuck's voice in her head talking his race talk, pulling her back to home base and pushing her out into the world—to the south—at the same time.

J.D. the painter had gone to Paris for the summer. Here she was in Mississippi, in a cab going she knew not where, embarking on an adventure that had death written in the small print. According to Shuck, even as a kid she'd always had a deep sense of justice and fair play. He was pushing her to go to law school. She couldn't see it. Wilamena, her mother, thought it silly of her when she wanted to share her dolls and candy with other kids, Negro kids, who didn't have the abundance that she had. Told her she was a fool to think they'd ever return the favor. Surely there was enough injustice in Mississippi to validate her coming, and she didn't consider it a favor. Or did she? She tied her reasons for making this sojourn to all of that, and to Shuck, her father—her so wanting to be like him and so wanting to be unlike her mother who'd spent her life running away from Negro people. From herself.

Celeste's head popped up from the seat back. That woman had squirmed back into her mind, in spite of her prodigious efforts to keep her mother at bay. Her memories of Wilamena had a blurry quality. She didn't leave Celeste's mind for long, though, like a touch of arthritis that flares and subsides in an aging person's body (Momma Bessie called it her new friend, "Arthur"), unannounced and unapologetic.

The cabby caught her eye in his rearview mirror. A crooked smile emerged on his turned-down mouth. She returned it, tight and small. Wilamena had moved to New Mexico with Cyril Atwood, her second husband. When they'd first gotten married, ten years ago, they'd lived in Chicago. Then Atwood got tenure at the university in Albuquerque, with research perks in Los Alamos. Away they went. She'd spent the years before her second marriage running in and out of town, more out than in, always with a suitcase packed and ready. When she and Shuck divorced, Celeste and her brother Billy stayed with Shuck. Since her remarriage, she'd never come back to Detroit, not even for Celeste's and Billy's high school graduation ceremonies.

Wilamena never did like Detroit—too blue collar, too Negro, too much of the blues underneath the city's swagger. She used to say Detroit had a veil of soot that most people couldn't even see. Of course, she never tired of asking her children to visit her in New Mexico, but Celeste pulled the curtain down when Wilamena didn't show for the graduation. She had no desire to spend weekends in a *cavernous* house (as described by her mother in one of her letters) making graceful conversation about weapons research and Indian art. They wrote and talked on the phone from time to time, curt little conversations that crunched rather than flowed. She sent turquoise jewelry (that Celeste kept packed in velvet bags and rarely wore) and boxes of etched stationery. Celeste figured it was her mother's investment in their continued communication.

Prickly Wilamena's escape to New Mexico suited Celeste fine. Now, she could be Shuck's daughter and be done with it. No more rough ride with Wilamena, not knowing whether she loved you or wanted to be rid of you. Besides, what Negro person moves to New Mexico? But then, what Negro person moves to Mississippi?

"We's y'here." The old man aimed his taxi to the curb.

Thank God, Celeste thought, shaking off her reflections. New people, new meanings. It was all perfectly timed. J.D. gone to Paris, Wilamena stashed in New Mexico, Billy living in New York, Shuck cool and easy in Detroit. And she was in Mississippi, of all places.

The cabby pulled in front of side-by-side storefronts on a commercial stretch near downtown Jackson and Celeste leaped out, the lights of the capital building haloing in the midnight sky a few blocks away, it seemed. Two police cars were parked across the street, the officers sitting there watching. Inside the well-lit One Man, One Vote office, heads and bodies moved around behind windows plastered with flyers and posters.

The old man carried her suitcase to the door. "Thank y'all. Thank y'all fer comin' down y'here." He doffed his cap and smiled a broken-toothed smile.

Celeste paid and tipped him like Shuck taught her to do, then walked in, the reflection of the police cars in the glass door, fear crawling into her like vine tendrils creeping up the back fence in Momma Bessie's yard.

2

Heat sizzles jitterbugged off the pavement on Lafayette Street. Shuck ma-neuvered his sleek white convertible Cadillac into *his* parking spot a few steps from the Royal Gardens door. On Shuck's map this bar, as much as he loved it, was just a mark in pencil, a stepping-stone to a New York–style supper club. Women would sing blues and jazz with gardenias in their hair. Men would blow heartbreak licks on burnished horns, feet tapping to the beat. If he could fit Count Basie's whole band in there, he'd book them in a New York minute. He flicked his cigarette to the pavement and walked inside, the late afternoon sun warming the back of his head.

In the cool uneven bar light, Shuck nodded to his soft-talking regulars already curled around their first drinks of the day. The blown-up figures in his custom-made "best-of-Negro-life" wallpaper stepped out of hard-glossed cars in tuxedos and draped white dresses; Duke Ellington, Paul Robeson, Dorothy Dandridge, Lena Horne and Louis Armstrong were there. Shuck clanked change into the jukebox, punched in Gloria Lynne, the Modern Jazz Quartet, and Coleman Hawkins. Posey, his bartender, nicknamed the big Wurlitzer the "party girl" because it lit up the alcove where it stood like a hooker caught in a police car's siren light on a corner in Paradise Valley. He took his usual seat at the back end of the bar with Gloria Lynne singing "I Wish You Love." He stacked his mail to the side and skimmed the front page of his *Detroit News.* The Tigers left for St. Louis. The mayor huddled with business leaders on Mackinac Island. Lenny Bruce's trial convened in New York City.

"Kids from all over the country going to Mississippi to register Negroes to vote. Negro *and* white kids. Volunteering." Shuck realized he'd said it out loud after he said it, then checked to see if anyone had heard him over the music. He'd been following the news about the happenings in the south. Rosa Parks had left Alabama to live in Detroit. Martin Luther King had come through there, too. But the newspaper specifically said "Negro and white kids volunteering to go to Mississippi," and that was a whole different thing.

Millicent sat on a stool at the other end of the bar fingering her pearl-plated cigarette lighter. "I'd kill my children myself before I'd let them go to Mississippi." She punctuated this with a good swallow of her drink before thudding the glass down on the bar top. Millicent was a supervisor at the main post office, dressed well, nursed her drinks, and went home early.

Celeste had been so impressed by the speakers coming up from the south, full of talk about the new, nonviolent revolution. She told Shuck about the organizing on campus. He shuddered as a tremor of dread moved through his body. He remembered her awe, her naïve view of the south apparent in every word she spoke. He stared at the newspaper and ducked his head, sorry they'd heard him before he finished the article. They chimed in just like they did when anyone brought up some tidbit of news in the bar. You could barely get a thought out before they jumped all over it.

"They won't treat those white kids the way they treat us." Iris sipped gin and tonic from a tall glass, eyeing the opulent Negroes on Shuck's wallpaper. Her hair sat in the neat rolled curls left by the curling iron. She more than likely had plans for the night and didn't want to comb it out too soon in the summer humidity. Iris, with three boys and a teenaged daughter, didn't have a steady man and wasn't going to get one. No matter. Going out and having a good time after working all week long precluded the need for a man.

Posey, his waist wrapped in his bar apron, brought Shuck's orange juice. "In Mississippi, a nigger lover and a nigger's the same damn thing."

"Not just in Mississippi." Chink sat with Rodney at a small bar table near the juke box, smoking his filter tipped cigarettes, taking shallow inhales because the doctor told him he wasn't supposed to be smoking at all.

"That's the truth." Millicent's lips pursed in finality or dare.

Iris looked out the front windows of the Royal Gardens. "You wrong."

Shuck lowered the paper a bit, then turned to the continuation of the article. "Says here they added one hundred new police officers, bought a truckload of new rifles, and they're using the fairgrounds as a prison in Jackson. The governor's hired seven hundred more highway patrolmen. Damn." Shuck's butter-cream, short-sleeved shirt flared against his dark brown arms like a lantern burning yellow in the back corner. He wondered if all those new hired hands had any training and what kind of training it could possibly be. He didn't want to think about it. Figured they were just a bunch of southern white boys whose main job would be to crack heads all summer long. "Go to Mississippi and end up like Emmett Till. They don't even kill like normal people," he mumbled, putting the paper down.

"Man, y'all need to forget Emmett Till. That shit happened a long time ago." Rodney, ever vigilant and eternally afraid of the wrath of white people, shook his big surly head in little swipes. He must've been reading Shuck's lips.

"How you gon' forget that, Rodney?" Shuck stepped on Rodney's words and didn't apologize, wanted to tell him to shut up, but he was too good a customer to insult.

No Negro person in his right mind would ever forget Emmett Till. Back in 1955, the regulars from the General Motors Cadillac Body Plant stumbled in the door of the Royal Gardens with a *Jet* magazine wedged in their back pockets. They told Shuck they'd done what they always did every time the new *Jet* came out—bought a copy and immediately flipped the pages to the centerfold photo of a big-legged, tiny-waisted, soft brown girl in a bathing suit. This time, they never got to the centerfold. Emmett Till, pressed into his fourteen-year-old's coffin, a bullet hole one inch above his right ear, body beaten and bloated from its dead-boy float in the mud-brown waters of the Tallahatchie River, jumped out and grabbed them on page six. It was their most god-awful nightmare come true, and not one of them had ever even been in Mississippi.

Like every Negro in America, Shuck had heard the story of Emmett Till, how he'd whistled at a pretty white girl in Money, Mississippi, and that was the last time he ever whistled. But he hadn't seen those pictures. It was like Cassius Clay had sucker-punched him hard in the stomach. With Billy and Celeste drinking soft drinks on two stools at the back end of the bar, Shuck wiped tears from his eyes and vowed he'd never let a child of his go below the Mason-Dixon line in this life or any other. Later, he talked to Billy about what had happened to Emmett Till in

Mississippi. Billy told Celeste, who hadn't understood his words, but she peeked at the photos in the magazine. The kids didn't so much as mumble on the ride to Momma Bessie's that day, as if they too had come to understand something that was way beyond their age, visceral and eternal. He chastised himself for letting Celeste see those photos. He questioned himself about Billy seeing them, too, but he was older and he was a boy. The images mesmerized everyone who saw them and there was more than one lesson in them, he knew.

Big Rodney's knees bounced up and down, vibrating the ashtray across the small Formica table. "What happened to the nonviolence? Sound like they ready for war."

"Nonviolence's for us." Chink sat slouched over his ginger ale, seeming smaller than he really was next to big Rodney, and lighter, too.

"White folks not giving up a thing to Negroes without a fight." Shuck knew nothing came easy except the sweet money from hitting a dream number. "Mississippi's gonna be a bloodbath. Worse than Birmingham."

Chink uncoiled, shaking his head "no." "Nothing worse than Birmingham, man." He steadied his ice-clogged glass so Rodney wouldn't bounce it right off the table. "They bomb so many houses and churches, people callin' it Bombingham." Chink harbored a deep interest in the city where he'd been born, though as time went on he admitted it less and less.

"Man, no place is as bad as Mississippi. You know that as well as I do." They didn't know it from firsthand knowledge, but they sure knew it from myth and whispers and the running feet of all the Negroes who'd piled into Detroit. "Who knows how many Negroes been killed down there, or how many houses been bombed? Bet your sweet ass they'll know this summer with all those white kids running around. Bet you the whole damned place will change." With Shuck, everything presented itself as a possibility for a wager. He slid the stack of mail in front of him, slapping through the bills and stopping when he saw Celeste's large but even handwriting on the front of an envelope postmarked Chicago. She hadn't said anything about going to Chicago.

"See, they not going to let white kids be strung up and shot down. They not gon' do that." He tore the envelope open and pulled out the one-page note. "Anybody wanna bet?" Nobody said a word.

She'd written June 13 on the top of the letter. It was already the fifteenth.

Dear Daddy:

By the time you read this, I'll be in Mississippi volunteering for the Freedom Summer project to help with voter registration.

Shuck double-checked the envelope and looked hard at the handwriting. It was Celeste's. No doubt about it. He reread the date on the top of the page, the first line. She was already in Mississippi.

I know you know what's been going on down there. Lots of kids from schools all over the country are going down. It's a big thing. Maybe by the end of the summer, the whole racial thing will be different in the south, the rest of the country, too. This will be great if I go to law school, don't you think? I'll be fine. Don't worry. You can leave a message for me at the One Man, One Vote office in Jackson, Mississippi. Will call as soon as I can.

Love,
Celeste

Frozen where he sat, Shuck heard the flattened-out voices of his customers talking about rights and wrongs, about the tangled history of Negroes and white folks, saw them gesturing in the air, smoke curling up and away from their faces. Coleman Hawkins sounded like heaven must feel. Posey stood behind the bar, hands on hips, farther away than he should be. Sitting there, Shuck tried to come up with one good thing he could say about Mississippi. Everybody including his mother, Momma Bessie, would think Celeste had lost her mind leaving her good life to go to that godforsaken place. He could go down there and get her, force her to come back.

Rodney tapped his near empty glass of ice and bar bourbon, his eyes darting towards the door. "Don't y'all have nothing else to talk about?"

"Rodney, man, stop shaking the table." Chink pressed his weight against one of the table legs. "What you want to talk about?"

"The weather. That's all he ever wants to talk about." Millicent's iridescent pink sundress and matching jacket soft-lit her face in sunset rose. Shuck looked at her down the bar. She wasn't a pretty woman, but she fixed herself up so well, you didn't even notice unless you stared at her.

Rodney's eyes snapped from the jukebox to the front door and back to the jukebox. "I don't give a damn what's going on down there." He rocked back on the chair's hind legs.

"You already broke one of my chairs, Rodney." Shuck held onto the bar to keep from going over and crashing a pitcher on Rodney's head.

Rodney leveled the chair on the floor, gave Shuck a sheepish look.

"Posey, give Rodney another drink. He's scared I got a white man from General Motors behind the walls listening." Shuck tapped the envelope corner on the bar top. "And bring me a Crown Royal on the rocks." He labored to even out his breathing, not sure if Posey heard him.

"I told him two or three times, the only white man comes in here is that mafia trainee takes the coins out the party girl." Posey's arms, sinews taut and black as raven wings, moved like precision blades setting up for the night crowd. "He's in and out so fast, I don't even know what he looks like. Shuck, you know what he looks like?"

"Posey. Bring me a Crown Royal on the rocks." This time he knew Posey heard him because Posey's eyes narrowed and clouded over with a question. Shuck drank from his private stock on momentous occasions. He tilted his head so the customers wouldn't see his eyes.

Posey stood there. "Who died?" He grabbed the Crown Royal bottle from its sacred place beneath the bar, scooped ice into a short glass, and brought it down to Shuck.

Millicent swiveled on her barstool. "Remember when Kennedy got killed? The only thing Rodney wanted to know was if a colored man had done it. Afraid every Negro in America was going to pay, especially him." She released a streamlined breath of smoke that drifted and dispersed in the space between Rodney's table and the bar.

"Celeste left school." Shuck drank the smooth whiskey down in one swallow and hit the bar top with the bottom of his glass. "Gone to Mississippi." Shuck could feel the confusion at play across his own face, muffling the clarity in his eyes.

Posey stepped back like he'd been hit, then seemed to sway with the realization. "Well, I be goddamned."

"Who's in Mississippi?" Millicent jerked around, leaned on the bar top like she might slide down to Shuck and Posey, save whoever it was in Mississippi.

"Shuck's daughter." Posey poured Shuck another drink, brandishing the elegant bottle of Crown Royal.

Shuck felt the question-marked faces of his regulars all turn to him, stare like they'd just heard some apocryphal madness. The regulars knew his kids, had watched them grow up.

Iris, her little curls and scalp parts looking like a road map to nowhere, glanced at the lush Negro images on the walls. "Well, baby, you got a problem now." She finished her drink and lit a cigarette, holding it like one of the elegant New York–looking women in the wallpaper.

"Shit's going on all over the country. She could come here and be in the Movement. Everything ain't that great right here." Shuck didn't know if the words came out of his mouth or not, but he sure thought them hard. The only thing to do with Mississippi was to leave it, to run away from it as fast as you could. Or, better yet, blow it off the map of the United States. Not one more Negro person had to die in that place for the point to be made. Then a gnawing thought took hold. More than likely that paintbrush-wielding, blue-jeans-and-sandals-wearing white boyfriend had something to do with this decision. Shuck's teeth clamped down until his jaw muscles hurt. Just like a white boy to lead his daughter to hell, a hell he more than likely would survive without a scratch but where she could die in a split second. He was white. He could fade into the woodwork of Mississippi or any place else for that matter. Celeste couldn't.

"Now, see, that's what I mean. You can't control these kids nowadays. That girl's had the best of everything from the day she was born, and look at her." Iris sucked on her cigarette, now the authority on raising children, satisfied, as if she and Shuck had something in common because her seventeen-year-old son had already been arrested for stealing a car.

Shuck sipped his whiskey and thought of a thousand places Celeste might've gone starting with right there in Detroit. But he knew that in some way he had something to do with this, that by being a race man himself, he allowed for the possibility of his children seeing things just like him. Only he hadn't counted on it going so far. Could be the white boy had nothing to do with it.

And what about Wilamena? Celeste had a way of not telling her mother the big things. Wilamena would call him looking for Celeste. He needed a double shot of Crown Royal. Now Celeste had run off, just like her mother. No. This wasn't like that at all. Celeste was doing something big, not just running off. He caught himself feeling a moment of pride. Men went to war to find themselves, came back different people, some better, some not so good at all. He knew he wouldn't have gone down there for all the tea in China. Not to Mississippi. And what would it do to her?

Maybe he should've remarried, made a traditional home, instead of living his life exactly the way he wanted and pushing the mothering off on other people. Never saw any cracks in his way of raising his children until now. Billy rarely came home. Now Celeste had run to Mississippi and didn't even tell him until she was already there. That's not how things were supposed to be.

"Why we got to be the ones always fighting for something? Paying double, triple, quadruple?" In the thin light, Chink's yellow-tinged skin shone dingy white.

Shuck felt prophetic. "That's what the whole damned thing's about. Paying dues until they wear you down. What you need is a gun. You got the right gun, you'll get your rights. Now, you take those peckawoods in Mississippi. I bet you give those Negroes some guns, they won't have any problems registering to vote. White folks understand two things. Guns and money." He might take his own gun and go down there. That would be the end of it. Bring Celeste home. "Damn."

"You got a gun, Shuck, you better pack it up and send it down there to your daughter." Iris sounded delighted, gripping the rounded edge of the oak bar as if the room was spinning. "The government needs to take care of that stuff anyway."

Shuck put a toothpick in the corner of his mouth, twirled it a couple of times. "Whole lot of things they're supposed to do." He dropped the toothpick in the ashtray next to his empty glass, his hands trembling.

"It's those slow-assed niggers in Georgia, Mississippi, and Alabama letting crackers walk all over them. They the ones needing some rights. Not us," Rodney said.

"You need to leave it alone, Rodney." Chink's warning floated like a buoy at low tide. "When's the last time you stood up to one, huh?"

Millicent talked to her drink. "Nothing between them and us but a few miles."

"Not even that." Chink moaned.

Iris shot a look to Shuck. "Where in Mississippi is she, Shuck?"

What difference did it make where in Mississippi Celeste was? It was the same damned thing. Mississippi didn't have any good neighborhoods for Negroes. It wasn't like Detroit. Dearborn might be a bad zone for Negroes, but Detroit was a good one. None of that in Mississippi. No place to run. No place to hide.

"Down south, they have sit-ins, nonviolent stuff. Up here, we have riots." Millicent's cigarette created a small white crossbar to her brown fingers and deep pink nails, jabbing the air in Shuck's direction. "Nobody's thinking about nonviolence up here."

"I'm still happy to be up here." Rodney said.

"You one of them 'I'se-so-happy-to-be-here' Negroes, always saying 'thank you, massa' for something that was yours to begin with." Posey stared at Rodney without a hint of fellowship in his eyes. But no matter what anyone ever said to him, Rodney shrugged it off, burly and untouchable.

Rodney sneaked a look at the floor. "Well, I saw them dogs and fire hoses on the news. Where would you rather be?"

"Shut up, Rodney." Posey glared at him.

Shuck heard them and didn't hear them, jumping over their references, scanning his own life and past, seeing Celeste and Billy as children, each holding one of his hands, walking on the island park, Belle Isle, going to the movies, buying ice cream, sitting in Momma Bessie's rose-scented backyard.

"I remember *the* race riot, man. 1943. Now that was awful. June then, just like now and already hotter than hell." Posey sounded like he wanted to say it and didn't want to, like he was pushing a conversation about something else, anything in the past, to help Shuck.

Rodney yelled out above Posey, above the suction vents, air conditioners, icemakers, humming ceiling fans, jukebox. "Shit always happens when it's hot." He folded back in his chair.

Shuck let the memory of those old days float into his head. Back in the forties, waves of Negroes and whites from the south overwhelmed Detroit. Instead of Packards and Cadillacs, they built tanks, jeeps, army trucks, airplanes, and PT boats. People lived jammed too many to a room, slept in closets, on porches, wherever a mattress would fit, or just a folded blanket would do. Lines for food, for streetcars, for housing, for everything. Momma Bessie even rented rooms in the old house on Whitewood, bringing down the wrath of the few whites who hadn't run when they'd moved in. Rocks hurled into windows. It never ended.

Chink wagged his head from side to side like a sad-faced dog. "It was bad on Belle Isle. Never forget it."

Millicent and Iris faced the bar mirrors, thin hazy smoke threads winding from the ends of their cigarettes, heads delicately ticktocking back
and forth.

"People used to cart their picnic things out there on the streetcar."
Millicent's chin dipped.

"The day that riot started was no time to be fooling around on streetcars." Posey dried glasses with a vengeance, clanking them down on the bar
sink. "Peckawoods pulled people off, beat them in the street."

"Whole lot of Negroes got killed," Rodney said.

"Few white boys, too," Chink added.

"Right." Rodney's knee started twitching. "A few."

Shuck went to the jukebox and punched in "Take the 'A' Train" and
"Broadway," escaping to his New York dream. He sat again, looking at the
night-life Negroes with pearl white teeth and processed hair, Joe Louis
in the ring, Thurgood Marshall on the steps of the Supreme Court, Lena
Horne draped on a Hollywood post, Nat "King" Cole at the piano.

Evening trucks from the post office jarred the big window across the
front of the Royal Gardens. That big plate glass window irked Shuck, though
he liked seeing his Cadillac parked at the curb, the patterns of traffic, the
twist and turn of the seasons—women in their sundresses, hair up off their
necks, then later the first bustling skips of autumn, the snow when it came
lashing with the wind off the lakes, barreling back and forth across the city.
And spring—hard as it was to see spring on Lafayette Street, all black tar
and concrete. Smaller panes of leaded glass would be more elegant, more
mysterious, make the place look less like a dressed-up storefront.

The talk about the riot of 1943 went on around him, the voices heavier,
garbled, swimming in and out of the music, in and out of his thoughts. He
reminded himself that children were born to leave, the universe ordered
it, that Billy would stay in New York, that Celeste would run off to Mississippi. And always there was the thought of Wilamena with her new
husband in New Mexico. He kept thinking of the man as her *new* husband.
It had been nearly ten years. Longer than that since she'd pulled the plug
on Detroit.

3

A hard something landed in Celeste's lap, waking her from a doze. Behind the continuous murmur of voices in the office, typewriter carriages banged, bells sounded, and a radio played. "Sign that. I'll take you to the apartment in a minute. I'm Margo." Celeste grasped the clipboard, frowning up at the short, pretty, blue-eyed white girl with edge-straight blonde hair cut just above her shoulders. By the time she got "hi" to her lips, Margo had pivoted into a small army of coverall-wearing Negro and white young people moving around the airless office/storefront picking up papers, diagramming patterns on a blackboard, sticking pins in a map of Mississippi. Celeste wondered if the pins marked the locations of dead bodies, burned buildings, or some other horrendous occurrence. On the walls, pictures of Martin Luther King, Rosa Parks, Medgar Evers. Through the front windows, she saw that the police cars hadn't moved.

Margo huddled over a mimeograph machine near the back wall with a young dark-skinned guy, she cranking the handle of the old inky cylinder while he caught the copies. Celeste eyed them through slits. The last thing she'd expected in this office was a white girl telling *her* what to do, even if it was only signing some form. Mississippi *and* the civil rights movement meant pushing two years of Ann Arbor's surrounds of white people to the rear.

Here, both Negro and white student-types were working and talking together in easy familiarity. Hard to tell who was in charge. Serious faces, cigarette smoke spiraling up to the white-tiled ceiling, and music coming from a small radio in the corner, Wolfman Jack's gravel-choked voice punctuating the melodies. It had the feeling of a campus gathering, without the food and alcohol.

Celeste walked to the bulletin board to see the photos of rural-looking Negro people grinning with their arms around overall-wearing student-types. Everyone seemed to be old and young at the same time. And, photo after photo of burned down buildings. She went back to her folding chair.

A ballpoint pen dangled at the end of a thin string attached to the clipboard. A typed page and a carbon under it, the word "release" in caps across the top.

In the event of your injury or death, neither you nor your family or heirs to your family have a legal right to sue or to otherwise seek compensation from One Man, One Vote.

This whole trip was going to break Shuck's heart. Beneath the fine suits, the stingy-brimmed hats, the sleek cars, and the smooth demeanor, Shuck was a race man. But Mississippi was a different story. He'd want to come down here and snatch her back to sanity. She'd better call him soon. He'd need to hear her voice to know that she was OK. Wilamena would more than likely hiss and fume and blame it all on Shuck being a race man, constantly talking about Negro this and Negro that, filling Billy and Celeste's heads with all that Negro-ness. She'd have preferred to have them less anchored in things Negro. More classical music, less jazz, more London and Paris, less Harlem and Chicago. And for sure, less Detroit.

A line of typed dashes stretched across the bottom of the page. Celeste's full name was typed under the line and the dates of her stay in Mississippi. A note at the bottom: *Be sure to send one copy home to a parent or guardian before leaving for your project city.*

Celeste's departure date, the end of Freedom Summer, August 21, was two months away. She might be dead by then—or a hero, a northern agitator hero who'd managed to register an entire town of disenfranchised Negroes. She saw herself as a cross between Joan of Arc and Harriet Tubman, the fires of righteousness flaming in her heart stoked by the news reports that had been coming out of the south for the last three years. Her departure date floated on the paper as if the ink had run out, as if there'd be no leaving Mississippi. She signed on the line and pulled the copy from under the carbon, then slipped it into her book bag. Shuck said your decisions were your own when you crossed from teen to adulthood. Age eighteen marked the beginning of adulthood, but the years between eighteen and twenty-one were a kind of nebulous grace period you were given if you appeared not to have good sense. She'd be twenty in November.

The clatter in the office scaled down as the volunteers filtered out in groups of two and three. When Margo led her out to a 1960 Ford and told her to get into the back seat, the police started their engines, too. Had police cars, lurking around midnight corners, followed the other volunteers when they left? She'd seen enough squad cars on the way from the train station to handle it. Was this the routine or was special attention given to new arrivals? Her suitcase gave her away.

Margo's car stank of decomposing cigarettes and sweaty armpits. Celeste added her own train-funk to the haze of odors. From the dark of the car's backseat she watched the back of Margo's head as they rode through the deserted streets of downtown Jackson. The two police cars followed half a block behind them. More than likely, the police knew when she'd arrived at the train station, knew the volunteers' every move. Already Mississippi felt like a moldy hole, a long dark tunnel without enough fresh air, too much moisture, and no light at the end. This interminable night ranked as one of the longest of Celeste's life. When she checked behind them again, the police cars had disappeared. She wanted to relax, but something told her the effort would be a foolish waste of time.

"If you're with a white person and you get stopped by the police, let the white person do the talking." Margo's pure New York City accent leaned against the slow southern night as she drove well under the speed limit, checking to the right and the left and eyeing the rearview mirror at every intersection. Perspiration slicked her face to a moony shine. A dark bandana covered her blonde hair. "Act like you're the maid getting a ride home from work."

"Are you *serious*?" Celeste rolled her eyes at the back of Margo's head. "Nobody's that dumb, even in the movies." Then, she remembered the porter at the train station. Was he acting servile to survive? To get paid, for sure. Now she wished she hadn't looked at him so harshly. She might find herself bobbing and weaving, shuffling to save her own life before this summer was over. Could she do that? What would it do to her? She tried to follow the thought to its conclusion. And what in God's name would Shuck think about her riding around in the backseat pretending to be somebody's maid? He'd want her to survive, pure and simple. Pride could get her a one-way ticket to a tongue lashing, or a beating—or worse, get her tossed into a fast-moving river.

"You'd be amazed." Margo double-checked her rearview mirror, then accelerated. "Another car fell in behind us when the police cars turned around. He's gone."

Maybe it was still the police but in an unmarked car, Celeste thought.

At the next intersection, Margo slowed. "When it comes to the movement, every white person in the south is the police. They all follow us. There's no real distinction between regular white people and the police down here."

Celeste sank deeper into the backseat, her heart skipping through its beats like a drummer on smack. Margo knew what she was thinking before she'd opened her mouth. She dug her fingers into the crack where the seat meets the seat back and brought her hands out with dirt and lint pieces sticking to her fingers. "So what do I do if I get stopped with all Negro people in the car? Jump out and start tap dancing?"

"You might have to." Margo turned into a residential section of wood-framed houses set back beyond night-black lawns. "It's already happened. Some volunteers were stopped and the cops made them dance in the middle of the highway. Guns drawn."

Celeste's neck tensed as though her vertebrae were fusing. What to say now? Nothing. Just listen. Pay attention. She caught Margo's eyes in the rearview mirror.

"Be respectful and pray. Sing freedom songs in your head. By the end of orientation, you'll know the words to a lot of 'em." Margo let her eyes go back to scanning as they moved quietly through the streets.

No lamps lit the windows, no porch lights were on, and the shrubs and hedges were just dark shapes in the night. Not even the trees moved, just the car gliding in slow motion over the black tar. Celeste ducked her head well below the back window, gasping for air, legs sprawled across the bump, peering out like a child. She tasted again the train coffee and that mayonnaisy ham sandwich from the stop in Memphis.

Margo turned into what looked like a housing project of low, dark-brick buildings. "Try to get the name of the officer stopping you. The patrol car number, details that can be reported to the FBI. Try to stay calm. Try to stay alive."

Celeste bucked herself up a bit, and pushed aside her bristling self-consciousness at being a trainee with a white-girl boss who obviously knew more about staying alive in Mississippi than she did.

"Remember names and squad car numbers. Sing the words to freedom songs," Margo repeated. "As soon as I get you ready for Pineyville and the other straggler ready for the Delta, I'm going to Aberdeen." Margo put her arm on the car window ledge, the warm air fluttering her bandana. She looked so in control, she made it sound like they were going off to be camp counselors.

Celeste strained to sense Margo's fear. Maybe she was so afraid herself, no one else's fear had a chance. She glared beyond the car's front lights. "Pineyville? Where's that?" She checked the map of Mississippi in her mind. Greenwood, Vicksburg, Natchez, Yazoo City. Names like dreams that pillowed nightmares.

"Down below Hattiesburg, a few miles from the Louisiana border." Margo stopped the car in front of an apartment building with windows across the front, then turned off the engine and the lights. The engine ticked down to nothing. "Used to be the Piney Woods before the loggers cut down all the trees." She sat low in her seat but alert, head turning like a radar scanner. "The Gulf coast is nice, but it's still Mississippi, and when it's not, it's Louisiana or Alabama or Florida. Same goddamned thing."

How much farther *down below* could they go? Where did Mississippi end? Celeste stopped a moan that formed in her throat, and said, "Aren't you afraid?" She didn't want to be the only one afraid.

"Yeah." Margo turned a little in the car seat and looked directly at her, and Celeste saw a wide-eyed girl very much like herself. They were about the same age. They had come to Mississippi for the same reasons. "Only a nut wouldn't be afraid in this place."

Celeste sighed, thanked God she wasn't alone. "That helps."

The shrieking of cicadas and mole crickets swelled, aroused by the sound of the car, the low-talking voices. Nothing romantic about it. No harking back to benign nighttime stories of the sounds of the south, no animated crickets and puffy-haired Negroes with smiles and songs on their lips. This was a tunnel of death. Her mouth tasted like sandpaper. Then, suddenly, the quiet mushroomed around them. Celeste heard her own heart beating. All she could see were dark trees, hedges near windowpanes lit only by the reflected moon. She sat up a bit to see the surrounding area.

"Stay low." Margo's voice was sharp. "There's a car under the trees across the street. It's always there." Margo turned to Celeste and smiled a creepy smile in the soupy darkness. "The Klan shot out the street lights when they found out we were housing volunteers here. We think that's one of their cars."

Celeste glared at the car, caught between wanting to thump Margo on the back of the head for scolding her like she was a child and being thankful that Margo had warned her about the lurking danger. Nothing moved inside the dark car. Just black windows and no heads.

"How long've you been here?" Celeste's voice crackled between her true voice and the hoarse whisper of fear.

Margo pulled a single key out of her bag and held it up in the streak of moonlight coming through the front windshield. "Six months." She sounded proud. Celeste didn't want to look up to a white girl, but she had sense enough to know that Margo had already passed tests that she hadn't even studied for. She had to give Margo her due, relax inside for a moment, and listen to her as she would her teacher.

"For the next few days, you go through nonviolence training with the stragglers. Y'all are the last group. We need to get you going to your projects so you'll have time to do what we're here to do." Firm-voiced, Margo laid it out, though the "ya'll" was a tight fit with her New York accent. "You'll be running your freedom school and your voting project at the same time. The voter education classes take priority. That's pretty much it. Oh, and try not to get killed." Straight faced and no nonsense. She handed the single key to Celeste and indicated with a nod that it was time for Celeste to get out of the car.

Fear approaching terror hurtled through Celeste. She opened the door and hunched over to climb out of the backseat. The civil rights demonstrations on campus seemed so harmless. That was another world. This was the real deal. Run a freedom school and try not to get killed. She'd read it in her packet of materials, knew the school was a part of the summer project, couldn't remember precisely what she was supposed to do. She needed to sleep, to bathe, to eat a meal that had a green vegetable on the plate. Negro people were *her* people. She didn't want a white girl from New York to be more courageous on their behalf than she was. She had to submit, though, because it might be the difference between life and death. Mississippi wasn't Ann Arbor or Detroit, and she needed to keep that foremost in her mind.

"Your contact's Reverend Singleton." Margo never stopped scoping the darkness, even as she leaned across the front seat and talked to Celeste out of the car window. A real soldier. "He's the point man in Pineyville. I'll fill you in over the next few days."

Celeste tried to gather up some mettle for her cracking, slipping voice. She leaned down, head in the window, wanting to crawl through the window back into the car. "When do I go?"

"As soon as I see you're ready. Stay low to the floor at night. That apartment's been shot into. Grab the empty mattress. There's another volunteer in there."

Celeste hefted her suitcase and book bag out of the back seat, wondering how long it would take her to get ready. Ready for what? Nonviolence training, of course. Practice being oppressed, practice not getting killed. Taking low to keep the peace, removing chips from shoulders, anger from lips, history from heart. She lingered by the side of the car, afraid to walk through open space. Afraid she'd end up like Medgar Evers, shot dead a few feet from his front door. Across the street, the dark car waited. "What about the police?" Celeste heard her own dumb question too late to pull it back. They'd just been followed by the police. The police were all over Jackson waiting.

"Forget the police." Margo sighed on the verge of impatience. "I'll pick y'all up in the morning. White volunteers have to sleep in another unit. No integrating. Not yet anyway." She started the car, staying low, her parchment-white face surrounded by her dark bandana and the night. "I'll wait 'til you're in the door. Go on."

Celeste hunched over and scurried for the door as Margo started the engine. Her suitcase and book bag scraped along the walkway. She might've crawled on her hands and knees, anything to not be a walking target. She found the door knob and felt around for the keyhole, then finally got the door open. When she turned around, Margo gave her a quick wave and headed, it seemed, almost directly for the dark car across the street, going so slowly it seemed to be a taunt.

A miniature lamp sat on the floor next to the mattress but barely lit the dark corner of the living room. Two folded sheets and a flat pillow with no case lay on top. In Ann Arbor, Celeste's mattress was on the floor, too, but not because it had to be, not because someone might shoot at her through the windows. She positioned her suitcase and book bag at the end of the mattress to form a footboard, or at least a blockade, then undressed down to her underwear before pulling a light cotton nightgown over her dirty body, keeping low the whole time. The jumper and the blouse were going in the bottom of her suitcase, never to be seen again until she got home. No, better to air out the sweaty clothes before putting them into her suitcase. She laid them on the wood floor. To take a bath or even to just wash up in the face bowl meant turning on lights, which would locate her for the mystery men across the street in the dark car.

She sat on the mattress and leaned against the wall staring at the small, bare living room. Always she had a sense of waiting. It went way back. Waiting for Wilamena to shower her with the hugs and kisses she saw other children receive from their mothers, waiting for Shuck to pick her and her brother up from some relative's house, waiting for Shuck's numbers to fall. Waiting for her life to begin. Now she'd begin her own journey with no clue as to how it would end.

"Your name better be Celeste." The voice wavered, followed by the padding of bare feet on wood. "Otherwise, I'm going out the bedroom window."

"It is," Celeste called in a whisper. She had hoped the other volunteer would be sleeping, giving her time to just sit there and mull over the possibilities of what lay ahead.

"Good." A door closed and in seconds there was the sound of a flushing toilet. A young woman crept into the living room, walking squatted down. "Ramona Clark."

Ramona sat down on the floor and leaned back against the door frame. Her hair was a mass of wooly kinks, round like an upside down bowl. Celeste could make out a small brown face, big oval eyes. "Haven't slept since I got here."

"Celeste Tyree." She felt her dirty, frizzled, humidity-inflated curls and waves, every strand symbolic of a contorted family tree. "That car across the street might keep anybody from sleeping."

"Amen to that." Ramona said. "Where're you from?"

"Michigan. Detroit. Actually, I'm in school in Ann Arbor." She tried to see more of Ramona's face in the dim light.

Ramona's head moved back and forth, her big bowl of kinky hair swaying. "Ooo wee. Not many black folks up there."

"Not many." Celeste heard the "black." Speakers from the movement who came to campus said it too. She hoped Ramona wasn't excluding her, tossing her in the "other" pile—the "good hair" pile, the light-eyed Negro pile. Negroes used to be "colored." Kids used to fight over being called black. It was the new title, the new calling. Black folks. She wanted to be in it. Shuck would be. Wilamena wouldn't. Celeste herself hadn't gotten comfortable saying "black."

"I'm at Howard with the black intelligentsia, the so called 'high-yellow first line of defense,' no offense intended." Ramona's voice eased out, consonants hit then released very quickly, sliding softly off the edges of her words.

Celeste bristled and lied. "None taken." Shuck was in her head telling her there was no high yellow, no low yellow, or anything else. There were just Negroes. Now, just black folks. Period. Celeste gave herself a point. Shuck was always ahead of the pack, in the vanguard. And she always trying to catch up.

"Where're they sending you?" Ramona stretched her legs out on the wood floor.

"Someplace called Pineyville." All she could see was the bowl of hair and flashes of the whites of Ramona's eyes. "I never even *heard* of it."

"Boy, you hit the jackpot." Ramona's eyes flared wide. "That's where they lynched Leroy Boyd James."

"Jesus." Celeste's train-weary mouth dried like dusty bones. She'd never heard of Leroy Boyd James, either.

"It was in the fifties. I did a paper on lynching in three deep-south states since World War II. I'm a sociology major." Ramona leaned her head back against the door jamb.

Every Negro in America was a sociology major, like it or not, college or not. You had to be. "What happened to him?" Celeste knew before Ramona said a word.

"They say he raped a white woman. Never got to court. Got kidnapped from the jail down there, beaten, shot, and dumped into the Pearl River. The sheriff said it never happened. A fisherman pulled him out. Body got caught on some tree roots or something. Otherwise, he'd have been swept down to the Gulf by the currents. Disappeared. A prisoner told the FBI that the sheriff there opened the door to some men. Nobody was charged with his murder."

All the air sighed out of Celeste's body. This wanting to know could definitely give you nightmares. Maybe Ramona exaggerated. Maybe there was more to the story, but she couldn't fathom what that might be. She'd seen the photos of Emmett Till. She'd seen the range of horror when it came to white women and Negro men. She tried to stir up enough saliva in her mouth to swallow. "Where're they sending you?"

"Indianola. In the Delta." Ramona sighed. "Plantation country."

Wasn't Mississippi *all* plantation country? And what was Pineyville? A lot more than the Piney Woods, evidently. Leroy Boyd James. A new wrench of fear cranked her stomach, sent the acids churning and the ghost of that ham sandwich flying.

"You running your project by yourself?"

"Unless some more volunteers show up. They've got a pretty active bunch of black folks in the town." Ramona got into her squat-walk position. "Oh, the lady across the way brings biscuits and jelly in the morning. We've got coffee. The phone in the hall is for emergencies. They said we can call collect anywhere. The FBI numbers are right next to the phone there." Ramona disappeared around the corner. "I hope *you* can sleep. I sure can't. Don't forget to stay low."

"Goodnight." Celeste shriveled down the wall, legs spread out on the mattress. She felt like she'd been awake for days. Too many thoughts swirled in her head.

Sporadic dog barks, crickets, the creaking of trees. No low music in the background. No laughing voices with conversation riffs in between. It had to be three in the morning by now. A thickness in the air that made you think you were hearing things, but when you really pressed your ears to it, there was nothing there.

Celeste squat-walked to the open front windows, sat down on the hardwood floor, and pushed on the screens. They were locked in place. Light-colored curtains waited for a breeze, any slight shuffle of air. The car across the street glimmered in a sliver of moonlight. Ghosts with guns. Sweat bubbled out on her forehead, under her arms, between her legs. She smelled her own body, the dampness curdling into a pungent aroma.

She crawled back to the mattress. The heavy air weighted her down on the thin bed, the hardness of the floor rising into her spine. What had Leroy Boyd James really done? Was it like Emmett Till? A whistle, a nothing whistle? She knew there were white girls in Ann Arbor who loved the easy grace of long dark arms and lips that felt like pillows in heaven. But this wasn't Ann Arbor. Margo standing at the mimeo machine with that guy?

What was that about? Maybe nothing. Margo was from New York. No big deal. But where was he from? He's the one who'd pay the price. Down here, death came hunting when you reached across the lines of demarcation. In Ann Arbor, maybe just a hateful look, a bad name slung across some busy street. She and J.D. turned heads. Here, crossed love got dropped in the cracks of old storm shelters, locked away with warning signs marked Danger. People died for flirting. She'd read enough to know this was the real deal. Mary Evans's voice in her head, *You be careful, girl, you hear? Miss'sippi ain't nothing to play with.*

4

Michael Schwerner, James Chaney, Andrew Goodman, and their blue Ford station wagon disappeared near Philadelphia, Mississippi, on the night of June 21, gone like a moonlight rainbow after a summer evening storm. The news flew through the trees, over the creeks, and down the mud-brown rivers on the rhythm of a talking drum. By afternoon of the first day, the news was on the dinner table in Jackson. By evening, it was in the fingers of the lady pressing hair in Canton and on the lips of the waitress in Greenwood. On Tuesday, the second day, their station wagon was pulled from the swampy waters of Bogue Chitto Creek near Philadelphia. The car had been burned to a crisp.

Wilamena's admonition about Negro people—*they'll never return the favor*—darted through Celeste's mind as she stood on the baking mid-morning pavement in front of a local shoe store in downtown Jackson. She'd brought no wristwatch to Mississippi, had no idea of how fast time passed or if it passed at all. Judging by the displays in the shop windows, the out-of-date dresses and rigid hairstyles on the women walking by, Celeste had a feeling that time was going backwards. Confederate flags adorned the fronts of every store for as far as she could see. Not a flag of the United States of America anywhere.

She'd been directed by Margo to hand out flyers for a voter registration meeting. She was to do this in the shadow of the Mississippi state capitol. She thought Margo was joking. But there wasn't the slightest smile on Margo's face. She thought of declining, of begging off, but knew how that would be perceived and talked about in the One Man, One Vote office. Besides, Ramona had been standing there when the assignments were given to the last group of volunteers, and she wasn't going to cop out in front of her, or them.

A police car with two officers pulled in across the street. She caught her peach short-sleeved cotton dress, her pony-tailed hair, even her tight-lipped fear reflected in the plate glass window of the shoe store. Celeste frosted a smile on her face as her fear petrified.

She'd been told to hand the flyers to Negroes and whites with no distinction. When a flyer was begrudgingly accepted or snatched, it got a quick glance and a quicker toss into the city trash can, as if the flyer and the message were contaminated. Negro people stepped wide of her, offering furtive takes to passing whites that said, "I ain't in it." Margo wouldn't be back to pick her up until noon so there was nothing to do but keep trying. She shook off thoughts of Wilamena's simmering disdain, her assumed superiority, as if every kind or giving gesture toward another human being qualified as a favor that had to be reciprocated. Wilamena never got what the gesture did for the person offering—not as something to lord over others, but as an expression of one's own humanity. Just like the graduation.

Wilamena couldn't put herself out to attend her own children's graduations from high school, and yet thought it just fine to continue asking them to come to New Mexico. Some people got it and some didn't. There was no blessed community in required reciprocity, but there certainly was in just flat-out giving. So many people had made the commitment, had put their lives on the line. Wilamena had to be wrong.

Already, Celeste had adapted to her Freedom Summer orientation schedule. Classes in nonviolent philosophy and action every day. *Drop to the ground, protect your head, go into a ball. If the fire hoses come out, forget it. There's no protection.* Voter registration booster meetings were held every night at local churches with speakers from the clergy and from the leadership of One Man, One Vote. The Mississippi State Constitution of 1890 and its strictures on Negro voting were featured at the meetings. The sermons, the boosting part, were designed to keep the brethren riled up and raring to go on the march toward enfranchisement. The brethren included the volunteers. At the end of each meeting, the church body stood to sing freedom song after freedom song, just like Margo said. Celeste garbled the words, reading sometimes from a mimeographed sheet, trying to catch the passion of the more experienced summer volunteers, the dedication of the locals.

To calm herself on the pavement, she quietly hummed "We Shall Overcome," feeling more and more like a fanatic whose beliefs separated her from the rest of the world. She spotted a suit-wearing white man coming toward her and opened her face to respond to his queasy smile, thinking this brave soul was about to break the barrier, to step up, take a flyer, and maybe even have a conversation about what was going on in Mississippi. She plastered some terrified version of love on her face to accompany her limp smile. He zoomed by, grabbed the flyer, and hissed "Jiggaboo" in her ear all in one seamless motion. She dropped a handful of flyers to the pavement as she spun around to see him scrunch his flyer into a ball and lob it gracefully into a trash can. He disappeared into the bustling morning flow of pedestrians.

Jiggaboo? A stinging rippled around the coils of her brain, igniting tenuous but deceptively wiry ganglia of self-hatred. From a long-ago joke, a lampoon, the ever-vibrant denigration of Negro people, that word, *jiggaboo,* sneaky thing, still lived in a backyard shed. *You can't hate Negro people and not hate yourself, Wilamena.* Celeste heard Shuck say that on a long-distance phone call years ago. Now, she was the alone-on-a-strange-street-jiggaboo girl a.k.a. Celeste Tyree. She'd been caught and stripped naked, revealed, branded out there on the street. *Call a spade a spade.* Did anyone else hear him? And why did she think about that at all? J.D. had pulled the cover off of her, showed her she was passing—not like Wilamena, but in a more subtle way, a more dangerous way, because she didn't think she was. She came down here to right her rudders, to get straight with herself. Jiggaboo Girl. She smiled.

The flyers scattered on the pavement, got caught up in the shoes of passersby. No one offered to help gather them. They stepped on them, kicked them away from their shoes. Lines drawn in the red earth. She'd come here to shore up her own Negro-ness, to plunge herself into the real deal after lounging on Shuck's racial cushions for her entire life. For too long, she'd thought she was above it. Wilamena stood in the wings. Shuck was right. They were all Negro people. *Black folks.* But why did no Negro person stop to help her? Wilamena had walked away, married a man who looked suspiciously white, though he wasn't, and escaped to a more pliable place. Wilamena wasn't going to be a Jiggaboo Girl for anybody or anything.

A sleight of hand, a face without stereotypical earmarks. Wilamena could slide by. Shuck couldn't. Wilamena wanted to be out of it more than she wanted to be with her own children. That was the rub. Escaping the *jiggaboo* meant more to her than anything. Celeste couldn't escape even if she wanted to. When the sun hit her, she went dark.

"It's against the law to throw trash on the street. Step this way." She hadn't seen the police car U-turn, hadn't seen the officers get out and walk up to her, so busy was she trying to gather up the errant flyers from the pavement.

She would willingly have gotten down on the pavement to retrieve the remaining flyers, but now the officer had her by the elbow, ushering her toward the open back door of the squad car. She lumbered into the back seat, closed her eyes, praying and stumbling around for the words to a freedom song, something to hold on to, remembering Margo's admonishments. *Sing the freedom songs, try to stay alive.* When she opened her eyes, she saw nothing but the cold-eyed stares of pedestrians. Now she was a jiggaboo criminal in the back seat of a police car.

It was a short three blocks to the police station. As they drove into the underground garage, Celeste's mind swirled with a collage of stories she'd heard from Margo and other volunteers who'd been arrested, a couple of them raped or beaten or both before they got to whatever floor they were being taken to. Celeste tried to make herself disappear, to curl up into a tiny ball on the back seat of the car. The garage was dark, dank, and smelled of layered exhaust and cigarette smoke. Police cars parked at angles. Uniforms walked and talked, all with white faces, all giving her hard looks. She was the enemy in her peach summer dress.

The two officers, young and scrub-faced, sandwiched her between them as they entered the elevator. Celeste drifted to the back wall as the doors closed and the airless box lifted, her eyes focused on the lighting floor numbers above the doors. Margo had walked them through the arrest procedure all week long. She had to stick to what she'd learned. *Stay calm. Stay alive.* Sweat poured out of her body. On the third floor, the officers again directed her between them as they exited the elevator and strolled ever so quietly into a square interrogation room. They sat her at a small wood table. High windows, too high to see anything but big blue sky and grand puffs of white clouds sailing by. Nothing on the walls. The room was close. She needed air.

"What's your name?" The taller of the two spoke. He'd removed his hat, which left a red line imprinted across his forehead and whiter skin between the line and his hair. His eyes were blue-gray, his hair black and shiny as a new forty-five record.

"Celeste Tyree." She trapped his eyes then looked down quickly. "Am I under arrest?"

"We ask the questions." No cartoon accent drawling across the air. Just straight talk, hard. Clipped. Where was he from? Had he come south, too, just like she had, only on the opposite side of the line?

The other officer floated to the back of the small room, put his foot up on the seat of a chair. He looked younger; maybe he was a trainee, too.

Neither officer had on a name tag. *Okay, Margo, now what?* Just dark blue uniforms with metal buttons, clanking handcuffs, billy clubs sticking up in the back, the gun, all hard, all opaque. She looked at their shoes, black thick-soled things with shoelaces.

"Where you from?" The questioning officer frowned into her face in a dare. *Careful, girl. Miss'sippi ain't nothing to play with.*

She wanted to ask him the same question. Insolence, she knew, would not be tolerated. Survive. Remember the porter at the train station. Take low to keep the peace. Tap dance if you have to. "Detroit." She kept her eyes down, the Negro look. She'd been warned about locking eyes with southern cops. It's cause for a hit, a punch. Margo told her that. Keep your eyes down to camouflage anger. When you look them in the eye, make sure there's no anger, no resentment, no harshness in your eyes.

"You a communist?" He put his strong hands on the table near her. She could see his hands. Sun-tanned. He was nearly the same color as she, but not quite. He had the golden brown skin, like Momma Bessie's turkey at Thanksgiving. She had already passed that.

"No, sir." In another place, she'd have laughed at the question. He was standing so close to her she could smell his sweat and soap. Early in the day sweat. Thick sudsy-smelling soap, mixed with salt sweat. By evening he'd be rank.

"Your parents know you down here stirring up trouble? You could get hurt down here." He moved back a step.

"My parents know where I am." She'd been told to say no more. If they kept her, Margo would know when she went back to the corner to pick her up. She wasn't supposed to leave that corner. She'd know. She'd come to the police station to get her. They hadn't said she was under arrest.

In truth, they didn't have to. They could keep her and tell the world they never picked her up or that they released her and all the while she could be rotting in a cell or worse, released into the hands of the Klan in the middle of the night.

The two officers left her sitting in the little room. She blessed her sweating body—at least she wouldn't have to go to the bathroom. The officers came back, directed her up and out the door, back into the elevator. Down they went into the garage, into the car, and back to the same corner. The older officer opened the car door for her, careful not to touch her, and told her to have a nice day. Her imagination had scurried to outrun reality. The officers rode away. The box of flyers was gone. Celeste waited for Margo in the brilliant sun. She'd survived her first encounter with the police in Mississippi. Not even a hit. Lucky she was, just like Shuck. She felt proud, standing under the awning of the shoestore waiting for Margo, praying she'd be on time.

That afternoon, Margo took Celeste and Ramona around Jackson like they were junior high school children on a field trip, showing them the city itself, pointing out the churches that were pro-movement and those that were not. They were the sideshow at a circus as they slow cruised around the city. Celeste, her confidence brimming over, told the story of her trip to the police station, which didn't really compare to the stories being told of real beatings, of terrified runs for one's life, of real arrests. But it was her story to tell.

That evening, they ate rich southern food at Mercer's, the Negro-owned restaurant near the One Man, One Vote office. They felt free and good even living under such a clear threat from the police and the local whites. They were watched, and they knew it. They were followed, and they were sneered at on the streets. They stood in the pro-movement church and listened to speakers and sang freedom songs until their throats went raw.

The day after the news hit about the three missing volunteers, mimeographed copies of new check-in procedures were posted on the bulletin board, stuffed into every mail slot, and taped to both sides of the bathroom door. A shrill quiet fell over the bustling One Man, One Vote office. After less than a week of orientation, Margo told Celeste and Ramona they were ready to go to their project cities. They hugged their goodbyes, waved their copies of the new check-in procedures in the air, and tried to ride high over their feelings of dread. With three of their volunteers already missing, the summer camp illusion was completely gone. Ramona left for Indianola in the Delta and Margo for Aberdeen.

The Mississippi sun pounded Celeste and Matt Higgens as they loaded her suitcase, along with two boxes of children's books for her freedom school, into the trunk of his late model Dodge. Matt told her he was from Kansas City. He had a round face and a stocky build, and was dark as live oak bark. He wore his de rigueur movement overalls over a white dress shirt with the sleeves rolled up to the elbows. Celeste felt her scoop necked tan cotton dress would ignite if she didn't get into the shade. She'd dressed to meet the woman who would be her hostess in Pineyville, and wanted to be spiffy looking when she stepped out of that car.

They headed out, Matt crawling through Jackson. They picked up Route 49, leaving Hinds County for Rankin. Route 49 would take them south to Hattiesburg, where they'd pick up Route 11 to Pineyville. It might have been out of the way, but nobody in their right mind was going to take any shortcuts over the back roads. Celeste had shoved her copy of the new check-in procedures into her book bag along with a postcard from J.D. that she'd taken from her mail slot in the One Man, One Vote office. She pulled out the new rules, which were full of emphatic capitalizations: (1) If you travel away from your project city, call before you leave, call the Jackson office when you return. (2) Keep vehicles serviced by friendly mechanics. (3) Drive UNDER the speed limit at ALL times. (4) If you blow a tire, ride on the rim until you're in a safe place. (5) NO TRAVELING ALONE. (6) Report any harassment or violence to this office first, the FBI second, and the local authorities third. (7) STICK TO THE MAIN ROADS.

Celeste shoved the sheet back into her book-bag and turned off the crackling radio, leaving the noise of the engine and the sound of the wind whipping along the sides of the car.

"You don't *look* like the kind of girl whose parents would let her be a civil rights worker. You down here looking for something to fill yo' hot pussy, or you here to get these niggers off their asses and out to vote?" Matt dipped his head twice and chuckled. If he'd been walking, it would have been a dipping stroll, the words spoken out of the side of his mouth from a face beneath a greasy do-rag holding the processed hair in place. He either longed to be a thug or he'd already made it.

Celeste stared at him over the top of her black-framed sunglasses, which continually slid down her nose on a river of sweat. Her forehead wrinkled in disbelief, and her neck stiffened like it was being held in a brace. "Jesus. What kind of looks *would* qualify me to be down here, Matt?" She thought he'd run the car into a ditch the way he kept turning toward her. She remembered Ramona's comment about the "high-yellow first line of defense" at Howard. Was that where he was going with this, too?

"I been to Detroit, baby, I know. Yo' momma would shit a brick if she knew someone as black as me even *sat* next to you. You a red-bone. That suntan ain't hiding much." He bumped onto the gravel shoulder, then bumped back onto the pavement. Sweat pebbled across his dark forehead and began to stream.

Celeste slashed him a look, then rolled her eyes so hard she thought they'd lock into a hateful glare. "If we're fighting for rights, I guess that includes my rights, too, hot pussy, red-bone looks, and all." She'd never said the word *pussy* in her life, and now she'd said it to a honcho movement guy. "You may be a big time civil rights movement veteran, but you sound like a street thug to me." She gave him one more serious eye-roll and turned to stare out the window, tears burning just behind her eyes. Shuck had taught her well how to back people off of her, but it felt like she'd damaged something of herself in the process. Shuck never wanted her to wear her heart on her sleeve. *Don't let 'em see you cry.* All she could think now was that she'd been in Mississippi a full week and not called him like she knew she was supposed to do. Didn't matter where she was—she'd promised to call and let him know she was all right.

On both sides of the highway, flat farmland spread as far as the eye could see, vegetables wilting in the heat of midday. Giant live oaks cornered frame houses with deep porches sitting at least a half-mile back from the highway. Nothing moving but the car. Celeste never felt so alone.

Another sneaked glance from Matt. "Bet yo' daddy's a doctor, huh?"

"He's a numbers man. Owns a bar." The blustery air shredded her words, and she didn't care. She mumbled, "If he was here, he'd kick your ass all the way to New Orleans." No way he heard her, and good thing he hadn't.

Matt's head whipped around. "You *jiving?*"

"Why would I be *jiving?*" Celeste folded her arms across her chest, her hair flying around her head, the ends slapping her in the face curling into her mouth. Forget looking nice for her arrival in Pineyville.

"*Yo'* daddy's a gangster? Back-up a minute, let me take another look at you." Matt's disbelief insulted and diminished who she was minus Shuck.

"Girl, you hot. You got all kinda shit going on, sitting over there all quiet and fine." Matt patted his hands on the steering wheel in time to some unheard rhythm. "Bet he drives a Cadillac."

"Yeah, he drives a Cadillac. So what?" She eyed Matt quickly; suddenly she wanted to say that as much as she loved Shuck, he wasn't the one riding down a forlorn highway in the middle of Mississippi, laying his life on the line for the cause. That Cadillac was safe and sound in Detroit. And so was Shuck.

"Probably been in more gunfights than John Wayne. I love me some gangsters." Matt nodded his head up and down, dropping the corners of his mouth into a fake frown.

"You don't know what you're talking about." Celeste wanted him to shut up, to get her to Pineyville in one piece and say a quick goodbye.

"Girl, you probably don't know your own father. He wouldn't tell you everything. Want you to grow up all proper. Go to the right schools, be around the right people." Matt was on a roll. What did his father do, she wondered? Kansas City wasn't that far from Detroit.

"You gonna sit there and tell *me* about my own father? You need to quit." She wanted nothing more than to get away from this movement honcho who seemed like he wanted to break her down. Something in it sounded like J.D. telling her he knew more about the blues than she did.

"All right, now, don't go getting huffy with me. We in Mississippi. I might be the one who saves yo red-bone ass. Know what I mean?"

"I might be the one who saves yours, too." Celeste sucked her teeth. She had wanted with all her heart to say, *I might be the one who saves your black ass,* but didn't. She was sitting in his car, at his mercy, on a road going to what sounded like hell, with no way to do a thing about it if he put her out of that car.

This wasn't the movement she'd spent months thinking about in Ann Arbor. The speakers who came to campus talked about the awakening of the south, the drive to register millions of Negro people who hadn't voted since Reconstruction. They spoke of courageous young students, Negro and white, from all over the country putting their lives on the line for what was right and just. Joan of Arc and Harriet Tubman. Now here she was stuck in a car with a guy who wanted to talk about gangsters, red-bones, and her sexuality.

They drove deeper into trench Mississippi, gutbucket Mississippi, the baking red earth stretching out on all sides, armies of insects slapping into the windshield. At this rate, by the time they got to Pineyville, they'd be driving blind behind a crust of dead bugs. Celeste closed the window half way to soften the beating she was taking in her face and hair. The car butted over the unevenness of the pavement. No smooth expressway here. Keep a good watch on the road, they'd said in Jackson. The three missing boys might have been held captive in some storm shelter or basement— maybe their captors moved them from place to place. Maybe they were free, escaped, trying to flag a friendly soul down. She stared, searching the landscape as if the very act of looking might conjure the missing three. Anything but having to deal with Matt anymore.

The thumping tires and the press of warm air lulled Celeste, and she rested her head back, strengthening herself with memories of Shuck and summer rides in his Cadillac with the top down, cruising the Detroit streets, stopping at his stops, the men back-slapping and number-writing, always happy to see Shuck. *Hey man, how you doing? How them kids? All right now.* Starched collars and cuffs, cufflinks like gold nuggets in the sunshine, stocking-capped-slick hair, pinkie rings and wide movie smiles. Smelling like heaven came out of an Old Spice bottle. Smooth. Shuck stepping up on the shoeshine stand, the crack-slap of the rag as one of his cronies gave him the best shine on the west side of Detroit, and Billy and her sitting up on the high seats, feet dangling, watching, listening to every word of the repartee. That was a long time ago, she thought, and opened her eyes. No place to hide in Mississippi.

Matt was eyeing his rearview mirror. He slowed, though they'd never reached the speed limit. "There's a state trooper behind us. If they stop us, let *me* do the talking."

Celeste turned to see the trooper's flashing lights, following so close it seemed it would touch their back fender. Celeste reached for something, anything to hold onto and came up with the mumbled words to a freedom song. She spoke the words as if they were a prayer, pushing the meaning up into her head and down into her stomach just like blonde-haired Margo had taught her. This wasn't Jackson. Out here, things were different. The melody came into her voice and she sang quietly. *Ain't gonna let nobody turn me round, turn me round, turn me round.*

Matt snorted quietly. "That shit works in church." He pulled onto the gravel shoulder. "It don't do a muthafuckin thing out here." He took a good breath, then sighed deeply. "No strong black woman smart talk cause they'll kick my black ass. You hear?"

For a fleeting second, she wished they would.

The trooper's brown uniform was pressed and crisp. He yanked open the door, his steel gray eyes piercing in a slash of sunlight under the brim of his cowboy-style hat. The billy club was in his hand, and she saw the black handle of his holstered gun, the silver handcuffs like Indian jewelry shining on a brown blanket. He pulled Matt out of the car, and Matt's limp body nearly fell to the ground. No resistance. Remember that. *Do not resist.* The trooper dragged Matt along the side of the car, and Celeste heard his shoes scuffing and grating over the gravel. She lifted out of her seat, twisting around to see, didn't know if she should get out of the car, try to talk to them quietly, plead for Matt. Matt had told her to let him do the talking. She'd heard around the office that he'd been arrested more than half a dozen times.

"Turn round and face front," the trooper barked.

He shoved Matt into the hands of the other trooper and came back to the opened door.

"I said, turn round, less you want some of this!" His lips were drawn up into hard lines making his teeth look big. His arm muscles pressed against the fabric of his shirt. He cracked his billy club against the side of the car. It sounded like a gunshot. Celeste's spine jolted like a steel rod had been shoved through her body. *Ain't gonna let nobody turn me round, turn me round, turn me round.* She sang softly, her breath coming in frightened pants. Fear deadened her memory so that she could only recall two lines of the song. Matt said it didn't work out here, but there wasn't anything else. The words drifted in and out of her mind like a ghost echo as if they weren't really coming from her at all.

A thud and the car lurched. She had to be still, be quiet. They had guns, billy clubs. Cattle prods. Margo always said if you got stopped like this, hold onto your training, pray and sing, otherwise you'll only make it worse. You can't win by fighting here. They have all the guns. Celeste kept singing. *Gonna keep on walking, keep on talking, on my way to freedom's land.*

"Bet you got them three boys right here in this car, nigger." The trooper spat the words out, his accent chopping off the consonants.

An excuse to open the trunk. Sweat poured into Celeste's eyes. Her hands gripped in tight fists in her lap. She sneaked a look back. The trooper stood to the side of the car. Matt and the other, the one holding him, were hidden by the opened trunk. She hoped they wouldn't take the freedom school books or her suitcase. The trunk slammed shut, rocking the car. Then the sound of punches, and a sharp crack. Matt moaned. His nonresistance didn't stop the blows that followed. Now she didn't want to turn around, didn't want to see what they were doing; she set her eyes on a black-barked shade tree marking the turn into a dusty side road. Beyond it stretched rows of crops, peanuts maybe or beans. Neat. No dark people cranked over at the waist between the rows.

"Nigger. Go back where you came from."

She'd love to be gone. Far off in the tranquil blue sky, rain clouds began to pile up like scoops of vanilla ice cream. There was the sound of air expelled in a moan. They must have hit him in the stomach. She didn't know which trooper was talking now. One of them snarled at Matt about *niggers chasing white women.* If they got on that, Matt was doomed and so was she. Better to be anything else, to have horns even, than to be accused of chasing, whistling, winking, even looking at a white woman. For a moment she thought of J.D.—those last times together, when a kind of desperation perverted their lovemaking, changing it from the joyous connection of two people clamped together by a fierce electrical charge into something dark and painful that they both identified as the falling away of love and attraction. She had hardly believed they could go from one to the other so fast. In the end, there had been silence. J.D. went back to his studio and she cowered in the apartment on North Oak Street, depleted and sad. Celeste felt pitiful and weak now again, sitting there by the side of the road listening to two white Mississippi troopers beat the shit out of a black man. Her head down, she prayed they wouldn't kill him.

"You just a bunch of communist outsider agitators. Come down here to stir up our nigras. Everything was fine til y'all got here." After each phrase, Celeste felt the car rock.

There might not be anything left of Matt to drive her to Pineyville. If he needed a doctor, what could she do? Drive to the next town and call Jackson, or just turn the car around and go back the way they'd come? She knew how to drive. And where was the traffic? It was midday. There should be cars driving by. The troopers must have stopped traffic in both directions so no one would see. Had they been followed all the way from Jackson?

The troopers shoved Matt back into the driver's seat. His shirt was missing two buttons and one of his overall straps was hanging off his shoulder. "Git in that car and you niggers git going. Next time, it'll go harder for you."

They slammed the door, then swung their billy clubs like bats, smashing the front and back driver's-side windows. Celeste turned her face away from the shards of flying glass and covered her face with her hands. Crystals landed in her hair, pricked her legs, hit the seat, bounced off the dashboard. They were booby-trapped in glass. The troopers got in their own car and pulled alongside. The trooper in the passenger seat slowly raised his gun and pointed it at Matt's head. She opened her mouth to scream before tearing her eyes away from the awful black hole of the barrel. Across the fields she saw a quiet tree, heard the whistling of a errant bird. She grabbed at the door handle, ready to crawl out of the car, roll onto the ground, and run for the tree's shelter. But Matt pulled her down on the seat under his arm so fast it took all the air out of her body. He held her underneath him, her snot and tears spreading across her cheek, little pieces of glass sticking into her arms and scraping her face.

"We know y'all hiding them boys. Trying to make us look bad."

She heard the cops laugh, and then the loud blast of the gun firing. Celeste expected Matt's warm blood to come streaming down over her. The troopers sped away, the acrid smell of burning rubber wafting into the car.

Matt sat up slowly, releasing Celeste. She looked up at him expecting the worst, but there was no gush of blood. A thin line of it meandered down her forearm, about to round the curve there and drip onto the car seat. There were shallow scratches in crazy patterns on both of her arms. She sat still, afraid any movement meant another cut. She touched her face for more blood, then climbed out of the car to shake out her clothes and hair. The troopers might turn onto a side road and come at them again or call ahead to the next town, tell the local police to stop them this time. They needed to call Jackson, call the FBI, call somebody to let them know they were in danger on the road to Pineyville.

Matt tossed glass out of the front seat of the car, making quick glances ahead, behind, furtive takes, fear all over him. She wanted to tell him it was okay that he was afraid, he didn't have to be a hero for her.

"Welcome to Mississippi." His voice hollowed over cracked lips. His breath came in quick pants. A knot glistened on his forehead.

"You need some ice for your head." She reached in to throw more of the broken glass out of the car then climbed back in.

"No stops until Pineyville. Be all right." Matt bumped the car onto the road. No smart lip now. His mask-still face stared at the highway ahead.

Celeste wanted mercurochrome for her scratches, a drink of cold water, an aspirin, a gin and tonic. She pressed Kleenex on her cuts, smelling Matt's aroma encasing her, drowning out her own. Animal as prey. She smelled her own stink beneath his, all anger and fear. Her mouth tasted dry, her tongue like a salt cake.

"Did you get a name or a patrol car number, anything we can report to the FBI?"

Matt sat like stone. "No."

She wondered where else they'd hit him. In Jackson she'd learned that the cops go for the organs—the kidneys, the liver—and bone structures like the spine and the kneecaps. Orientation. What to do? No ice. Try to get Matt to talk. "Don't we need to call Jackson? You need to see a doctor. What if you have a concussion or something?"

He said nothing.

Way off to their right, a train sped over the baking red earth, a toy to dream on. Was it going to New Orleans? The City of New Orleans, Ltd. Her train. Name like a lure. Music, dancing, freedom, water. That woman in the station had said to her, "Don't want to miss my train." Celeste was sad to see it go past, knowing that whatever sanity was left in the world went with it. She wished Matt could speed up, catch the train, throw her suitcase and book-bag up and help her get on board. So long, Mississippi, see you later.

They passed through Collins. Hattiesburg was thirty miles ahead and from the looks of things, there wasn't going to be anything much in between. Celeste scoped each side road, each driveway, looking for patrol cars, cars with white men in groups, panel trucks with loaded gun racks. The pain in the little cuts on her arms quieted to a dull prickle.

Matt's eyes shot back and forth from the rearview mirror to the highway. He steadied his hands on the steering wheel, his jaw dropping, his lower lip slack, his body braced.

Celeste sank in her seat. "What now?"

Matt kept his eyes dead forward, slowing as a car pulled around to pass them. A white sheet flung across its front seat-back lifted in the draft of the car's acceleration as it went by. It billowed gently, like Momma Bessie's bed sheets on the backyard clothesline. Then, like a crumpling parachute, airless, quiet, the sheet relaxed. A stretch of red satiny fabric lay next to the snowy sheet. Four white men, two in front, two in back, glanced at Matt and Celeste. They wore short-sleeved shirts, relaxed ties, narrow-brimmed straw hats. Their eyes were flat. They went by, a blurry glare of recognition passing between them.

"Klan meeting in Hattiesburg tonight." Matt smiled a creak of a smile. "You hear about them Negroes in Louisiana?"

"What about 'em?" Celeste was so happy he was talking, she didn't much care what he said.

"They arming themselves. The Deacons for Defense and Justice. Don't want to hear another word about nonviolence." Matt stared ahead, watching the car that had passed them disappear on down the highway, driving a good deal faster than they were with no fear of being harassed.

After what had just happened to Matt, she had her own new questions about the payoff for nonviolence. Matt had gone limp, never spoke a provocative word, and they beat him anyway. You might as well have a gun. This waiting for the spiritual power of nonviolence to tame the opponent was already running short. So many people had already been beaten and jailed and the summer was just beginning. And now those three volunteers were completely missing, just gone, disappeared like vapors. Two Jewish students from New York and a Negro kid from Meridian.

Celeste had a sudden overwhelming feeling that she'd never get back home, never sit in Momma Bessie's kitchen again or picnic on Belle Isle or walk along the shore of the river, looking across and seeing Canada as a benign restful place across the way. She'd never sit at the bar with Shuck and pretend she was more grown up than she really was, sipping the alcohol-free concoction that Posey used to make for her and for Billy. Now she could drink real drinks at the bar, drop quarters in the party girl, swap stories with the regulars and tap her feet to Shuck's jazz favorites. It seemed so far away. That wallpaper Shuck had ordered especially for his bar with all those fine Negro people who seemed to have the world in their hands, bigger than life up there on the walls of the Royal Gardens, smiling and reminding everyone that they were real. It was all on another planet. She had dropped into a foreign country, an alien place filled with death and pain. She felt the scratches on her arms, the tiny nicks in the skin on her face, pressing them, feeling the pricks of renewed pain.

South of Hattiesburg, the rust-red soil changed to orange. Along the

road, the gravel shoulders gave way to soft sand, then rolled off into a
shallow depression. For a few miles, the land up-hilled into a forest of long-
needled pines that blocked the sun and perfumed the air like a thousand
women wearing fringed-green dresses, laughing. Margo had called it the
Piney Woods.

Just after Lumberton, with the speedometer marking them at still well
under the limit, they entered Pearl River County as if on tiptoe. Celeste
felt coolness in the air, felt it on her stinging face, prayed it would last. But
within minutes the long-needled pines gave way to hundreds of decaying
stumps, dead logs scattered in the open spaces. The barren expanse screamed
beneath the peacock-blue tropical sky, a sky fit for an island paradise in the
Gulf of Mexico. The sun pounded down on it all. She flinched but there
was no getting away from its rays.

Before they reached the Pineyville town center, Matt left the blacktop
for a part-sand, part-gravel side road. No alluvial plain, no cotton plantations here. Power lines, but no phone lines. Matt pulled up and stopped
near a stunted water pipe with a spigot that seemed to periscope up out
of a square concrete platform. At the turn-off, Celeste saw a large country mailbox attached to a leaning post, beneath a street sign that read,
"Freshwater Road."

5

Detroit summers pulled thick, water-logged air from the lakes, boiled it with car and bus exhausts, mixed in smokestack poisons, then asked you to inhale. At Shuck's house, on an island boulevard lined with red maple, elm, yellow birch, and hickory, the trees saved the day, so that on the ground you could breathe in the scent of roses, lilacs, and wet, fresh-cut June grass.

The first thing a city does when it knows Negroes are moving into a neighborhood is cut down all the trees. Thank God they'd done little of that on the West Side except over by the projects. Not a tree in sight there. Outer Drive, where Shuck lived, had the feel of a rich man's street, lush and green in summer, vibrant red, orange, and ocher in autumn, and quietly carpeted with snow in winter. The trees made the difference.

Whatever went on in those perfect houses stayed neatly behind closed doors. None of that sitting out front loud-talking. In fact, Shuck barely knew who his neighbors were; he nodded and greeted the people from those quiet houses without ever thinking about who lived in which. He preferred it that way since his life was still the nightlife. His neighbors lived and worked the nine to five or something close to it, or so he thought. For those who blue-collared at the plants, they put up such a good front of middle class respectability, of nine to five instead of shifts at the plants, you missed the blue of it all together. He appreciated that.

One night a new customer happened into the Royal Gardens still wearing his work clothes, a familiar face but Shuck knew not from where until in conversation it came out that the man lived right around the corner from him. The man seemed embarrassed to be seen in his work clothes and he never came back to the Royal Gardens again. Shuck's regulars worked blue-collar, too, but they wore sports jackets and slacks to work and at home and changed into their work clothes at the job. Those blue-collar clothes were not for the streets.

Posey gave Wilamena's first phone message to Shuck. Shuck decided, without telling Posey, that he wasn't of a mind to return the call. She called a second time and a third. Posey said she was hot on the phone, fussing at him as if he hadn't given Shuck the message. Posey told him to take care of it because he didn't want her calling and cussing him out. Shuck knew Wilamena never used that kind of language, but she could make you feel like she did.

He propped the little square of paper with her name and phone number written in Posey's grade-school scrawl against the base of his bedside lamp. When he opened his eyes, the black ink vibrated on the white background of the paper. In the shade of his secluded room, the drapes drawn tight for daytime sleeping, he eyed the numbers and considered selecting two sets of three and playing them on Monday. If he played the area code boxed, and the numbers fell, he'd get a hit regardless of the configuration. Funny that Posey thought he didn't have his ex-wife's number. Maybe he figured with the kids grown and gone, it had faded from Shuck's mind. But Shuck was good at remembering numbers.

He dozed until afternoon, surface dreaming of a Wilamena who gave him kisses that spun him out of control, flew his heart on a balloon caught in a sailing breeze. When he woke, he'd dreamed so hard he shuddered to find she wasn't sleeping beside him.

Wilamena had been in the Outer Drive house only once. She'd breezed into town for her own mother's funeral and stopped by on a moment's notice to see Celeste's new bedroom furniture. She'd spent most of her time there pacing in the foyer waiting for her husband, Cyril Atwood, to pick her up. She never saw Shuck's room with its wall of east-facing windows, the tan and blue silk comforter spread, and the matching drapes. She never felt its deep carpet under her feet. Maybe she didn't want to see what his life had become. But he hadn't even been home that afternoon, and he always kept his bedroom door closed.

Shuck showered and threw on his blue summer robe over a pair of black slacks. He went downstairs and headed straight for his high-fidelity record player in the dining room. He stacked on two LPs, staring at the machine until the needle locked into the vinyl's grooves. Count Basie's downbeat sounded through the silence. He retrieved the morning paper, dropped it on the kitchen table, then went out the backdoor to the expanse of yard, the smell of grass and leaves like a new world coming. Wilamena loved this afternoon light, the light that signaled the softening down of the sun as it dipped behind the giant elms and maples standing in rows all over the neighborhood. Back in the kitchen, he fried himself three pieces of bacon, scrambled two eggs with a splash of milk, salt, pepper, and half a palm of grated cheddar cheese, made toast, and perked two cups of good strong coffee. He sat in the kitchen and went through the newspaper with flat, focused attention. After scouring the front sections, he turned slowly to the sports page. Neighbors along Outer Drive dreamed of supper as he sat down to his first meal of the day.

Shuck spent the two weeks since he got the first message kiting through an assortment of reasons for Wilamena's call, knowing all the while that it had to be about Celeste. The thought that distracted him as he drove back and forth to the club was that Wilamena's husband might be lying in a hospital bed holding on to life by a breath. Wilamena might just need Shuck's support.

She'd meet him at the Albuquerque airport, her dark hair in wavy lengths to her shoulders, wearing a dress the color of the New Mexico sky on a postcard she'd sent to Celeste. It would sway gently as she walked. Her golden brown eyes would flash her need for him. She'd be darker than she'd ever been in Detroit, and he wouldn't stop looking at her. They'd rush to the hospital, but it'd be too late. Over drinks at his deluxe hotel, she'd ask if he was involved with anyone, tell him they should rescue their own love. He'd sit there with a long face and hold back his heart. For once, with Wilamena, he'd hold back his heart. They'd order more drinks, and he'd take her up to his room without saying anything about the future, knowing that would only ignite her passion. They'd make love like they'd done a long time ago.

When he looked down, his plate was empty and he hadn't tasted a thing. For years, he'd worked at convincing himself that he no longer loved Wilamena, that he only *remembered* loving her.

New Mexico, the wild land of the southwest with little water and fewer Negroes, was an impossible concept to grasp. Wilamena might as well have gone to the moon. On the postcard, the place looked all dark pink and white hot, but the color of the sky, the dense blue of it, was new, had a light behind it that didn't diminish the depth of color. No skyline at all. He pictured a long, low-slung house with sand right up to the doors and windows, cactus plants everywhere. Albuquerque.

Shuck put his dirty dishes in the sink, then splashed a generous jigger of Crown Royal over ice cubes and carried it to the foyer, where he sat in the upholstered chair by the window. After Wilamena remarried and settled out there, Shuck made sure she knew that everyone in Detroit was doing fine without her. Cyril Atwood. He rolled the name around in his mind. He was the quiet type, an engineer, tall and lean with deep-set eyes. Not a smile in sight. He wondered how Wilamena, who he knew had a need for grandness and flash, could stand to live with a man who barely spoke and didn't like music. He'd never met a Negro man who didn't like music, but Cyril was as close to white as Wilamena could get. She had to be going crazy with boredom out there.

The occasional car leisured by out on Outer Drive, the driver no doubt admiring the thick, deep, shadowed grass, the height and fullness of the grand elm trees up and down the street. He slowly dialed Wilamena's number in New Mexico, one number at a time, each one making him feel like he was slipping on ice, smooth but cold. He left his finger in the rotary dial, let the machine take his finger all the way back to the metal stop. What if Cyril answered the phone? So what? He had every right to call Wilamena. She was the mother of his children. But something in his voice might reveal his morning dream. He sipped his Crown Royal for cool and courage, the ice cubes cooling down the sting of a day's first drink. The ringing echoed on the other end of the line. Shuck focused on the lush music rolling through his house, the memories that came with the sounds.

"Hello?" Wilamena's voice pitched forward, startled.

"It's me." Shuck held his breath, flutters winging in his stomach. He didn't want to stumble over his words like a tongue-tied kid. It had been months since he'd heard her voice, close to a year. Even her "hello" was like no other. Strong, present and turning in on itself at the same time. Like a girl.

"Well, I'm glad you returned the call, finally. I was beginning to think you never got my message." Wilamena paused.

Not an iota of Negro in Wilamena's voice. Nothing of Detroit lingered. The music twisted a breath out of him. "No, no. Posey gave it to me." He sipped his drink. His foot tapped on the plush carpet to the beat of the music, the husky voicing of saxophones, the graceful piano licks. "I'm a working man." Wilamena thought that outsmarting the police who pursued gamblers like they were murderers and outrunning the Italians who coveted his lucrative numbers business didn't constitute real work.

"And, how's Posey doing?" She made an effort to be mannerly. Posey knew them both in the old days, but she'd never asked about him before. It was her way of apologizing for bringing Posey up short on the phone. Shuck knew that asking about Posey wasn't necessarily about Posey. She wanted something specific. He didn't know if he wanted her to get to the point quickly or if he just wanted to linger there with her voice and the music.

"Fine. Everybody's fine, Wilamena." Shuck sat back in the chair, settled in, and let the memory of her body smooth out inside him.

"Are you at *home*?" Wilamena sounded doubtful. "You were never one for hanging around a house."

She nailed him. But that was all in the past. These days, he searched for reasons to stay home. He just couldn't find any. Behind her clipped speech, he saw the smile of even teeth and how her eyes sparkled when she danced the jitterbug in the aisle of the Fox Theatre. When Duke Ellington eased into "Mood Indigo," she closed her eyes and leaned into him. They were slow dancing in the blue-speckled light of a spinning globe. Now, he hoped she could hear the soulful recording of Coleman Hawkins's mellow horn all the way to the desert.

"Shuck?" A softness in her voice.

Shuck stared out the foyer window, lost in the deepening shade.

"Are you there? Shuck?" By the second time she said his name, the old Wilamena had seeped in, demanding, self-important.

"Yeah. I'm here." He wasn't yet ready to let go of the fantasy he'd created in his mind about his ex-wife. "You oughta see the club, Wilamena." He'd said too much. Wilamena was a married woman. Better that she stay out there in New Mexico, stay out of trouble. Nothing out there for her to do. Shuck thought of her dressed in a light blouse that revealed her perfect shoulders, a skirt that rounded her hips and thighs. She had a real woman's figure. Where was she sitting or standing? Where was Cyril? In the pause, he put his dream words into her mouth and answered in his own head.

I'd love to see the Royal Gardens, Shuck.

It was supposed to be us, Wilamena. Walking down Seventh Avenue, hanging out in Harlem.

"I tried to call Celeste but her phone's disconnected." Wilamena's actual words broke through his reverie. "I thought she was going to summer school."

One thing Shuck knew for sure: Wilamena didn't like unearthing their daughter through him. He stopped himself from saying she'd gone on a trip to Europe, or even Africa, somewhere far away where Wilamena couldn't reach her. He settled for the truth. "She's in Mississippi. Doing voter work for the summer." He sipped the smooth liquor, and hoped the sound of ice cubes clinking on glass made it through the wires to New Mexico.

"Why would she do that?" A true wonderment arose in her voice.

"They call it Freedom Summer, Wilamena." Shuck knew well that she didn't own up to being connected in any way to any Negro in Mississippi. To any Negro anywhere.

"Who calls it? Who's *they*?" Wilamena's voice seized like a shallow pond freezing over in a blizzard. "She needs to see a psychiatrist. What's she trying to prove? How Negro she is?"

Shuck laughed. "Celeste is fine." Without giving her credit for it, he accepted Wilamena's appraisal as at least partly true. But no matter. Celeste needed to be in the real world. Just maybe not the Mississippi real world.

"It's not funny, Shuck. Mississippi, of all places in the world? Voter work? You both need to see a doctor." Wilamena didn't get it. Never did. Something missing in her view of things. Like she saw herself in a Hollywood movie playing the white girl. It was the thing Shuck disliked about her, what he'd always wanted to protect Celeste from becoming.

"It was her decision to make, Wilamena. College kids from all over the country are down there. White and Negro. Lot going on in Mississippi." The trees on Outer Drive formed swaying shapes against a tilting gray-blue sky.

"I don't care about them." Her tone arched into a point, a blade.

"Tell me something I don't know." He nearly said, you don't care about anyone but yourself, but he pushed it down his throat, and it nearly gagged him, that little truth he'd been dying to report for all those years. He'd spent years trying to protect Celeste from the ravages of her own mother, knowing all the while that Wilamena didn't intend to hurt, she just couldn't help it. The music lay back against the walls and carpet. He tried to find the beat again, the sleekness in the sounds, but had lost it.

"Well, did you even try to talk her out of it? What if she gets killed? Negroes die down there for looking the wrong way. Are you crazy? She doesn't owe those people anything. You *let* her go?" Wilamena hissed in a whisper.

Shuck wondered if someone had come into the room where she was. He listened for footsteps, doors. "She was already in Mississippi when I found out." He wanted to shake her through the phone, tell her it was way too late for all this caring.

"What a stupid idea." Wilamena dismissed the entire meaning of Freedom Summer in one short phrase. Shuck recognized the throwaway. She banished the notions and feelings. Freedom Summer withered and fell away in her disdain.

"She's fine. Leave it alone." He wasn't going to let on as to how frightened he was for Celeste—how he scoured the papers and television broadcasts to keep up on Mississippi news, the shootings and burnings and bombings. It was a small war. If Celeste died in Mississippi, it would be on him.

"Is there a phone number where I can reach her?" She sounded officious now, like she and only she had the capacity to correct a situation that had spun out of control. Of course, he'd been waiting on a phone call himself.

"You can call the Jackson office of One Man, One Vote. They'll pass a message on to her." A delight the thickness of a blade of grass in his voice. He knew the conversation was over, but he refused to let go. "She's doing what she believes in. Can't fault her for that, can we?"

"Passing messages along. How absurd in this day and age." Her exasperation singed the air. "Well, where is she living? You're telling me there's no phone?"

"Some people don't have phones, Wilamena. Pure and simple." In truth, he didn't know if Celeste had a phone or not, but assumed she didn't since he hadn't heard from her. Now he wanted to let Wilamena go. He told her again to go ahead and call One Man, One Vote in Jackson, and then told her goodbye.

He drank the rest of his Crown Royal in a gulp, then walked a circle through the house, laughing to himself that he was still in love with that wrong-headed woman. He turned off the record player, poured himself another drink, then bore down on his scalawag memories, forced them back behind their gates. Some were still running in place no matter how many years went by, no matter how many fine women smiled his way. Alma was a good-looking woman, an educated woman, steady and straight, but she paled beside Wilamena. He'd be late getting to the Royal Gardens tonight. Something must be going on out there in New Mexico. She's lonely again, miserable, trying to stake a life in the unknownness of the southwest, in that dryness. Shuck liked to think of her pacing around like a caged pet, thirsty for music, for dancing, for an edge to her life. He could have her back, he told himself. She always ached for what she didn't have, never satisfied. Nothing had changed.

6

Bony dogs ran up and down barking at their arrival, then skulked off into the woods that stopped some yards from the back of the plank board house. White paint peeled off the boards. Those great long-needled pines, a thickness of them, stood arrow straight and seemed to grow out of nothing more than the peachy barren sand of a tropical island. The house with a down-leaning screened-in porch balanced on stacks of cinderblocks, with a good two feet of unprotected crawl space underneath. Off to the back and to the side, well beyond a vegetable garden, was a lopsided playhouse-looking structure, like a way station before the start of the forest. A rusted-out tiller lay crippled in the sandy earth a few yards down Freshwater Road. The next house, slightly larger, was a good half of a city block away. A pile of wood planks and cinderblocks on the ground across the road appeared to be the remains of another house.

Matt climbed out of the car and walked to the spigot, dropped his coverall straps, and took off his shirt. He bent over, flinching in pain, and stuck his head under the water, which first splashed its yellowish spray in all directions, then settled into a clear steady stream. He washed his upper body using a piece of soap from a small metal plate beside the spigot, gulping water between scrubs.

Celeste stayed in the car, her wind-whipped hair standing in spikes and corkscrews around her head, sweat caking on her skin, the little glass cuts like so many pinpricks on her arms and face. There'd been no mention of outdoor baths. How could she do this? She saw herself spooning beans from a tin plate and drinking muddy coffee from a dented cup. The only thing missing was a wood-wheeled wagon and an old mare. She eyed the patches of flaccid vegetables interspersed with drooping flowers. She remembered Margo cautioning the new volunteers against acting as if the things they were accustomed to at home might be better than what was offered here.

Matt replaced the soap and rinsed the sudsy residue from his upper body until soap scum floated on a moat surrounding the platform. Celeste searched Matt's body for signs of the beating he'd taken. His chest and arms were hairless and smooth, dark and muscular. He was shining wet. When he turned to the side, she saw a swelling near his waist.

Celeste stepped out of the car, feeling creaky from clenching with fear for so long. She joined Matt at the spigot, hiking up her dress to keep it dry. She too gulped the mineral-tasting water, felt its cool splash on her legs and arms, and finally put her whole face under the faucet before grabbing the soap bar and lathering up her face and arms.

"There's ice water in the kitchen." An older woman came out of the screened door talking, holding a towel, eyes averted from Matt's naked upper body. "You coulda waited til tomorrow with that Klan meetin' going on in Hattiesburg and all."

Mrs. Geneva Owens stood barely shorter than Celeste. Her unpressed gray hair was bunched into a fat french twist, and her dark eyes were not too old to flash. She wore a waist-tied apron over a soft yellow print cotton housedress. Her skin was dark brown though not as dark as Matt's, and her laugh lines were deep grooves that kept to their places, didn't creak off into small lines and wrinkles. She looked dutiful, alert, and invigorated.

"I didn't know a thing about it til Matt said something. We were almost here by then." Celeste spoke by way of introducing herself. "We saw a whole carload of them on the other side of Hattiesburg. Had their sheets and robes thrown over the seat back." She sounded like an excited child, as if this woman had never seen the likes of that in her life. She quickly remembered where she was.

"No need to be worrying the life outta me. What's left of it, anyway." She gave Matt the towel, then walked right back into her house as if she'd handed it to him through a bathroom door, never even acknowledging that Celeste was standing there.

Matt dried himself then tossed the towel to Celeste. He shielded himself from the house and lowered his coveralls to tuck in his shirt. "Don't go bringing that siddity Detroit shit down here. I know you got it in you." He spoke very quietly as he slipped the overall straps up onto his shoulders.

Celeste rolled her eyes at his back, water still dripping off her face and knowing full well she wasn't going to dry her face with a towel he'd used to dry his body. She'd never even done that with J.D.

"That's better." The woman came out again, walked straight to Matt and squinted at the knot on his head. "What's that on yo head? Look like you been in a fight with the devil."

"Wasn't no devil, Mrs. Owens, just a man. And I wasn't doing none of the fighting." Matt's eyes clouded and dropped in embarrassment.

"State troopers. Two of them." Celeste worked to get the attention of the older woman off Matt, who seemed to shrink at using the word "fighting." It had been a beating. She struggled, too, for some acknowledgement of her own presence. Here she was, ready again to prove she belonged exactly where she was standing. No way around it.

"Well, you won cause you here." Mrs. Owens heaved out a breath and put the positive note to it that Matt so desperately needed.

The quiet ride through the surrounding pine forest had calmed Celeste, blocked out the beating and the gun pointed at them before it was fired into the air, but it all came back when the woman said, *you won cause you here.* If they'd lost, they'd be dead.

"I got you a towel in your room, child." She took the damp towel from Celeste and smiled the slightest bit as if something was holding her back. But Celeste seized onto her use of the word "child" and knew she was going to be fine with this woman. She also figured that by the time they got into her room, the sun would've dried her off well enough. Mrs. Owens's reserve reminded her of Momma Bessie. Older Negro women notoriously favored boys. Always trying to make up for the brutalities of the world outside. Celeste had traveled that road, had seen Momma Bessie do the same thing her whole life not just with Billy and Shuck but with every walking, talking Negro man who came in her door. The men came first.

"You right about that," Matt said, remembering his manners at last. "This is Celeste Tyree. She's gonna be staying with you over the summer."

She gave Celeste a sideways glance. "You welcome here."

"Thank you, Mrs. Owens." Celeste's head bobbed with a serious expression. Full-out smiles were a long time coming in Mississippi.

"Y'all hurry and come on in here and eat this food 'fore it spoils. And I got something for that knot on your head." Mrs. Owens walked inside, the screen door giving a muffled version of a slam.

"Hey, Celeste, you got runnin' water—you just got to run outside to use it." He said it in a husky laughing whisper. "Hasn't been that long they've had electricity out here. Whole lot of white folks in Mississippi got no toilet plumbing either." As if that was supposed to make it all right. She got a better look at the small leaning structure near the pines. She didn't want to believe it was an outhouse, but what else could it be? Outdoor spigots and outdoor toilets. She hadn't connected the two when they first drove up. *You missed something, Margo.* If the One Man, One Vote office told the truth about the living circumstances, some of those volunteers would've taken a pass and stayed in the cities to do their volunteering. She checked herself. She, of all people, needed to do the harder thing, and this was going to be it.

A dark wire traveled from the house to a T-shaped pole in the back. The same poles stood all along the road as far as the eye could see. The wires were relaxed, swinging between the poles like skinny black hammocks. They never looked so naked as this back in Detroit. Mrs. Owens's pole had a transformer—close to the corner, so the power company people didn't have to venture too far down Freshwater Road, this neighborhood of glorified shacks. Matt said the houses were built by the loggers back in the days of the timber boom, when the piney woods stretched across southern Mississippi. When the forests were cleared and the loggers departed, Negro people squatted in the houses, painted them, made them into homes. It was as if the slave shanties of a hundred years ago had been painted and electrified. Not much else had changed. In clearing the land for the houses, all the shade trees had been cut down too and no one had bothered to replant them. No lounging under live oaks on Freshwater Road. If you needed to hide, you had to run through empty space like a moving target, racing for the remains of the pine forest.

"More thunderstorms through here than anywhere. The lightning fires burn those trees. They call 'em stags' heads." Matt grabbed Celeste's suitcase and walked into the house. He came back for the boxes of children's books. Celeste imagined the burned trees as escapees from some miserable past who hadn't made it out. They were caught in the moment of agony as if they'd reached their scorched hands up to a God who'd turned his back on them. She went inside.

Mrs. Owens met Celeste on the screened porch, and Celeste noticed her charcoal black eyes had a blue ring around the iris. Celeste followed her inside, noting too the lone rocking chair on the porch. She was directed to put her book-bag in a small bedroom where her suitcase and the children's books already sat just beyond the curtain that took the place of a door. There was a small sitting room directly across a hall of sorts from the bedroom.

In the kitchen, Celeste joined Matt at the small table dressed with a checkered cloth. She pushed her memories of home and Momma Bessie's china and crystal out of her mind as Mrs. Owens set down a plate of food then took the seat between them, closest to the hot gas stove. She grabbed their hands and prayed over the food. Beyond the back door and some yards from the house, that cool-looking patch of woods beckoned. Great, grand trees with delicate branches and long, long needles. They were the only thing she'd seen that reminded her of Michigan, though these pines weren't shaped like Christmas trees. A mysterious wood. How far back did it go? Was there another road beyond those trees, another cleared stretch of sandy soil with shanty houses up and down?

As hungry as she was, the hot biscuits oozing butter, pork-laced greens, and smothered chicken gave Celeste pause. Even Momma Bessie lightened her cooking in the heat of summer. But this was a special meal for Mrs. Owens, and she should eat no matter how it made her feel. She drank the iced tea and ate the food, staring out the back way and praying silently for a breeze. There was a wide work counter on the rear porch with two tin tubs, one inside the other, beside a big box of Tide and a jug of bleach. A water pump. Off the kitchen, another floral curtain marked a door. It had to be this woman's bedroom.

"They're probably going to dredge the rivers up around Meridian if they don't find 'em soon." Matt chewed and drank his iced tea in long gulping swallows. Periodically he took breaks from shoveling food into his mouth and pressed a knot of towel-wrapped ice cubes to his head. "Those boys went missing over by Philadelphia." Celeste thought again of Matt's beating on the road. Only the grace of God protected them from some unknown fate. There was no other help on that highway.

"They start looking in all those rivers and creeks, they gon find plenty people supposing to have left here for someplace else and never heard from again." Mrs. Owens ate sparingly. Dribbles of sweat sprouted on her upper lip. "Nobody speaks it, but they all know."

"They've already found some remains. There was a photo in the Jackson paper of the police throwing some bones in an unmarked grave." Celeste's words hung over the table like a dead calm on the ocean. She wiped her mouth on the thin paper napkin, wishing she'd kept her bone story to herself. Bones all over Mississippi. "Those cops who stopped us said we had them in our trunk."

Matt reared back in his chair, surely tight with all he'd eaten. "They didn't believe that."

"I didn't think they did." Celeste picked up her fork and plowed into the rich hot food again.

"They was just trying to make life hard for you is all. Slow you down." Mrs. Owens took a long swig of iced tea and poured more into her jelly-jar glass, taking a dainty sprig of mint from a saucer and shoving it down into the tea. Just like Momma Bessie did in summer, only there were no lemons on this table and Momma Bessie's house had never been this hot. Out the back door in Detroit was a spread of green grass and roses, peonies, an apple tree. Mrs. Owens would be the same kind of woman if she lived like Momma Bessie lived. Stark but warm at the same time, loving but severe. What brought these women to that place? Bones, Celeste thought, the lost and the found.

Then there were only chewing sounds and the small clanks of forks on plates and ice in glasses speaking into the dimming evening air. The red and white checkered table cloth danced under the plates of food. Celeste held onto her iced tea. It was the only cool thing. She gripped it, hoping the chill would work its way up her hand to the rest of her body. Seeing the trees out the back door made her dream of the shade, quick breezes that shook branches, rustled leaves. It was a memory.

"Those white boys po' mommas and daddies never thought this place could be so hellish as it is." Mrs. Owens got up from the table to spoon out three servings of peach cobbler. She put them on the table just beside the still-working dinner plates. Matt eyed the cobbler and continued piling in the food. His stomach didn't seem to have a bottom, or maybe he was being polite to Mrs. Owens, since she'd cooked all that food in honor of their arrival. With that thought, Celeste ate more of the dinner, already feeling stuffed, sure now that she'd have to use that dreaded outhouse before this night was over.

"You sure right, Mrs. Owens," Matt said. He looked at Celeste then took a toothpick out of the little box on the table and openly picked his teeth. She knew that was for her—his way of telling her again not to get Detroit-siddity in this house. "That Chaney boy grew up here so his people know all about Mississippi. They been living it."

Celeste wanted to roll her eyes good and hard at Matt, but instead she studied the kitchen with its shelves—some doorless, some with lopsided doors—not wanting to see if Matt dislodged some slight string of chicken or torn piece of collard. The enameled gas stove with side-by-side oven doors looked rich and out of place. The refrigerator, too. Matt twirled the toothpick in his mouth like an old man at a shoeshine stand or a would-be gangster leaning against a corner on some big city summer night.

"Still and all, nobody wants their child to be hurt whether they been living here or not." Mrs. Owens's eyes grew sad. "That's why I sent my boys away from here."

"Mrs. Owens got two boys up in Chicago." Matt continued picking his teeth.

Celeste wondered how anybody kept their children with them in this place. They should all have been sent somewhere else, especially the boys. It was right out of the Bible, only Negro people didn't claim it as so. *Kill all the boy children. Find the baby Jesus.* Hang them, shoot them, beat them to death. Not just in Mississippi. All over the place. It was the boys, the men who brought down the wrath of white people. Leave the women to manage on their own, to make do, to be the disconnected maids needing to be familied-in somewhere, somehow. The isolated woman in the small house on the barren road.

"Anyway, we prayin' they hiding somewhere, scared out of their minds." Matt put the used toothpick on the side of his plate next to the low hill of chicken bones, slid the dinner plate to the side, and dove into the cobbler.

"I hope so. I pray so. I just don't think so." Mrs. Owens spoke with a dreadful finality. The three were dead and Mrs. Owens knew it.

Matt didn't say a word. Celeste did her best to clean both her plates and felt like she needed to go somewhere and lie down. Early evening light cut in through the small kitchen window and threw shadows on the walls.

Matt wanted to get on the road to Bogalusa before dark. He hugged Mrs. Owens at the front door. The older woman remained stiff but needing at the same time. Celeste walked him to the car, carrying a large metal pitcher to fill with fresh water from the spigot for her bedroom. He told her to find the pay phones in Pineyville and to check in with the Jackson office as often as possible. Her church was southwest of the center of town. Reverend Singleton would be in touch with her tomorrow.

"Be careful." Sudden tears stung her eyes. She wanted to say she was sorry he'd been beaten, sorry things had gotten so testy between them in the car. "What about money, Matt? Should I give her some money for food?"

"Naw, naw. The movement's taking care of that from donations. If you want to help her out on the side, suit yourself, but be easy with it. Wait a while. But make sure your daddy's got that bail money ready for when you get your project up and running." Matt leaned on the side of the car.

"Forgot about that." She hadn't forgotten about it. She just hadn't come up with a way to make a call to Shuck and say it. He needed to send the bail money to the Jackson office in case she got arrested. She'd already been close. But saying that kind of thing to Shuck meant risking the possibility that he would come down there and check on her. She needed to see this through on her own.

"The Sheriff here's Trotter. Don't play with him. Make it count or don't do it at all." Matt folded his arms across his chest, his shirt and overalls not looking too bad considering all they'd been through. "You be all right."

She felt like the small girl who got dropped off at a camp she didn't want to go to. Shuck got back into his car and she was supposed to be grown up and stay there with all those strange kids for two weeks. She knew before he turned the key in the ignition that she wasn't going to make it. She bit her lower lip, tried to hold it together feeling all the while like throwing herself down in the dirt and screaming to Shuck to please take her home. But she was grown now and it was Matt, not Shuck. She had to see it through.

Matt patted her fly-away hair, put a frizzled lock behind her ear. "You almost got you a natural there." He laughed, the knot on his head less conspicuous now.

"Right." She smirked, thinking of Ramona's soft bowl of hair, and of what that word meant. No pressing and curling. Just natural. She liked it, but knew she'd never have that look.

"Pineyville's bad, but it ain't no worse than anywhere else in Mississippi. Just be mindful of where you're at." Matt's eyes rambled over the ground near his feet, the house behind them, then off down Freshwater Road.

"Yeah." She wanted to hug him, but she didn't want to aggravate his bruises. "But, Matt, every town hasn't had a lynching." They stood in a southern Mississippi road in the waning sunlight, facing each other like students on the green in Ann Arbor, but here they talked of lynchings, of disappeared people.

"You talking about Leroy Boyd James?" He knew she'd roomed with Ramona during orientation and that she was an authority on that lynching business. "Well, we don't know all the towns that have had 'em."

Matt put his hand on the car door handle and opened the door. "Ramona doesn't know it all because the news about a lot of lynchings never left the small towns where they happened. There wasn't nothing to research. People never fessed up that a murder had even taken place. Negroes just disappeared. Mrs. Owens said it."

He was right, of course. What difference did it make where in Mississippi she was? Emmett Till had been in Money, Medgar Evers in Jackson, Herbert Lee in Liberty. Ambushed and shot, beaten to death and thrown into a river for organizing for voter registration, standing up to any white man for any reason, winking, eyeballing, accused of raping a white woman, whether ever proven or not. Pineyville was in no way special.

Matt sat in the driver's seat. Celeste put her head through the busted-out window, wanted to climb into that car with him. She kissed him on the cheek. "All right now." Matt said. "Don't be startin' something you can't finish." He grinned. "Miss Detroit. You all right, girl."

She'd won him over. She'd never be what he assumed she was at first, a pampered shallow girl from Detroit. Maybe it had as much to do with Shuck as it had to do with her. But she'd held up her end, too. They went through the fire, and they survived. The next step was on her and her alone. She'd earn the badge of courage or she wouldn't. But still, she'd gladly get into that car with him. A big part of her didn't want to stay in this house on this lonely looking road.

Matt maneuvered the dusty Dodge around, tires grinding gravel, grains of sand flying back, and made the left turn onto the black top going toward Pineyville and then Bogalusa, the heat of the day softening into the slippery humidity of a long summer evening. That blazing sun was gone. Celeste watched the dirty car with the broken-out windows until it disappeared down the highway, feeling like there'd be no leaving Mississippi, that Freshwater Road was all there'd be to her life She filled her bedroom pitcher at the spigot, wondering when Sheriff Trotter would make himself known to her and how.

The aroma of pine disinfectant permeated the bedroom. No closet, only three nails driven into thin wallpapered walls and a brass clothes tree with bent wire hangers on which to hang her dresses, slacks, skirts, and blouses. Celeste dropped sleep shirts and underwear in the four-drawer dresser and buried her small make-up case behind the underwear, relishing the thought of going au naturel for the entire summer. She slid her gym shoes, white pumps, and sandals underneath the dresser, then shoved her suitcase under the high-sitting bed, everything moving easily across the worn linoleum, so cool under her bare feet.

A fading, rose-tinted photograph in an oval-shaped wood frame leaned in from the wall above the bed. In it, a tall dark man wearing a baggy World War I uniform stood with his hand resting on the shoulder of a seated young woman. Celeste barely recognized Mrs. Geneva Owens, her hair parted in the middle and pulled back, a high-collared Victorian blouse touching her chin, a black skirt hitting her at the ankles. They sat like people of means, rigidly straight, content and proud.

"That's my husband, Horation." Mrs. Owens stood in the doorway between the parted curtains. Mississippi Negroes floated like ghosts, tiptoed through life as if to pass unnoticed, so unlike those boisterous Detroiters shouting from cars and buildings, from street corners in summer, bragging of conquests, loud-talking each other into crescendoes of noise, like the regulars at Shuck's Royal Gardens Bar hashing over the day's events, not a shy one in the bunch.

Mrs. Owens's eyes fluttered then settled on the photograph. "He died nearly ten years ago. Had a piece of something in his head from the war. Just fell down and died." The woman's tone was matter-of-fact, as if his early death had been inevitable.

"I'm sorry you lost him." Celeste knew from orientation that hospitals in Mississippi wouldn't have treated Mr. Owens anyway. Nowhere was segregation more strict than in hospitals. No one would ever know how many people had died because of that.

Mrs. Owens pressed the front of her apron with her hands then let them drift. "You need anything else?"

"I'd like to open the other window." The front one over the screened porch was raised, but the side window was shut. Maybe the nearness of the Gulf of Mexico and of Lake Pontchartrain meant cooler nights in Pineyville. No sign of it yet, but Celeste prayed for it anyway.

"I been in here by myself so long, I just leave it closed. Let me see if I can find a old screen or something so the bugs don't eat you alive."

"Thank you, Mrs. Owens." Celeste didn't know what else to say. The woman lingered, then patted the lace doily on the dresser like Momma Bessie would do, eternally smoothing the bumps, beating back all signs of life's irregularities. You knew how to make do, and you learned how to make better. She scanned the room, then pulled a wrinkled photograph from her pocket. "This here's my two boys. They living in Chicago." She handed Celeste the snapshot.

Celeste turned on the small bedside lamp. The woman's sons were plain young men whose shirtsleeves hit above the wrist bone, making their hands seem unnaturally large. They stood grinning with uneven teeth. "Handsome." She glanced again at the wall-photo of Mr. Owens. "Like their father. Have you been to Chicago?"

"I visited them. Never seen so many people. Too many. They took me ridin' on that train? Above the streets? My, my." Mrs. Owens's eyes sparkled with her memory. "Didn't much like it."

"It's beautiful, by Lake Michigan." Celeste regretted saying it. Those boys probably didn't live anywhere near Lake Michigan or in the beautiful part of Chicago, from the looks of that photograph.

Mrs. Owens pocketed the picture. "Well, I'm glad they're up there."

Celeste heard the emphasis on "up there." The woman could say it a million times, but she must never sound as if the north was better. It was this place that had to be made more livable.

"You mighty welcome here." She floated through the curtain-door, a heartfelt greeting in her voice.

"Thank you." Celeste wondered if something she'd said had relaxed the woman. Certainly not her talk of unidentified bones at the dinner table. Or the woman might well have been wrought up because they arrived a little late. That was cause for grave alarm in Mississippi. Then too there'd been a lot of talk in Jackson about manners during orientation. Already, complaints had come in about some volunteers being too aggressive and even condescending. So far, she'd stayed away from any of that.

Celeste leaned a snapshot of Shuck and her brother Billy against her small rubber-band jar on the dresser top and a square silver-framed photograph of Wilamena and Cyril Atwood standing near a blooming saguaro. She switched the photos back and forth then put her toothbrush, toothpaste, and other necessities between the photos. Wilamena had a tight smile on her face as if she'd just been pricked by the cactus spikes or perhaps was seeing out of the photo into this room on Freshwater Road. She never would've stepped in the door of this slat-board house with no bathroom. But here she was. Celeste chuckled.

Cyril Atwood's face had not a hint of Negro-ness, certainly not in that little photograph. Celeste searched his face with her racial Geiger counter, the one that Negro people keep revved and ready for those quick identifications of passing-for-white-Negroes who were everywhere. Not once did the machine go off. Nothing Negro there. Wilamena swore he was Negro and then fussed at Celeste for making so much of it. *What difference did it make?* Shuck mumbled, keeping his cool, shook the man's hand and soon after excused himself. She hadn't packed another photo of Wilamena. This was it. No photo would be worse. Just because she'd been a motherless child for most of her growing years didn't mean she had to advertise it.

Lace curtains winnowed the last gray streaks of evening as she scooped cool water from the metal basin onto her face and soaped her arms, the tiny abrasions from the car window glass already dried over. In the cracked mirror, she checked her face for cuts, then poured pitcher water over her toothbrush, squeezed out a line of toothpaste, scoured her mouth, and spit in the basin. The scummy basin water now had toothpaste froth floating on top. She rinsed the toothbrush with clean water, poured a small amount in her glass and gargled, spitting again into the basin. The old woman had cautioned her about pouring dirty basin water near the house—best to take it to the outhouse, far clear of the flowers and vegetables.

Mrs. Owens knocked on the doorframe, called quietly, and came in with a large pitcher-shaped container and a removable screen.

"If you need to go in the night." She put the jar on the floor on its own throw rug in the corner. She raised the side window and adjusted the portable screen, then turned to leave again, eying the photos on the dresser. "Your people?" There was a slight surprise behind the question.

"My daddy and my brother." She said it too fast and didn't know why, felt foolish, and cast her eyes down. "That's my mother and her second husband. Out west." She wished she had a photo of her mother alone, it would be easier to explain. Wilamena looked like she could be anything.

Mrs. Owens continued towards the door. "Nice looking people you have. You favor your mother."

"Thank you," she lied. "She's out in New Mexico. I'm going out there for Christmas." She lied again to design a tradition that didn't exist. Christmas and family closeness, all those occurrences went with Momma Bessie, not with Wilamena. No way she'd slave in the kitchen fixing a massive dinner for a steady stream of people all day long.

"New Mexico. I guess I heard of it." Mrs. Owens closed the curtains behind her. "Nighty night."

Celeste stumbled over her own "Goodnight." She "favored" her mother. She'd been hearing that all of her life, though she couldn't see it herself. She cast it off to a genetic tree whose root system snaked into unknown soils for more years than anyone could remember. *There's some Cherokee back in there. There's a few different white folks, too, and some blends of this and that, some African.* She should've said something more about her mother and her second husband, anything. She could create whatever mother she wanted for Freshwater Road. No one would ever know. She thought again of storing the Wilamena-Cyril photo in her drawer or her suitcase. Too late. Mrs. Owens had seen it, was surely thinking her mother was married to a white man. God only knew what she thought of that. She left the photos on the dresser. This was the south, and slavery was about more than economics. There probably wasn't much that Mrs. Owens hadn't seen or heard before.

Night jar. Momma Bessie had used that term when she talked about the old days in Kentucky. If she used it, she'd have to empty it in the outhouse in the morning, but she'd have to smell it all night in the stifling heat. There was a kerosene lamp by the back door for night trips to the outhouse. Celeste grabbed up her metal basin of dirty water, shoved a wad of Kleenex into her pocket, and walked through the short hall to the kitchen. A narrow line of light angled out from under Mrs. Owens's curtain-door. She lit the kerosene lantern and made her first trip to the outhouse in the dead of night, walking hard on the sandy earthen path to scare off any night creatures lurking along the way.

The shed-like room was small and had one curtained window. She held the lantern high at the door, stepped up the one step, and entered what would be her toilet facility for the rest of the summer. There was a roll of toilet paper and a stack of newspaper torn into uneven squares. She poured out her dirty basin water then lined the wood platform around the black hole with toilet paper and sat, the lantern in her hand like a weapon. She heard her urine fall into the pit. Thank God, she thought, it's too dark to see. She hurried back to her room.

The slightest catch of a breeze whispered in the curtains as black night leaned against the house. She pulled J.D.'s postcard out of her book-bag. He chided her to be careful, wrote of the humidity in Paris, said to write him, and ended with *Wish you were here, J.D.* Not *Love, J.D.* The love was over. One year of love. The return addresss was c/o American Express, Paris, France. The color picture on the other side showed a narrow winding street. The designation read "Montmartre, Paris." He said there were streets so old and narrow you had to walk sideways to get through. She could see him in some window, large canvas on an easel, the light streaming in.

She put the postcard back and shoved her book-bag under the nightstand. What would she write him? Of how Matt was beaten at the hands of state troopers on the way down from Jackson? Or of humidity so thick her body felt clumsy when she stood perfectly still, heat so ferocious her internal organs struggled to function? Of outhouses in the back, water spigots in the front? He wouldn't be able to say a word about how Negro she was or wasn't now. A calm settled over her that made her feel giddy. She had the distinct feeling that she was knocking them dead all over the place. She'd won Matt over, Mrs. Owens had softened, and now J.D. would know who she really was. To say nothing of Wilamena.

Finally, Celeste pulled on a sleep shirt and settled on the bed, which felt more broken-down than broken-in, lumps leading to a caved-in middle, thinking that here, where bodies disappeared like lunary rainbows, containers of human waste sat around in plain sight all night long. The old photo above the bed told her Mrs. Owens had vacated her own room. Such a private place, so much of the past wearying the corners, hanging on the walls, dappling the well-worn bedspread. Old beds hid great secrets of the mind, body, and spirit, prayers at night and in the morning, loving for pleasure and for child-making, ceiling-staring thoughts that hung like crystals in a cave, and Bible reading by the dim of old lamps.

Celeste felt sleep coming, her ears pressed against a quiet so profound she thought she heard the stars twinkling in the sky. She focused on a memory of cool weather, that last ride on J.D.'s motorcycle in a late spring snow, the sideways skid near the apartment in Ann Arbor that had them laughing and crying at the same time. Would these plank-board shacks provide any protection from wind and rain? There were no basements, no fireplaces or furnaces, just kitchen stoves. The people must huddle around them if the air blows cool. She imagined people hibernating like the exotic koi at the botanical gardens on Belle Isle, sleeping at the bottom of a frozen pond, their eyes closed, their senses curbed. A solemnity of need, a ritual of denial.

A car turned onto Freshwater Road, gnashing the gravel. Celeste turned out the light, her heart in a gallop. Matt wouldn't dare come back here from Bogalusa in the dead of night. The car passed the house, tires pulverizing small rocks and any shell-backed night creatures. She slid off the bed and crawled to the window. No lights. It might be a truck with guns racked across the back window. Maybe Sheriff Trotter himself. Not a streetlight anywhere, but a sky of stars, a quilted sky, and a moon so clear and white it seemed it really was a face. No competition from the haranguing neon fractures of Detroit, advertising everything from White Castle hamburgers to laundry washing powder. She listened until her ears ached. The sounds faded. It was the slow pace of the vehicle that riveted her mind, as if the driver designed a return, scoping the darkness. Freshwater Road went somewhere, though when you stood outside, it seemed to be a road without end, or a road to nowhere, just narrowed into its own horizon. She crept back across the linoleum and climbed onto the high bed. Perspiration pooled and soaked her thin cotton nightshirt. This mattress smelled old, though she had seen the sheets were clean.

Matt said Reverend Singleton would be in touch tomorrow, come to take her to the church where she'd be working. There was no phone here. Mail would be forwarded down from the Jackson office. What would the Freedom School children think of her? Would she be able to get through to them? Who were these people in this godforsaken place at the end of the earth? The Freedom School books were stacked close by. If she read, it would calm her down, help her sleep, but she didn't want to turn on the light. She began counting backwards from one hundred, her ears keyed to the sounds outside. The power lines crackled in a high pitched staccato. She got lost dreaming of cool-edged winds on tree lined country roads, the soft spread of new snow.

7

Shuck dressed in a pale yellow summer shirt, brown slacks, and a tan linen jacket. He lowered the convertible top sitting in the driveway, cruised the tree-lined streets to Woodward Avenue, and turned south. Early evening was his afternoon. When he passed the old Fox Theatre, he slowed. There were days when he avoided this stretch of Woodward Avenue altogether. Too many memories. He and Wilamena used to dance in the aisles to Count Basie, Duke Ellington, and Cab Calloway, who wore a big white suit and smiled across the whole damned stage while jamming the night away. The palace had fallen on hard times. Shuck continued south on Woodward to Jefferson and out East Jefferson, the radio music a monotone in the wind. Nothing in the world as fine as the breeze on his face riding in that Cadillac toward the water on a summer evening.

The river air whose glory lay in Lake Erie and Lake St. Clair struggled between the buildings and warehouses before succumbing to the unforgiving concrete, black tar, and car fumes. By the time that air got to Grand Circus Park, not an iota of coolness or freshness was left in it. To penetrate the city, it needed a cold rush from Canada or some ghost-blast from the Upper Peninsula. In summer, you had to get up close to the water to know it was real.

Belle Isle was a good place to find some relief. Relief from the heat of summer and from the twist of old memories and new worries that crowded his mind. He was in a perpetual state of distraction, and he didn't like it. Before he turned to go over the Belle Isle Bridge, the signal light changed to red and caught him. A rabbly group of boys, their loud voices sounding in eruptions of profanity as they dip-walked in circles in the street, oblivious to the summer evening traffic, stopped in front of Shuck's Cadillac. They evil-eyed him, licking their lips at the brilliantly white car. High on "boy," Shuck figured, arms loping up and down, dancing in place like marionettes whose strings had too much play, carrying on their pitched conversation as if they were alone in the world. Shuck clutched the steering wheel, the quiet idle of the sleek car's horses ready to blast ahead, run over their drug-wired bodies. In that moment, he hated their listless, undefined existences, their shirts slopped out of their pants, their pants drooping down like they might fall off, their conked hair with do-rags askew and congolene dripping. He wondered why these boys burned their own brains with drugs, ground their parents down to powder, dishonoring their lives with not a thought to history or tomorrow. They probably couldn't identify one person in his best-of-Negro-life wallpaper at the Royal Gardens Bar. Wouldn't know Lester Young from Earl "Fatha" Hines and forget Thurgood Marshall. Probably couldn't even say it. When the light changed to green, the boys stayed in front of his car like they were on stage about to break into some rag-tag dancing doo-wop song. Shuck watched them, his breath lifting up to a shallower place, heart beginning to pump harder. He put the car in park, revved the engine, foot solidly on the brake. "Get the fuck out of the street. You don't own it. You don't own a goddamned thing including yourselves." Shuck stared at them with ice in his eyes. It was as if they were the reason for his summer anxiety, as if it was all their fault. He could blame them for the plight of the city, for the spiraling downward of the good things he'd hoped for. He could step on them like they were roaches. But in one of their young faces, he saw himself as a boy who had a choice to make, who knew that something in the air meant him no good, that too much stood to break him down. Shuck lowered his head.

Cars lined up behind him waiting to make the same turn, horns honk-ing, people hot and impatient, wanting a breath of relief from the humid stifle of the city. This new breed of unused young men drifted and turned rancid before they reached eighteen. "Bad pennies," Momma Bessie called them. "Too many boys coming up under women." They'd kill their own mothers for drugs. It was all he could do to not get out of the car, drag them by their shirttails to the curb, and beat the shit out of them. He locked his doors and wished he'd put the top up on the car. Beating them would make no difference at all. The world as he knew it was stacked against them, and there wasn't a damn thing he could do about it.

The boys jerked around, faces frozen in a sneer, seemed to float for a moment. "Old man, what you looking at?" one boy yelled. "You better watch who you talking to."

Shuck wished he'd brought his gun. He would've shot into the air, tried to scare them sober. He caught himself thinking like a young man, a man ready for a fight. Reality hit him like a thunder clap. He *was* old, certainly too old to fight five young men whether they were high or not. He tightened his hold on the steering wheel, his foot ready to accelerate. "I may be old, but I can run your asses over with this car." He didn't yell it this time, said it out loud to himself.

With all the traffic, no telling who would get out of a car and join in and whose side they'd be on. They might side with him, they might not. The boys doubled over laughing, fell against each other then moved to the curb. The streetlights flared on. Their faces stretched like reflections in a funhouse mirror.

Shuck turned onto the bridge. In his rearview mirror, he saw the boys climb onto the bridge railing and fake throwing one of their group into the river. He wished they'd all jump. He had an urge to go back and help them, and in the same heartbeat, he wanted to take them all over to Momma Bessie's, clean them up, and set them straight. Shuck's heart beat like he'd just played a Miles Davis high note for one long breathless year. He wanted a cigarette but his hands were glued to the steering wheel. His fingers cramped from the pressure. If he didn't loosen his grip he'd break something. Wondered if he could break the steering wheel. He remembered when he and Posey had been offered a so-called opportunity to sell drugs and had turned it down. Praised the day they turned it down. Back in the forties and fifties, when musicians nodded out on stage or found themselves soaked in urine in Harlem doorways, in the alley leading to Manfred's After Hours Joint, in back bedrooms all over town, he knew then that he didn't want to have anything to do with selling something to Negro people that killed them. He wanted to sell them dreams, numbers, at least a chance for a good time, not this—this sinking down to the pavement with drool at the corners of their lips and eyes hooded in an odd sleep that might leave a man with one foot just hanging in the air. He lit a cigarette, the smoke curling down his throat. What difference did it make now? He didn't sell the stuff, but somebody else sure did.

Shuck drove around the still-crowded island, the river breezes holding people reluctant to return to their hot houses and airless apartments. Their trash lay in crumpled bits near cans, as if the effort to put it in the can required one step too many. Shuck parked, put the top up, walked to the river's edge, and sat down on a picnic table. The city lights of Windsor sparkled on. Hard to fathom how this strait of water separated two places with such different histories. What, he thought, were Negro people doing here, struggling and fighting for a place to be after all this time? The numbers rackets never as lucrative there as here. Not as many desperate Negro people playing hunches, studying dream books like pocket Bibles. Whiskey came across this river during Prohibition. Even now he'd go over to buy booze and cigarettes, too. Cheaper and calmer over there.

Shuck knew this island, this Belle Isle, had come here on summer days for his whole life, swam from the beach to the city side and back, rode horses, canoed and ice-skated in winter. Momma Bessie called summer to order with a picnic on Belle Isle and dismissed it the same way every Labor Day. These were the things to look forward to until age and death crept in with a different plan. Momma Bessie couldn't stand in her kitchen making potato salad for fifteen people anymore, packing picnic baskets, ice chests, gathering everyone around, cooking ribs on the park grills. Sometimes they'd be on the island for breakfast, too, then a day of softball, swimming, walking through the zoo and dinner outdoors. It was an all-day thing. But the children grew and left, the old people started dying off, and those who remained sat on porches all over the West Side wondering what the hell was going on. Shuck felt a slipping away like the muddy riverbank at his feet.

Sailboats lined up on the river heading in for the night, bows shadowing as the last orange streak of light sank beneath the horizon. He remembered that day years ago when he and Wilamena carved their initials in the gray bark of an old beech tree. He always loved the way she looked in the shade with sunlight filtering through the trees, her skin browner in summer, dark golden brown.

When he first saw Wilamena at Lakeview High, he thought she was a vision from some island paradise. She stood out. The other boys circled, asking her where she lived, and could she go to the movies or for a ride on the streetcar. The white boys stole glances at her, too. He stayed back. Almost lost her when her head starting turning this way and that. He found out she was a small-town girl who knew how to climb out of a bedroom window. Wilamena had an edge. She wanted out in a way he didn't understand.

Shuck walked along the riverbank. No sand beaches on this side of the island. Too much water moving too fast. A quick look back at his Cadillac gleaming in the near dark. He hoped those boys wouldn't come this far around the drive, find it, slash his convertible top. He pushed forward, the water sploshing up on the grass and rocks making a small slapping sound. Cars on the drive lolling by, radios loud, voices kicking through the evening air. Then quiet. The light dimming to true darkness. He stood in a small grove of mature trees yards back from the river's edge, went from tree to tree tracing his hands on the thin bark, searching for the initials he hoped would still be there, fingers gliding towards the past. He saw himself, a well-dressed man digging around for the past like a teenager who still loves the girl he took to the prom. He laughed then ignited his cigarette lighter and went from tree to tree until he found the beech with their initials carved, bigger now, stretched in effigy. They'd dug deep with his pocket-knife. He stood there tracing the initials and finally snapped his silver-plated lighter closed. In the dark, he walked on the grassy earth away from the water toward his car, his creamy yellow shirt a soft light in the night.

Celeste was the ghost-sister of her own mother, headstrong, wily, and only just beginning. He didn't know what to warn her of anymore, didn't know how to protect her. She'd taken herself to a place beyond anyone's protection. Not something Wilamena would've done. He saw Wilamena in Celeste sometimes, the way she said a certain word or how she moved her hands, but they were oceans apart. But how had she put it together to go to Mississippi? He caught himself. If white children had the courage to put themselves on the line, why not his own? *God bless the child.* His heart gave a different answer. Negro people had paid enough. Their ancestors paid with the lash and the rope and no money for hundreds of years of backbreaking work. If anybody on earth had a right to be tired, it was Negro people in America. It wasn't enough and he knew it. The struggle would go on until the end of time.

Celeste had a rebellious streak and that would bring her pain, the kinds of pain he could not protect her from. He told her that when he met that white guy with her. He came down hard on her because he wanted her to understand she was treading on shaky ground, bound for the big fall, the kind of hurt that destroyed a spirit. He didn't want to see that happen.

Like her mother, Celeste was restless. They were women who stared into space, loved cold winds, storms, and deep colors. You couldn't hold them too tight. A man who was like a rock, Wilamena had said, was there to catch her when she spun one last time out of control. In the old days, Shuck knew he was too much in the streets to be anybody's rock. He'd forgiven Wilamena's wandering because he hadn't been there himself. He had to forgive her whether he wanted to or not. He prided himself on being a stand-up kind of man.

He scraped his shoes with a tree branch, left the top up, and locked his doors. He drove around the island, passing the all-white yacht club, the beach, and headed back to the bridge, then turned to go across downtown and over to the Royal Gardens. Maybe it was time to keep a gun in the car the way things were playing out in the city, hard to know where it was safe and where it wasn't these days. He was a businessman who made bank drops with zippered bags of cash. Easy to explain to the cops why *this* Negro man traveled the city streets with a gun. Then he remembered those boys high-dancing in front of his car. He didn't know anymore what he'd have done if he had his gun.

8

The driver, "Middleman," grinned at them in his rearview mirror. He ferried a steady stream of girls from campus to the abortion doctor in River Rouge, charging fifty dollars for door-to-door service in his customized hearse. He collected the three hundred dollars for the doctor's services. Back-alley entrance, no-nonsense Negro nurse as cold as Celeste's feet in the icy stirrups, body open like a cave, cramping, feeling the scraping and hearing the flushing. You had to have an appointed time, and the doctor was always busy. Images of clothes hangers, mangled girls, and dead babies skydived in her mind. Momma Bessie put the fear of God in you, but you couldn't stay scared forever. Lying on a sheet-covered table, half-asleep in the dark, Celeste waited for the other two girls who came from Ann Arbor that day. They sipped orange juice and took huge white pills with five more to take. She wouldn't tell J.D. and not a thought about telling Shuck.

Geneva Owens's voice and a man's voice, too, wafted through the house, seeped into her dream, riding on the aromas of frying bacon and strong coffee. She woke fighting to free herself from the dream's residue, knowing she'd revisit it, like it or not. She lay there listening to them talking about a neighbor woman, Sister Mobley, who had half of a job, three small children, and a long-gone husband. Her hostess sounded chatty, saying she took food to the bereft family whenever she could. Her slow and easy vocal gait was a counterpoint to the strong, stage-savvy male voice. He said the church was doing all it could for those in dire straits.

The nearness of the Gulf, of Lake Pontchartrain, and God only knew what other bodies of water had directed no cool air to Pineyville. Maybe the talk in the kitchen would go on, they'd forget her, let her drift until she adjusted to the swelter, the smallness of the thin-walled house, and the lack of an indoor bathroom with a toilet or a tub. She was learning the stillness of the south, the slowness. Less racing around, less body heat. She had a thought that she might not get a full bath until the end of the summer.

She threw the top sheet aside and studied the color schematic of her body. Her arms and lower legs were well past a shade that would be acceptable to Wilamena. Good. She knew her face was beyond the pale and laughed at the double meaning. Wilamena had been known to grow impatient when Celeste played too long in the sun. *Stay out of the sun, girl.* A tad too much curl would sneak into her hair in the summer humidity. As she matured, Wilamena's coolness became profound, the physical distance a true rendering of the emotional. Eventually Celeste lost interest in struggling to make herself Wilamena's adored child. Maybe it wasn't that at all. Maybe Wilamena just didn't know how to love.

When she could lie there no longer, she planted her feet on the cool linoleum floor. The tiny, healed-over cuts in her skin had the crusty feel of minute scabs. She used every drop of remaining pitcher water to wash herself from face to feet, realizing too late that she had no clean water with which to brush her teeth. She dressed in a sleeveless blouse and a skirt and tiptoed out the front door to the spigot, squinting in the hard sunlight, beckoning to the distant clouds to bring shade in God's name to Freshwater Road. She eyed the long-needled pines. No shade trees near any house that she could see. Where had that car or truck in the night gone? She stared at the empty road. The two-lane was a short city block in the other direction, the road Matt had disappeared down. With the sun like a hot iron on her neck, she bent over to refill her pitcher.

Mrs. Owens stood at the stove frying eggs. Celeste downed a waiting glass of ice water as the smooth-voiced man rose from his chair. "I wasn't sure until last week if they'd send someone. We're on the low rung down here. I'm Reverend Singleton."

"Celeste Tyree." She joined him at the table. What was the high rung, she wondered? Jackson or even Hattiesburg. "I was with the last group. They called us the stragglers." She might've said she was happy to be there, but Leroy Boyd James's name leaped into her mind, followed quickly by the prowling car. This Pineyville was a lynching town, and 1959 wasn't that long ago. She needed to talk with a local about the real deal in Pineyville without being rude to the person who'd guide her to what she was there to do. "The work's the same wherever it is." She said it thinking that maybe it was true and maybe it wasn't.

"We're so happy that you're here." Reverend Singleton resumed eating, cleaning his plate. "We'll take you, straggler or not, and we'll show them a thing or two in Jackson."

"Thanks, Reverend Singleton. Nothing would please me more." It felt good to say his name, to hear that he understood the undertow of competition between the volunteers to register the most people to vote.

That got things off on the right foot. He had the cheerleading enthusiasm they'd need to get up and running. The question remaining was who was good for the long haul once the going got rough. She'd learned enough about Pineyville to know that it wouldn't be a cake walk.

The kitchen vibrated with heat. The coffee smelled bitter, and the plate of food Mrs. Owens handed her swam in a shallow of yellow grease. Margo had admonished the volunteers to not waste the hosts' hard-to-come-by food. Celeste forked in a small bite of fried egg, then ate a corner piece of biscuit. Thankful she was that the woman had given her less to eat than she had last evening, when Matt shoveled in food like it was his last supper, and she'd tried to keep up with him. She chewed a piece of bacon that gloriously melted on her tongue after a crisp beginning, and waited patiently to pounce on the Reverend about that lynching.

"If Etta'd allow it, I'd eat over here every day, Sister Owens." Reverend Singleton pushed his empty plate forward. "You make a biscuit that brings tears to a man's eyes." He reared back in his chair, brown face glowing in satisfaction. His neatly trimmed moustache camouflaged full lips, and his thick eyebrows set off dark brown eyes.

"You and Etta both come over here to eat anytime you feel like it." She took his dirty plate to her pump and washing tub on the small back porch. She gave the handle a few brisks pumps and sulfur-yellow water belched and spewed over the plate. "You did real good for a second breakfast, Reverend." She wiped her hands on her apron, eyes bright and strong, her face ten years younger than yesterday when Celeste and Matt had arrived. Her hair was tucked into a bun at the back of her neck, her housedress crisp and fresh.

"You're right. Etta won't let me out of the door without breakfast." He had the sated tone of a well-cared for man. Sweat creeks trickled from his cropped sideburns, beaded on his forehead. He took a handkerchief from the jacket hanging on the back of his chair and mopped his face. Every man who sat at Momma Bessie's table in Detroit got that look and sound. She took good care of them. Negro men triumphed in the kitchens of older Negro women, if nowhere else. Celeste ate slowly. The coffee was too hot and acrid-smelling to drink. She sipped more water with a thought to the outhouse.

"That chicory might take some getting used to." Reverend Singleton smiled and pointed to her steaming cup. His hairline receded slightly at the temples, his hair cut close. Celeste figured him to be in his late thirties or early forties. "I imagine this heat does, too."

Celeste nodded, wondering what chicory was. "I'm getting used to it," she lied.

"Been getting the church body ready for you. Telling them what I see for all of us here in Pineyville." His eyes were set just a bit too far apart.

"You be comfortable starting up by say, Thursday?" He put his elbows on the table and clasped his hands, his gold wedding ring a beacon on his finger.

"Just want to see the church and figure out what we might need to get going. I've got books for the children." Celeste felt the effects of the food drugging her brain, a slow caving in of her energy. She'd have to learn to eat differently or risk dozing the summer away. Here was the full meaning of porches and rocking chairs. Idle time after each meal. Mississippi siestas. Whites only. Everybody else had to march back to work. Maybe Mrs. Owens would allow them to eat on the screened porch, as far away from that stove as possible.

"Good, good. We'll be all right. Today, I'm taking you sightseeing." He had a city way about him, polished, a smile at the mouth corners and thinking with his whole face, clear enough to grasp. "I told the church that we'd start the classes come Thursday."

"I'm ready." Not sure she knew what *ready* meant anymore. She'd been ready for her final exams, ready to get out of Ann Arbor. But this place called out for a new kind of ready. "They told me in Jackson—there was a lynching here in '59?" She blurted it out, fear like a river undertow right beneath her words. She hoped she sounded like a researcher, like Ramona. She couldn't have stopped the question if she'd wanted to.

Mrs. Owens whisked her dirty plate off the table. "They do that all over Mississippi. Always have." Mrs. Owens said it like she was playing a trump card and the game was over.

"Don't fret. We'll be all right." Reverend Singleton sounded like a leader man talking. He'd said, *"We'll be all right."* He wasn't going to talk about that lynching. Maybe, after they left the house, he'd tell her the story, maybe he didn't want to ruin Mrs. Owens morning by going into the details.

Just like home. Momma Bessie and Grandpa Ben, even Grandma Pauline, Wilamena's mother, all clammed up that way when it came to the details of the old days. Now she was living in the old days. When she'd asked questions about those times, the older ones paused as if gathering enough air into their lungs, enough cushion to even think about the old days. They'd packed those times away. It was too painful, too backward-facing to go digging around unearthing whatever had been.

Celeste's last stop before getting into Reverend Singleton's car had to be that outhouse. She collected her basin of scummy water and came back through the kitchen, letting the screen door slam. She walked on the dirt path beside the small vegetable garden toward the little shack near the tree line. The garden segued into an expanse of pale-orange, sun-drenched, sandy earth.

The daytime smell escaping into the morning air wasn't as rank as she expected. She took a deep breath and went into the little outhouse, her sandals and feet powdered with a film of dust. Sunlight shot through the small window above the plank-board platform with its smooth round hole. She poured the dirty basin water in just as she'd done the night before. What lurked in that black abyss, and could it creep up? If Shuck found out about the bathroom facilities in Mrs. Owens house, he'd be down there in one snap of his well-manicured fingers. She did her business and rushed out again.

One stop in the kitchen for breakfast, one trip to the outhouse, and she was already in a full sweat. At the spigot, she scrubbed her hands with soap, patted her face with cool water, and washed her basin. Mrs. Owens had placed a clean towel on a tin plate. The morning air smelled of old wood, mold, and mangy dogs. But when you turned in the other direction, it smelled of a sandy beach, like shells and kelp. The freshest air, with that faint aroma of pine, whiffs of magnolia and jasmine at the edges, would tumble into a moving car with all the windows down. She couldn't wait to get going.

After Reverend Singleton cleared the DeSoto's front passenger seat of his papers and Bible, putting them in the back along with his suit jacket, he held the door while she climbed in. His starched white shirt was brilliant in the harsh sunlight. Her pale green blouse and tan skirt gave in to the humidity, wrinkles softening into damp furrows, and the day just beginning. They rolled away, pulverizing the gravel as they made a left turn onto the blacktop leading into Pineyville. She'd listened for that sound all night, even in her sleep. She hugged the passenger side window, arm on the opening, air already breathing up into her armpit.

The tall thin pines decorated the nearly barren landscape on the road, throwing a few delicate shadows here and there. That tropical breeze swept in. Such a relief to have moving air on her face. She sat buttoned and demure beside this man of the cloth with his wedding ring on. She was a stranger in town walking a thin line toward what she hoped would be acceptance. She wanted to release the rubber band holding her tight ponytail, pull her skirt up to her thighs, unbutton her blouse down to her cleavage, and let the fresh air blow over her clammy skin. But in the south, you kept your buttons buttoned up to your neck and your skirt down below your knees. They'd been told in Jackson that the women in the south kept to a rigid standard of comportment. The female volunteers, especially the ones from the north, had been warned not to bring their college campus freedoms down here because they wouldn't sit well at all with the locals, Negro or white.

They drove through the center of Pineyville, a one-stoplight affair. Reverend Singleton pointed out the Pearl River County Administration building, which housed the office of the registrar of voters, Mr. Heywood. By the end of the summer, she imagined she'd know that future-denying fortress well enough. A sheriff's car parked as they floated by, an officer stretching his neck to see inside their car.

"That's Sheriff Trotter." Reverend Singleton didn't turn his head. "He's rock hard and full of hate."

"I heard." She nodded to the uniformed man, felt momentarily powerful sitting there beside the reverend and watching the sheriff's face freeze over. He knew she'd arrived. The Jackson office informed the FBI of the whereabouts of every volunteer. At least then there was a starting point if a volunteer turned up missing. Some FBI men hated the movement as much as the local whites and passed information on to local law enforcement. It traveled from there to the White Citizens Councils and the Klan. She was marked, set to be watched for the entire summer. The Reverend and his car, too. They'd both be under scrutiny, targets for any backward-thinking person in the area. A bullet might fly from the black hole of a gun and shoot one or both of them dead. She saw Matt's body going limp beside his car yesterday on the highway from Jackson. What good had it done? The troopers beat him anyway.

"Story goes that his daddy had a Negro worker on his place who he abused unmercifully for years. Seemed he couldn't get it through his head that slavery was over. Never wanted to pay the man a decent wage, called him out of his name. One day, the worker ran him through with a pitchfork. The son blames the entire Negro race, never given so much as a mumbling thought to how mean-spirited his daddy was. He's a chip off the old block." Reverend Singleton drove slowly on, Celeste twisting to get another glare at Sheriff Trotter, who'd gotten out of his car and was walking up the front walk of the County building.

They passed a cluster of small storefronts, a grocery, a drug store. Awnings and nicely spaced magnolias shaded the storefronts with slashes of sunlight baking the curb-less pavement between. You might run from tree to tree or awning to awning escaping the sun, much like ducking the rain. White people in shade hats went in and out of the few stores and the county building.

"Now, Celeste, the phone company removes our request to the bottom of the list for phone lines at the church. That means you have to use that phone there by the gas station to check in with Jackson and make your calls to home." He drove by the gas station and the pay phone. "We have a phone at our house, but it's too far for you."

She spotted a red Coca-Cola machine against the side wall of the gas station and wondered if they could get a cold drink. But that might necessitate a bathroom stop somewhere, and God only knew what that might mean. She had a thought that one of the distinct pains of the south was the constant necessity to plot your way from one accepting place to the next, for bathroom facilities, for lodging, for travel, even for shopping. You had to have it on your mind at all times.

"Where are the Negro people?" She hadn't seen one since they got into town.

"They come into the grocery and the gas station when they have to. Town's not too friendly to its Negro citizens."

At orientation, they told her that in Pineyville, Negroes stepped off the sidewalk to let whites go by. No wonder they didn't come to town. What would she do if she passed a white person on the street? Margo said it was a decision you had to make at that moment, careful of everything going on around you. No matter what you decided, she said, remain respectful. If you stepped off the sidewalk, keep your head up and say a "good morning" or a "good afternoon." If you decided to cross the street, say your greeting and keep going as if you'd planned to cross the street anyway. She saw herself zigzagging back and forth at a dizzying pace to somehow avoid the obeisance but keep the peace. She almost laughed out loud at the ludicrousness of it all, but underneath, another layer of fear crept into place.

Reverend Singleton circled a block of neatly painted wood houses with shaded porches, deep green lawns, magnolias and dogwood. "This is where the white folks live," Reverend Singleton said. A woman working in her flower beds stood to watch the Negro man and the young woman driving by. No smile, no greeting. Celeste knew that look, called it the Grosse Pointe stare. *Nigger, what are you doing in this part of town?* She hoped the woman wouldn't call the police, accuse them of casing the neighborhood for a robbery.

"Do any Negro people live in town?" She stared at the set-back houses, the neatness and calm beauty of it all compared to the drab, rundown look of Freshwater Road.

"Not in the town limits."

Reverend Singleton came back by the Pearl River County Administration Building. The sheriff's car sat in front of it. "Can't go in that front door, either. But that's exactly where we're going when we're ready." People glided slowly in and out in their light-colored dresses, white sandals, summer suits, straw hats. Celeste wanted to walk in with them, stop the insanity of some people trooping around to some other inconvenient door. Not yet. Probably cool and dark inside there, clean and with echoes like City Hall or the Court Building in Detroit.

"I'ma pick you up every morning at nine and take you over to the church for freedom school, then take you back to Mrs. Owens in the afternoon."

"You sure I can't walk there from Mrs. Owens's house?" Celeste was hoping he'd say that during the daylight hours, it would probably be fine.

"Not here. My wife, Etta, will fetch you for the voter registration classes in the evening or I will, and we'll both be driving you home after that." He was back at the traffic light. "Most important to stick to the routine. If you break it, that means something's gone wrong."

"I understand." Gone wrong meant gone missing. It was the breaking of the routine that alerted the Jackson office that Schwerner, Chaney, and Goodman were in trouble. No phone call. No check-in. Three gone in one heartbeat.

They passed a road sign: Bogalusa, East, 25 miles, New Orleans, South, 65 miles. Reverend Singleton headed south. Matt had passed this way yesterday, taken the road to Bogalusa. She wanted to tell the reverend to keep going all the way to New Orleans, take her to the airport, and send her home.

In what seemed like a mile or so, he made another turn into a rough sand and gravel road leading to the St. James African Methodist Episcopal Church. He told her they wouldn't stop, but he wanted her to see it. He had pride in his voice. The whitewashed church with a stocky bell tower in the center of its roof sat in a clearing with spurts of weedy grass and gravel, surrounded on three sides by dense stands of long-needled pines, live oaks, and a magnolia or two. The trees stood as shelter from the badgering sun. They offered dark passages of seeming coolness where not a ray of light shone through. She searched the grounds for the outhouse but saw only a water spigot on the side of the building. "The church has a real toilet?" She couldn't contain her excitement at the prospect of working every day in a place with a real toilet, then chastised herself for making such a big deal out of indoor plumbing.

"There's one off my office. I couldn't manage with no phone and no toilet either. Unfortunately, the church body still must use the outhouse. It's well behind the building. *You* and only you can use the toilet whenever you like." He drove back over the bumpy church road.

"What about the children, Reverend Singleton?" She knew she'd let the children use that bathroom when he was away from the church, make them promise with their blood that they wouldn't tell.

"It's a very small toilet, Celeste. And children can be messy." He turned back on the highway heading in the direction of New Orleans.

She'd be the one cleaning after them, but she didn't care. A toilet meant luxury here and the children should have the experience. But then, she thought, that might create a problem in their own homes, dissatisfaction with what they had. Perhaps she wouldn't let them use it after all, but she'd never let them know that she sometimes used it. The last thing she wanted them to think was that she saw herself above them, more worthy of the nicer things in life than they.

Reverend Singleton drove her by his own neat, flower-fronted house on another side road off the highway to meet his wife. Etta Singleton, a plain woman with a quiet demeanor, was conservatively dressed in a belted day dress with a white collar and mid-arm sleeves with matching white cuffs. She was small next to him. She spoke with no accent at all as she welcomed Celeste to Pineyville and told her she looked forward to seeing her in church on Sunday. She couldn't have been more unlike the city man who was her husband. Riding with Reverend Singleton was like driving the Detroit streets with Shuck, making all of his stops, greeting his friends. It seemed he knew the entire world, and they knew him as well. This world was smaller, but it was the reverend's domain.

The highway out of Jackson had been wide open, all but treeless. This same road, Route 11, out of Hattiesburg yesterday had been lined with pine trees, but never so eerily forbidding as it now was. Celeste felt the nearness of water, but she couldn't see it. She wondered how this inauspicious road led to someplace as joyous sounding as New Orleans.

"We got stopped yesterday on the way down from Jackson." She kept her eyes peeled to the road, to the turn-offs. No surprises, please, she prayed.

"Mrs. Owens told me." He turned his head toward the window and nodded at an inlet of water edged by wild grasses, trees with moss hanging like ragged curtains, a hint of mystery in his voice. "No bayous in Michigan."

Reverend Singleton wasn't going to dwell on the negatives. He was right. If you started thinking of all the beatings and killings, you'd pack it in. Celeste's skin itched. She stared at the marshy land. The earth seemed to tip off into water until finally it was impossible to tell where the land ended and the water began, with roots and tall grass interwoven.

"Along here, it's spurs of the Pearl River. Creeks and bayous." Reverend Singleton enjoyed showing her the sights around Pineyville. He was a take-charge kind of man. That, she thought, seemed deeply southern, too.

The landscape had a dreamy quality. She imagined stepping on what seemed to be grass and then sinking into the black watery muck. What a place to bury the mysteriously disappeared Negro men of Mississippi—the ones who ran terrified in the night, caught by bloodhounds, beaten, shot, thrown into this swampy marsh. She saw again in her mind the photo of Emmett Till's battered and bloated body pulled from the Tallahatchie River, thought again of Leroy Boyd James and the unnamed others. And at no hour of the day or night did she not think of Schwerner, Chaney, and Goodman, disappeared from the face of the Mississippi earth.

On the east side of the road, the land was planted in neat orchards of trees that were as different from what was on the other side of the road as night from day.

"Tung trees." Reverend Singleton must have been watching her out of the corner of his eye because he certainly never seemed to take his eyes off the road, never stopped checking his rearview mirror.

Celeste heard "tongue" and had a quizzical look on her face. Reverend Singleton spelled the word.

"The oil from the nuts goes into paints and varnishes. Not as beautiful as the piney woods, but they bring money to the county." He was sweating unmercifully, even with the thumping breeze blustering in the opened windows. He kept his handkerchief at the ready.

By the time they reached the towns of Derby and McNeill, Mrs. Owens's breakfast had drugged Celeste into lethargy. In Carriere, they turned off Highway 11. Her eyelids lowered to half-mast and her head bobbed to the seat back. They turned away from the deserted town center, less interesting looking than Pineyville's, and drove on an alarmingly bumpy blacktop road through a jungle of trees and hanging vines before turning in through an iron gate surrounded by tall iron fencing, rust patches up and down the bars, that went as far as she could see to the right and left.

They drove up a hard-packed earthen road bordered on both sides with immense live oaks and stopped on the gravel driveway in front of a house that stood high above the ground with steep stairs leading to a deep wraparound porch. It couldn't have been more unlike the leaning shanty houses of Freshwater Road and even the "white folks" houses in Pineyville. It was a plantation house, a grand stark white mansion with black shutters nestled in a forest of liquid green. Palms and banana trees nestled in bunches near the base of the porch. The land around the house was overgrown with foliage and vines, and it was all strangely beautiful. Celeste imagined a slave girl in a cotton smock would emerge to direct them to the back.

Instead, a large dark woman in a blue tent dress, with a brilliant blue and gold cloth around her head in a kind of citadel, came out of the carved double

doors. She beamed a canyon of a smile that seemed to be studded with diamonds. Her gold hoop earrings and her finger rings glittered in the snatches
of sunlight that filtered through the shade trees. She waited for them at the
top of the stairs, her remarkable teeth whiter than Momma Bessie's sheets.

Celeste stood on the stone walkway staring at the immense house and
the grand woman at the top of the stairs. She turned to see again the godly
live oaks they'd just driven under, the branches on either side overarching to
form a tunnel of iridescent green with black veins branching through. The
sun shrank back, rebuffed by the power and grace of those trees. The balmy
air had a streak of coolness in it. This was far away from the beach-like sand
of Freshwater Road; she was standing in a primordial forest where anything
that dropped to earth took root.

Reverend Singleton took the steep stairs two at a time. The woman
hugged him and kissed him on both cheeks. Something in her eyes when
she looked at him, powerful enough to read even from the bottom of the
stairs. Celeste walked up to greet the woman, who had the smooth face
and vibrant eyes of a precocious teenager. She ushered them into the house
speaking in French, laughing through the few words of welcome that Celeste
could understand.

A foyer with silent ceiling fans whirling and great potted palms in every
corner opened onto a living room with shuttered French windows and
polished hardwood floors. The large room was filled with an assortment of
furniture—an overstuffed chaise lounge with a bright print fabric thrown
over it, a Victorian sofa, floor lamps and fringed table lamps, an antique
record player with stacks of records in brown paper covers next to it, and a
grand piano in the center of the floor. The room's coloring reminded Celeste
of a Cézanne still life. She gathered herself, remembered she'd been to the
big-time cities with Shuck, knew how to walk into a luxurious place. But
she never expected all this in Mississippi.

"Celeste, I want you to meet Miss Sophie Lewis, as she's the one who's
helping finance our church. Now, if I could only convince her to come on
a Sunday morning and sing for us." Reverend Singleton's face expanded to
hold his enormous glee at being in the presence of Miss Sophie Lewis.

Celeste had heard both this woman's name and her luxurious voice
somewhere along the way. She knew her to be an opera singer of world re-
nown, but why would she live in the swampy primordial forest of southern
Mississippi?

The woman evaded a direct response to Reverend Singleton's invitation as her arm swept them toward the sofa. She pulled a fabric cord beside the fireplace mantel and within seconds, a starchy looking Negro man in a white waistcoat served them iced tea with tiny cloth napkins and a plate of thin irregular cookies. He bowed as he left the room. Celeste gawked and had the feeling she'd dropped into the rabbit hole.

"Pralines." The woman nodded at the cookies. "You're from Michigan, then?" She sat on a high-backed, wood-framed chair that might have come from the court of a Spanish queen. "Reverend Singleton told me."

"Yes, ma'am." Celeste straightened her spine and set her iced tea glass on the small lace doily atop the mahogany coffee table. She wasn't sure if the question had to do with the state or the school. She thought of launching into her usual recitation of planning on law school. It's what she always said though she barely believed it herself. Her choice of classes for two years had ranged from anthropology to Middle Eastern Studies to English literature. In truth, she didn't have a clue as to what lay ahead.

"That's good." The woman nodded, taking Celeste in. "And has the good reverend told you of his own illustrious background?"

Before Celeste could open her mouth, the woman told her that Reverend Singleton had a master of divinity degree from the University of Chicago and that he'd been offered a position at a church in Seattle that boasted a large, integrated congregation. He declined it to come back south to lift his people out of despondency. Sophie Lewis's pride in Reverend Singleton beamed out of her like a searchlight. Celeste caught something else in it, too, that the woman wanted her to know she wasn't the only one here from a big white northern university.

Miss Lewis kept her attention on Reverend Singleton, whose chest protruded through his buttoned suit jacket. "Now, what's new in Pineyville?" She said it with a rumbling mirth just underneath. "How you manage to stay there is beyond me, though I'm glad you do. If I couldn't escape every few months, I don't know..."

"But your house—" Celeste imagined herself ensconced on the chaise with a stack of books and a telephone. She noticed that she wasn't sweating for the first time in over a week, and wondered dreamily if there was a way she could do her work from this place. The thought drifted through her head like a fantasy.

"My father built this house, Celeste. He came here from New Orleans when Storyville closed down. I bet you don't know anything about that?" She smiled an alluring kind of smile.

"No, I don't." She sure liked the sound of it. Storyville. A land just off the map of Oz, a place with houses like this one, cool and calm, rich and sensual.

"It was a red light district, so to speak, with grand houses of ill-repute—free flowing sin, you might say. My father owned houses in the area. He sold them all and built this. His hideaway. Nobody knows, including me, how he survived it all as a Negro man. I'm not sure I want to know. My mother's a good deal younger than he was."

Reverend Singleton's head went from side to side in the "it never ends" wag. Celeste wanted to hear the whole family saga.

"I won't stay here after my mother passes on. My father sat on that porch with a shotgun daring anybody to cross his gate until the day he died. I remember that. He was an old man."

Celeste wondered how many times he'd had to shoot. She imagined the old Negro man sitting on his wide front porch with a shotgun across his knees, sipping a mint julep with a servant by his side. From his porch, he had a clear shot straight up that alley of live oaks.

Reverend Singleton cleared his throat and ferried the conversation toward an update on the movement in southern Mississippi and the plans for Pineyville. He ended by telling Miss Lewis that the timing of the summer work had to do with the Democratic National Convention coming in August in Atlantic City. "We have to do our best to register as many Negroes as possible, be ready for the November election."

Celeste joined in. "One Man, One Vote will challenge the all-white Mississippi delegation in Atlantic City." She eyed the pralines.

"I see. The signatures of registered Negro voters will be needed for the challenge." Sophie Lewis knew the plan. "But the point is to get them registered for the next election and beyond."

Celeste nibbled a praline. "Yes, ma'am." The cookie turned to pure sugar in her mouth with pecans all through. She wanted to wrap a few of them in a napkin to eat later that night, her mind wandering around the cool room and examining the vases, the fabrics, the still life paintings on the walls. Had Geneva Owens ever been invited here? What other connections did this woman have to Pineyville? Maybe she was just a woman of means who wanted to stay in the background but tried to be involved in her own way. There were whites, too, all over the South supporting the movement with money for lawyers, calling in favors to protect people. Why not a Negro woman doing the same thing?

When Reverend Singleton said they'd have to be getting on, Miss Lewis took a thick envelope from the pocket of her great tent dress and gave it to him. "This is from New Orleans. I imagine some from other places as well. And, from me."

Reverend Singleton stuffed the plump envelope into the inside breast pocket of his jacket. "We'll be starting on Thursday. This will give us bail money and help the ones who get fired from their jobs once we go to see Mr. Heywood. Maybe even another row or two of pews. And thanks to Almighty God for sending us this young woman to help with this work."

Celeste nodded to him, the weight of it pressing down on her again. It sounded so grand, so important, and she just a nearly motherless child from Detroit. He spoke as if she was a seasoned volunteer like Matt and Margo. The instructions from orientation squirmed around in her mind, alternating with feelings of fear and general ineptness toward what lay ahead. She was crawling toward the moment of absolute engagement, and the movement had already taken her by the elbows and rushed her to the starting line, her feet dragging in the dirt. What if she registered no one? Would Miss Lewis understand? Would Reverend Singleton think of her as a failure? Would Pineyville be the same in August when she left as it was right now? The questions single-filed through her mind.

"May I use your restroom?" She wasn't going to leave this house without using the restroom. She wanted to flush a toilet, to put her hands under a faucet and turn on the water, have the water pool in a real face bowl.

Sophie Lewis directed her to the foyer and to the center of the house. She entered a guest restroom completely encased in white marble with gold fixtures molded into leopards. There were tiny balls of perfumed soap piled on a gold-rimmed dish and satin-inlaid guest towels fanned out on the marble sink. Silk flowers in crystal vases decorated the marble top. She flushed the toilet and saw the clear water enter the bowl, then flushed again just for the hell of it. Finally, she sat on the toilet seat, not even bothering to line it with toilet paper. No need for squatting here. She washed her hands using the perfumed soap and let the water run into the porcelain face bowl, then dried her hands on a guest towel, folding it neatly and placing it to the side. She had an urge to lock herself in the bathroom and never come out. She stared at her darkening face in the oversized gilded mirror, remembering the week of life under the scorching sun in Jackson before she came to Pineyville. *Jiggaboo girl.* At this rate, by summer's end she'd be as dark as Ramona. No high-yellow quips then. Wilamena would pass her on the street and not even know her.

Reverend Singleton and Miss Lewis waited for her in the foyer. At the top of the porch stairs, the woman pinned Celeste with intent in her big eyes. "You've taken on a great challenge, young lady, and you will succeed. I will hear of nothing less." She kissed Celeste and Reverend Singleton on both cheeks and said, "Adieu."

She *expected* success. Celeste's eyes burned. The woman suddenly struck her as both in touch and out of touch at the same time. Elegantly dismissive. Wilamena in a grand dress and a head wrap. Miss Lewis would be off on one of her tours when things came to a boil. But she'd given the Negro people of Pineyville her support in that envelope. Still, Celeste knew they needed people, bodies to line up. Bodies ready to take a beating. She knew also that people did what they could, and it all mattered.

From the car, Celeste and Reverend Singleton waved to Miss Sophie Lewis. She watched them from her porch, a great statue of a woman, her blue and gold head wrap striking against the white of the house, the deep color of her skin. It wasn't easy to leave the cool luxury of that place. Celeste wondered what must it have been like to grow up there, to live there now, leaving and coming back to this grandness. They'd turned back onto the earthen road under the alley of live oaks. The DeSoto barely made a sound.

They drove through Carriere as a thick warm rain smeared the dust on the windshield, shining the green of the trees and grass. Celeste opened her window and stuck her head out to let the rain fall on her face, then cupped her hands and smoothed the lotion-like rainwater up and down her arms.

"You got some country girl in you." Reverend Singleton smiled as he turned on his windshield wipers.

"That's what my grandmother used to say." She cranked the window up when the rain turned to a downpour. "Why won't Miss Lewis come sing at the church?"

"Well." Reverend Singleton's mouth seemed poised to say more. "It's a long story. When all the pews are in and we're as good as we can get, perhaps she will come and sing for us. I certainly hope so."

Celeste stared across him to the sinking land, to the tilting willows at the edge of the bayou. Reverend Singleton pointed out the swamp oaks, sweet bay, and yellow poplars with flowers like big tulips as they drove north towards Pineyville.

9

The next morning, Reverend Singleton drove Celeste to see the dilapi-dated Negro elementary school. Negro students had to take one of the old school buses parked on the grounds to Lumberton for high school, and he told her what few teachers they had lived in Hattiesburg. He then drove her to see the sturdy brick buildings that housed the whites-only school and its well-maintained grounds and play areas, including a bright green baseball diamond. He didn't need to point out that this was where all of Pineyville's children should be going to school. Celeste stared out of the car window; the effort to push down her anger was making a bother-some knot in her stomach.

When he turned onto the church road, Celeste expected to see a group of excited children waiting on the steps anticipating the start of freedom school. Not one child waited. She didn't blame them. It's a rare child who wants to go to school all summer long. Hard enough to be in there during the regular year, especially in this place of few books and broken-down facilities. They didn't yet understand how very different this school would be. How to get that message out, she didn't know.

Inside, pull shades controlled some of the sunlight roaring in the tallish windows. The side aisle floors were finished wood. The pulpit area, up two steps from the floor, and the center aisle all the way to the door had a thin layer of dark blue carpet. An organ sat to the side of the pulpit area and the preaching stand was off to the other side. A thick rope, the bell cord, was hooked to the side wall and, high above, extended into the small bell tower.

There were five rows of wooden pews followed by a few rows of assorted folding chairs, and then more rows of all manner of hand-me-down chairs. It was a work in progress.

"I'll need a chalkboard." Celeste paced across the front of the church, glancing to the front door and praying for the arrival of a child, any child, for her freedom school. "And a couple of boxes of chalk and an eraser or two."

Reverend Singleton sat on the front pew. "Hattiesburg." Celeste thought him so well-dressed in a suit and tie, a spiffy shirt. He still had Chicago in his veins. She wondered what his plan could be, where he saw himself in the future.

"I'm going to need a daily newspaper, too. We'll use it for reading exercises and civics lessons." Celeste sat on the pulpit step.

"We can pick them up in town every morning. I might try to find a couple of nice standing fans to sit on each side here. Give you a little cross breeze." Reverend Singleton leaned over, his arms on his thighs, studying her.

The overwhelming quiet of the place seemed to settle on them. The church clearing was far enough from the highway to shelter them from any sound of cars or trucks. And at just that moment, no birds sang, no insects moved, no breeze stirred the trees. Even the wood snakes stopped to hear the great nothing. Reverend Singleton was openly staring at Celeste.

"Is something wrong?" His stare didn't make her necessarily feel uncomfortable. There didn't seem to be anything lascivious in it. His look was at her and also very far away.

"You remind me of someone I used to know." Reverend Singleton shifted on the pew ever so gently as if to break the spell. "I didn't mean to stare. Forgive me."

"It's all right." Celeste walked to the window to give him a moment to himself. She tried to imagine what had his life been like before he came back south. He'd lived in Chicago, gone to school there. He'd lived a life as far away from life in Pineyville as possible. How in God's name had he returned to live here? Was it only about the dreadful things going on in the south? Or had he come to mend himself, as she had? She was a visitor, an interloper who'd be gone by the end of August. He'd still be there with that other life spinning around inside him. The stare had been about a woman. She wanted to ask him how long he'd been married to Mrs. Singleton, why they didn't have children. She wanted to pry.

"How many children do you think we'll get?" She walked toward him, the light behind her slanting in from behind the shades. Her questions helped ease her own anxiety about the responsibility she had for the job ahead.

"Hard to say. Some folks are plain scared, and some have to negotiate transportation." Reverend Singleton rested back against the pew, and seemed himself again. He knew that she was trying to take the reins.

"How do we get around their fear? I mean, there's good reasons for it." Celeste sat on the pew near him.

"At some point, the fear becomes more of a burden than the action it forestalls. People get tired of being afraid." He angled his body towards her, comfortable.

"I can see that." She'd already felt it since coming to Mississippi, a coupling of fear with fear-fatigue. But she was from the north. It was a shorter trip to that fatigue for her. Not so for the locals who'd learned to live with it morning, noon, and night as a survival mode. The lynchings, the beatings, the scoffs, the many deprivations and denials over years sealed that fear into the human heart, and surely had, at times, saved lives, too.

They waited, Celeste thinking they should grab the bell cord and ring the bell to call the children to the freedom school. She sat gazing at the cord then up into the small bell tower, which really was just an alcove in the ceiling. It was a primitive affair but the church was small, so it was sufficient. They weren't in Paris in a cathedral. They were in a modest, whitewashed church in southern Mississippi. Having a bell at all was remarkable.

"I'll show you my office and my treasured bathroom. I saw that look on your face. Don't you let those children go in there and mess up my privy." Reverend Singleton walked toward the side aisle, a knowing smile on his face.

"Now, Reverend Singleton, I'm gonna do exactly as you tell me." Celeste followed him. They passed a door opening onto the grassy clearing that led off into a thick stand of trees, a deepening forest. His small office had one window with its shade pulled down, the room in shadow. He opened the lavatory door and showed it off. It was indeed small, with the tiniest face bowl Celeste had ever seen. But there was the toilet, and she intended to use both every chance she got. Out the side door, he pointed to the back and a path that led to the outhouse. Stepping outside was like stepping upright into an oven after being in the relative cool of the church.

By noon not one child had come. Reverend Singleton took full responsibility. When the heat pressed down like the sun had mistakenly moved too close to the earth, they left the church.

Reverend Singleton drove down Freshwater Road, well past Mrs. Owens's house, turning on and off of side roads until she had no sense of where they were. They passed clapboard houses and scattered shanties, some painted bright pastels and some raw cypress wood, some with jalopies parked at odd angles or rusted out trucks. The few people there waved their hands and arms at Reverend Singleton and stared at the girl sitting in his front seat who surely was not Etta Singleton.

Just after six that evening, Mrs. Singleton picked her up to go back to the church for the first voter education class. Not one adult came in the door.

Dear J.D.,

I couldn't have imagined this place. Nothing I read, nothing I heard from any speaker on campus, no Bob Dylan song, no blues song, no photograph tells the truth about Mississippi. It's between the monster things that happen, it's in the air. It's the place where hideous nightmares rupture to life then breed and hide behind a cloying magnolia veil. An archeology of hatred, bones in the earth, sowed under the cotton, fed into the roots of live oaks, men, women, and children for over two hundred years.

Mrs. Owens's rocking chair ground against the sagging porch planks just outside Celeste's window. The grating sound roared in her head as she sprawled and sank into the soft mattress, writing to J.D. After stuffing little pieces of tissue into her ears, she took her freedom school books and voter registration materials to the kitchen table. She put her head down on folded arms, small twists of tissue sticking out of her ears. Oceans coursed through her head.

I am so lonely here. There are no paintings, no movies, no bookstores, no fast rides on two-lane country roads with sharp winds in my face. There are trees and cloud-skies and rains that come fast and hard and then disappear, taking all relief with them. The heat is a stockade. I'm bending from the torture of it. I don't know if the people see the sky.

Night had spread its country dark canopy. Celeste took the plugs out of her ears, heard the ritual locking of the front doors as if those frail pieces of wood and puckered screen could protect them from anything but a few flies and summer gnats.

"Mrs. Owens, is that one mailbox for everybody on Freshwater Road?" She counted houses. Maybe ten or so spread way down the road.

"Uh-huh." Mrs. Owens came into the kitchen. "They take they time putting anything in it." She checked the latch on the back screen and locked the back door, cutting off the minute catches of air that sometimes whispered in. "You want to send something out, just raise up that red arm. They'll pick it up directly." She passed behind Celeste and went into her room.

All those people who'd moved to Chicago, Detroit, Texas, and California must send something back, even a scrawl telling where they were and how they were getting on. "They told us in Jackson the post office workers might not give us our mail."

The old woman brought her pitcher to get spigot water from the tiny lip of the kitchen that passed for a back porch. The goal each night was to have enough fresh water on the back porch so no one had to go out front. Celeste watched her ladling the good water from a big bucket. "They just slow."

Emmett Till's mother must've wished with all her heart that she'd sent a letter to Money, Mississippi, instead of her flesh and blood teenaged son, all Chicago sharp and cool, no Mississippi hanging off his shoulders. She wanted her back-home relatives to see her spiffy boy, but she must've forgotten how that look, that free way of being in the world, made white men in Mississippi seethe. Maybe she just believed things had gotten better.

"I'm gonna be coming to that voting class tomorrow evening. I thought by keeping you here, it would be my way. But I need to go on and try to vote before I'm too old to care."

She'd paused in the middle of the kitchen between the refrigerator and the stove, her intense face and eyes plowing into Celeste with years' worth of meaning.

Mrs. Owens read the Bible every evening, and Celeste needed readers. From what Reverend Singleton said, not many folks here did much reading. The Mississippi State Constitution was written in 1890, the same year Pearl River County was created. Its text was one gnarled paragraph after another. Now, in order to pass the voter registration requirements imposed by the state, the Negro people of Pineyville would have to sit in a hellishly hot church and memorize whole sections of a document that had been used for years to grind them into sediment. There was no time to teach remedial reading to an entire group of people. Mrs. Owens would help bring the rest of the group along. "That's good, Mrs. Owens. I need you to come."

"Count on me." Geneva Owens walked into her room. "Nighty night, now."

Celeste heard the gentle washing sounds as the old woman prepared for bed, of water pouring into her basin, the cloth being wrung out and rubbed over aging skin, sloshing in the water again and repeated until the final wringing out, until only drips fell into the basin. She wondered if the woman had ever bathed in a real bathroom. Then the old mattress springs spoke briefly as she lay down. These small sounds were her only radio, with the sounds of the country night, distant chirps and calls, a barking dog, a lonely car on the blacktop, a subtle keening always in the background. Country quiet was like no quiet she'd ever heard in her life.

Celeste gathered her materials, went to her bedroom, opened the Mississippi State Constitution, and then shut it again. She wanted to take it outside and drop it in the outhouse hole.

She poured pitcher water into her basin, careful not to splash and waste it because every time it was empty, she had to either go out to the spigot and refill it or go to that bucket on the back porch and ladle fresh water into her pitcher. She refilled at the spigot unless it was raining, giving Mrs. Owens use of all the bucket water. She washed the day's caked sweat and dust off of her body as best she could. She needed a shower, a bath, wanted to feel clean; she hadn't had an all-over bath since the little apartment in Jackson nearly a week ago. Back home, she bathed in a green and white tiled bathroom, then soundlessly walked into a carpeted bedroom with a canopy bed and flows of drapes and sheers.

There must be women in this world of tight-lipped lies who defied the curtained doors and the penitent preachers with their Bibles and shadow swords, women who bathed in the streams naked, who walked the banks of the Pearl River and the Bogue Chitto with their dresses tucked into their undergarments, who loved with abandon in stands of pecan and magnolia trees, propped upright by live oaks like dolls, so overwhelmed by the sweetness that they lost themselves. Did they all leave town? They probably escaped to New Orleans. They collected tiny hand-painted matchboxes as souvenirs and wrote notes home on hand-painted cards with scenes of New Orleans life. That's why Mary Evans was so excited to get out of Mississippi, to breathe a free breath. The workers in the post office probably hid those cards, kept them for themselves to take out on Saturday nights when the moon freed their lusts. In church on Sunday morning, they raised their Bible hands to God with images of courtyards, lapping fountains, gardens of night jasmine, and naked bodies just behind their eyes.

Celeste paced, her own body smells adding to the dank vapor that lay over everything. She felt like a lonely prisoner in the house, as if the walls, as thin as they were, had already begun to close in on her. She was angry at Margo and the office in Jackson for sending her to such a blighted place with not even so much as a radio. How could she make it through to August like this? She couldn't hold herself still in that cell of a room. She grabbed her towel and tiptoed outside, gym shoes in hand, sliding the bolt back on the front door so as not to wake Mrs. Owens. Before any thought of danger crossed her mind, she went to the water spigot. Her ghostly white sleep shirt would be the only thing visible about her from a distance. She took it off and stood naked, the warm night air like hands on her body, and turned on the spigot, which spewed and evened out into a cool stream of water, splashing on the concrete platform, on her legs and feet.

She soaped herself from head to toe using her hands and the piece of soap Mrs. Owens left on the tin dish. She prayed no one would hear the splashing water in the quiet night, prayed no errant car turned into Freshwater Road while she stood there naked. She bent down to get as far under the flow of water as possible. She rinsed her hair. The cool water assuaged her anger. At least now she felt clean for the first time in days, pulled her sleep shirt over her towel-wrapped hair, and sat down on the steps of the leaning porch, slapping mosquitoes. How, in God's name, did people live here? She removed the towel and let the warm air begin to dry her hair. The new moon seemed lost in the starry country sky. Not a light on all the way down Freshwater Road.

Mrs. Owens came through the short hallway and onto the screened porch. "What you doin', child?"

"I felt so sweaty, and my hair needed washing." Celeste stood up on the bottom step.

"People clean themselves down here. I got a tub for that. No need to be washing your hair out in the front yard." Mrs. Owens was sharp and clear in her disapproval.

"I'm sorry, ma'am." Celeste knew she'd stepped over the boundaries of what was acceptable. "I'm sorry." She flushed with embarrassment and felt like Shuck's little girl again, scolded for stepping out of line.

"Mrs. Owens, I need to talk to my daddy." If anyone had told her that she *couldn't* talk to Shuck that night, she'd have wept in distress. "I should have called him before now. I promised." Maybe if she talked to Shuck just the sound of his voice would calm her down.

"You caint go to that pay phone this time of night." Mrs. Owens's voice broke, her words coming quiet, fast and fear-tinged.

"I can run it and be back before anybody knows I'm out there." Celeste knew she had an edge in her voice, too, from her desperation.

"Then I'm goin' with you, and that means you cain't run." Mrs. Owens turned to go into the house. "Cause I cain't."

Celeste hadn't been in this house a good week and already she was wearing thin on Mrs. Owens with her petulant need for things to be the way they were at home—exactly what the office in Jackson warned them against. It would be dangerous enough for Celeste alone, but she surely didn't want to be the cause of any harm coming to Mrs. Owens. She wanted to run the whole way and run back. She needed the run, too—forget the heat, she needed to push out, press herself into another mindset, another place. She went to her room, pulled on cotton slacks and buttoned on a short-sleeved shirt, laced up her gym shoes, clutched some nickels and dimes so tightly in her palm she felt the indents in her skin. If anyone in Jackson found out about this, they'd send her packing back to Detroit.

Voter registration projects were supposed to have cars. She needed one, didn't like feeling so cut off from the rest of the world. With a car, the trip to the pay phone would be nothing. She sat on the side of her bed and closed her eyes, slipping into a reverie of freedom, aching to get out of Pineyville even for a few hours. New Orleans wasn't very far away. There had to be a museum, a park, places to take the freedom school children, a city street to walk on, store windows to loiter in front of. She pictured the wide Mississippi River like the Detroit River at home, a bridge like the Ambassador to Canada. Ramona and Margo probably had cars for their projects. They were in bigger towns. But a young woman driving around the countryside in a marked car would be vulnerable. And, there was no safety in numbers. Schwerner, Chaney, and Goodman didn't make it back to their project. Every sheriff and highway patrolman in Mississippi knew the movement cars. They were all registered vehicles, all the plates were known. Easy prey.

"I'm sorry. I might be better off on my own. I can move faster." Even this, she knew, was against the rules.

"I'm goin' with you if you have to go." Mrs. Owens came from her bedroom, buttoning her housedress, a light scarf tied around her hair and looking like she could shake Celeste senseless. She had a white scarf in her hand.

There was no way Celeste could force her to stay in the house.

"You best put something white on so drivers can see us in the dark." She held the bandana towards Celeste.

"Maybe it would be better if no one saw us, don't you think?" Celeste read the look on Mrs. Owens's face to say, how are you going to come down here and tell me what the best thing to do is? Celeste shrank and took the scarf.

Mrs. Owens stood there. "You best to put something light on so some tired truck driver on his way to New Orleans don't run over us." She repeated it in a voice that defied misinterpretation. Celeste tied the white scarf around her damp hair, feeling reined in by this woman like Wilamena never seemed to be able to do. Wilamena might've tried when she and Billy were very small, but she never seemed to have the will to carry it through. If you pushed against Wilamena, she fell. Celeste pushed. Wilamena didn't want to be bothered with the day to day. She had glamor days left and two children were stealing them from her. Mrs. Owens had drawn a line that said, *I'll do this with you but you'll do it my way.*

They went out, closing the doors quietly behind them. When they got to the mailbox, Celeste stopped. The arm wasn't up, but she figured the post office workers wouldn't put the arm up anyway even if they did deposit mail in the box, especially mail with her name on it.

"Go 'head, child." Mrs. Owens had a kindness in her voice now as if she understood how lonely Celeste felt, how cut off.

Celeste opened the oblong mailbox, wishing now she'd finished her letter to J.D. to put in it, and that by putting something in, maybe she'd get something out. She reached her hand and half her arm inside, scraping her fingernails on the back wall, then slid her hand along the bottom in case she'd missed something. There was a thin envelope. She pulled it out, and it was addressed to her. Even in the dark of night, she knew Wilamena's elegant swirl. The Jackson office had forwarded it to Pineyville.

"It's from my mother." She hoped Mrs. Owens didn't hear the distance she felt when she said "mother," a person she rarely mentioned. The older woman just nodded and adjusted herself for the trek.

Celeste shoved the letter in her pants pocket. Wilamena and her cool words, reserved and formal, that always sounded and felt like obligation. No doubt it was another invitation to New Mexico. She'd read it later.

"Guess you right about them post workers not wanting you to get your mail. They didn't even put that arm up. That's not right." Mrs. Owens sighed with exasperation.

"No, it's not, Mrs. Owens, and it's probably against the law." Celeste saw it as a part of the grand cover-up going all the way back to slavery times. It happened, but let's *pretend* it didn't. *Let's pretend those Negroes aren't even here unless we need them to do some menial back-breaking work.*

They took off, two women walking through the night darkness on the side of the road with crickets crying and dogs barking and the loneliest new moon Celeste had seen in her life. No beaming headlights. She thought of nightriders, flaming crosses, and panel trucks with loaded shotguns. Mrs. Owens breathed steady, her eyes straight ahead. Celeste sensed the woman heard every sound, from the soft scratchy thuds of their feet on the dirt and gravel shoulder to the siren barks of dogs tied, she hoped, behind fences.

Their mission to reach the pay phone, make the call, and return home safely propelled them along the road. Celeste heard the sound of a car behind them and turned to see two globes of light coming their way. Mrs. Owens moved over on the shoulder and walked behind her. Celeste held her breath as the car drew closer. The sound of it moving on the uneven road drowned out all other night sounds. She didn't know if they should duck into the trees and let it pass. The car was near now, could see them for sure, and in seconds had passed them by without so much as a blare of its horn. Mrs. Owens sighed deeply. Celeste did the same. They didn't speak, just kept hiking along at a good clip.

The tall pine trees were black against the deep blue-black sky, their guardians in the night. She thought of turning around, of apologizing to Mrs. Owens for dragging her out of her bed to walk a dangerous road, but something else had taken over. Now, it was more the idea of doing it, of not caving in to the terror that lived in the Mississippi air, of not letting the disappearance of the three boys and all the other dead and disappeared stop them. She believed Mrs. Owens felt the same thing though she never said it.

They reached the solitary pay phone at the corner of the gas station with its small convenience light, highlighted by the one swinging traffic light blinking yellow all night long. There wasn't a car in sight.

Mrs. Owens took up a position a few feet away while Celeste deposited a dime and dialed the operator, asking to make a collect call to Mr. Shuck Tyree in Detroit, Michigan, giving her name, clear and quiet, saying the phone number of the house on Outer Drive in a gamble that he was there. If the music on the party girl went too current and the crowd too young, Shuck might leave for an hour or two and stop by Alma's or go home before heading back to the bar to close up. If he was home, he wouldn't be there long. She heard the phone ring on the other end and prayed Shuck was there so she didn't have to place another call. Mrs. Owens stood still a few feet away watching the empty street. Celeste heard the clicking of the pick up and breathed a sigh of relief. The operator announced that she had a collect call from Celeste Tyree in Pineyville, Mississippi, for Shuck Tyree. Her thick Mississippi accent cut "Shuck" into two syllables.

"Yeah, this is Shuck Tyree." He cut the drawling operator off, all expectation in his voice as he yelled into the phone. "You all right? Sure, I accept. That's my daughter."

Celeste never felt so good hearing his voice. He was her home.

The operator clicked off. Celeste hoped she wasn't listening in somehow.

"Daddy. It's me." Before the words were out of her mouth, she felt the burn of tears coming to her eyes and blinked them back.

"I know who it is." He sat on his excitement, trying to be the cool guy. "You think I don't know who it is?"

"Thought maybe you forgot me." She joked to harness her own loneliness, knowing Shuck wasn't going to get sentimental with her or anyone else and wasn't going to allow her to, either.

"I know you not in jail?" He questioned and dared at the same time.

"No, I'm on a corner pay phone. The lady I'm staying with, Mrs. Owens, is here with me being the lookout." Celeste tried to put a wry joking tone in her voice then angled herself to see down the main street of Pineyville, acting cool and nonchalant. Street lights blazed down in front of the County Building, the blackness just beyond it.

"You need a lookout to make a phone call?" Shuck's voice rose up in disbelief.

"I could've come by myself." She lied. There was no way. She wouldn't be at the phone if Mrs. Owens hadn't come along. She'd have turned around in five minutes.

Mrs. Owens stood a few feet away, the signal light blinking yellow on her deep brown face.

"Listen to me. You can always get on that train. Don't have to stay there. Get on a plane. Don't make me have to come down there and kill somebody." Shuck took a breath. "Pineyville. Of all the damned places." The cool guy had ducked and run.

Did Shuck know about Leroy Boyd James? Is that why he said *of all the damned places?* "It's going well, really." She gave it her best pleading. That *going well* helped his breathing slow to normal. No need to say anything about the ride down from Jackson with Matt, that would upset him too much. The only thing he'd say about Miss Sophie Lewis was that the woman ought to pack up and get out of there. She let the *going well* stand.

Shuck grunted. "When's this damn thing over?"

"August. I'll be home sometime in August." She started crying, didn't want Shuck or Mrs. Owens to know, turned herself away from the older woman. "You tell Billy?" She sounded like a criminal talking on a phone from behind bars, tears running down her face.

"He thinks you lost your mind." Billy didn't know her now, anyway. He knew her to high school, then he was gone to college, and now she had come to this place. He didn't even know she'd had a white boyfriend in college unless Shuck told him. Unlikely.

"I don't think he'll be living in New York long." Shuck implied that New York was kicking Billy's behind. "Wilamena called here looking for you." He was letting her know that he'd told Wilamena where she was.

Celeste stopped crying, wiped her face on the back of her hand.

"You know about how that went over." He was chastising her for not staying in closer touch with her mother. She knew very well that Wilamena didn't like searching for her.

Celeste felt the letter in her pocket, a warm weight against her body. She hadn't called her mother "momma" since she was a little girl. The grandmothers, Momma Bessie and Grandma Pauline, had subsumed the mother notion, taking up so much space in her mind that "momma" receded to a small place. But, it never disappeared. Didn't even know if Wilamena minded being called by her first name. Wilamena in her house with no music wouldn't want to know too much about Mississippi.

"Make sure you write her." He paused. "You catch more flies with honey." Shuck chuckled in the back of his voice.

Celeste rode over what he said, didn't want to spend her whole phone call talking about Wilamena. "I need you to send bail money down in case I get arrested. Send it by Western Union to the Jackson office of One Man, One Vote. They'll take care of it from there. Five hundred dollars." She'd been told to make this phone call while she was in Jackson, then Matt told again before he left, and now, finally, she was doing it. She'd lived that first week wondering if she was going to stay in Mississippi long enough to get arrested. After the police picked her up in Jackson then let her go, she'd felt lucky. Then with Matt on the road down, she'd missed the blows and knew she was lucky. She felt like she was running on Shuck's luck. "This is costing a fortune, Daddy."

"I don't give a damn how much it's costing." Shuck held on and let go at the same time. "I'll take care of the bail money. You be careful, you hear?"

She heard the pride in his voice and the warning, too, like she had from the lady in the segregated bathroom in Jackson. "I will."

Shuck hung up.

Celeste in that one little moment felt so alone that hanging up the phone seemed like disconnecting herself from her own life.

Mrs. Owens nodded in the direction of Freshwater Road. "All right now, child, let's go."

Celeste figured she'd pushed Mrs. Owens right to her limits and that she'd had all she was going to take of doing things Celeste's way. They took off, walking fast, their footsteps cracking over the gravel, thudding on the sand shoulder, sometimes scuffing quietly on the blacktop. Celeste listened for truck tires, for wild men who didn't need to be drunk to do horrendous things. She smelled pine and felt mosquitoes but didn't even bother to slap her arms, just kept moving, making sure Mrs. Owens breathing was deep and strong.

When they arrived at the big mailbox, the house with the slanting porch looked like home. Millions of bright country stars tiptoed across the sky, running from the cloud banks that never stopped moving through, creating dark rooms of night.

They headed straight for the kitchen and tall glasses of ice water. The old woman drank hers then said goodnight, closing her curtain door behind

her. Celeste stood at the opened back door. The pine trees rustled in a
slight current of air, like water sliding over old stones. At night, the aromas
of rotting wood, outhouses, and meals cooked every day for years settled
over and nearly obliterated the subtle scent of pine. Insects whistled in full
knotty cries that thinned to aches. And always, the sporadic barking of
the skinny dogs who scrammed under the houses of Freshwater Road or
hightailed it into the pines when cars and trucks rolled by on the two-lane.
They knew when to hide.

Wilamena's thin slip of a letter pressed through her pocket against her
thigh. With her mother, Celeste felt out of place, never knew how to crack
the cool veneer. She scratched and pecked at the enclosure of Wilamena
and got crumbs or nothing at all. *Nobody owes you anything because of how
you look.* Wilamena'd written that after Shuck mailed her photographs of
Celeste dressed in green taffeta for the junior prom. She'd responded in
a phone call admiring the dress and Celeste's hair, then ended with that
deflating scold. Finally, Celeste surrendered to her mother's coolness, let
her be, held close to Shuck.

She locked the back door, turned out the kitchen light, and went to
her room. She was relieved. The walk and the phone call had given her
energy. Had she not bathed naked, had she not gone to the phone, she never
could've stayed in this house for another week, forget until August. Some
prisons were worse than others. She pulled the sweat-damp letter out of her
pocket. The return address was written on a beautiful linen envelope, the
tiny numbers marking a house she'd never seen and a street name she only
knew from the upper corner of other envelopes. Wilamena would berate
her for going to Mississippi in the first place. After that, the invitation to
New Mexico would sit like a sour candy at the end of a bad meal. She put it
under her underwear in the dresser drawer as if it were a treasured heirloom
to be touched ever so delicately, not breathed on, not dropped or dirtied,
polished only with the softest of cloths. Wilamena in a glass cabinet with
the door locked. She needed support, encouragement, and the strength to
see the summer through, not lectures about her decision to do this work.

The next day when Reverend Singleton left her alone in the church while
he went to run an errand, two children came in as quietly as if they were
ghosts. The girl, with blond curly hair and blue-gray eyes set in a reddish
brown face, handed Celeste a piece of paper with a note introducing them
as Labyrinth and Georgie. She read the names over, said them to herself,

wondering if the child had any idea at all of what her name meant. The girl had a dare in her eyes, so Celeste figured she must know something of her name's impact on people. The boy and the girl had no resemblance to each other at all, he being dark with intense brown eyes. The note said that their mother, Dolly Johnson, or her sister, would come back for them around noon. The more she looked at the girl, the more she understood what a brilliant stroke it was to name this strange-looking child Labyrinth.

When Reverend Singleton returned, Celeste begged him to ring the bell in celebration of the beginning of Pineyville's Freedom Summer project and he did, laughing and protesting that he hoped the Negro people who heard it wouldn't think the place was on fire and come running with their buckets. Dolly Johnson's sister honked her car horn around noon, and the two children ran out the door yelling back to Celeste that it was their aunt come to get them. No lingering there that first day. And no wonder. They were the only children in the freedom school class so far.

On the ride home, Reverend Singleton told Celeste that Labyrinth and Georgie had different fathers and that Labyrinth's father was Percival Dale, the white grocery store owner in town. Georgie's father was a Negro man named Hiram who Dolly had met in Hattiesburg, where she went around with him for a while. When she got pregnant with Georgie, Hiram took off for California. In his defense, Reverend Singleton said, Hiram had found work there and sent money on a semiregular basis for the care of his child.

Dolly worked for a white family over in Hattiesburg, and was doing all right considering the situation of most Negroes in that part of Mississippi. Everyone suspected that Mr. Dale had secured her job for her. It was also rumored that he periodically sent bags of groceries to Dolly with cash money hidden under the potatoes. Mr. Dale was married and had white children. She asked Reverend Singleton about the child's name, and he told her the nuns at Charity Hospital in New Orleans had suggested it to Dolly after they saw her child with that head of blond curls crowning brown skin. Percival Dale had been there with Dolly for the birth, too, and of course the nuns took notice of that. Reverend Singleton went on to tell her that situations like that had always been quite common in New Orleans and there were many people with strange names there. He himself had baptized Labyrinth right there at the St. James A.M.E. Church.

10

If any pitiful drafts of night coolness lingered, Geneva Owens annihilated them by turning on the stove before daybreak. The aroma of collards with ham hocks wafted through the house, and something so sweet smelling that Celeste's stomach rumbled like rolling thunder before she even opened her eyes. On Sunday in Mississippi, church predominated. She hoped it would be another step forward in her work, a baptism in the fount of Pineyville.

Celeste washed herself as best she could before putting on one of her scoop-neck shirtdresses. She went straight to the kitchen and grabbed a cup of chicory-laced coffee, then stood at the back door trying to catch a breeze. Back home, on this kind of lazy summer Sunday, she would put on a strapped sundress and go to an air-conditioned movie. Or Shuck would take her and Momma Bessie on a ride over the Ambassador Bridge to Canada for lunch, the cool breezes off the river quelling the rages of summer.

Mrs. Owens moved around behind her curtain door off the kitchen. The steaming room pushed Celeste to the back steps, her brain struggling to stay alert. By midweek, the whole town knew who she was and why she was there. The local newspaper carried stories about the invasion of northern "rabble-rousers." She never thought of herself as a rabble-rouser, and she didn't think of Pineyville's Negroes as rabble. She saw the Freedom Summer volunteers as right up there with the great patriots, the idealistic founders, supporting the idea of one person, one vote, making America more true to itself. She felt good about being in Mississippi. Even her fear—lodged so deep inside, it had become a part of her being—had stopped interrupting her every thought. Her dreams were another story altogether.

Coffee acids churned her emptiness to a wrenching depth. She didn't mind being hungry because Mrs. Owens's cooking had a tendency to create hunger when there was none. Smothered chicken and gravy, red beans with pickled pork, stewed okra with shrimp, all of it over rice, fiery hot and pepper laced, bringing on eruptions of sweat. Oh, for a glass of ginger ale with mountains of ice cubes and a cold chicken sandwich with lettuce and snappy pickles. Yesterday they'd eaten bacon drippings over rice. Never had so much rice at home. Momma Bessie cooked southern, but this was a new level of southern. The only dish she'd never even heard of was red beans and pickled pork over rice. It all tasted like heaven, even though it sat high and hard in her stomach for hours after each meal. The iced tea was so sweet it made the sides of her mouth cave in. But it was cold.

Mrs. Owens came through her curtain door, a hint of plum rouge on her dark brown cheeks, a hint of a smile wrinkling the corners of her mouth. "We riding to church with them Tuckers from down the road in the best-looking and fastest car in Pearl River County. At least that's what everybody calls it."

The old woman grew more conversational as the days passed, as if she'd saved words to spend at a sale and now was on a spree. She lifted the lid from her collards, giving escape to a grand whoosh of the pork-infused aroma, then turned off the flame. The kitchen steamed.

"It's a pretty car." The pay phone Celeste had used to call Shuck stood just a few feet from the gas station where Mr. Tucker worked. She'd never walked there again in the night, but she had used it to check in with the Jackson office, let them know she was still alive just as Matt had told her to do. Mr. Tucker's maroon 1954 Hudson Hornet was parked behind the garage, a big chrome fender peeking around the corner. At night she saw it parked down the road next to the Tucker house, had watched the Tucker children play close to their front porch, never running up and down the road, never venturing close to this house.

"Some colored boys from over in Purvis stole that car in broad daylight." The old woman poured herself the last of the coffee.

"In Pineyville?" With one slow swivel of the head, you could see everything going on in the town center. Celeste couldn't imagine something as big as a car theft taking place right there.

"He had the car up in Hattiesburg when it happened." She sipped, perspiration rising on her face like ground water swelling. "On business." There was a slight note of disdain audible in the word *business*. "They caught 'em. Those boys still in Parchment Prison for all I know."

When Mrs. Owens gossiped, Celeste wished they could sit there all day long and chew the fat about everybody. What kind of business had he been doing? Why did she sound like that? Mr. Tucker must be into something. And where did he get a car like that to begin with? And Sophie Lewis? She wanted to ask Mrs. Owens about the grand lady in the big house. Did she even know her? What if there was bad blood between them about the church? Jealousy? Did Reverend Singleton tell everybody about the money and where it came from? Maybe Sophie Lewis didn't want anyone to know about her involvement in the movement, maybe it was safer for her to be quiet and in the background.

"They once had some white boys take it, too. From the gas station where Mr. Tucker works. Right from under his nose. Newspaper say Sheriff Trotter put the white boys in the county jail. They were out before the sun went down." Mrs. Owens took two dishtowels, tied them together end to end, then tied them to the handles of the pot of greens, securing the lid. "Sheriff said they didn't have enough evidence to hold *them*. Probably never saw the inside of a jail."

"No witnesses?" Though the Tuckers lived right down the road, before this morning Mrs. Owens had barely mentioned their name.

"Oh, they had witnesses. Colored." She brought the sugar-brown bread pudding out of the oven. "Anyway, he got that car back."

"Do those white boys live around here?" The memory of the creeping car that grated down Freshwater Road on her first night rose like a specter in her mind. If the police never really arrested the white boys for taking Mr. Tucker's car, they were the ones to watch. She thought of the lessons from orientation. *Keep your eye on the police, but notice, too, with whom they have coffee, whose backs they slap, what car windows they lean into with their hats pushed back, black billy clubs, cattle prods, chromium-plated handcuffs and flashlights clanking and shining in the sunlight.*

"Sure do. Mr. Tucker got to look at 'em every time they go in there to buy gas or a Coke Cola."

Celeste knew the red Coca-Cola machine standing beside the gas station wall, used it herself. She tried to remember the white men who'd come into the gas station while she stood there on the phone watching Mr. Tucker pumping gas or cleaning the "whites only" bathroom. Plenty of white men filling their tanks. Negro men, too. How to know who was friendly and who wasn't? And Mr. Tucker? What did he do in Hattiesburg?

Celeste had marked the distance from the church to the pay phone, about a mile. An easy run. She'd already walked the distance from Freshwater Road to the phone and knew she could run it easily. She'd memorized the phone numbers for the FBI offices in Hattiesburg and in Jackson. The numbers rolled through her mind. The problem wasn't the distance, it was the danger from some local hiding in the trees, or some truck that might drive by and run her down. She needed to know who those locals were, what they looked like, what kind of vehicle they drove. Keep an eye on them. She'd ask Reverend Singleton after church. No matter how fast she ran, she couldn't outrun a truck, let alone a bullet. She already had nightmares of being thrown into the Pearl River like a sack of trash, floating with the current down past Pearlington into Lake Borgne and on to the Gulf of Mexico.

When Geneva Owens turned from the stove again, the sun caught the crystal brooch pinned near the collar of her cotton print dress and sent shafts of light in all directions. It made her look very dressed up. "I guess he probably feel they always plottin' to take that car again. Maybe that's what makes him so hateful."

Celeste startled. What did that mean? Was Mr. Tucker hateful to everybody? He might be working for the police for all she knew, or even worse, for the Klan. Not every Negro in Mississippi was for the movement. During orientation in Jackson, this had been a touchy subject for Margo to discuss with Celeste and Ramona, but she said she had an obligation to tell them, alert them to keep an eye out for Negroes who might take information to whites who paid them to stand against the movement. Celeste remembered bristling, later whispering to Ramona that she didn't like hearing about that from a white girl. Ramona had told her to take it as gospel.

"Where did he get it in the first place?" There were plenty of panel trucks with gun racks, and rusted-out wrecks on thin tires, but there were no other big shiny cars on Freshwater Road.

"His brother died up in Memphis." Mrs. Owens picked up the pot of collards and went to the front of the house. "It was his." Celeste heard her rest the pot on the screened porch, heard her say, "...and Lord only knows where he got it."

Celeste imagined that Mr. Tucker's brother made his money running numbers or even drugs, or maybe he owned a nightclub, lived on the edge like Shuck used to. Who was the brother? Maybe he'd been a musician. Memphis had music, blues, rhythm and blues.

"Now, Celeste, I want you to handle that bread pudding." Mrs. Owens went into her room and came out with a small black straw hat with a piece of netting hanging off the back. "It'll be cooled enough by the time them Tuckers pull up. Take that dishtowel and lay it over the top. There's another towel over there for underneath it. Mrs. Tucker gon' have to hold it in her lap. I put that pot of greens on the floor by me. As shiny as that car is outside is how dirty that trunk is inside." She put the hat on without a mirror, tightening the net under her unpressed hair and anchoring it with a pin. "If you take that bread pudding into the back seat with those Tucker boys, won't be none left for the church picnic."

"Yes, ma'am." Celeste's mind went on whirling with the possibilities of the life going on in Pineyville, with the things she needed to learn. She went to her room to muscle her swollen feet into her white pumps, happy they weren't walking the nearly three miles to church. Her light blue dress already had large perspiration patches under the arms. She stood in the middle of her bedroom and fanned the skirt to dry her thighs, then changed her sweaty underpants. In Mississippi, she changed her panties at least twice a day, rinsing and hanging them on one of the nails on the wall of her bedroom.

The Hudson Hornet roared to a stop in front of the house. Mr. Tucker blew the horn hard and long. Celeste wondered why he hadn't sent one of his sons up to knock on the door for them.

"Ain't no need for all that." Mrs. Owens went out with her purse and her Bible, hoisting the pot of collards on her way, Celeste right behind her.

She helped Mrs. Tucker get the bread pudding situated on her lap, then climbed into the back seat with the Tucker children, Sissy, Darby, and Henry. The big Hudson turned onto the two-lane leading into town. Not a puddle anywhere though it rained everyday. Southern pines flashed their green in the sunlight. Pink and white crepe myrtle burst out from the ground all the more brilliant against the green and the orange tint of the soil. In great stretches, there were no trees at all, just sandy earth and stunted plants as if the desert crept in then retreated, then came in by another door.

The Tucker children hadn't come near her in the brief time she'd been

living with Mrs. Owens. Now they sat beside her, the boys flipping through
the pages of a half-rolled comic book they hid on the seat between them, the
girl sitting with her head leaning back, quiet. Celeste was wedged into the
corner, with no room to spread her legs or smooth out the skirt of her dress.
Her big sunglasses perpetually slid down her sweaty nose. She wondered
how the locals managed without sunglasses at all.

The little girl, Sissy, reached across her to roll down the window. A hot
sandy breeze roiled into the car, pumicing the sweat-salt on her face. The
swirling air brought the food and body aromas together as if they were
tumbling in a mixer. When the boys lowered their window, the cross-breeze
blustered into a full-fledged wind, though Mr. Tucker drove slowly. After
his impatient horn blaring outside Mrs. Owens's house, Celeste expected
him to take off like a spooked stallion. Maybe with her in the car, he figured
he better not do anything to provoke any attention from the sheriff.

Out of the corner of her eye, Celeste caught Sissy staring at her. She
placed her big sunglasses on the girl's face, and Sissy gazed up to the aquamarine spread of sky.

"Now you look like a movie star, Sissy." The wind whipped Celeste's
everyday ponytail into a scattered catastrophe.

"What's a movin' star?" Sissy sat up, leaned towards the window, searching the shapely clouds lolling atop one another.

Celeste didn't know if the child's accent was getting in the way of her
saying *movie* instead of *moving*. "A beautiful lady on a big screen in the dark.
Dorothy Dandridge or Marpessa Dawn." In truth, Sissy's face reminded
her of a Modigliani portrait, only one with smooth chocolate-dark skin.
Her slanted eyes carved ovals above high cheekbones. Her hair was braided
so tightly it looked vengeful, made her all face and eyes.

"They ain't got no movies round here, Miss Celeste." Mrs. Tucker's flower-
encrusted felt hat bobbed, making the silky flowers rustle like leaves.

Celeste wished the local people would drop the "Miss" business. It
separated her from them, the very thing she was trying to get past. They
spoke to white people that way. She'd heard it in Jackson and in Pineyville
on the street with Mrs. Owens, who mumbled her greetings to white
people, swallowing the ends of their names after getting out the "Mr."
or "Miss." She eked out enough of what passed for respect to keep retribution at bay.

Sissy stared away then up to the heavens with an eight-year-old's imitation of adult seriousness. "Where do they live in the daytime? Do they movin' fast or slow? Where'd you see them? I wanna be there." Her intense voice swelled in breathiness as if Celeste had confirmed a dream of something imagined that she'd never seen.

"I'll find a picture show with movie stars, and I'll take you." She said *movie* slowly so the child could hear the word, the letters.

"Give those glasses to Miss Celeste, Sissy." Mr. Tucker glanced in his mirror. "Aint no movin' picture round here. No movie stars neither."

Celeste stopped herself from telling Sissy to keep the glasses, then took them and put them back on to hide the narrowing of her eyes as she glared into Mr. Tucker's tight, kinky hair nobbling down his head to his stiff, starched shirt collar. He needed a shape-up.

"They got a picture show over in Gulfport." Mrs. Owens invaded the parched silence.

"They got one in Hattiesburg, too. Don't mean Sissy's goin' to it." Mr. Tucker's hard eyes in the mirror warned Celeste.

She held Sissy's hand; the girl's high smooth forehead slowly tilted down, her eyes glassy with tears. Celeste had an urge to wrap her hands around Mr. Tucker's neck and squeeze. He took the air right out of the car. Mrs. Tucker's hat looked clownish now, its autumn-colored flowers jiggling in the hellish heat.

They rode silently through the town center, the big Hudson engine humming, the tires rumbling over seams in the concrete and black top. Mr. Tucker made a left and within minutes turned into the rutty road leading to the St. James A.M.E. Church. She'd been coming here every day with Reverend Singleton, but this was Sunday. They joined a near-parade of people walking or jostling over the bumps in old trucks, dilapidated cars, even a horse and wagon. Women carried large lidded pots and bowls covered with white cloths and waxed paper. More than one balanced containers on their heads. It was the day of the church picnic, a celebration. The maroon Hudson stood out like a slickly dressed visitor from the big city come to lord it over a bunch of country kin.

Women wore hats over braided kinky hair. Others wore their hair straightened and flattened on their heads with a spike sticking out here or there, no fancy curls like the Detroit Sunday-go-to-church women. Some wore lacy white handkerchiefs on their heads, others makeshift straw hats with flowers dangling off the brims. A few carried umbrellas against the sun. Parasols in Pineyville. Their pastel dresses were bright against the mahogany tones of their skins. Only when you drew closer did you see that some of the dresses were threadbare and patched. The men's suits were too large or too small, wrist bones poking out. The older ones walked slowly, some bent, others proud and upright. They grubbed an existence in the weather-beaten, no-industry towns of Southern Mississippi all week long. This church was theirs and they came to it for rest and reprieve. All Celeste could think was God bless Sophie Lewis.

She reminded herself that it was 1964, that she wasn't watching a film based on a history often distorted and mostly forgotten. This obsolete place lived, and it *was* like a movie. What might have been quaint looked dispossessed up close with living, breathing people. This wasn't some anonymous village in Africa or South America where people washed their clothes in a stream, emptied their bowels just yards away, and drank the water from the same stream a few yards in the other direction. It was too close. She remembered Wilamena years ago fussing against the way Negro people were portrayed in films. She refused to go see them, said she would not support some "catfish row" rendition of Negro life. Maybe the realities and the images became too overwhelming, too close to the truth for her. This is what Wilamena ran from and once she got going, she couldn't stop. Jettison the whole thing. Too much lacking, run. But Detroit had scores of well-off Negroes. Celeste knew what drove Wilamena was deeper than money.

"That bell given to us by a gentleman from New Orleans." Mrs. Owens spoke with the clanging of the church bell.

Celeste wanted to bolt from the car and find a spot in the forest, lie down on a bed of pine needles and see sky slivers and sun dots, only what the thick green branches allowed. Instead, she and Mrs. Owens carried the bread pudding and the pot of collards to the shady side of the whitewashed building, where tables of all sorts had been set up to hold the food, shaded by rain umbrellas propped up by food containers, rocks, bricks. A small group of women hovered around the tables with fans—homemade of giant plant leaves attached to spindles of thin wood. There was one small electric fan with its cord running into a church window. Celeste wished she could stay outside with them, be a food fanner. Anything but sitting in the hot church at close quarters with well over a hundred other sweating people. But she dutifully followed Mrs. Owens inside.

Reverend Singleton nodded to the two women as they took seats midway back on the left side, the last two openings on the smooth wood pews, as close to the open windows as they could get. The shades on the tall thin windows were pulled halfway down to block the sun, the windows open in hopes of a breeze. The church was a perpetual work in progress—though the floor was carpeted on the center aisle and in the entire pulpit area, the side aisles were bare wood. The Tuckers had gone on toward the front and seated themselves on the opposite side. Mr. Tucker probably wanted to get his children as far away from her as he could, afraid her northern ways might rub off on them. Probably afraid they'd end up running from him yelling "free at last" at the tops of their lungs.

The churchgoers took up their balsa wood–handled cardboard fans advertising the Morris Family Mortuary in Hattiesburg just as soon as they were seated. There was enough fanning going on in the church to create a windstorm, but nothing cool came of it. Celeste moved hers with a sultry motion, as she'd learned in Detroit churches that any fast fanning would only make you hotter. Before one complete pass of her hand, her entire body broke out in a second wave of sweat. Her cotton dress would soon be soaked. It was already sticking to her skin.

The small choir sang and swayed through "Rock of Ages" and "Old Rugged Cross" with Mrs. Singleton leading on the organ, her hair wound up into a mound on the top of her head, her small body laying into her instrument. Reverend Singleton respected women who made music, Celeste thought.

With his eyes focused on his flock and his mustache glistening, Reverend Singleton launched into the sermon of "people get ready, there's a train a'coming." Celeste had heard similar messages at the nightly orientation meetings in Jackson. Exhilarating calls to action, cheerleading lifts meant to rouse the doubtful, fire people up for the task at hand and maybe the beatings and arrests they might suffer in the process. The sermons stoked the burn and led the way, and the way was nonviolence. The road was steep and hard, but no other road offered redemption to the oppressed and epiphany to the oppressors. The old way reiterated bad treatment, deception, and deprivation.

Reverend Singleton paced, stomped his feet, his electric-blue preacher's robe open down the front, flying behind and around him like a celestial cape. His dress shirt collar absorbed perspiration that dripped down his face and sprayed off in all directions when he made quick turns. He kept a handkerchief at the ready to keep his eyes clear of the pour. Reverend

Singleton yoked a kind of rural earthy drama to his well-honed intellect. He appealed to the people's hearts and souls and pricked at their brains. And it all had rhythm. He wanted the Negro people of his town to get on board, to stop standing around studying the dirt. His congregation called back to him, urging him on, clapping, speaking to God directly on their own behalf. Celeste thought he was too good at the big sermon to stay long in this town. He was right up there with the best she'd ever heard, not far from the range of Martin Luther King Jr. himself.

There was urgency in the calls to action. She heard a cleaving in the voices and stood up with her hands thrown into the air as she had never done in Momma Bessie's church at home; she'd never felt so bound to a moment in church as she did to this one. This was her moment, and she threw herself into it with energy. Wilamena would've had a heart attack seeing her standing there waving her hands to the heavens. The music so profound it brought tears to her eyes. Mrs. Singleton was to the music what Reverend Singleton was to the word. It all cut to the heart of the matter. He bound the old lessons to a new message and his listeners followed. Celeste was swaying with the Negro citizens of Pineyville, felt she was becoming one of them.

"Sister Celeste Tyree." She heard her name called from the pulpit. Reverend Singleton beckoned her forward.

He hadn't warned her. Maybe he hadn't decided to bring her up before he saw her standing, her arms reaching to Heaven. With her sweat-soaked dress clinging to her body and the straps of her bra slipping off her sweaty shoulders, she walked toward the pulpit, focusing on Reverend Singleton's beaming face, then on the color painting of Jesus on the wall behind him. Mrs. Singleton played chords to cover her walk. Celeste hadn't been in the pulpit of a church since she was baptized.

Across the center aisle, Sissy leaned forward, her mouth open, caught in surprise. Mr. Tucker's eyes were locked in a straight-ahead stare. Mrs. Tucker's chin lifted, haughty and disapproving. Darby and Henry looked confused. The white railing across the pulpit area had entrances on each side and one in the middle. It seemed to not be getting any closer. People coughed and shifted in their seats. The sounds rebounded in Celeste's ears, made her feel as if something in her life was about to change forever. She was walking down the aisle alone. Finally, she stepped up into the pulpit area. Reverend Singleton received her with a two-handed handshake and guided her to the podium to face the congregation as Mrs. Singleton played a chord of presentation. Her mouth went completely dry.

It all looked different from up here. She'd held freedom school in the church for a few days now, but this was an entirely new experience. During freedom school she stayed down front, never so much as referring to the pulpit area. In her mind it was off-limits. It was Reverend Singleton's domain. The choir and Mrs. Singleton seemed squeezed in behind the preaching area. No stained-glass windows, no vaulted ceilings, and only a few rows of polished hardwood pews. She cleared her throat softly and clutched the podium with both hands. The body of the church came into clear focus. A sea of sweat-glossed country Negro people stared up at her.

"Thank you, Reverend Singleton, for inviting the movement into your church." Her voice sounded puny and distant, disconnected from who she thought she was. She'd practiced selling the idea of voter registration in front of small groups during orientation, but that was nothing like this. She pushed her voice out. "And thank *you*, Mrs. Owens, for allowing me to come into your home to do this work."

The words lay like rocks. She regretted saying Mrs. Owens' name, for though she figured by now most everyone knew where she was living, she didn't want to call unnecessary attention to it. She didn't yet know who was with them and who wasn't. She had no idea how far anyone might go against them.

"I hope you will visit the freedom school." Celeste paused to clear a nervous tickle from her throat. "We meet here every morning from nine o'clock until noon. Voter registration classes are held here, too." She didn't want to hem and haw, tried to keep the flow of her sentences even and clear, but the endings kept diving down into near inaudibility. "In the evenings as close to 6:30 as we can get. We want to present the lists of new registered voters at the Democratic Convention in August." Her fingers dug into the sides of the podium.

Celeste prayed Reverend Singleton would rescue her. He stood, chest out, nodding his head in agreement. "Does anyone have any questions?" Her clipped speech and college girl manner weren't translating well. All was quiet but for the hand fans waving through the heavy air, small coughs and grunts. Everyone sat there staring up at her like she was a ghost—or worse, a Negro ghost who didn't look quite Negro enough to be accepted into the ranks. She had a lot of work to do. Reverend Singleton stepped closer.

"We got a distance to travel 'fore we get to the eating." He'd dropped his voice an octave and grinned. "If that's what's on your mind."

It was nearly noon and just about time for the daily rain. The food was on tables under the eaves of the church with umbrellas placed strategically to protect it. Celeste knew she'd have to eat or risk offending the women of the church who, just like Mrs. Owens, had spent the early morning frying, baking, and boiling all that hot food.

A wiry, light-skinned woman stood up in the back. "Sister Mobley," Reverend Singleton introduced her. He called the people Sister this and Brother that, corralled them in his own brotherhood, hoped it would steel them against some of the fear and deprivation in their lives. At least they belonged to each other. Celeste remembered that kind of calling at Momma Bessie's church in Detroit. She was Sister Tyree.

"I don't wanna cause no trouble. My chirren wants to come to learn with you, but I'm afraid for 'em." The whooshing fans nearly drowned her out. Three children sat close to her, a boy and two tiny girls. Sister Mobley sat down and fanned.

Reverend Singleton gave Celeste a prodding nod.

"So far, we've been okay." She shied away from revealing that nearly a week into her project only two children had come to freedom school, and no adults at all had shown up for voter registration classes. She searched for the faces of her two students, Labyrinth and Georgie. Hard to miss Labyrinth's head of blond curls and brown skin, Georgie there beside her with his eyes glowing like a cat's in the dark. And beside them, the woman who had to be their mother, Dolly Johnson, young and strong looking, sitting up straight and tall, the woman who sent her children to freedom school first. She wanted to wave to Labyrinth and Georgie, their eyes piercing, searching for recognition. *J.D.'s child would have been a Labyrinth.* Shuck would've laid down and died. She thought that, too. The children smiled at her as if they recognized something in her face, something of themselves in her. She held onto the podium so tightly her hands seemed to be leaving impressions there.

Again, Reverend Singleton moved closer to her, and she inched more to the side, releasing the podium, giving him room to stand with her, realizing that he was her ticket to acceptance.

"Amen." Came a voice from the other side of the church. Celeste didn't know if that "amen" was the signal that they didn't want to hear anymore from her or a validation. An "amen" could be a period as much as anything else.

Sister Mobley waved her hand, popped up again quickly. "I'm sho glad you come here to Pineyville."

"Thank you, Sister Mobley." Celeste nodded to the frail woman. "And please do send your children to the freedom school. We're moving along in our work."

A white-haired man sitting by the window spoke up, fanning himself. "If we come in here fa dat registering, de white man gon tell us not to come to work no mo."

"Sho will." A youngish voice from the back.

That was followed by a few grunts and uh-huhs. Mrs. Owens's brooch flashed in the sunlight. Celeste followed the flash to find her face, serious and set with satisfaction. It made her feel she was doing okay up there in the pulpit.

Reverend Singleton spoke. "Now Jesus is in here, moving around from one to the other and when he stopped by *me,* he told me to tell *you* that sometimes you got to walk through the darkness to get to the light." Reverend Singleton walked to the center of the pulpit area. Every face turned to follow his movement. He hadn't warmed up to this thought, just dove in at full emotional pitch, grabbing the attention of the church, waking those who'd started to drowse with Celeste talking to them. "I said, you got to walk through the darkness to get to the light." He cut through the heat and lethargy like a lightning strike. "Think about that, now." He came back to her.

"Go 'head now, Sister Celeste." He spoke under his breath. "You got to break it down." Mrs. Singleton hit a minor chord on the organ, sending goose bumps up her spine, then slowly and softly started playing "How I Got Over." Celeste needed all the help she could get.

"The people in Jackson want to end this summer with voter registration for all the Negro people in Mississippi." The thumping music got into her. She reared back a bit and took a good deep breath. "If we do *that,* it will make a great difference in *your* lives—these roads will get paved, the schools will be improved, these children will be able to go into the library and read the books or take them home." Mrs. Singleton wailed on that organ and Celeste rode the rhythm like a ship on a wild sea, hanging on. "There's churches being bombed, people being shot at, so this registering to vote is causing a lot of trouble for everyone. That's how important it must be."

"Yes, it is, Lord."

"Amen."

"Speak on, chile."

They expected her to stir them as Reverend Singleton did. They wanted to lift her up, but she had to help them.

"Don't feel mad at yourself if you can't do it." She pushed the queasiness down in her stomach and went on, feeling a kind of power. She still clutched the podium, and her voice streamed on without breaks. "This summer is the beginning. Your children can grow up feeling the vote is their right." She nearly bit the "t" off the word "right." "We're learning that today is not tomorrow." She was running out of things to say while rivers of sweat ran down her neck.

Sissy inched forward in her seat. The only thing keeping Mr. Tucker from snatching her backwards was the fact that he couldn't reach her through the barricade of her brothers and mother.

"And it ain't yesterday neither." A heavyset man stood up fanning himself with his hat then sat down. Everyone was within the rhythm code of the song. It was call and response, like a symphony.

"Thank you, sir." Celeste reached for the red farmer's bandana she'd picked up in Jackson. It wasn't the thing for Sunday church, but it was in her pocket, and it was all she had. She balled the bandana into her fist and wiped her perspiring neck, not wanting to bring the red up near her face while she was in the pulpit. Negro people put great significance in symbolism, and red was the sign of the devil. For a brief moment, she didn't recognize her own hand it was so dark. Reverend Singleton moved in again while the small choir joined the organist humming the song. She was grateful he looked as if he was about to take the reins.

"Yes, Jesus. I know we been walking through fire for a long, long time. I know you praying the hard times coming to a end." Reverend Singleton was going to finish it, put the parable to it, give the people an image to carry them to the next point. "The hard times not going nowhere lessen you help 'em along. I can't pray you into registering, I can't shout you into it. You got to think about all these young people come down here, like Sister Celeste, Negro and white young people from all over this country down here to help us do this, now, make something different happen here."

Celeste stepped back from the podium, allowing Reverend Singleton all the space he needed, feeling like his protégée. She had raised the stakes, broken through the barrier, and felt redeemed. Whatever happened from this point forward, she now had become a part of them.

"You know, me and my wife, Etta, was ridin' through Alabama back in April. We took a different road going to Montgomery and passed a sign said, 'Kill a Nigger Creek, Alabama.' Now, that's the God's honest truth. A *place* called 'Kill a Nigger Creek, Alabama,' and it was right there on the road sign. You voting, that kind of thing won't be there. Whole lotta other things won't be here either. It's not free. Somebody's gon' die. Somebody's already died. A whole lotta somebodies already died."

The responses were flying around the church. There was "Sweet Jesus," "Lord, have mercy," "They done died," and "Save us, Lord," and little rapid claps of hands.

Celeste moved farther away as Reverend Singleton flailed his arms, the blue robe flapping. She picked up the rhythm of the choir's sway, feeling as if she belonged right there with them, seeing the faces of Schwerner, Chaney, and Goodman in her mind, wondering if Leroy Boyd James's people still lived near Pineyville or had they run away from the horrid memory of how he died. All the things she'd learned in orientation, the memories of Emmett Till and Medgar Evers, all of it came to a peak of clarity there in the pulpit of the St. James A.M.E. Church. She believed that she could change the world, and she believed these people would be with her every step of the way. Tears ran down her face, mingling with the sweat.

"You know it, and I know it." Reverend Singleton wrapped the church body in his hands, his face shining with passion. Mrs. Singleton seemed to know his every inflection before he hit it and masterfully accompanied him on her organ. The small choir hummed under him. Celeste felt like she might swoon, she needed something to hold onto. The responses from the church rang out, some sweet and calm, others filled with resonance and even anger.

"I tell you, the life everlasting is a sweeter life anyway, and you can make *this* life a whole lot sweeter, too. But, you got to stand up for it. Say, 'Life, you're mine, for as long as I'm here, you're mine, and I'm gonna live you better than my ma and pa did, better than those sharecroppers, better than those slaves, better than I *been* doing!"

By the time he got to the end of his sermonette, everyone was full of will and desire. He could've led the churchgoers right out the door and down to the courthouse to register to vote. But it would have been for naught on a Sunday morning. *Lord,* Celeste prayed, *help me to do this with these people I see in front of me.* Shuck would chuckle at her calling on the Lord. He'd say the Lord helps those who help themselves. Then he'd say God bless the child who's got his own. He said that all the time. She wanted to shout it out to the congregation, get them in the habit of thinking precisely that.

Celeste returned to her seat while the church hummed through another verse of "How I Got Over," Mrs. Singleton laying on the downbeats until the organ sounded like an entire combo. The people shifted, fanned a bit faster, and took quick looks to Celeste and Mrs. Owens.

"That's that same song Mahalia Jackson sung out there in Washiton with Martin Lutha King," Mrs. Owens announced in a low voice as Celeste sat down. There was a new intimacy in her tone as if they were now compatriots locked in a dangerous mission that might end in catastrophe, but might, too, end in triumph.

When Mrs. Singleton hit the opening chords for "We Shall Overcome," Reverend Singleton invited the congregation to stand and join hands. Celeste took Mrs. Owens's hand on one side and on the other, the hand of a man who appeared to be as old as the live oaks in front of Sophie Lewis's big house. She hoped this song, this joining of hands would invigorate the people, give them the courage for the long walk ahead. ... *Oh, oh, oh, deep in my heart, I do believe....* She believed it or she wouldn't have come down here. The church hummed another verse as Reverend Singleton walked down the center aisle and opened the double doors, inviting the last row out first, backslapping and shaking hands with the men, politely hugging the women, and nodding in the direction of the church picnic.

The sunlight was staggering after the shady respite of the church. The daily quick rain had left a glisten on the trees and grass. Celeste eyed the food. No one in the food line seemed bothered by the fat flies and silk-winged vagrants flitting over the fried chicken, greens, red beans, cakes, cobblers, and pies. They filled their plates, swatting, fanning, talking quietly, nodding at her shyly as they meandered onto the grass to sit on a variety of chairs, at tables or on the ground, which the sun dried in moments. She'd have to eat something soon or risk offending Mrs. Owens and the women of the church who'd gone to so much trouble.

"What you think?" Celeste kneeled down to Sissy's size when the girl approached, at ease as if they already knew each other well.

"I think I wish you was my cousin." Sissy searched her face. "Then I could come to yo' school."

"Did your momma say you couldn't come?" They'd barely begun. How could a parent deny a child freedom school when regular school was nothing *but* denial?

They walked to a small square table and sat on wobbly wood folding chairs, side by side, facing out. To the east, she could see the backs of the shady rain clouds hastened away by lazy breezes from the Gulf. Nothing now but a clear sapphire sky.

"My daddy say it." Sissy swung her legs, the toes of her shoes surfing the grass. "Say don't want you teaching me nothing."

Celeste tried to fathom his fear or whatever it was, remembered his face in the rearview mirror of the big Hudson. "Is that all he said?"

"Yes, ma'am." Sissy didn't seem to mind the sun, looked straight up to the heavens again, like she'd done in the car with her sunglasses. She seemed on the verge of flight.

"We'll try to get him to change his mind. Don't say anything else. Promise?" Something tugging at Celeste in her eyes as if she expected her to give her wings, a way out of Pineyville, a way from a father who already was bearing down on her in a dream-smashing crusade. Surely Sissy didn't understand all those things yet. "Go ahead now and sit with your momma."

She pushed her gently in the direction of the Tucker table just as Mr. Tucker came out the side door of the church, anger flashing in his eyes, Reverend Singleton right behind him. He spotted her and paused for a quick second, face tight and hard. She watched him until he sat with his family, returning his anger with her own defiance. All that from the car, she thought? No. Sissy must have been bristling under his clamped-down rearing for a while. Asking too many questions, gazing too far off. Now here came Celeste, the freedom loving rabble-rouser in town to put the finishing touches on Sissy's rebellion. Freedom School. In his mind, it had to mean liberation in a visceral sense. He was right. He had reached his limit. Celeste closed her eyes, dropping her head. She wasn't supposed to look at anyone like that, Negro or white. Too much violence in the tone of her eyes behind those sunglasses, but she knew her body said the same thing. Reflecting that kind of uppitiness to a white person in Mississippi might mean a hit or hot spit in her face.

"Mr. Tucker says his children won't be coming to the freedom school."

Reverend Singleton sat where Sissy had been, his church fan pumping, reaching for his necktie, pulling it away from his sweating neck.

"She told me. Sissy." The shade trees just beyond the clearing drew Celeste like a magnet. "Did he say why?" Her tone all flat and dry.

"Well, now, Sister Celeste, some of these people got some old-timey notions about all that's going on. I'ma keep working on him." Reverend Singleton got up. "But in the meantime, you need to be patient. These people been living in this place a long time. They know it better than you can ever have learned it in a week-long orientation."

Celeste felt the chide. "I'm sorry." She was thinking maybe she could teach Sissy at Mrs. Owens's house after freedom school, when Mr. Tucker was stuck at the gas station working. How had this animosity grown up so quickly? She didn't understand.

"I don't see Labyrinth and Georgie." She searched the crowd for Labyrinth's hair, a standout in this sea of dark-haired, dark-eyed people.

"It's hard for Dolly Johnson to mix out here in the open. She comes to church every Sunday but she leaves right after. People swear she's still having to do with that white man fathered Labyrinth. Course, they don't have a thing to say about the Negro man who fathered Georgie. They are afflicted with a double standard and it's easy to see why, I guess."

Celeste let go of a long deep sigh, shook her head from side to side. "Is their coming to freedom school keeping the others away?"

"That child, and that white man, are nothing new here." Reverend Singleton's face tightened the slightest bit and he spoke low. Celeste wondered if he was hiding his true feelings or maybe hinting at something from his own life in Chicago.

"I don't understand, then." Celeste pushed him for more. She knew so little for sure about these people, knew only that white Pineyville hated her being there and the reason she was there. All else was up for interpretation.

"Well, she gets favors. You know. Money from him. Or so people think. Plus she's got that job over in Hattiesburg and those white folks are good to her." Reverend Singleton shook his head.

"Oh. You're saying there might be some jealousy in it?" She grabbed the thought as if it was a life raft in rough water.

"I am. That's not native to Mississippi, I'm sure." He said all he was going to say about that.

"No, sir, it's not. My daddy says you have to be strong as acid to deal with Negroes, and there's no words to describe how strong you have to be to deal with white people." Celeste felt grown-up and full of wisdom quoting Shuck.

"He's so right." Reverend Singleton softened.

Celeste wondered if she should befriend the outcast woman. But if she befriended Dolly Johnson, the other women would read into it. She had to be careful, needed to bring them all in without dragging the quibbles and tensions that divided them. Like Reverend Singleton did from the pulpit, preaching to everyone, bringing everyone along equally.

"Don't you worry. Be some more children in there tomorrow morning. And some grown-ups in that voting class, too. See there, Mr. Landau, and Sister Mobley's gonna come. Truth be told, that Dolly Johnson's a good candidate for voting, too. It'll be a start." Celeste followed where he gestured and saw Mr. Landau walk away from the group heading for the parking area in front of the church. He was an African-Indian looking man, tall, carved, and dark. "Have to keep an eye on Landau, though, he's partial to those Deacons for Defense over in Bogalusa. They don't believe in taking a lot of crap off of white folks."

Celeste wanted to stand up and yell for Mr. Landau to come back, to sit down and talk a while. Matt talked about the Deacons in the car and had even gone over to one of their meetings when he dropped her on Freshwater Road. Reverend Singleton left her to float from group to group, nodding, shaking hands, being the good minister.

Still, Sissy wouldn't be there, and that bothered her. She sat sideways on her wobbly chair, wishing she'd brought the fan from inside the church but too lazy to walk back in there to get it. She watched the crowd in their dresses and suits, jackets off now, tie knots loosened. Her dress was damp, her hair a mad mix of humidity-induced curls and straight sticks. She'd wanted it to be contained for church, had released the rubber for a few seconds to sort the mess out, and in that instant of time, it rose and puffed up all over her head until she had to work to wrestle the rubber band back on it and finally gave up and put the rubber band in her pocket.

Mrs. Owens chatted with a group of women, glancing over from time to time. Celeste hoped she was convincing them all to come to the voter registration class. Peaceful on the surface at least. A country painting, *The picnic at the church*. J.D. could paint it, but it would never show the night-mare living just beneath the skin. The people holding their picnic plates and sipping sweet drinks had been terrorized into stepping off the sidewalk when a white person came down the street. They entered the county court-house through the back door. They drank water from the colored fountain and sent their children to the broken-down colored school—as Labyrinth had called it, the school with no books. They assumed the face of serenity while they seethed inside, until they succumbed to a childish inferiority or stepped out of line. God only knew what that might mean. Some became what white people called them. Others never bent. She needed the unbent ones to help her through. In church, their response had been spirited, with the music lifting them like a soundtrack. She had no idea if that was enough to bring them in to do the real work of breaking down the old ways. She didn't know if someone was going to die.

Celeste turned her chair to stare into the woods. Piles of cool stones nestled in low ferns, shaded by the modest live oaks and tall pines. The oak branches reached out from the trunks for yards, strong arms offering shade and solace. She could see the tops of long-needled pines way back. She walked to the edge of the clearing to get a better view, hoping to sit out of the withering sunshine. As she eased into the wooded area, a high-pitched scream rang out, stopping her in her tracks. She backed out into the clear-ing and turned to see the entire congregation gawking at her, some with mouths open, some so stunned they appeared to be marvelously life-like statues. Mrs. Owens hustled over, grabbed her arm, and snatched her from the grove.

"Chile, you can't go in there." She pulled Celeste back to a table and sat her down forcefully enough to let her know the old woman still had muscle. Mrs. Owens tore to the food table and came back with a cup of punch, then retrieved her own plate.

The punch was so sweet Celeste smacked her lips. "Was it a snake or something?"

"Drink it down, settle your stomach."

She had the exact opposite thought. The sugar might make her sick.

"You didn't eat nothing all day."

"Too hot to eat, Mrs. Owens. Was there a snake or something?" The screech still lobbed around in her head though all was quiet except the murmur of voices in the background. She wondered if the churchgoers were talking about her and she didn't even know what she'd done.

"There's a coupla graves back in there. Can't go there. Have to go around the other way. A few yards in it's sacred ground."

"Nobody told me." She felt weak, the syrupy liquid oozing into her stomach, shivering her, making her nausea rise, hold there on the ledge waiting for the next surprise. "Who screamed?"

"Sissy." Geneva Owens talked softly. "She got a big voice for a little girl."

Celeste sipped the grapey sugar water thinking she probably needed salt more than sugar to offset what she was losing in perspiration. The older woman ate as if she'd just been sitting there sunning herself on a quiet summer afternoon, flowering beads of perspiration forming thin, slow-moving streams that traced her gray hairline, seeped down her forehead.

Celeste drummed the paper cup on the table. "Who's in there?"

"Don't make no difference who's in there. It ain't for sittin'." Mrs. Owens finished her food without another word.

It was hard to tell if Mrs. Owens meant to ever reveal the truth or just didn't want to talk about it right at that moment. Reverend Singleton might tell her, she thought, but that wouldn't be until tomorrow morning when he opened the church for freedom school. She prayed she hadn't lost the favor she'd gained by standing with Reverend Singleton in the pulpit. Again, she felt the sharp yearning to go home, to ride with Shuck in his convertible Cadillac all over the West Side, visit his friends and cronies, stop at Momma Bessie's to rest in the shade of the apple tree with a tall thin glass of minted ice tea and a long slim handled spoon.

The picnic carried on and people ignored her as long as Mrs. Owens, her guardian and supporter, was there with her. She saw Sissy across the way trying not to look over at Mrs. Owens and her. Mr. Tucker sat with his back to them. Reverend Singleton mingled with his congregation as if nothing had happened.

Later, the Tucker boys, Darby and Henry, barely opened their eyes when the Hudson stopped short in front of the house. A quick hand squeeze for Sissy, who didn't have a smile anywhere on her face, a grunt from Mr. Tucker, and a nodding rustle of fake flowers from Mrs. Tucker passed for goodbye as Celeste and Mrs. Owens got out of the car, the empty bread pudding pan and the giant collard greens pot smelling sour now. Just as Geneva Owens's hand reached the screened door handle, Mr. Tucker lurched off leaving a train of orange dust and gravel bits. Celeste had a flash of that flowered hat falling down on Mrs. Tucker's face as she stepped into the house behind Mrs. Owens. They headed to the back porch, Mrs. Owens to scrub the pots and Celeste to dry them. "That man from New Orleans give the church the bell, he's buried in that sacred ground. Can't talk about it cause it's against the law to bury white in a colored cemetery. But it's what he wanted."

Later that night, Celeste climbed onto her bed thinking how it was that every Negro in town knew a white man was buried in the Negro cemetery, knew that if the whites learned it, they'd dig him up and throw him away, his white bones floating down the Pearl River. How long had he been there, who put him there, how had they pulled this off without anybody telling? Was his the only white grave back there? Was it the secret that made the ground sacred? A curl of a smile at the corners of those lips, those sun-ravaged faces, saying that white people didn't know it all, hadn't made every decision for every life in Pineyville. They must have other secrets, too.

11

Shuck had written "Pineyville" on a slip of paper and pocketed the note. Mississippi was as bad as a good number was good, but Pineyville had locked his mind even tighter than Mississippi itself. The name brought his teeth together in a grinding gnash, his mouth so clamped he had to jab a cigarette between his lips. But it refused to crystallize, just pricked and poked uselessly at his memory.

At the Royal Gardens, he moved fast along the bar, nodding and "hey-ing" to the slow night crowd, the jukebox blaring, Posey working easy. Shuck's only thought was why weren't they at home.

In his small office at the very back of the Royal Gardens, behind his desk, on a secondhand bookcase that he'd salvaged from Momma Bessie's attic, Shuck kept old copies of *Jet* magazine. He brought the little magazines over to his desk in bunches, flipping through the pages, not knowing what he was looking for but knowing that whatever it was, it pressed him to the search, and Pineyville was the reason.

The magazines didn't stack well, kept sliding away from each other until his entire desktop was a mass of them. And, there it was, dated 1959, a short five years ago. Leroy Boyd James, charged with raping a white woman, lynched before he got to trial. The Pearl River County grand jury in Pineyville, Mississippi, refused to acknowledge that the lynching had taken place, though his body had been fished from the Pearl River and he was supposed to be locked in jail. Negro prisoners told of hearing him screaming and fighting his abductors, heard his feet dragging along the concrete floor, his hands grabbing then slipping their grip on the bars, his fingernails scrabbling the bare walls near the door. They said they heard his shouts in their dreams. Celeste had taken herself to a lynching town.

Shuck drew a thousand dollars in cash from his safe. He put five hundred in an envelope along with the little slip of paper. He marked it *Celeste,* and pocketed it. The other five hundred he put between the pages of the *Jet* magazine, his idea of insurance, put a rubber band around it all to clasp those two things together as if they had been conjoined at some point in the past, separated and reunited now. He took out his loaded gun, turned it over in his hands, checked that there were bullets in a small box inside the safe. He secured the sorry history of Pineyville to Celeste's hope for the future, bound by money and a gun. It was the riskiest bet he'd ever made in his life, but he believed in her like he believed in himself. He locked his insurance in the drawer of his desk. He'd tell Posey what was going. They'd be ready if the call came, ready to take guns and money and go to Pineyville.

Shuck drove north on West Grand Boulevard, passing the deep-porched houses not destroyed by the expressway. At night they were presentable, but Shuck knew in the light of day you could see the disrepair creeping around the eaves, the paint chipping off the wood trim, the old people let go of by their delinquent children. Old people with no one to leave their hard-won victories to. But at night, the summer smells of fresh cut grass sweetened the breeze and mixed it with the scents of a thousand dinners, the smoky residue of backyard barbecues. He smelled chicken, ribs, maybe even turkey in a smoker. Whatever, it was leftovers now, sitting on a plate in the middle of the stove for the last one home, or stashed in the back of the refrigerator for tomorrow's lunch.

Finally, Shuck pulled up in front of Alma Weaver's two-family flat in a neighborhood already too far gone to save. Isolated apartment buildings were tended to as they had been years ago, but much of it all had sunk into disrepair. In the middle of the day the discarded young men stood around on corners, and women ran from the bus stop to their front doors, hands in their purses, clutching kitchen knives or sewing shears to ward off junkies. Shuck closed the convertible top.

Up and down the street, cars parked bumper to bumper, porch lights on, nothing moving. Monday nights were quiet in Detroit. Dinners eaten early, television, and off to bed so you could be up to face the job the next morning, if you had one. Too many didn't have one. Shuck was an escapee, a free-flying bird. The numbers racket had saved him from daily confrontations with white folks, especially white men. He was as free as a Negro man could be in 1964. Now, Celeste had bound her fate to Mississippi, taking his precious freedom with her.

The narrow stairwell led up to a spacious well-lighted hallway with a window through which he could see his car. He didn't like parking overnight on this street. Out of habit, he wiped his shoes on the welcome mat. The climb had taken Shuck's breath, paused him outside her door to regroup before putting the key in the lock. She'd awaken as soon as she heard the lock turn, meet him somewhere between the living room and the kitchen. He waited in the dim light for his heart to slow, his breathing to ease. She'd chastise him for smoking too much, staying up too late. He used to ice skate on the Detroit River, ran track in high school, but now a walk up one flight of stairs jumbled his heartbeat. Mississippi.

He tipped into the living room. A small tabletop spotlight was aimed at a huge dark-leaved plant standing in the corner near the front windows. The primeval plant took on eerie qualities in the uneven light, a dark green centurion guarding Alma's jungle. She had plants everywhere, and polished their leaves with minute dabs of mayonnaise and a cotton cloth until they reflected like glass. She also had plastic covers on all of her living room furniture. The covers made him feel the furniture fabric was more important than anyone's comfort, crunching and whooshing when he sat down, sweating under his seat in summer, sticking to his skin. He hated those covers. On the walls, she'd hung colorful paintings by local artists, giving the living room a tropical look but for those plastic covers.

She jokingly told him if he moved in with her and stopped smoking, she'd take the plastic off the furniture. He said it would be like going backward to move to that neighborhood. But he couldn't tell in all the laughing if she was waiting for an invitation to move to Outer Drive.

Alma came out of the bedroom hallway tying her robe at the waist, looking good, he thought, even in the middle of the night. Smooth light brown skin, dark hair brushed back and looped behind her ears. A frown across her face. He knew she was comfortable with his late arrivals, but this was a work night.

"You hungry?" It was what women always asked when they sensed something was wrong. The solace of food. Shuck wasn't sure if they intended it to ease the disharmony of life, or if they had become skittish about so many things that they just wanted the food to fill their mouths rather than the words.

"If you cooked." Shuck followed her into the kitchen, passing through the dining room. More plants. The dining table lived under a covering of homework assignments, textbooks, newspapers, bills, her purse and keys. She insisted on teaching summer school.

He washed his hands before sitting at the small kitchen table, ducking so he wouldn't hit his head on the big fern hanging from a ceiling hook. She even had plants on tall stands in the bathroom. Every time he went in there, he was afraid he'd knock them over. Shuck peeked back into the front of the apartment. It was a jungle all right. Maybe she needed the quiet of the plants after teaching those wild teenagers all day. He wondered if she talked to the plants, and how much time it must take to water them all, polish all those leaves. There was a mayonnaisy smell in the apartment sometimes when the windows hadn't been opened. It made his stomach turn. He bought her an air conditioner for the bedroom, more for himself than for her. It was powerful enough to cool the whole back of the apartment including her second bedroom, which she used as a television den. She needed a bigger place.

Alma foraged around in the refrigerator, the light showing the silhouette of her curvy body under her summer robe. Shuck figured Alma to be about forty-two or -three though they'd never discussed it. She'd graduated from Lakeview High School three years after he and Posey took to the streets. She knew about Wilamena, but Shuck led her to believe it was all in the past. Alma pulled out a waxed-paper-wrapped loaf on a plate and a bottle of milk.

Shuck eyed her behind as she brought a glass out of the cupboard.

"Meatloaf okay?" She unwrapped the loaf and put a sandwich together, going back to the refrigerator for lettuce, tomato, and mayonnaise. Shuck loved watching her standing in the refrigerator light. He didn't have to answer. She knew it was better than okay. He watched her working quietly, feeling guilty that he'd gotten her out of bed in the middle of the night when he knew she had to teach in the morning. Alma was committed to teaching kids who acted like getting an education was an imposition. Celeste could work out her need to help Negro people right there, too. He understood that part of it. Mississippi was what he didn't get. Of all places on the earth, why Mississippi? She'd have been better off going to Africa in the Peace Corps. Contracting malaria was better than going to Mississippi.

Alma put the food in front of him, smiling, and poured the milk then sat down. Shuck drank in one long chugalug, leaving milk residue lining his upper lip.

"I got to get up in a minute and face those kids." Alma just said it, straight out and blunt. Just like when she'd asked him if he was still running numbers, back when they bumped into each other at the Lakeview High School Class of 1939 twentieth reunion. Shuck and Posey had stopped by dressed like Wall Street bankers, smelling of ease. Shuck had his chest out when he told Alma he owned his own bar, but that he still played the numbers on occasion and probably always would. He'd noticed that she kept glancing over to him even though she was the date of one of his classmates that night. When he and Posey left the reunion, Posey said Alma Weaver had a reputation for being an upright, straight arrow, knees-locked kind of woman. Shuck didn't have any problem with that.

Shuck wiped his mouth on a paper napkin he took from the plastic holder on the table. "Celeste's in Mississippi."

Alma stopped drumming her fingers on the tabletop. Her mouth dropped open a bit and she sat back in her chair. "Well, I never thought she'd do anything like that."

Shuck wrapped his hand around the empty milk-coated glass. He'd known for weeks that Celeste was in Mississippi but hadn't told Alma. He didn't know why not. Alma refilled his glass. "Is she all right?"

All summer long, people had been asking Shuck the same question. *She all right?* "Her all right and my all right are two different things." There was an unintended edge in his voice.

Alma rubbed the front of her head like she was trying to remove a layer of skin. "You have to be proud of her courage." Her hands dropped to her lap and she tilted her head a little to the side. She seemed to be straining, crinkling her forehead, squinting her eyes. "Shuck Tyree, I know you're not thinking about going down there."

"If she gets arrested, I'm going. They still haven't found those three boys. You know they're dead by now." Shuck hunched over the table, his hands loosely clasped. If he tightened them the least bit, they'd be in prayer.

Alma folded her arms so that the fabric of her nightgown and robe pulled tight around her breasts, making her nipples show through. "Anybody in their right mind knew someone was going to die down there this summer. There's so much attention on the place now with the television, they're not going to hurt anybody else. I don't think."

"Nobody knows what those crazy people will do." Alma might know the history, but she'd never had a child. That changed everything.

"Well, I'd sure like to be a fly on the wall when those white folks look up and see you pulling in front of the courthouse in that Cadillac with that diamond ring sparkling in the sunshine." Alma put her hands over his hands and spoke to him in a coaxing voice. "I know you'll keep worrying, but she's going to be all right."

Shuck nodded, barely. "They had a lynching in that town where she's working. In Pineyville. You remember Leroy Boyd James? Not that long ago."

"I guess that says it all about Pineyville. But, truth be told, they've had lynchings some of everywhere. Thank God I'm here." Alma sighed.

"You sound like Rodney at the bar." Shuck smiled at her.

"The truth is the truth, Shuck." She had sleepiness in her eyes.

"You're right." He looked down at the sandwich knowing he couldn't eat a bite and felt bad that she'd gone to all the trouble.

"Don't worry about it." She put the glass in the sink and slid a piece of wax paper over the sandwich.

"Go on to bed." His eyes felt wet and tired. "I'ma sit here for a while." She kissed his forehead and went back to her bedroom.

He raised the kitchen window. On the counter Alma had a bread box and ceramic canisters with the words Flour, Sugar, Rice, Coffee. Momma Bessie had the same things only they were in the pantry. When you sat at the table, you couldn't see them. This apartment-sized kitchen was tight.

Shuck walked to the living room, the plants hovering like dreams in the low light. She needed room for her jungle of plants to spread. The emptiness of his house had begun to give him hollow answers. Some nights, he didn't even like going home to Outer Drive. But he didn't like staying here either. Things he'd been doing like clockwork over more years than he could remember now seemed caught and blown around in gusty winds. He knew for sure he'd never allow those plastic furniture covers.

He tried to sweep an ache from his mind, a whisper that perhaps the good days had passed. They'd begun to mark the corners of his mind like some nearly forgotten expensive shoes in a mildewed corner of the attic. You never took the time to check, though you had a suspicion that the roof leaked. You just didn't want to come to the conclusion. Shuck wondered if his mother, Momma Bessie, was about the same age as that Mrs. Geneva Owens down in Pineyville, and what on earth could a woman that age be counted on to do to protect anybody. He stood at the window looking down on his car, everything quiet on the street. Alma was probably asleep by now. If he smoked, she'd smell it in the morning. If he crawled into bed beside her, he'd disturb her rest. If he tipped out and went on home to Outer Drive, and she awakened on her own, she'd worry that something was wrong. Something was.

Shuck turned out the kitchen light and eased out the front door, turning the key in the double lock quiet as a thief.

12

Gunfire cracked, high-pitched and fast, through the quiet country night. A crash of broken glass. Celeste sat upright in her bed out of a deep dream-forgotten sleep. No dogs barking. Bits of gravel-rock flew from under the wheels of a moving car or truck. Silence. The skinny mutts knew when to hide. She rolled off the bed onto the floor as Margo had taught her to do, tried to get herself under the bed, pushing her suitcase out of the way with her feet, her heart leaping in her chest like a ball being batted furiously against a concrete wall. Everything quiet. "Please, God, don't let Mrs. Owens be dead. Don't let them kill us." She reached around for a viable bargain to make with God. "Dear Lord, I promise I'll go to New Mexico to see my mother. I'll stay as long as you think I should. I'll do better, Lord. Please, Lord."

The second round of bullets flew right through the house as if God had said, "Not good enough." She heard the ripping sound of lead shattering wood. Bullets exploding through this fragile place not even built strong enough for winter weather. The abrasive smell of burning metal trailed into the open windows. Gun powder. An engine revving. The sliding scream of rubber tires on solid road. Someone's turned onto the two-lane. She wanted to scoot from under the bed to see. *Stay put.* Engine gunning harder. Burning rubber smells perfuming the night. *No need to run from us. We don't even have a gun.* It wouldn't take much to end this terror. Shoot back. Defend yourself. You may die, but you die with dignity, with muscle in your jaw, no staring down at the ground. No more turn the other cheek. Matt had run out of cheeks to turn. That beating on the side of the road sealed it. That's why he went to Bogalusa to meet with the Deacons for Defense and Justice. Defend yourself. Celeste could hear her own heart pounding.

"You all right in there, child?" Mrs. Owens called out coming down the short hall.

Celeste scooted from under the bed, giddy with relief that the woman walked and talked, wasn't splayed out on the kitchen floor with blood oozing from her body and not a doctor anywhere who'd touch her. They met at the splintered front door, Celeste's mouth dry and eyes so wide open they hurt. "I guess so."

Mrs. Owens held a low-burning kerosene lamp, her tremoring hand making their shadows move on the wall. Celeste took the lamp from her, held it to the splintered cypress wood door. Her own hands shook. The older woman stepped forward onto the screened porch.

Celeste hung back. "We should stay inside." She racked her brain for the lesson from orientation. Stay in the house? Go outside? Stay under the bed? What to do now, Margo? In Jackson, she and Ramona were ordered to always stay low in the apartment at night, to keep the front lights out or very dim. Don't make yourself a target. But, this was the country, and Mrs. Owens seemed to know that the coast was clear.

"They gone." She walked around the screened porch checking for damages like she already knew the map of terror. "Bring that lamp on."

Celeste, hunched over and listening toward the two-lane, stepped out onto the porch to bring the small lamp close to Mrs. Owens, who'd now found the ragged holes in the thin screen. She unlatched the screened door and started down the porch steps, Celeste behind her with the lamp but otherwise useless. Mrs. Owens took the lamp and blew it out, walking on the path toward the gravel road, seeing just fine in the darkness with only the moon to light her way. Celeste followed her slowly, stopping where the path flowed into the gravel road, her ears still ringing with the sound of guns firing. After that sharp noise, the stillness hurt when it was supposed to soothe. More noise would've deadened the echoing sound that cracked the air, not this interminable country quiet. The violent noise had nothing to slink away into, nothing to be camouflaged by, nothing but crickets and pitiful dog barks that sounded more like moans now.

Mr. Tucker appeared in the middle of the road. "Look like they shot the back window in my car." He came closer, clothes thrown on carelessly, his sanctimonious face becoming visible as the darkness stepped aside to allow the moon and stars more play. "Geneva, you okay?"

Mrs. Owens continued toward him. "Been better."

"Sure you right." He walked with her toward Celeste, never looking at her. He probably blamed Celeste for this, since she was the rabble-rouser, the person coming around to stir everybody up to action. Now he'd been attacked, too, even though he didn't side with the movement. He'd given her a ride to church in his big Hudson. Now he was a marked man, too.

"You all okay?" Mrs. Owens placed herself between them, Celeste's protector. Celeste stayed still, shielded by the older woman.

"Just tense is all. I'ma drive down and check on Sister Mobley and them kids." He walked heavily back toward his house and car. That spark of kindness confused Celeste. He was acting like the protective man of Freshwater Road, the only man around, checking on all the women and children after the raid. How did that instinct live inside that man? How could he be that and the dream killer, too?

Mrs. Owens and Celeste turned to go inside. "Ain't nothing new. At least this time they think they got themselves a reason." Celeste knew that she was the reason. Her presence was already bringing the wrath of those who wanted things to remain the same in Pineyville. She wanted to ask when it had happened before but stayed quiet as they went through the house checking for bullet holes. The only gunshots she'd ever heard before this sojourn in Mississippi were fired on New Year's Eve and smoked through the snow drifts in the backyard of Momma Bessie's house.

Mrs. Owens brought the light to every corner of the kitchen looking for bullet exit holes. The refrigerator and stove were fine. Celeste figured the bullets probably went right through the thin-walled house to the line of long-needled pines beyond the clearing. The holes would become visible when sunlight shined through them in the morning. Mrs. Owens checked the locks on the back screen door, closed the inside kitchen door, and put a chair in front of it.

"Celeste, take one of those kitchen chairs and brace that front door. Best to sleep on the floor now. Just pull that mattress off. Stay down low and don't turn on the lights. Night, now." She went into her room and closed the curtain, sounding more like Margo in her soldier way than the Mrs. Owens she'd come to know. Mrs. Owens had been down this road before and though she might be concerned, she wasn't going to alarm her guest.

In the torpid heat of midnight, Celeste's teeth chattered uncontrollably and her hands and feet shook. She lay on the mattress in the close dark room, the white lace curtains reflecting the only light, and that was from the moon. No bullets to duck in her bed in Ann Arbor. Cozy in the corner behind the door, the French windows open. Momma Bessie's quilt. She couldn't stop shaking.

Her night jar sat across the room near the side window, but she couldn't get up, felt the warm run of urine on her upper thigh, running between her legs onto the mattress beneath her. The shaking stopped.

She crawled to her washstand, still listening hard through the pour of water from the pitcher, the squeezing of cloth and droplets splashing into the basin. She cleaned herself, changed her nightgown, and pulled the sheet off the bed, put the wet area in the wash basin and did her best to rinse it, then spread it to dry by the window. She listened with her innermost ear for tires crunching over gravel, feet tipping over soft, sandy soil and then thudding off in a run. Next time, maybe they'd throw a bomb. She put her towel over the mattress's wet spot, covered it with her top sheet, and closed her eyes trying to fool herself into going to sleep.

13

Shuck sat in his car parked outside the Western Union office on Bagley at Grand Circus Park, the air conditioner blasting and the radio tuned to the news station. Celeste hadn't been arrested yet, but it might happen soon. He'd send the the five hundred dollars she'd asked for and hold the other five hundred as his hedge against disaster.

Shuck had it in his mind that the whole summer of violence and death would end up being about the politics of people who already had the power. Not wanting to take a swipe at Celeste's idealism, he kept that to himself when she called. He had an inkling that surviving a summer in Mississippi would pretty much demolish her rosy view of what could happen and how much time it would take. Why hammer the point home? Experience was the better teacher. He'd spent his life preaching to his children that their generation could do anything they wanted. Even as he said it, he knew it wasn't entirely true. It didn't mean the sky was now the limit for Negroes, but it was getting close. For him, luck had been pivotal. That's the path he'd taken. He wanted better for his children. Luck had a way of running out.

Celeste just needed to finish her work and get the hell out of Mississippi in one piece. That's all he asked. He turned the radio off, hummed Dakota Staton's "Broadway," saw himself walking on Seventh Avenue toward the Sheraton Hotel and the cabaret with live jazz and dressed-up women.

The heat wave was setting records for the summer, and an anxiousness for change bubbled up to the surface. Detroiters grew weary of summer, secretly pined for new seasons to tidy through, clean out the wilted flowers, re-dress the trees in bursts of color, and lure the winds that swayed the branches. They ached for summer all winter long, but didn't mind when it left. There was Indian Summer to look forward to, that last warm spell, and after that the very first snow, which draped the city in a spectacular white gown. You just wanted to stand and look at it, pray everyone stayed home, didn't go out there driving and walking and dirtying it. But life went on. After a while, you prayed for a break from the slush and bitter cold. Then you dreamed of spring, pined for buds on trees and soft-voiced birds and little whiffs of warm air returning. He realized that he really wanted this summer to be over, that he was pushing it along too fast and with it, his own life. Better to take it slow, make it last, but Mississippi loomed, confusing even his sense of time and the good life.

Shuck leaned his head back on the soft leather of his seat, watching through half-closed eyes as other cars pulled into the small parking lot to the side of the building. Negroes with big cars and tiny houses, or one-bedroom apartments in working-class neighborhoods, bringing cash money to wire to the south—not for daughters and sons working for "the cause," but for relatives left hanging on by a breath and a thin dime in Alabama, Mississippi, Kentucky. They might be sending money to a household like the one Celeste lived in right now. Shuck watched them get out of their cars dressed in house shoes, do-rags on their heads, the sometimes-employed with cigarettes smoked down to the filter, loud-talking and back-slapping.

The city had been a mecca for black job seekers since he was a child. Truth was the slots had been filled for years, but no one knew how to close the doors and the leftover people stayed on. He saw the For Sale signs on houses all over the city, the boarded-up buildings along Dexter and even on the side streets downtown. A slow, slinking decline. Every week, the newspapers—the white ones and the Negro one—talked of businesses closing. The business to be in right now was moving and storage. Shuck imagined white people scattering out of the city so fast, pieces of their clothing dangled out of their suitcases and car trunks, overstuffed boxes bumped the trunks open. They snatched their children off the playgrounds of schools that had remained integrated right up until the last great migration of southern Negroes in the late 1950s. Then it was, "Let's get the hell out of here." Southern Negroes coming in the back door while home-owning, tax-paying white people ran out the front. Even the experts couldn't keep track. It wasn't that there were no tax-paying, property-owning Negroes. There were plenty. But not enough to support the city.

Shuck didn't know if he should hit the road out of Detroit or stay put with a prayer. And where would he go? Follow the white folks to the suburbs? Move the Royal Gardens out there, too? His New York dream of a supper club with live entertainment languished. The music he loved lived in whispers. Old people's music, Posey called it. You barely found it on the radio, and most of the clubs in town, white-owned or Negro, were filling their jukeboxes with the new music. Young people liked the singing groups, the dance-stepping, shantung-silk-suit-wearing men who crooned love songs in rhyming couplets, and the girl groups with their sleek gowns and puffed hair singing gaunt lyrics. He never got enough of Dinah Washington and Sarah Vaughan, Gloria Lynne and Ella; he put his ears to the speakers for Count Basie, Oscar Peterson, and Jimmie Lunceford. His springtime music would always be dancing in the aisles with Wilamena to the big bands swinging at the Fox Theatre. Shuck felt like a throwback in his own city, in his own life.

He checked all around for any lurking do-nothing men, then chastised himself for having the thought. After all, he was downtown on a street with traffic, pedestrians going and coming in and out of office buildings. Teenagers who might be troublesome slept later than he did.

He patted his breast pocket for the envelope of bail money, then glanced down at his newly polished gray leather loafers, in perfect blend with his light gray jacket and dark gray slacks. He preferred fall and winter clothes. Camel hair and wool gabardine, dark suits with French-cuffed shirts. Silk ties. Didn't like wearing galoshes. First thing was to get this money to Jackson before the shit hit the fan. If Celeste got arrested, he wanted the money to be there to get her out right away. No Negro person was Mississippi-jail material. Nothing but nightmares. He didn't want Celeste to see the inside of a jail in Mississippi or anywhere else.

Inside, the Western Union office smelled of stale cigarette butts. There were trash bits in the corners, yellow paint going grimy. The big plate glass window hadn't been washed in a month and featured all sizes of hand prints, smudges wiped this way and that. Up high, a good half of the yellow lights on the Western Union electric sign were burned out and the dark brown writing needed repainting.

Shuck, a standout of perfect elegance in a throwaway-looking place, stepped into the short line of patrons, angling himself so he could see out of the front window while he waited. Traffic moved around the circle of Grand Circus Park like a silent movie—Fords, Plymouths, Chryslers, delivery trucks of all kinds. A halo of decay veiled all of it.

At the counter, he opened his envelope and took out five crisp hundred dollar bills and splayed them out like cards in a good poker hand, took the paper napkin on which he'd jotted the One Man, One Vote office address, and laid it beside the money. He'd send the money and keep praying Celeste made it through to the end of this Freedom Summer thing. Wouldn't do for him to go down there. They'd all be dead.

The young woman behind the counter smiled. "Morning, sir. May I help you?" She had a crispness in her voice. Her Western Union uniform fit, yellow shirt tucked into dark slacks, her hair pulled back away from her pretty brown face. He was relieved, not up for any double negatives, any slack-jawed southernisms. Not that he considered himself a man of words.

"Good morning to you. I want to send this to Jackson, Mississippi, as fast as you can get it there. Here's the address."

"You want to send a message with it?" The woman slid him a pad for writing out messages. Her nails were neat and clean. She must be a college student at Wayne. Very professional, he was thinking. The kind of young person he'd hire to work in the Royal Gardens, part-time. He figured he could pay more than Western Union.

"I do." Shuck wrote Celeste's name on the message next to the amount he was sending and what it was for. Then he wrote, "Come on outta there, now. Love, Shuck." Then he remembered she'd probably never see the note. He didn't care. He left it.

The woman totaled his costs and gave him a receipt. "Have a nice day, sir."

Shuck made a snap decision, tore off a piece of paper from the pad and wrote his name and phone number, the name of the bar and the address. "You need any part-time work, give me a call. It's a nice place. You in school?"

The girl blushed, eyes tracking quickly down the row of patrons behind Shuck. "Yes, sir. I'm studying at Wayne."

Shuck lowered his voice. "Call the place. My name's Shuck Tyree. I'm the owner." He felt so proud to say that to that young woman, knew his eyes twinkled when he said it.

She took the piece of paper, slid it into her pants pocket, eyes nervous, darting, as if she wanted Shuck to get going. "Thank you, sir."

Shuck nodded to the mangy man in line behind him and walked out to his car. He had choices. To live out the next few years grabbing all the joy he could from the life he'd built, or make some big changes, not knowing what might be on the other end. He knew he'd take care of Momma Bessie and the old house for as long as she wanted to live in it. Alma would stay in his life whether she moved to Outer Drive with that jungle of plants or not. Leave those plastic covers behind.

Shuck drove around Grand Circus Park to Woodward and went toward the river, passing Hudson's department store, the traffic slowing him to an easy summer crawl, his Cadillac gleaming in the afternoon sun. One worry left. Every time Momma Bessie asked him about Celeste, he told her she was doing fine. If he told her where Celeste was, there'd be a long thick pause as if Momma Bessie expected him to announce he was getting on a plane and flying to Mississippi. Celeste wouldn't leave Mississippi until she finished what she went there to do, whether he went down there or not. And how would he get to that god-forgotten town anyway? A flight to New Orleans or to Jackson, then a car ride to Pineyville. What car? Would he be able to rent a car in either city? Better to close the Royal Gardens and drive down, take Posey and all the guns and bullets they could find on the west side of Detroit. Put a sign on the door, "Mississippi or bust."

The regulars were already inside when he pulled up in front of the Royal Gardens. They knew not to park in his space just outside the door. Rodney's old Cadillac and Chink's new Mustang were parked front to back just beyond Shuck's space. Iris parked her old hunk of junk Studebaker more than half a block away. Shuck never told her, but he didn't want that car near the front of his place, attracting the wrong kind of customers. She must have guessed it after looking at his best-of-Negro-life wallpaper. Millicent's sleek Chrysler was parked back of Shuck's spot. He didn't mind that at all. Posey always parked his Oldsmobile across the street from Shuck's Cadillac, said he liked to park in the direction he was heading when he left, didn't want to be out there U-turning like Shuck did every night.

He walked in with a smile on his face for the first time in weeks. The money was on its way to Celeste. For now, that's all he could do. The rest of the summer would be a waiting game. As soon as he walked in the door, he heard the new music on the jukebox and began to shake his head.

"Posey, that music's for children. Nobody in here right now qualifies." He went to his seat at the back of the bar, newspapers and mail in his hands as usual.

"We just tryin' to keep you from getting too old, too fast, that's all." Posey prepped the bar for the evening. "Isn't that right, y'all?"

"Sure is, Shuck." Iris jumped in. "We been worried about you. You walking slower, head all down, look like you lost your best friend. These kids' music put a skip back in your step."

Iris had on her work clothes, a man-looking shirt with the sleeves rolled up over something he couldn't see. Compared to the women in the wallpaper, Iris looked like she was on work detail as janitor. Shuck didn't like it. With her teenaged children, this new music was right up Iris's alley. She couldn't get away from it if she tried. She wasn't the type to teach her children about Duke Ellington and Louis Armstrong, take them places so they knew where they came from.

The voice in his head told Iris she'd better be worrying about herself. He wouldn't say it, didn't want to hurt her feelings. "I'm all right."

"Celeste doing okay?" Millicent sat quietly smoking, twirling that luscious pearl-plated cigarette lighter, sipping a Tom Collins, looking good in a low-cut summer print dress, gold bangles on her brown arms, matching gold hoop earrings, hair pulled back and up against the heat. "I know it's on your mind." Shuck could see in a minute how she made supervisor at the main post office. She carried herself very well.

"Thanks for asking, Millicent. So far, so good. Be glad when it's over."

Chink nodded down to Shuck. "I know that's right."

The thumping bumping new music from the jukebox swelled between them. For a moment, Shuck saw them all as foreign, as if he'd entered a world unknown to him, incomprehensible. He didn't want to be old yet, didn't want to be thought of as out of it, but things were slipping. How did these people fit into the new sounds, the new thinking, when he did not? Why now after all these years was he feeling out of step? He picked up his newspaper and thumbed through as much to hide as to read.

"Posey."

Posey walked down to him, white shirt agleam against his night black skin.

"Hey."

"You up for going to Mississippi? If it gets necessary?"

Posey rubbed two fingers down on both sides of his mouth as if he were smoothing a moustache. "I'm in."

"Keep it to yourself. May not be. Just checking."

"All right, man." Posey slapped a flat hand on the bar, nodded and went back to his work.

They could do some real damage in Pineyville. Posey was mad enough at the world about losing his house to a scheming ex-girlfriend, he'd be perfect for the job. Shuck sensed Posey was humoring him, but he didn't care. He knew this idea of going to Mississippi was a flight of fancy, but one he needed to scope out. He was too old to be fooling around down there, but if push came to shove, he'd go. They'd go. Celeste was nobody's wimp, had taken the bit between her teeth in a way he never dreamed she would. But not like that, not in that place. You had to be young to do something like that.

14

In the hottest hour of the afternoon, flies, crickets, birds, and even the dog-day cicadas all stopped, leaving only phantom movements, elusive echoes. Celeste sat on a stiff chair in the kitchen with the back door open, the long-needled pines like a fortress wall less than a city block to the rear. Her voter registration study materials lay helter-skelter on Mrs. Owens's table.

By now Dolly Johnson was attending the voter registration class regularly, Mr. Landau, too, and Sister Mobley and Mrs. Owens. Others, more tentative, more afraid, ventured in, too. Each evening, one, sometimes two new people appeared in the back of the St. James A.M.E. Church, knotting their bodies into self-effacement, heads hanging low as if to be there and not be at the same time. Celeste beckoned, cajoled, even begged them to join the small group down front, those few who'd decided to risk life and limb for the right to vote. They moved up when they felt comfortable moving and not a second before. They remained wary of Celeste and of the work she was doing, unsettled by the air of threat that hung over Mississippi like an iron veil. Celeste couldn't separate the ongoing historical fears from new ones the movement brought with it.

Her daily routine leaned toward the grueling. Teach the children at freedom school in the mornings, home to eat, wash the sweat off her body, put on fresh clothes, rinse her morning clothes in the tin tub and hang them out back, then prepare for voter registration classes in the evenings. Some days, she swept the sandy dirt out of the house. On others, she walked into town to help Mrs. Owens carry groceries back to Freshwater Road, relieved to change her routine in any small way. No movie theater to slink into, no television, no radio (not in this house anyway), no cool library or lofty museum to amble through—just a front porch with a hard-seated chair waiting at the end of each long day.

Celeste stood from the table to stretch, the pale blue mimeograph ink and small print of her copy of the Mississippi State Constitution a burr in her brain. In Jackson, during her orientation week, the idea of the freedom school had baffled her most. How would she teach children from different grades at the same time? What would she teach? Now, she found the hardest task was preparing the beaten-down older people for voter registration. She walked to the door praying for a breeze from beyond those fragrant pines, her hand smoothing the cypress wood repairs over the bullet holes in the door frame. No breeze came, but Sissy Tucker sped through the heavy air creating a zephyr that bounced her tight braids up and down, almond eyes wide, running across the orange sandy earth out of the trees and heading right for Mrs. Owens's back door. Celeste remembered the hateful fire in Mr. Tucker's eyes the day of the church picnic, the warning he cut her in the rearview mirror of his big Hudson after she told Sissy she'd take her to see a movie. "Sissy! How are you, come in, come in." She quickly unhooked the screen, and Sissy darted in like a panicked bird.

Celeste sat the panting child at the table and gave her a glass of ice water, remembering the tears that welled in Sissy's eyes after her father crushed her dream of going to see a movie. Sissy was throwing down her gauntlet by even coming to this house. Celeste had to buck up. She glanced down the short hall to the porch where Mrs. Owens dozed in her rocking chair. Sometimes there came an easing of the day's heat, arriving like an unexpected check in the mail late in the afternoon. The sun's rays somehow shifted to a less abusive angle; the temperature didn't change one degree, but it seemed the full fire of the sun had inched farther away. Sissy had a patina of sweat on her oval face. Her hibiscus-yellow summer dress had broad straps across her dark little-girl shoulders. Her yellow socks looked purposely dyed with orange splotches, and her black Mary Janes were scuffed and scratched but not a bit run over at the heels.

"Thanks again for warning me about the sacred ground." Celeste stood opposite her in the tight kitchen. What if the big Hudson with the blasted-out windshield pulled up? She glanced out the small window. What would she do with Sissy? "You can sure holler."

"You welcome, Miss Celeste." She sipped her water carefully. Although Sissy's eyes were anxious, there was a soft belligerence in them, too. She was proud that she'd warned Celeste with her big voice at the church picnic and maybe even prouder that she was doing what she wanted to in spite of her father.

"Reverend Singleton said he was going to speak to your father about you coming to the freedom school." Celeste listened for the sound of wheels on gravel. Now that the house had been shot into, Mr. Tucker would never allow his daughter to participate in anything that had the word "freedom" attached to it. No doubt she'd been told that this house, with its boarder and her freedom songs, was completely off-limits to her.

Sissy stared over the papers on the table. "You a real teacher?"

"I'm a student. College." Celeste imagined Sissy seeing Ann Arbor, the green of it, the richness, too, with a library bigger than any building in Pineyville and students everywhere with their easy familiarity.

"Cause you too young." The girl nodded. "I sure liked you talking in the church that time." She wagged her head like an old woman for emphasis, as if thinking, I want to do that, too.

A car crunched by on Freshwater Road, grating over the gravel and sand, and Sissy's eyes grew wide as she jumped towards the door.

Celeste looked out the window again, this time to see a rusty chrome back fender, not the big Hudson's, disappearing down the road. "I was scared to death. Never done anything like that before." This house, closest to the turn-in from the blacktop and only half a block from the Tucker house, wasn't a good choice for this clandestine meeting. "Let's go for a walk. You got time?"

Sissy had her hands on the doorknob. "Yes, ma'am."

"Yeah, let's go." If Mrs. Owens woke, she'd see the spread of papers on the table, the unlatched back door, and figure she'd gone to the outhouse.

Celeste followed Sissy across the sandy earth towards the pines, both of them checking back in case the Hudson turned onto Freshwater Road before they made it to the trees. When they entered the deep forest, there was no real path, just breaks among the trees. Sissy wound around, heading away from Freshwater Road so that nothing could be seen of them, Celeste knew, because she could no longer see the houses or even the electrical poles. They slowed and walked side by side, the heat infiltrating the trees, thick but less intense than in the open spaces. The scent of pine laced the air without the overlay of must and funk.

"What's your college?" Sissy led them through the piney woods like a scout, stepping slowly, cautiously, eyeing the needle-laden ground. Celeste wondered if snakes slithered through those woods and what other wildness lived in this place, so close to the house and yet foreign and strange. She'd never been a girl for the countryside, not on foot anyway. "It's a big school. Up north. It's called the University of Michigan, after the state." Mrs. Owens never spoke of the woods, never set foot into them though they were practically a part of her backyard. Celeste heard the slightest moan of the trees, the subtle movement of branches high up in the air, responding to a breeze that never made it to the ground. She didn't want to go too far from the house, but she didn't want to show her fear of the woods to Sissy.

"My teacher says she went to school in Jackson. At Tougaloo College. You ever seen it?" Sissy talked easy, slow-gliding between the trees, sure-footed and carefree.

"When I was doing my training to come here." Celeste nodded, stepping gingerly over piles of browning pine needles, seeing things that were not there. "It's a lot smaller than where I go, but it's nice." Margo had taken her and Ramona on a sightseeing trip to see Tougaloo College and the state capital. She and Ramona had sat in the front seat with Margo driving, a visual anomaly for sure. It had to be a challenge to local whites to see them riding around chatting like it was the most normal thing in the world. Even as they did, Margo stayed vigilant and so did she and Ramona, checking behind them and to the side in traffic as heads whipped around watching the three northern interlopers. It was nerve-wracking even while it was funny. Margo had a streak of the wild. Sissy had it, too, apparently.

"You got a boyfriend?" Sissy's voice lifted up, nearly sang it.

"I had one. He went away for the summer." She had been thinking of J.D. less and less frequently.

"You went away, too." Sissy laughed, then stopped short and stood quietly listening.

"You're right." Celeste whispered, not about to tell Sissy that her boyfriend was white or that one of the reasons she'd come south was to get J.D.'s white world out of her system. Sissy didn't say a word for a moment, just stood there looking up into the pines at the streaks of blue sky showing through.

"Is he cute?" Sissy took off walking again. "Where'd he go?"

"He's good-looking. But he's not my boyfriend anymore." Celeste figured after this summer, if she survived it, they'd at least talk again. "He went to Paris, France."

"How come?" Sissy pressed her with little girl questions. "Where's that?"

"Well, he comes from a different kind of background. He paints pictures." Celeste struggled to cast J.D. in a light that revealed and secreted him at the same time. "Paris is a city in another country. Across the ocean."

"You have a lot of places in you." Sissy's voice dreamed again as it did in the car when she tried to grasp the concept of movie stars on big screens in the dark. "I never knew someone who painted pictures." Said as if a child her age should've known someone who painted pictures.

Celeste smiled at the thought of the woman Sissy might become. "I never did either 'til I met him at school." She remembered the day she'd first seen J.D. all set up with an easel on the campus green. She'd stopped to see what was on the canvas. Trees, but not representational. Greens in all shades and bricks it seemed of black and brown. He'd asked her to have coffee with him.

"What about your daddy and your momma?" Sissy kept walking.

Celeste didn't answer her right away, listened to the whistle-singing of birds like she hadn't heard since Ann Arbor. She thought of the idea of a daddy and a momma as a grouping, a framework. She'd barely known it before Wilamena took off, had lived all the intervening years with that slight hollow in the idea of *parents*. "My mother lives in a place called New Mexico. My father lives in Detroit. Before I left for school, I lived with him. Me and my brother." She felt a pang, a prick every time she thought of how her life had played out so far with a distant mother who always seemed to be looking in her own mirror. *Father.* She held onto Shuck. She'd missed something, she knew, but it was hard to fathom exactly what it all meant.

"By yourself?" Sissy eyes got bigger and cloudy. "Just you and your daddy and your brother?"

"Well, my brother left for college first. So, yeah, for a while it was just me and my father. He's a lotta fun." Celeste saw Shuck in her mind, all crisply dressed, pinkie ring shining, Cadillac gleaming like a white-iced cake in the sunshine. Whatever oddness there was in Shuck being a single parent faded. "My parents divorced when I was younger than you are now."

A slippery feeling of unease went right down her spine. She tried to grab it, make it speak to her, but it was gone. She didn't know if Sissy understood the concept of divorce. Not sure she understood it herself.

"You got a daddy who's fun?" Sissy stopped in her tracks. "My daddy ain't no fun."

Celeste heard the child's vehemence, saw the anger in her eyes. "I can see that. He's protective of you, that's all." Celeste didn't want to get off on a tangent about Mr. Tucker the dream killer. People were possessive of their children, though Wilamena had never been particularly possessive of hers. If that was what it was. She'd seen it in her cousins and in friends, always felt a draft of loneliness in those moments. Wilamena would drop her and Billy off at a cousin's house and never seemed to miss them, never seemed to care if they came back or not. Shuck had never been so dismissive; he'd made himself a presence no matter how late he stayed out at his bar or with his pals. That only drew her tighter to him, and to Billy, too. When Wilamena left for good, that same lonely draft blew even harder, but Shuck took up the space with his warmth.

Celeste had been walking behind Sissy again. She had no idea of how far they had gone. "Maybe we better get back."

"Yes, ma'am." Sissy turned and led them unerringly back to the place where they'd entered the piney woods. Inside the house, the child sat for a moment at the table with Celeste. Sissy must know the forgotten paths, Celeste thought, all through the remains of the piney woods. When they said goodbye, Sissy re-entered the forest, taking the long way around toward her house by walking parallel to Freshwater Road through the pines. Celeste stood at the back door and followed the yellow of Sissy's dress until it disappeared in the trees. She didn't have much hope that Reverend Singleton would be able to convince Mr. Tucker to allow his children to come to the freedom school. Not now.

15

The five children who now came to freedom school every day were ages six to eleven. They were Labyrinth and Georgie, her first students, and Tony Mobley and his two little sisters, Hattie and Marge. Other children attended on different days, dictated by the ability of their parents to get them to the church. On some days, Celeste had as many as fifteen. Sissy occasionally appeared at the church door, but never came inside. Mr. Tucker had expressly forbidden it. If there'd been any hope that he'd soften, the gunshots that blasted out his back windshield put that to rest. But Sissy had shown up again at Mrs. Owens's back door and taken a furtive lesson from Celeste in the kitchen. And then another.

Celeste stood near the wood railing separating the pulpit from the rest of the church, her portable chalkboard leaning on a chair, the children squirming on the hard pew. Though Reverend Singleton's two big fans created a meager cross breeze and the splotchy window shades were rolled down against the sun's assault, the late morning swelter made her feel that she would surely faint if the temperature rose one more degree. She and the children grew lethargic near noon, the end of the freedom school day. She longed for a thin current of crisp air, a Canadian breeze with chills at the outer reaches.

In Jackson Celeste had been taught how racial oppression made children think less and speak little, bending many of them into the hunched old people they would eventually become. Celeste added parental oppression to that list, thinking of Sissy and her clamp-down father. When Sissy appeared outside the church, she would spend the morning opening and closing the church door, spiraling in and out of the parching sun, her bright-colored dresses blinking light into the shady church cavity as she kept an eye out for her father and his big maroon Hudson.

"The first time Frederick Douglass escaped from slavery, he was captured and sent to jail." Celeste's voice bounced limply off the wood walls and beams, barely breaking through the retributive heat. "He didn't give up just because he went to jail." She raised her voice so Sissy could hear the lesson back at the door, hoping the children would connect Frederick Douglass's journey to what was going on in Mississippi that summer. Sissy had read Frederick Douglass in the kitchen, but that was their secret.

"Pass it down." She handed the picture of Frederick Douglass to the boy sitting on the end of the row. "Stand and say your name." She asked them to stand and say their names before speaking when it became very clear that they seemed to feel more comfortable staring at the ground when they spoke. It was a way of encouraging them to inhabit the space they lived in, a way of for them to plant themselves in the earth and say, "I'm here and I matter."

The boy jumped to his feet, grinning. "My name be Tony." Tiny white beads of sleep nestled in the corners of his child eyes and bed lint speckled his tight kinky hair. Ashy from head to toe. No shoes or socks, toenails dirty, ankles marked with insect bite scars. Celeste fought an urge to take Tony straight to Reverend Singleton's lavatory, wash him, rub lotion on him, comb his hair, then take him shopping for new clothes. "Your last name, Tony?"

"Mobley, ma'am." He took the picture, gave it a good look then passed it down.

Sister Mobley, his mother, had committed to the voter registration class after Celeste spoke from the pulpit. She'd sent Tony and his two sisters to the freedom school the next day. Sister Mobley and her children lived farther down Freshwater Road in a raw wood house with a sinking porch that had spaces wide enough to slip a foot through. Sister Mobley had no husband. She worked in service part-time and, in her mind, had not much to lose. Registering to vote and freeing her children from the thinking they'd been born into had become a small obsession for the thin woman.

Labyrinth and Georgie stared at the picture of Frederick Douglass. Labyrinth stole a peek back to Sissy at the door. "May I take it to Sissy?"

"Stand and say your name." Labyrinth knew the ritual.

The blonde-haired child stood, looking like a creature from another planet. Celeste felt an odd kinship and a small revulsion at the same time. The similarity between them had to do with their overall difference. In truth, they looked nothing alike. Not many blond Negroes in Mississippi. Not many green-eyed Negroes either. One thing was for sure, though: Labyrinth was nobody's fool.

"I'm Labyrinth Johnson." She pursed her lips, not in the least cowed by the fact that she used the last name of her mother and all the other children used a father's surname whether or not that father had disappeared from their lives. "Now, may I take this picture back to Sissy, ma'am?" Clearly, she felt she didn't need to stand up and say her name every time she spoke. She knew her name and knew how to be in the world, whether her daddy was white Mr. Dale who owned the grocery store but didn't own up to her or not.

"Sissy, do you want to see Frederick Douglass?" Celeste called to her, coaxing. Sissy stepped just inside the church door, her eyes like the wings of hummingbirds fluttering back to the ominous road. Her thick hair was braided tightly, Vaseline glistened on her scalp in the parts. Her face was scrubbed, elbows and knees oiled every day.

"I do want to, Miss Celeste." Sissy's voice trembled. Her almond eyes grew so large Celeste could read the fear in them all the way to the front of the church. Then Sissy smiled, acknowledging their secret lesson in Mrs. Owens's kitchen. Celeste nodded to her. If Sissy saw her father's Hudson turn into the church road, her cotton dress metamorphosed into wings as she took off flying through the long-needled pines and wax myrtles, plaited hair coming undone as she navigated the back way to Freshwater Road. From the church, running through the woods she arrived at her house more than five minutes before her father. She'd already told Celeste that she'd rather be punished by her mother for coming in with her socks and shoes coated in orange dust, or even mud, than have her father find her at the freedom school.

One time Sissy hadn't run. Mr. Tucker left the car idling in front of the church, while he got out to grab Sissy's thin brown arm. He pushed her roughly into the front seat of his big car, yelling the whole time in his seething Mississippi drawl that women belonged at home. Celeste, helpless to do anything about it, stood in the church door watching the maroon car disappear back down the church road, Sissy's little body bouncing in the front seat next to him.

Later that day Mr. Tucker paid a visit to Mrs. Owens, who met him at the front screened door and invited him in, but he stayed on the dirt path at the foot of the leaning stairs looking up at her. He told her that no daughter of his was going to be learning anything from a loose young woman like that Celeste Tyree. He said that when Sissy left his house, she'd be leaving with a man she was married to. Not like Celeste Tyree, unmarried and not living in her parents' home. He called her *that unbound woman, coming and going, talking from pulpits like a man, taking long train rides alone, living like she was a young widow woman ready for anything.*

Celeste heard it all from inside the house. She marveled at his perception, having never had more than a one-minute conversation with him. She walked to the front and stood behind Mrs. Owens like a child. Mrs. Owens shushed her before she opened her mouth, waving her back with her hand. Mr. Tucker said that he'd already warned his daughter to stay away from that freedom school and Celeste Tyree. He must never find out that Sissy was coming to the house having Freedom School lessons in Mrs. Owens's kitchen.

When the Hudson took off down Freshwater Road, Mrs. Owens told Celeste to be careful. Mr. Tucker made her think of the devil, and she added in a low voice that she'd seen little pitchforks in the lights of his eyes. Celeste said she needed to find a way to liberate that child from her own father before her spirit shriveled. Mrs. Owens told her to stay out of it—that Celeste would be gone at the end of the summer, but Sissy and Mrs. Tucker would still be there, dealing with that hateful man. Mrs. Owens didn't say a word about the kitchen lessons, but Celeste figured the old woman had been feigning sleep on the afternoons when Sissy came to the back door. That way, she was free to say she'd known nothing about it.

"Go, ahead, Labyrinth. Take the picture to Sissy, and thank you." Celeste thought of scenarios for Mr. Tucker's next trip to the church. She wasn't sure that if he came again and caught his daughter at the church door that she'd stay back like a helpless bystander. She saw herself standing between Mr. Tucker and his daughter, having a full-out argument with him about the value of the freedom school for Sissy's future, the value of freedom, period. She'd put her heart and soul into trying to convince him of the good of it all for Sissy.

Labyrinth marched down the center aisle of the church, her sun-dress straps sliding off both shoulders, her blonde curls bobbing like a headful of big yellow daisies. She stayed with Sissy while they both handled the picture of Frederick Douglass. Sissy checked for any sign of Mr. Tucker on the church road, then Labyrinth dragged a chair to hold the door open, looking back to Celeste as if to say, "Why didn't you think of this?"

"Frederick Douglass eventually escaped in 1838 and went to live in New York, starting a newspaper called the *North Star*." She'd already talked to them about what newspapers were; she used the New Orleans *Times-Picayune* for reading exercises. She spoke loudly enough so that Labyrinth and Sissy could hear her back at the door.

The children were respectful of her whether they were getting the point or not. Just like the adults here, they treated her not quite like she was a white person, but certainly not like one of them, gazing at her as if she were on the other side of a plate glass window. In the first days of freedom school, they didn't look at her at all. Except Labyrinth. Everything on her face was a challenge. Dolly Johnson was training her child for what was coming. She was rearing a half-white no-father child with a strong name like Labyrinth, endowing her with an attitude strong enough to back people off of her. It was working, because the child was strong, unbent but in a different way than Sissy, who was a delicate dreamer. Labyrinth dug in her heels and wouldn't take no for an answer for her life.

"He was like a movin' picture star." Sissy seemed to float herself inside the color picture of Frederick Douglass, his wild, full head of hair and beard making him look staunch and sturdy.

"They didn't have no movies in those days, girl." Labyrinth rolled her eyes at Sissy.

"I know that." Sissy stood her ground.

Celeste heard the two of them sounding like grown women fussing over a backyard fence.

"He named his newspaper the *North Star* because the slaves used the North Star in the night sky to guide them to freedom," Celeste explained. "Today, he'd be like a movie star because he was very famous. Only he was famous for fighting for freedom."

"See." Sissy sucked her teeth at Labyrinth.

Labyrinth looked up at Celeste and shook her head. "Whatever you say, Miss Celeste."

Say the word freedom over and over again until it becomes like the hair on their heads and the brown in their skins. Say it for yourself. Say it for yourself.

"So, it helped to move people, Sissy, to guide them from a bad place to a better place. Like the star of Bethlehem at Christmas time."

While Celeste focused too much on Sissy back at the church door, the other children grew restless. With dark flashing eyes and sun-brown skin that was as smooth as Momma Bessie's gravy, the children played a toned-down version of musical chairs to little stanzas of church songs that they sang out in bursts. Their clothes were nearly tattered. Next to Sissy and Labyrinth, Tony might be the one to make real strides in reading and Negro history, in seeing the possibilities of life. He had curiosity. But it was Labyrinth who was already feisty. Celeste wished they all had her spunk, because they were going to need it.

The children perked up at the mention of Christmas with little pinches and whispers. Their high-sounding voices sparked the front of the church. Tony popped his head around towards Labyrinth and Sissy.

"I see you, Tony." Labyrinth stuck out her tongue then wiggled her hips.

"Okay, Labyrinth, come on back here and sit down." Celeste had to keep a handle on Labyrinth. "Sissy, leave the chair in the door so you can see from inside."

Sissy smiled her distant smile as if she'd been piloting a group of escapees by the light of the North Star herself. She checked for the maroon car, caution clouding her face with the worried look of a grown woman. Sissy seemed to dote on Frederick Douglass from the first time she saw his picture on the book cover.

When she called to Sissy to take her turn reading from the Frederick Douglass biography, Sissy was gone. Two men stood inside the door in shadow, one holding the chair that had braced the door open. They disturbed every mote of dust, every wilted and solemn molecule of air in the church as if the building itself held its breath. From the height and slight thickness of one of them, Celeste thought that Shuck had found his way to Pineyville to take her home.

It wasn't Shuck or anyone like him. They were too young, with short-cut kinky hair, white T-shirts under their bibbed overalls lighting their dark, sweat-shiny faces. No curls and waves pomaded to flatness with a stocking cap, no diamonds sparkling, no stingy-brimmed hats, no suits and ties complementing pastel dress shirts. The men weren't like her brother Billy, either, or his friends, the ones she called the work-hard, party-hard set from Detroit. Nothing about them resembled the Negro boys who crept around campus, the big-muscled athletes or the brainy types whose sports jackets drooped off one shoulder and whose shoes were run down at the heels.

They were calm, standing in the shadows neither smiling nor frowning. She saw now that the taller of the two wore wire-rimmed granny glasses. She fumbled, shuffling papers, beginning to feel that she'd conjured a mirage in the afternoon heat. But the children had grown quiet, too, waiting for a cue, eyes darting back and forth between the men and her. A child should speak up, calling to an uncle, an older brother, someone they knew. No one spoke. Instead, they left their seats to be closer to her. She put her arms around them. Tony took a step towards the men. Labyrinth was right behind him. Celeste grabbed the girl back to her.

"Miss Detroit. How you doing?" Matt Higgens's Kansas City twang rang out in the still church. Matt and his friend came out of the shadows down the church aisle.

"You checking on me?" Celeste said, smiling. She saw his friend was Ed Jolivette, who she remembered had spoken at one of the orientation meetings in Jackson. He'd quieted a packed church with a soft voice. She'd sat in the back of the church that night with Margo and Ramona, and hadn't gotten a clear view of him. In the One Man, One Vote office, everyone spoke of him as "Jolivette" because the movement seemed to be so full of guys named "Ed." Ed Jolivette was different—that night, his quiet speech had set him apart from the other speakers, who beat you over the head with the obvious.

Their self-possession frightened the children because they intuited already that Negro men with that air died fast in Mississippi. They knew it whether they could speak it or not. These two men were the strangers in town, the threat to all that had been before, gunslingers with no guns. Their eyes had no fear, no rancor, no need to please or displease.

Matt seemed older than he had just the few weeks before when Celeste had last seen him. "It's okay." She said it to Tony. "Go on home. Be here on time tomorrow."

Labyrinth pouted. "That your boyfriend, Miss Celeste?"

"Go on home now, Labyrinth." Celeste gave her a chiding look, wondering which man she was referring to. "And be careful." In Detroit, it would've been, "be careful of the traffic crossing the street, be careful of

bigger kids on the prowl to toy with little ones." In Mississippi, it was a
general be careful of everything.

The children walked out slowly. Tony lingered, eyeing the two men and
her as they started to straighten up the church. Tony studied Matt and Ed
like they were ebony carved statues.

Ed Jolivette smiled at Tony and said, "Hey now, where you at, little
man." Tony grinned.

She knew he'd never seen anything like them, not even Reverend
Singleton, but surely he'd heard stories and knew how those stories ended.
Negro man stands up to white man and is killed, disappears without notice.
These were the "stand up to" kinds of men. Even Reverend Singleton had
to do a lot of bending to keep a church going in this town. Finally, Tony
grabbed the hands of his two sisters and strolled out.

"Pick that up, could you?" She pointed to the portable chalkboard. "It
goes in the back office. You're Ed Jolivette. I heard you speak in Jackson.
You were good." He seemed to move in a cocoon of stillness, as though
there was some kind of seal around him, an invisible wrap with electricity
running through it. She felt the charge.

Matt took the front end of the chalkboard. "He's all right." Matt glanced
away from Ed when he spoke.

She led them to the back with the chalkboard balanced between them.

"I try not to do much of that." Ed sounded comfortable with his own
reluctance to be in the public eye at a time when new leaders were springing
up like weeds. His voice was low and smooth, with an accent she couldn't
trace. He had thin lips and dark red-brown skin. Everybody was dark
down here. Celeste couldn't figure out how the white people stayed so
white in all the sunshine. Maybe they had some secret balm they used to
keep themselves white and separated. Negroes soaked up the sun—but
not Wilamena, she remembered. Celeste wondered what she did in New
Mexico to hide from the desert sun.

"So you got five kids in here," Matt sounded like he wanted to say "only,"
but didn't. They came back into the church after leaning the chalkboard
against the wall in Reverend Singleton's office.

"Six, really, but one's got a daddy problem." Sissy must've seen Matt's car
turn in off the highway, thought it was her father's, and taken off running.
"He won't let her take the classes so she sneaks in and out. Some days, I
have as many as fifteen." She grabbed her book-bag and felt Ed watching

her, the way her yellow cotton dress fit. She realized she'd been in a kind of neuter zone since J.D., a place that quieted her sexuality in a way that seemed readable to any man who might've shown interest. She'd wanted time, and perhaps she got more than she'd bargained for. "What? That not enough?"

"You can do better." Matt chastised her gently.

"One would be enough in this town," Ed spoke quietly, defending her. But she resented his speaking of Pineyville this way, even though she felt the same. It was her town now and her project. They were ganging up on her. She decided to ignore both of them and turned off the fans.

"Matt, I know y'all are giving me a ride to Mrs. Owens's house so I don't have to sit here waiting for Reverend Singleton." She sounded flagrant and strong and liked it. "Couple of times I just walked it because I got tired of sitting here."

"You not supposed to walk from here to Freshwater Road, chère, no matter what. It's too dangerous," Ed chided. "You tryin' to get killed?"

"Not really." Celeste said it loud. What was that "chère" business?

"Big city impatience don't work down here." Matt harped. He sounded the way he had when they first started driving down from Jackson, *before* they were stopped on the road. Matt was supposed to be her ally. He was showing off for Ed, being harder than he would've been alone.

The men's voices conquered the space, devoured it. Their long arms dangled, their big hands gripped the pew backs and folding chairs. They walked around the small church, their footsteps thudding on the boards. She felt relegated to the side, part of the backdrop. Women only rented the space when they sang on Sunday morning, rearing back, dropping their jaws, pushing their music and their hearts toward Jesus. Then they sat down and shut up. Men just spoke into the space any time of the day or night and owned it.

"What the hell am I supposed to do?" She started toward the door but stopped and turned to Matt, the impulse to put her hands on her hips like Labyrinth strong enough to make her clutch her book-bag instead. "I'm sorry." She said it to the church more than to the men. "Must be the heat."

Matt and Ed had crystallized here as if they were characters out of a Bible story, disciples winding through the land provoking a man here, a woman there, goading all who'd listen to reexamine everything they'd heard for the last one hundred years about the way life was supposed to be lived. She stood at the door, digging around for her place that seemed to evaporate the longer she stayed in a space with Matt and Ed.

"Her daddy's a numbers man." Matt said nonchalantly, cocking his head back to look at her.

"Is that true?" Ed nodded his approval, his accent sending a whistle of air on the "t."

"He owns a bar. Numbers are a side thing." She slid it out there, claiming Shuck for all he was worth, proud.

"You been into Hattiesburg, yet? Yo daddy got the coin, you can take *us* out." Matt put his hand out to Ed for the slapping five, something in his tone putting her down. She couldn't have been more disappointed in Matt.

"Haven't been anywhere." She rolled her eyes at both of them as she held the door open. "The last time Hattiesburg came up I was with you, remember? I don't have a car, you know."

"Don't need one if you do what you supposed to do." Matt walked out on a roll now, as if everything they'd been through together had created no kind of bond at all. He swaggered around like he owned Pineyville. She bit her tongue, not wanting to get into a verbal snarl with Matt in front of Ed Jolivette.

As oppressive as the church was, when she stepped outside in the direct sunlight she flinched like she'd been hit, and squinted so hard she lost track of where she was until she got her big sunglasses on. The sun burned the oxygen out of the air, scorched the lungs. Breathing became a cumbersome act.

"I better put a note on the door for Reverend Singleton so he won't be worried." She was thinking she'd better tell Reverend Singleton to swing by and tell Mrs. Owens, too, so *she* wouldn't be worried if they were really going to Hattiesburg. She pulled paper and tape out of her book-bag and watched Matt and Ed head for the dusty Dodge, noticing the back of Ed's tall body, the balance of it and his easy gait as he strode over the white rock gravel. Her cotton dress suddenly felt like burlap scraping the surface of her skin. She unbuttoned another button, revealing the round of her modest cleavage. If Reverend Singleton drove up before they got out of there, she'd have to rebutton it. She knew better than to test those boundaries in this Bible-toting place where innocent gestures carried the weight of sin. If Mrs. Singleton happened to be with him, she'd button the dress up to her neck.

"Mrs. Owens said you could cook ribs on the church steps this time of day." It was just about high noon when she joined them at the car, tossed her book-bag into the back seat, climbed into the front in the middle. She glanced back to see her note taped to the church door, clearly visible to anyone coming up the church road. "Glad you got your windows fixed, Matt." She tried to put some smart jokiness in her voice, remembered that glass flying across the front seat of the car, wanting to remind him of their history together. "Now, that was something else."

"It's been worse." Matt said, backing the car around, heading down the bumpy church road.

Celeste knew he was stifling her allusion to their camaraderie in the trenches. She'd kept her wits about her while he got a real Mississippi beating. "Well, that may be true, but that trip ranks up there at the top of my bad list. I was scared they were going kill you, and God only knows what they might've done to me." Just in case Matt hadn't told Ed about it, she wanted to be sure he knew she'd earned her stripes. She sat up straight, holding her own, feeling good that she hadn't let him roll over her life's experience for the sake of making her look wimpy in Ed's eyes or even in her own.

"By the end of the summer, that ride down from Jackson will look like child's play." Matt couldn't resist, she thought, letting her know he was the one with the notches on his belt in Mississippi. She was still green and underneath, he seemed to be saying that no matter what she did, she'd never measure up.

"Somebody shot through Mrs. Owens's house the other night." She one-upped him right back. "We sleeping on the floor now."

"You and damned near every volunteer in Mississippi." Matt swatted her back down hard.

Celeste's blood rushed up to her neck and face. Why was he being so hard on her? He was tearing her down in front of a stranger. Was it Ed Jolivette? It clicked in. He didn't want Ed Jolivette to like her because she might like him back. She couldn't tell if Ed understood what was going on between them or not.

"How many you got in voter registration?" Ed brought them back to business.

"It keeps changing. I'm teaching remedial reading and civics at the same time. My core group is about four or five." She didn't finish before Ed broke in.

"What'd you expect?" It stung even though he said it quietly.

She ignored him. "Half the time, they can't get to the church for the class. I don't know." She'd had about enough of both of them. At the same time, she felt Ed's naked arm touching hers, so smooth she didn't want to say anything to make him move.

"Goes with the territory." Ed sounded like he'd seen it all, and there was no burden to it. He sounded almost apologetic.

Celeste didn't want him to see her face for fear it would reveal the charge she felt in being close to him, even though they'd been dueling since he walked in the church door. He *was* the movement; she knew he'd been arrested and beaten more than once. Like Matt, he lived in the frontline trenches long before Freedom Summer ever started. They exuded the same manliness, the same new root meaning of Negro man, but Matt had an edgy, street-wise side to him. Ed came off like a quiet bookworm, but maybe that was just the wire-rimmed glasses leading her off on a dead-end tangent. He'd taken them off. She glared at him. Clear boundaries, sweet eyes, but dread hiding way back in his heart. No compromising here. He'd walk away or die first.

"Trust what you're doing." Matt drove slowly north on Highway 11. "We need to see one of your voter registration classes." Matt backed down a bit. More than likely, he was following Ed Jolivette's lead.

She rested her head on the back of the seat. "Fine by me." The whip of the breeze patted her face dry. She spied the bend of Ed's long legs, the shape of his knee and his thighs beneath the denim overalls. His dark brown arms slendered into elegant wrists. No watch. No rings. He seemed older.

The air thickened like a pot of stew with too much flour. The sky opened and a hammering rain fell. They rolled up the windows of the Dodge, locking in the plump air. Lightning snapped at the crabby trees. Dry branches ignited, and when the quick fires died, the trees were leafless black embers, still standing upright.

The last time she was locked in a car with Matt, he'd assumed everything about who she was and what kind of family she came from because of the way she looked. *I been to Detroit, baby, I know. Yo momma'd shit a brick if she knew somebody as black as me was this close to you. You a red-bone.* By the end of that trip, she believed they'd gotten past all that. He'd accepted her. But now she wasn't so sure. Why did she have to prove how Negro she was to the Matts of the world? Shuck would say that was his problem, not hers. She wanted to ask them if there was anything new in the search for Chaney, Schwerner, and Goodman. She'd read in the local newspaper that their burned-out car had been found, containing Mickey Schwerner's wristwatch stopped at 12:45. Dead time. These deaths, these unfound bodies, made gargoyles of men who turned their eyes away, pretending this thing made a man truer to himself and to his God. The women who slept with the men who did the killing knew what happened to those boys. If you listened to men, they told you everything. Who were these women, who slept with death on their lips and woke up silent?

The countryside whizzed by though of course they drove well under the speed limit. Crows jostled on the telephone lines and cross poles, breaking for chatter before another sally into someone else's nest.

"Fish crows," Ed said. "Up from the Gulf."

"Really?" She took her eyes away from the crows. He'd seen her looking at them. Relieved to hear his voice, take her out of her own mind.

"Crows the most intelligent birds God made." He said it as if all the world should know it, and the sound of his words was round, open.

"How so?" He had her interest, easy to do now but she still tried to sound nonchalant, thinking how in the world did he know that. And, did he really know it or was he just talking?

"Trainable." That was all he said. She wanted to hear more, like did he have some hobby learning about birds? Trainable? Were these crows some metaphor for women? She already knew she wasn't trainable. And what did intelligence really have to do with being trainable? Some brilliance was wild and not trainable.

"Trainable, huh?" He sounded like he meant more than the words coming out of his mouth. Maybe it was the stillness around him that she was reading into. Crows. *Black like Negroes. Black as a crow. Blackbird. Ugly as a crow. Lazy as a crow.* Now, they're smart. Wouldn't you know.

Trying to be distant with Ed wasn't working. She had an urge to run her finger down his forearm, it was so even, the muscle against the slight indentation of bone. She wanted to stare into his face and not talk at all. She'd been isolated for too long.

"Y'all leave them birds alone. They not bothering nobody." Matt left the wipers going though the rain had slowed to a sprinkle. "Mrs. Owens doing okay?" With each wipe, another insect scrap smeared across the windshield. The rain and the wipers didn't clean them off, just smudged them around until there were bug remains and road dust wiped all across the windshield.

Matt and Ed had been driving around Mississippi checking on the various projects for more than a week. The car looked it.

"She joined my class." Celeste rolled a little with the car movement, her thigh shifting to touch Ed's leg.

"She read?" Ed rubbed the ridge of his nose. He was more serious than any professor she'd ever seen at school, like a scientist who lives in a basement lab. His calm made her jumpy.

"Reads that Bible every night. She's teaching me the Bible. I know she thinks I'm a candidate for hell cause I can't quote chapter and verse. She's saving me." She knew that kind of thing would impress Ed. Valuing the gifts of the local people was part of the mission. "I guess I need saving." She stared off into the distance chastising herself for saying that she needed saving when in truth she needed far less. What would he think of that?

They drove along, knowing their license plate numbers were on lists owned by the White Citizens Councils and passed to the police and the Klan. Three pairs of eyes scouring the air straight ahead, listening, watching out for panel trucks with shot guns loaded in the racks and too many men. They were outnumbered, maybe not by souls, but certainly by power, by guns, and most of all, by the sheer intensity of the hatred against them.

A sign read, "Hattiesburg, 5 miles." The rain stopped. The gray slipped off to the east leaving a cloudless, aquamarine sky and a freshly reignited sun. Within minutes, the clean post-rain air had siphoned moisture from the Gulf and the creeks, rivers, and ponds and spread itself heavily over everything again like quilts.

They rolled down the windows. She wished she was sitting in the back seat with Ed, closing her eyes, the air blowing her dress farther and farther up her thighs. She saw herself in a French movie with Ed Jolivette as her lover.

They were in Hattiesburg before the last raindrops dried off the hood of the car, creeping to the far side of town. Wood framed houses set back from the curbs, some with full wraparound porches, wicker furniture, porch swings. Squares of lawns with forest-green hedges. Splashes of color from dipladenias and geraniums. Sidewalks. Real pavement, not just dirt and gravel. Vast umbrella-like trees. Willows, live oaks, magnolias. They rode through the Negro section of town and they might well have been in another country. The poverty shocked Celeste to silence. She felt as if she was on parade driving through, not wanting to stare at the shanty houses built side by side, the barefooted children playing in the dirt. The picture of neglect was overwhelming and she realized that in Pineyville that same poverty was spread out over the countryside. In Hattiesburg, it was bunched together so that nothing of nature might soften the blow. The trees did nothing to assuage the picture, nor did the near-tropical sky.

Matt turned into a gravel parking lot. They walked into a cinderblock building with no sign. She followed Matt, feeling Ed's eyes on her back the whole way.

16

Celeste adjusted to the dim light, saw the cinder block walls painted glossy strawberry red, then spotted the aging jukebox sitting like a live band waiting to play a downbeat. There was a garish confusion of chromium-braced chairs featuring assorted orange, pink, sky blue, and milky turquoise plastic cushions and seat backs. The chairs surrounded kitchen-sized Formica-topped tables arranged near a small dance floor marked off by black and white oversized linoleum squares.

A freckly, beige-brown man stepped from behind the bar, smiling. "Hey, now. Ha' y'all during?" He wore a short-sleeved white shirt with a dark cowboy tie and a holstered gun on a belt.

"All right now." Ed shook both of the man's hands at the same time. Matt followed. Celeste nodded and beelined for the jukebox—she hadn't heard a note of music except church music and freedom songs for weeks. She scanned the selections. Rhythm and blues and deep blues. No Frank Sinatra here, no Dinah Washington, either. Wilamena would turn on her high heels and stride out the door. Shuck might handle it for a while, but he'd grow restless with all that deep blues. She'd left her book-bag and change purse in the backseat of the car. Ed Jolivette brought her two quarters and she pushed buttons until her finger hurt. "Gypsy Woman" flowed into her like an elixir, smooth and knowing, the words like her own personal anthem now. She walked to the bar with Curtis Mayfield's high sweet voice filling her ears and the backbeat releasing her hips, her head moving from side to side, her lips falling right into the words.

"Otis, this is Celeste Tyree, working with us for the summer." Matt barely glanced at her, then drank from a huge tumbler of ice water.

"Otis Gilliam. Pleased to make your acquaintance, Miss Tyree." He shoved a glass of water in her direction over his homemade bar, nodding his head.

Celeste sat on a barstool. "Mr. Gilliam."

"Oh, now, you call me Otis." He grinned. "Please, call me Otis, anytime, anywhere."

Celeste drank the water and eyed Otis's pistol. This must be the bucket of blood the old people talked about a long time ago. Then she remembered Sophie Lewis's father and how he sat on his front porch with a shotgun to protect his house. There was something coming into clarity here and it wasn't what it was supposed to be. Real men wear guns. Nonviolence had a boundary, a limit. Ah, yes, she thought, if a man had something he wanted to protect, without question he'd better be armed. Would nonviolence ever get them where they needed to go?

"Man, you better give us something real to drink. I know you got some gin back there even if you did make it in your bathtub." Matt's hand slid his water glass back across the bar. "I need a real drink."

"Cain't. 'Gainst the law." Otis gave Matt a serious look, winked at Celeste.

At the Royal Gardens, the long bar mirror and the mood lights reflected an assortment of liquors and ingredients that looked like a festival of alcohol, labels from Ireland, Kentucky, Canada, France. Shuck joked that his good stuff would kill a typical street wino. There wasn't a single bottle on the home-style dining room buffet behind Otis. What kind of bar was this?

Ed stood. "If the white man don't get you, the black man surely will. Let's go." He had a stony unreadable look on his face.

Celeste looked at Ed and Matt like they'd lost their minds, hoped this routine would soon end. She didn't move from her barstool.

"You let the young lady put money in the box and you gon leave before her records finish playing? You ain't got no manners. Neither one of you." Otis folded his arms across his chest.

"Thank you, Otis." Chuck Jackson swept her into "Any Day Now," the big bass drum vibrating right through her. She was just about as happy as she'd been in weeks.

Matt stood. "You the one. Break out the gin and tonic. We know you pay-ing off that sheriff. This young lady been in Pineyville for weeks. Ain't seen a drink, a television, even heard a radio. You know what that place is like."

"Pineyville? Lord, have Mercy. That's a shame. Sending a fine young woman like this to that godforsaken town? Y'all crazy. And Sheriff Trotter down there giving everybody hives. Oh, she need a real drink all right. Probably need two or three. Do it for her. Not for you two knot heads." Otis looked directly in her eyes, all robust charm. "What would you like, Miss?" He gave a little half bow. "Pineyville? You shoulda told 'em no."

"She's bad. She can handle it." Matt sucked air.

"Gin and tonic with lots of ice." Her mouth watered even as she laughed. She heard the joking seriousness of what he said. Part of it must have been his usual ritual and part of it real sympathy for her being stuck out there in Pineyville with a sheriff no Negro person had a kind word for. She didn't want to think about not being here in this red cinderblock place with its homemade bar and real jukebox blaring. It was a heavenly interlude and not a Bible in sight. And it was cool. Too soon she'd be back in Pineyville.

Otis reached under the bar and pulled out a bottle of gin and made three tall gin and tonics. The icy glass breathed onto her face like a chill wind off a frozen lake.

Matt and Ed sat again and took healthy swigs of their drinks.

Otis gave her the sideways look. "Where you from, Miss Tyree?"

She sipped. "Detroit. Please, call me Celeste." The tonic was too sweet, like every cold drink she'd had in Mississippi.

"I knew you wadn't from 'round here," Otis said, satisfied.

"My daddy owns a bar, too." She gulped now, wished she could take a thermos of the stuff back to Freshwater Road. Pralines from Sophie Lewis, gin and tonics from Otis. If she borrowed right, maybe she could make it through the summer.

"Got me a ally." Otis slapped the handle of his gun. "This young lady knows how hard it is to keep a bunch of wild Negroes patted down." He swaggered, nodding to her, teaching. "Now, this Miss'sippi's dry. Good business for someone like me." He reared back, adjusted his gun belt. Otis Gilliam was a saloon-keeper like in the old wild west of the movies.

"Yeah, it's been good to my daddy." The way she said *daddy,* she knew, made men want to have daughters when they notoriously wanted sons. She drank her gin and tonic. "Dry?"

"Like during Prohibition." Ed said. His body kept time gently to the music.

She glanced at the door. "If it's dry, what are we doing sitting here drinking?"

"I told you, he pays off the Sheriff." Matt said. "Hey, man, when's the next payment due?

Otis deadpanned his face toward her. "I'm gon' ignore him. You see, you can't just walk in a bar anywhere in Miss'sippi. Oh no. Not in Miss'sippi." He dropped the second syllable. "You out there in the boondocks. Ain't nowheres to get a drink out there." He made it sound like it was miles away, out west somewhere, in another state across plains and mountains. "Les' you in somebody's shack drinking out a jar, dipping out a crock. You in a different country here."

"Come to Louisiana. Got enough liquor there for everybody." Ed swilled his gin and tonic and pushed his glass forward.

Celeste searched through the too-sweet tonic for the gin. "You got any lemon or lime?"

"Girl, where you think you at?" Otis chided her and got a shriveled lemon out of his kitchen model refrigerator. "'Course I got lemon." He cut it into paper-thin slices and put them on a small white plate.

Celeste put one slice in her glass and started eating another, her head bopping slightly to the beat. The tart lemon tasted clean, cut the sweetness of her drink. She chewed the rind. Otis stared at her. "They not feeding you out there?"

"Damn, girl." Matt's head moved side to side to the bumping rhythm. "Maybe we should've gone by Short Sixth Street to feed you."

"Don't want to get scurvy." She laughed at herself going through the slices like they were candy-coated. She hadn't had an orange or a lemon in weeks. "What's Short Sixth Street?"

Ed caught her in the mirror, his face seeing her and turning from her at the same time. "Just a street. There's a black restaurant over there."

He said "black" like Ramona. A restaurant Negro people could sit in. She hadn't been in one since Jackson.

"See them chairs?" Otis waved his hand towards the jangle of chairs. "I bet you come in here, took a look, and thought I had to be crazy." He waited for her answer.

"I sure wondered about them." She played along. "Didn't know if I was coming to get a drink or to get my hair done on somebody's back porch in Black Bottom."

"What you know about some Black Bottom?" Total disbelief on Otis's face, his head going backwards a few inches from its normal position.

"I know where it used to be." She'd heard all about Paradise Valley, Black Bottom, and Hastings Street—the old Negro section of Detroit, on the East Side. Shuck had certainly warned against her and Billy even thinking about going over there. He knew teenagers came up with wild notions, testy things to do to just to prove they could.

"You don't know nothing about no Black Bottom." Otis talked to her like a parent might.

"I bet if you come to Detroit, I could take you over there." Celeste wiggled her head and smiled, proud she knew something that he thought she shouldn't know.

"Yo' *daddy* would take me. Not you. Anyway, already been. When it was the jumpingest place on earth. Been some of everywhere." Otis wiped their water rings from the bar. He was a countrified Shuck. Shuck always talked about the Flame Show Bar and Dinah Washington. She felt comfortable, spinning on her stool to face Matt. "I played 'Kansas City' just for you." The gin was creeping into her brain, and her tongue began a thick and lazy flop in her mouth.

"Can't wait." Matt looked at her in the bar mirror, sizing her up all over again. Ed eyed the multicolored chairs, said dryly, "They're different all right." Celeste wondered if he'd even heard the intervening conversation.

"You can't talk. You from New Orleans. Whole place is different. Rats big as cats running around, and dead bodies floating in the cemeteries." Otis leaned against the bar with his two hands. Celeste wondered if the whole thing might not topple over. Maybe New Orleans wasn't such a good-time place after all. Rats and dead bodies floating?

Ed laughed. "Only when it rains."

When Jerry Butler sang "For Your Precious Love," Celeste sat there, elbow to elbow with Ed Jolivette, hoping he'd ask her to dance. He didn't. The song sank into her in a a downpour of need, the husky voice as dark and strong as Ed's face. She dropped her head; she didn't want him to catch her eyes in the mirror, afraid she couldn't hide her desire to be close to him. She was afraid she might put her head on the shoulder of a man she'd met two hours before. She wanted the record to play again.

"And it rains all the damn time. Now, you, you from Detroit. A *real* big-city girl." Otis folded his arms across his chest again as if to say New Orleans didn't qualify and spoke in a tight-lipped, high-toned manner, the handle of his gun ready as a carpenter's tool, waiting to be swung into action. "Bet you never seen a Negro out his mind on corn?"

"Nope." Celeste went along at first confusing corn with corn on the cob, not getting it, then it focused in her mind: corn liquor.

Otis smiled, showing the two gold incisors in his mouth. "Lot of Negroes round here can't 'ford to drink bottled whiskey, so they get near drunk on corn then come through here for they nightcap." He'd gone back to his normal speaking. "Corn make you crazy. Laughin' one minute, tearing up the place the next. That's why I got them chairs. Cheap."

"No telling what's in that stuff." Ed's face went serious.

Matt laughed. "Aw, Otis, you know you like those chairs. You probably got the same thing in your living room. You probably got a barrel of corn back there, too."

Otis laughed big. "I do not." He slapped the bar with his beefy, freckled hand. "That's what I mean, Ed. See, you can have a conversation with Ed. You can't do nothing with that Negro." He nodded over to Matt. "How a Negro gon go pay they hard-won money for something to drink, and you don't even know what's in it, and you know the man selling it just as soon see you dead as standing there?" Otis filled the space behind the bar. "See, Negroes, even after all that's gone on, they still trust the white man too much. Not me. I never let 'em see my back. But you can't tell Negroes nothing. They keep drinking that corn."

"Probably peed in it." Matt examined his gin and tonic, holding his glass up to the light. "Wooweee, Otis, this gin's kinda yellow."

"What you looking at, boy?" Otis sounded like a southern white man when he said "boy." "That gin come from a sealed bottle. Sealed by the gov'ment. All these bottles got seals." He pointed under the bar to his stock.

"They wouldn't pee in it, would they?" Celeste wasn't sure if they were joking again.

"Never know." Otis swiped a rag across the bar and fixed them another drink.

"That seal's a tax. Nothing to do with what's in it." Ed drifted away, taking the fun with him. She felt his consciousness reaching out, to keep them from going over the line from self-mockery to self-hatred.

"They don't make two batches of corn, one for us, and one for them." She imagined ragged white men stirring gray liquid in vats out in the Appalachian woods and a beat-down Negro coming to buy, looking at the ground when they filled his jug.

"Don't want you drinking from the same fountain, using the same toilet, sitting on the same seat, hugging the same woman. What you think?" Otis put a toothpick in the corner of his mouth. "I wouldn't put nothing from no white man nowheres near my mouth. You hear me?" He slapped the bar again. Celeste's glass bounced.

Matt reached down the bar for a New Orleans *Times-Picayune*. "Otis been working with us since we came into Mississippi. He knows."

Celeste wondered if he could draw his gun fast like a cowboy in a movie. The gin picked up speed in her veins, flushed her body, made the music seep deeper inside her, sent it rippling down her spine. She shimmied on the bar stool, one foot tapping on the curved chrome footrest. She hadn't felt this good in a long time, sitting at Otis Gilliam's homemade bar with his old jukebox thumping and Matt and Ed on either side. Johnny Ace sang "Pledging My Love."

"You play that?" Otis screwed up his face at her. "You know that Negro killed himself playing Russian roulette? What a Negro doing sitting around playing Russian roulette? No telling what really happened."

The deeper-than-blues dirge quieted them. Celeste's eyes burned and she lowered her head. *"Forever, my darling, our love will be true..."* His voice was the haunt, not the words. It was the loneliest sounding voice she'd ever heard. She didn't know why she'd played it. It was some old collective memory song, a haunting thing whose strains never left you once you heard it. She couldn't even remember where she first heard it. Probably somewhere with Shuck. Maybe it had been on the old jukebox at the Royal Gardens, but it wasn't Shuck's kind of song.

"Kansas City" brought them back, cleared the air, pounded the red walls with rhythm.

"Things are changing," she said. Even Shuck talked about how things had changed in Detroit from the time of the big riot back in the forties, always talking about how she could do anything she wanted to do in this life.

"Changing? Drinking from the same water fountain? What's that do?" Ed pointed to his head while his eyes gazed into the interminable craggy cave of historical misfortune. "It's too late, we're already gone."

Celeste wondered if that was the gin talking, or did he have the gift of prophecy? Could he really believe that—and if he did, what was he doing in the movement? She couldn't spar, damage for damage, with anyone from the south. Maybe the gin got inside him and balled up all his bad experiences. But he wasn't talking about the dreadful confrontations. He meant a memory of death, the whole experience of slavery and its residuals. Neglect. Living in too small spaces. Curvature of the soul. Did he mean there was no repair? No hope?

"You don't believe that." She said it praying he didn't and wishing they'd stop this conversation.

Ed turned away from her. "If corn liquor doesn't make you crazy, all the stuff you can't do down here sure *will*. I'm not even talking about white against Negro." She tried to ease away from the challenge Ed had just flung onto the bar.

"You right." Otis dropped ice cubes with his bare hands into their drinks. "When it comes to some things, everybody in the same boat. Whole lot of Bible going on."

She wished he'd pour more gin into her glass, she felt dryness coming into her mouth. "White people bother you?"

"They always botherin' somebody." Otis sounded like Shuck. No rancor. That's just the way things were. A night man. Night men were father confessors, Buddhas in the temple, men who listened a lot and saw it all. Exemptions. They would kill, Negro or white, whoever crossed the line. The gun said it all.

"Keep on Pushing" came on loud and jumping.

"We supposed to just wake up one morning like it didn't happen?" Ed slid off his stool as if running from the thoughts drumming in his head. Something chasing him. She thought he was going to ask her to dance this time. He didn't even look back. But, he said something she heard loud and clear: *like it didn't happen.*

She watched Ed moving in the mirror. With his arm out as if he was carrying a staff or an umbrella, he did a high-stepping dance, moving around the perimeter of the dance floor, between the tables, all over the room. She swiveled to watch him, aching to join him, to release her own demons in a dance.

"You can't take that out of him. Don't even try." Otis read her thoughts, spoke to her like he knew her.

What was it that couldn't be taken out of him? The dance was beautiful.

Why take it out of him? Then she knew Otis didn't mean the dance but what was under it.

"He's one of them Creole muthafuckers." Matt whispered in a huffy voice.

Ed seemed to lead a line of invisible people who he turned and bowed to without missing a step. Leaning to one side and then the other, prancing a strut, swaggering, bending the music to his rhythm, he moved with a furious dignity, his head thrown back, his eyes nearly closed.

Celeste watched. Creole was a mixture. He didn't look in the least bit mixed, not mixed with white anyway. Maybe Indian. Maybe somewhere back there, something else. She glanced at her own darkened face in the mirror.

"From New Orleans." Matt leaned in to her. "That's a second line. They do that behind street funerals. A band plays and people dance. After the body's buried."

If that was a second line, what was the first? The trip to the cemetery? The band? He looked so free, she wanted to join him out there, second lining, but felt glued to the barstool. Something intimate and private about the way Ed moved through the air.

Otis read her. "Go ahead. Ain't nobody in here but us."

"In the Still of the Night" came on the jukebox before she moved off the stool. Ed walked over and took her hand. She stopped breathing as they slid onto the big black and white linoleum squares, fluid, like roller-skating, a breeze on her cheeks. But they were dancing tight, clinging body to body, feet barely moving, thighs clamped together, his arm down at his side clutching her hand. His heart still pumped the second line. He smelled of crisscrossing rivers. The room fell away, went black behind her closed eyes. He whispered, "Sugar," in her ear and she pushed her pelvis into him, felt him respond.

Spinning slowly on her own away from him, the red cinder blocks melted into wide brush strokes, slashes of red-orange paint on a giant canvas. Her dress flared, and she knew that the shape of her legs and buttocks showed. She moved her hips to the music and saw Ed watching her. She dreamed she was Marpessa Dawn dancing in the streets of Rio. Or it was a basement party in Detroit with dim lights, old furniture, and spiked punch. Hard boys and chiffon girls, afraid to go all the way, kissing until their lips cracked and peeled to rawness, rubbing each other to the corner of madness through their high school dress-up clothes. *If you do it to yourself, it'll drive you crazy.*

"You sure from Detroit." He brought her back to him just as she was feeling too far away.

The hard pocket of lonesomeness she'd been carrying around softened. The ever-present nagging fear released her. So many thoughts of death, jaws clenched at night for fear shots would be fired through the house again. The terror of Mississippi had tunneled into her. She felt worn down and lifted up at the same time.

"I think you got to come to New Orleans, chère." He made it sound like an inevitable direction, like this moment created a door that they stood in with New Orleans on the other side. She had blue sky and white clouds in her ears, the music thumping and her breath sinking into his.

17

But for the presence of the northern rabble-rouser, Celeste Tyree, a Pineyville local eavesdropping on the proceedings inside the church on these summer evenings would have heard Reverend Singleton teaching freedom directly from the pages of the Bible with a rawboned intensity. When he closed his book, Celeste opened hers—the Mississippi State Constitution and the One Man, One Vote study materials. Her lessons centered on the clauses in the constitution's 1890 text that had brought voting rights for Negroes to an end. She taught her small group about poll taxes, grandfather clauses, and literacy tests, the legal obstacles they sought to remove once and for all.

Celeste, Matt, and Ed made it to the church from their outing in Hattiesburg just as Reverend Singleton began the Bible-study portion of the voter registration class. Celeste ran for the outhouse. The greasy food from Miss Grace's Café on Short Sixth Street where they'd stopped to eat after drinking far too many gin and tonics at Otis's red cinderblock joint—it all kicked high. She threw up, lurching over the black hole, avoiding a look into the well of corrosion and quicklime as the last soft light of evening shafted through the wood slats and the small window. She lit a kerosene lamp, replacing the protector glass carefully, turned the flame down low. Her stomach felt queasy but no new wave of vomit came. She stopped at the spigot on the side of the church, already dreading a late night trip to Mrs. Owens's outhouse, but so thirsty she thought she'd never make it through the class without the water. She splashed it on her neck and face, head thundering as she leaned over. *Shuck said don't let me see you drunk.*

That meant don't get drunk. He never said, "Don't drink." Alcohol flowed like water on campus, but she'd never been drunk before. She dug around in her book-bag for a piece of stale Juicy Fruit, which she chewed and sucked nearly dry before coming in the side door of the church to take her place up front with Reverend Singleton.

Matt and Ed, cool and composed, had taken seats in the back as representatives of One Man, One Vote to size up Celeste's voter education class. In the car coming from Hattiesburg, they'd decided to ask Mrs. Owens if they could sleep in their sleeping bags on her parlor floor rather than risk traveling to McComb, their next stop, in the dead of night. Celeste imagined inviting Ed to sleep in her bed, but nothing would've been more out of the question in Mrs. Owens's house. She'd never do anything of the kind in Shuck's house, either. Something unmanageable had been let loose in Hattiesburg, her pent-up loneliness, her rebuke of the clamped-down world she was living in, so starkly opposite to the freewheeling life of Ann Arbor. Now she had to tuck that freedom taste away again.

Celeste slowly got into the rhythm of the class and only had the slightest feeling of being off-balance. She taught *Williams v. Mississippi,* the 1898 case that sealed the fate of Negro voters in the south when the United States Supreme Court decided in favor of the State of Mississippi. The rest of the southern states followed Mississippi's lead. A county clerk had the power to select a passage from the state constitution for a potential registrant to interpret. A black man was given a difficult technical passage. A white man, a simple sentence. It was the end of Negroes voting in the south. By Freedom Summer, very little had changed.

In the course of each class, Celeste laid out the sections of the constitution that would more than likely appear on a voter registration test. The sample tests from One Man, One Vote had questions ranging from extremely difficult interpretations of constitutional clauses to ridiculously obvious ruses meant to stump people. A question might ask how many grains were in a cup of sand, or how many bubbles in a bar of soap. These inconsistencies in testing procedures made some Negro folks the more determined to pass whatever test was put in front of them, and made others apply themselves only in a half-hearted, oh-what's-the-use manner. For many, it meant they'd rather not try at all.

Dolly Johnson attended the voter education class regularly by now. To Celeste's eye, she'd undertaken a broader personal transformation, going from a woman who wore low-cut dresses and tight-fitting slacks to more conservative styles. Dolly was evolving. Still, if Labyrinth was the apple, Dolly was surely the tree. At close to thirty years old (as Celeste found out from Etta Singleton), she didn't look a day older than Celeste, and she had the same feisty spirit as her daughter. Mississippi hammered women into a tight-lipped passivity, but not Dolly. Even Geneva Owens camouflaged her spunk and guarded her speech and demeanor most of the time. She'd survived a rugged life on her own after the death of her husband. She'd earned the right to be on the earth with a voice. But Mrs. Owens stayed quiet, until she decided to let her voice be heard in her will to vote. After making that decision, Mrs. Owens proceeded cautiously. Dolly spoke her mind at the slightest provocation. About the voter registration test, Dolly intimated that her good relationship with Mr. Percival Dale might offer her a leg up. Of course, this was exactly the wrong thing to suggest in front of the class, but it didn't stop her.

Mr. Landau brought the message of the Deacons for Defense and Justice to the meetings. He lived near Pineyville, but worked in Louisiana at Crown Zellerbach. He regularly went across the state line to attend the meetings of the Deacons, and he carried a rifle in his truck. The Deacons promised to defend themselves against any marauding whites, to protect their lives, their family's lives, their property, and the lives of civil rights workers who came to their towns. It didn't matter to them if the whites had on uniforms or sheets. Freshwater Road had been used as target practice in the middle of the night, the very kind of thing the Deacons for Defense and Justice defended against. Mr. Landau never would've allowed that, he eagerly reminded everyone in the church. He created a stir whenever he spoke. There were those who mumbled their agreement with the Deacons (still short of joining them or of starting a group in Pineyville) and those who stayed in lock-step with Reverend Singleton's strict adherence to nonviolence. The only self-defense was in spiritual and actual nonviolence. In Celeste's mind, the spiritual part required the greater work. A person might live a long time with a heart full of violent hatred, sing God's praises in church with vengeance and retribution just on the tip of the tongue. Reverend Singleton admired Mr. Landau and feared him, too. He thought of the Deacons as Louisiana Negroes walking a thin line that bordered on crazy. Wild Negroes, he called them.

Celeste believed in her heart of hearts that "Wild Negroes" were just what they needed, but she couldn't say that to Reverend Singleton.

Celeste couldn't imagine Shuck doing any violence to anyone first but she knew darned well he'd never walk away if he was attacked or, worse, roll into a ball on the ground. If he did walk, it would only be to get his gun. There was a code on the streets and without teaching it in words, he lived it. Celeste wobbled on nonviolence, worked hard to keep the principle focused in her heart. But she knew, too, that if she was alone, walking on a Pineyville street, and an individual assaulted her, that person might get a response and she didn't really know what that response would be. She felt very clearly a hardening of her anger over the situation in Mississippi. She also knew real fear for the first time in her life. She continually pushed it down, sat on it, buried it, but still, it was there.

Along with Dolly Johnson and Mr. Landau, Sister Mobley, Geneva Owens, and Etta Singleton rounded out the class. Mrs. Owens and Mrs. Singleton were the best readers in the group. Others came and went, taking it all in, nodding and rustling around in nervousness. This was a big step to take for people who had been denied the vote since the end of Reconstruction, for people who lost their jobs if they even whispered about voting, whose homes were bombed if they walked in the front door of the courthouse. They had no memory of the meager, long-ago days when they could vote. The people remembered being told by the registrar of voters that voting wasn't for them, that they should stay out of whites folks' business no matter how many times they tried to register. They had clear memories, too, of the men who'd been shot, whose homes had been burned to the ground when they pushed the issue of voting farther than white folks allowed.

The Mississippi constitution gave everyone a headache but they read and reread it. They studied it and they studied the United States Constitution, too. Celeste grilled them and Reverend Singleton quoted Bible passages that helped them stay with it. He knew his people well—he knew that he could slide a whole lot of new food onto a plate that had been greased by the Bible. It was a long class that night, interminable to Celeste, who fought the residues of the alcohol's effect and who never stopped feeling Ed Jolivette's body close to hers on Otis Gilliam's linoleum-squared dance floor. Behind her talk of voting rights and grandfather clauses, she conjured ways for the night to never end, for Ed to decline going on to

McComb in the morning, to stay there in Pineyville with her. She knew it wouldn't happen but she allowed herself the dream anyway.

Matt unloaded both sleeping bags out of the trunk and helped Mrs. Owens from the car on Freshwater Road. He'd been quiet on the trip back from Hattiesburg and nearly sullen after the class on the ride to the house. He'd seen with his own eyes how Celeste had danced with Ed. Celeste hoped it wouldn't influence his report on her project. Mrs. Owens chatted away in the car, grateful to have both men staying the night in her man-less house. When she closed the front door behind her and Matt, Ed and Celeste took off for the pay phone to check in with the Jackson office.

Celeste scrunched down in the front seat watching Ed on the phone. She checked the main street for headlights, movements. The Pearl River County Administration building and Sheriff Trotter's office were three short blocks away. She hoped Sheriff Trotter and his deputies had turned in for the night.

Her eyes came back to Ed, tall and leaning, skin nearly as dark as the night. He couldn't have looked more different from J.D., but something about him reminded her of J.D. regardless. Danger? J.D. loved to roar his motorcycle over those country roads even when they were wet and slick, hanging on to the edge, pushing it as far as he could, snuggling up real close to death. Then there was his pursuit of her; she hadn't thought about that kind of risk until Shuck had nailed her on the subject of Negro women with white men. J.D. never spoke of how it might've thrilled him to swim hard against the tide. She too felt that rush walking the campus with him, seeing the heads turn now and then, seeing even a scowl or two and sometimes a tight-lipped smile.

Ed stood there with one elbow on the metal platform holding the pay phone, open to her. He was no back-facing man. Another daredevil, but with a calm voice denting the quiet night. Mississippi made the motorcycle rides and dating a white boy feel senseless. What was it for? Personal excite-ment, a high like a ride on a roller coaster? This high was defying guns and beatings to stand up in the face of history. But was there still an adrenaline rush? Maybe that, too.

"Ed Jolivette checkin' in." Accent falling on the *Jol.* "Pineyville. All right, then." She loved the music in his way of speaking, thinking her own voice must sound very flat with its midwestern clip and drag.

"We going into McComb tomorrow." No fear, not in his voice anyway.

Death defying. Ed sounded generous, unruffled but wary at the same time. He stood perfectly still in his bibbed denim overalls and a light shirt. Any white man with a gun could shoot him dead right before her eyes. At least she could duck down to the floor of the car. She scanned the darkness beyond the circle of the convenience light.

"Everything else fine here. Project's going good. Saw it tonight." He put in the good word for her, though she wasn't convinced it was going all that well. Voter education needed speeding up, that's for sure.

With no exhausts from cars and trucks, no smells of cigarettes and cigars, no tumultuous breathing locals, the mawkish aroma of the magnolias lining the main street of "downtown" Pineyville clung to the night air like a cheap perfume. Just half a block from the pay phone was the stingy drugstore, the only place she'd spent any money since coming to Pineyville. Each time she'd gone in there, the straw-haired white woman, red-faced and plump, sat in the breeze of a whipping table fan behind a glass case displaying faded peach shelf paper and an assortment of odds and ends: toothpaste, Band-Aids, mercurochrome, hydrogen peroxide. The chewing gum and candy bars were arranged in designs on the top of the display case with a slight covering of orange dust. She kept the Kotex in the back. When Celeste had gone in, the woman smiled an empty smile that matched the coldness in her eyes. When Celeste left, the woman called her "y'all" and invited her to come back soon.

Ed turned the car around in the gas station. "Pineyville's so bad, black people better not even laugh when they walk down the street."

"Not much to laugh about anyway." She said. "It's not safe out here this time of night." Then, "You say *black*."

"Negro is their word. Black is mine." It sounded like a challenge, like he was trying it out on her to see where she was with it.

The thickness of the day's journey had thinned down to the two of them. She wanted to lean into him the way she had on the dance floor, rest her head on his chest.

"You know what running drunk is?" Ed smiled.

She checked behind them, to the front, and to the dark sides of the road. She hoped he wasn't going to lecture her about drinking too much in Hattiesburg. It seemed forever ago even though it had only been a couple of hours, long enough for the night to go from soft to deep black. She wanted him to find a place, some cluster of trees big enough to camouflage them while they pressed themselves together, rolled naked on a bed of pine needles, picking up scalded orange dust in their hair, in the creases of their elbows and knees. "Never heard of it."

"I got so drunk one night, my legs started running down Canal Street. I grabbed onto light poles and swung myself around to slow down. I was headed for the ferry to go home to Algiers. Thank God the ferry was at the dock, or I woulda run right into the Mississippi River." He glanced over at her.

She didn't want to talk about being drunk, but she had an image of what he said and it made her smile. He hadn't had as much to drink as she. But he hadn't been trapped in Pineyville for weeks either. "Algiers? Algiers is in Africa."

"Cross the river, where I grew up." His dark face glowed. "I go to a place in New Orleans got a man with two peg legs who stands on his hands on a table and tap dances on the ceiling." He glanced sideways at her to see her response.

"You're exaggerating." She laughed.

"No, chère, and that ain't the half of it. You ever hear of Plaquemines? Leander Perez country in Louisiana. They got a special prison for civil rights workers. Old French fort full of snakes and dried bones. Make Mississippi look like a vacation." He spoke as if he knew the place intimately.

She looked at him. "You been there?"

"Oh, yeah." He stared at the blacktop, the front lights of the car reaching ahead of them. "Two years ago. We tried to grow up a voter registration project down there. Never been so scared in my life. Couldn't hardly find a piece of dry ground to even sit on, and you better not go to sleep. We ended up hunched over on some stones left from the fort. Slept in shifts."

She didn't want to think about it but he'd put the picture in her mind, a snake-infested swamp prison with a bayou floor. Why did he tell her this? The guys in the movement swapped stories, one-upped each other when they sat down to drink and relax. She'd seen that in Jackson. Like guys in a war movie talking about the taking of this hill or that town. They spoke reverently of the injuries sustained by fellow fighters. The battles changed them forever. Ed was bringing her into his inner world talking about Plaquemines. It must be his nightmare place, the setting and time he'd never forget. One more nightmare, and she might not make it.

As they neared Freshwater Road, Ed turned off the headlights. There wasn't another car on the two-lane. The darkness of the night was astounding.

Her whole body sighed in disappointment when he turned into Freshwater Road. She had a thought to ask him to go back to Hattiesburg, go back to Otis's and finish dancing the night away. He parked near the remains of the house across the way, some distance from the front of Mrs. Owens's house. Stars like jacks, the moon a thickening arc that had been tucked away in a toy box of clouds. No rolling around on the earth making love in the pines. They were quiet. No lights down Freshwater Road, and it wasn't yet midnight.

"Other places are better." He paused and checked behind them. "Natchitoches, Evangeline, Vermillion, St. John the Baptist. Lot of places to see besides Plaquemines." The words rolled off his tongue like warm honey off the tip of a tablespoon. He enticed her with these place names, which called to mind bunches of blood-red flowers growing along the side of a road. "I take you to the bayous. Cypress trees grow out of the water, nets made of Spanish moss."

The words poured out of his mouth in a rush. She knew then that these words were a cover for his fear. He wanted to say words that sounded far away from this place, sweet story-sounding words. He'd been to that French fort in the swamps, and he'd made it out. A good ending. But with so much work still to be done, he might not make it all the way through. The aura that surrounded the volunteers was fear, shining like a halo. Good fear, walking-in-God's path fear.

"You come to New Orleans, we'll run on the levee." He'd captured her but showed no hubris, no swagger. "Better than running drunk."

"You're right about that." She was floating downstream in his river on a barge loaded with indigo-dyed cotton and peg-legged men who tap danced on the sky. "What'd they say in Jackson? You leaving tomorrow?" She knew she had to stay and do what she'd come there to do, but she didn't want him to leave her all alone in Pineyville. Promised God she'd never get drunk again if He'd make Ed Jolivette stay or take her with him.

"We got to check on McComb." He slumped down in the car, his liquid hands draped over the steering wheel. "Somebody threw a bomb in the voter education center. We got to stop by there and rev people up again. Scared some away."

She knew about McComb. Herbert Lee, Louis Allen. Dead. The dark unnamed. People beaten for working in voter registration. Children born of numb-mouthed parents, jailed for months, singing insane songs to stay sane. Bombs thrown into churches. Black smoke rising, leaping licking flames on a crusade of destruction. Fire on the cross. He knew where he was going, and knew he might not come back. No time for holding on.

"You gon come to New Orleans?" He said it again as if he needed to make appointments for *after* Mississippi to get through it.

She gave a short laugh. "If we live that long." They sat for a while in the car, slouched down in their seats, she over by the passenger door, window rolled down, slapping a mosquito on her calf. Still behind the wheel, his long legs sprawled over toward her side, his right knee crooked and touching her thigh like a heated rock. The car sat tilting into a shallow gulley separating the weed-choked vacant lot from the road. Celeste watched Mrs. Owens's house for signs of life. No lights came on.

Massive quiet coming now. Cicadas and crickets. Little eavesdrops of sound. Ed smiled, the space between his front teeth making him look like a boy who could spit for a city block with his teeth closed. "Mosquitoes like you. Must be sweet."

"Wish they'd find somebody else to chew on." She slid her hand into his. He squeezed it, his hand firm, the pressure sure.

He took his wire-rimmed glasses from his front pocket and set them on top of the dashboard. That was the move that propelled her toward him over the Naugahyde seat. She pressed herself against him until the only thing between them was a dream of moving water. She felt his body against hers, needing a rest from thoughts of death. He knew it—that's why he'd parked away from the house. The mass of loneliness inside her pushed outward, making her feel like a needy child. *Take me with you, when are you coming back?* Memories of standing by windows in solitary shafts of light waiting for the Cadillac, waiting for Shuck. Loneliness in the absent-mother world.

When are you coming back? The kids at school ask me where's my mother. I'm gonna start telling them she's dead.

Don't you do that. You hear me?

Ed unbuttoned her dress and kissed her humid skin, pushed the straps of her bra off her shoulders, lifted her breasts out of her bra, and stroked them until they swelled and quivered. He stirred the car moving to the middle of the seat, then unsnapped the straps of his overalls and pulled them down to his ankles. "Sit on me, sugar." His voice came from a hol-

low deep inside, his lips barely forming the words. She straddled him. He
guided her down slowly, his smooth hands around her waist until she felt
his full warmth reaching up inside her. He felt like dense morning mist
on a wide river softening everything in its path. The night and Freshwater
Road surrounded them. She didn't care that they were in a funky car on
a dusty road in a backwater town in southern Mississippi. She was glad
to be there even as the car seat burned her knees, the seam of fake leather
creasing to the bone.

She leaned over his shoulder and grabbed the seatback, then dug her
knees into the seat to brace herself. Sweat ran down her face and chest as
she began to move. She looked quickly through the back window and saw
no lights, no movement. They were safe for now. A moment. She checked
the house again to be sure no lights had come on, checked as far down
the road as the Tucker house. Nothing. He moaned into her throat, then
brought her face in front of his. She tasted his sweet salty sweat and probed
inside his mouth with her tongue, lingering on his lips and kissing him
hard then soft then hard again. Her dress fell away. He unhooked her bra,
bringing the straps down her arms and completely off. She smoothed her
hands over every part of his skin, as if to trace a memory for the hungry
nights ahead.

He laid her down on the car seat, opened her legs and kissed her thighs,
then ran his tongue up the middle of her body, his lips stopping on her
stomach, on her ribs, her neck and finally her mouth. He put himself inside
her and moved gently. She hugged him hard, stifling a cry tinged with
laughter that she buried in his chest.

"What's so funny?" He lifted his weight, his eyes the only lights on
earth.

"I'm not in Mississippi." Her head pressed into the car door, crooking
her neck. She tried to maneuver down. He held her still for a moment. She
didn't know how he'd arranged his long legs and didn't care. He sat up and
pulled her into him, taking quick looks in both directions up and down
Freshwater Road.

"No sugar, you with me and I'm sure not in Mississippi." He held her
close for a long quiet moment, his heart beating in her ear like the paddles
of a steamer.

A quarter moon traced in the sky. There was a sea of anxious night, too ominous for sitting in cars, talking in low tones. A slight salty breeze crept up from the Gulf of Mexico, rustled around, and quickly disappeared. She wished she could tackle it to the ground, make it stay.

"I'm sick of this heat. I need a real bath." She thought maybe she'd run away, run down to Sophie Lewis's house and take a bath, sit on the sofa and listen to music, pretend this whole time was something she'd conjured up while she stared out those big shuttered windows.

"Be careful you don't hurt Mrs. Owens's feelings, now." Ed chastised her.

"I won't. I was thinking of Sophie Lewis's house down near Carriere. You met her?"

"Sure haven't. But I heard of her."

"You oughta see that house. Never seen anything like it."

"These little old houses lean to the side because of the weight that's on them." He brought her back to the here and now. "Lot of people see this place, know what's going on, but they don't take the step to come here. You did."

"You did, too." She talked low, soft, sorting through the streaks of reasons why she'd come to Mississippi. "It was more than a step, Mr. Jolivette. It was a long bad train ride."

"Yeah, but I was born in it." His neck was arched, his head resting on the seat back.

She sat up, pulled on her panties, pulled up her dress to cover her breasts, and leaned her head back by his side, her legs heading toward the passenger door so he could rest his across the front of the car. He needed room. Ed was quiet, both of them staring at the ceiling of the car as if it held a starry night.

"Lot of speakers on campus talking about the movement. I heard them. I needed to get out of there." She closed her eyes, counting the days since her last period. She was safe. She had absorbed the lesson, taken it to heart. She'd not been with anyone since J.D. and that was a year ago now, but still she counted the days every month out of habit. The days ticked off inside her like a clock that was a part of her being and had to be paid attention to no matter what else was going on. She never wanted to see Middleman again. There would be no more trips to River Rouge.

"How long before you think you're ready to go to the courthouse?" Ed brought her life raft to shore. Back to the real deal.

"I guess a couple more weeks. You know about the Deacons?" Fear trickling in.

"Sure 'nough." He said nothing else.

She wondered if that was a tactical silence.

They stayed still for a long while, both of them teetering on the edge of sleep. She listened so hard she thought her ears would crack and inside that listening, she felt peace.

The night heat spread the smell of their lovemaking all through the car. She imagined it smoothing out over Freshwater Road like the smell of night jasmine, like the faint scent surrounding the stands of long-needled pines. She'd better check the seat before they went inside. Matt would be in the car tomorrow, ready to leave for McComb. Looking for signs, maybe, that they'd done it.

18

Goodman, Chaney, and Schwerner were found—or rather, their bodies were excavated from an earthen dam near Philadelphia, Mississippi. Celeste assumed the boys had been dead for a while. Mrs. Owens knew from the beginning that they were dead. She'd said as much on that first evening. She knew Mississippi like she knew the back of her hand. There was no surprise in the discovery. But if any people understood the need to nourish hope in the face of unfathomable distress, the Negro people of Mississippi surely did. Tears, anger, frustration, but still the work of the summer had to go on.

The dug-up bodies didn't create the slightest disturbance in the quiet, peaceful veneer of Pineyville. No ribbons or flowers, no stores closed; it remained like a model train village with plastic people in the identical places everyday. When Reverend Singleton and Celeste passed through town on the way to Freshwater Road, Celeste spotted Mrs. Owens stepping into Percival Dale's grocery store. She noticed there was no grimacing Hudson at the gas station, no stone-faced Mr. Tucker pumping gas and cleaning windshields. Perhaps, she thought, he'd gone home for lunch as a ruse to keep track of his wandering daughter. She relieved Reverend Singleton of the trip to the house and got out to help Mrs. Owens carry the groceries.

Celeste crossed the street to avoid an approaching white woman, then crossed back and headed for the store just as the registrar of voters, Mr. Heywood, came out onto the sidewalk eating an ice-cream sandwich that was quickly melting. He stuffed the whole thing into his mouth. Reverend

Singleton had pointed the man out to her more than once over the summer. Celeste refused to cross the street again to avoid him, and surely wasn't going to step off the pavement. Here was the embodiment of the reason there were no Negro voters on the rolls in Pearl River County. Lanky and smooth-faced, with brownish straight hair laced with gray strands, he wore a khaki-colored summer-weight suit with a tie, and carried a newspaper under his free arm. His angry eyes had sunk into their hollows so that Celeste couldn't see their color.

"Good afternoon, Mr. Heywood." She followed her orientation instructions, the protocol when encountering the enemy, plastering a crooked smile on her face while her insides churned. *Be cordial, extend yourself beyond what you thought you were capable of doing.* Even innocuous encounters lay the groundwork for the future south. *Be mindful of the future.* Let the hurts of today and yesterday be put aside.

Mr. Heywood scoffed at her, an unintelligible word tangled up with residues of ice cream that spewed out of his mouth and onto her face. She didn't understand the word, just felt bits of cool milky spit spray her. Another *jiggaboo* moment. But what was the word this time? A lexicon of epithets to select from. Of course, he could say and do whatever he pleased. He turned in a huff and fast-walked toward the Pearl River County Administration Building.

Mrs. Owens had told her that Mr. Heywood had been instrumental in getting the county to plant magnolia trees in the business district and that he wrote poems for the local paper extolling the beauty of the flowers, comparing them to his wife's white skin. He and his magnolia blossoms. If he got to the sheriff's station before she moved along, he'd have her arrested for loitering. It was an offense for a Negro person to idle on this street. If you weren't working, you best not be on any street standing around looking *shiftless.* Grandma Pauline used to say, "Everybody needs a shift." Celeste had a shift all right, as the outside agitator, the northern rabble-rouser. She stared at Mr. Heywood's back as he loped towards the sheriff's station, still stunned at the vehemence with which he'd greeted her. She touched the splotches of ice cream that clung to her skin, rubbed the sticky sweetness from her face.

Mrs. Owens came out of the grocery store empty-handed with Mr. Dale on her heels. "Now, Miz Owens, you sure you don't want to just go on and do your shopping?"

Celeste saw again Labyrinth's blue eyes and blonde hair in Percival Dale. Labyrinth's resemblance to him was quite remarkable, but for the color of her skin. His hair didn't have the depth of color that hers had. He was of medium height with a sturdy build and a pug nose. What had Dolly Johnson been thinking in this small town to get involved with a married white man? And did she ever bring Labyrinth into town? Mr. Dale nodded to her but focused on Geneva Owens and her empty shopping bag. Celeste had no clue as to how Mr. Dale viewed her and the work she was doing in Pineyville. She'd been in the store with Mrs. Owens before. He'd never been rude.

"You didn't buy anything?" Celeste asked. She wanted to get going.

"Mr. Heywood angered me so, I lost my train of thought." Mrs. Owens's eyes flashed in the direction of the county building. "I be back another day, Mr. Dale."

"All right, then." Mr. Dale glanced sideways at Celeste and went back into his store.

A few more steps and Mr. Heywood would arrive at the county building. If she told Mrs. Owens about Mr. Heywood scoffing ice cream spittle into her face, it would only make matters worse.

Mrs. Owens took off at a stomp. No sideways looks into store windows, no head nodding toward a living soul, just a marching forward under the magnolias, then out into the sunshine, then back under the luxuriant trees. Celeste kept pace. "What'd he say?"

"Say I should get you out my house or else." She marched on, her empty plastic shopping bag swinging, her black purse hugged into her body.

They left the little town center and turned into a block of houses where the air itself had taken on a greenish hue, grass that went from forest green to nearly black in deep shade held by the orange-tinted soil. It was a short-cut to the two-lane.

Celeste spoke under her breath. "You hear about the three boys?" Reverend Singleton brought the news when he came to pick her up after freedom school. She let the children go without mentioning it, sat in the church with the Reverend for a few minutes.

"After all this time." Mrs. Owens huffed.

Celeste didn't know if Mrs. Owens was talking about the civil rights workers' bodies being found or Mr. Heywood. *After all this time.* Every-

thing in Mississippi was a crisis of *after all this time*. Mrs. Owens walked
her down a block of houses at a good clip, sweat streaming down her body.
The houses here were wood framed with screened porches, painted white
with green trim. Rain gutters, plots of impatiens, giant yellow hibiscus
exploding through the green lawns. She imagined eyes peeking out from
behind curtains and blinds peering at the two Negroes hurrying over the
pavement. They weren't going to work anywhere, so they shouldn't have
been on this street. Mrs. Owens marched like she was in a demonstration,
telling all that she had a right to walk the sidewalks of a town where she'd
lived and worked for more than forty years.

"He can't tell me who I can have in my own house." Mrs. Owens turned
the last corner, a street lined with a sheltering of live oaks. Sunlight slanted
through the contorted branches. Celeste had an urge to sit on the grass in
the shade, lie down under the grand canopy of trees. Then she wondered
which of the town's old trees had suspended the dancing apoplectic feet of a
bug-eyed Negro man who had laughed walking down the street, or turned
his head to a white woman whose sweat-wet dress clung to her body, or
simply didn't step off the pavement when a white person walked by. And
the boys. What had been the last thing they heard or saw or thought? All
of life ahead of them, all the good in the world in them to give.

They turned onto the two-lane and walked down the gravel shoulder,
the sun like a blowtorch playing hide and seek with the darkening rain
clouds moving up from the Gulf. She watched for traffic, let Mrs. Owens
walk out her anger. The humidity thickened like wet wool. The village
crickets agitated. As she always did, Celeste checked each passing truck
and car for gun-toting white men. Small gusts lifted her dress then died,
releasing the fabric. Rain started falling in fat isolated drops, warm as a
shower. The two women made it to Freshwater Road as the downpour began
in earnest.

In the kitchen, Mrs. Owens rested from the walk, her usual glass of iced
tea nearby. "I'm 'bout ready to go on down there and register." She didn't
look at Celeste, instead stared out the back door as the water pelted the thin
roof and ran off in sheets. "You ready? You think the others ready?" Her
agitation fanned her courage to fight back in the only way she could. By
going to see the registrar, the man who'd insulted her dignity.

Celeste counted up her voter registration students. Sister Mobley and

Mrs. Owens. Dolly Johnson and of course Reverend Singleton, and maybe
Mr. Landau. But Mr. Landau didn't believe in nonviolence. No way he
could go yet. She would be there herself for moral support and any last-
minute instruction. Should have more people, though. "We all have to go
together. Reverend Singleton will have to okay us making our first trip."
The memos coming from the Jackson office over the last two weeks had
encouraged projects to go on to the registrar. Nobody registered on the first
try, and there might be arrests. It would take time to get people out of jail,
then back to the registrar. Get moving, they'd said. That was before the
bodies were found.

   Mrs. Owens swirled her iced tea and said, as if to herself, "Told me to
go on home and take care of it."

   Celeste poured herself a glass of tea, wishing she had a tall gin and
tonic. The whole town might erupt. No riots here. People would be arrested
before any riots had a chance to erupt. Mass arrests. Ed talked about the
special prison in the swamps for civil rights workers. Plaquemines. Did
Sheriff Trotter have some Plaquemines hidden out in the bayous near the
Pearl River? As the outsider, she'd be the number-one target when they
went to the registrar. She and one local person would take the brunt of any
physical attack. That's what orientation taught. "We can make our first trip
on Monday morning, depending on Reverend Singleton. Start the week.
It's going to take more than one try." She stopped before she said what she
thought—that it might not happen at all.

   "Yes." Mrs. Owens went into her bedroom and closed the curtain behind her. Celeste could hear her mumbling scripture.

   The rain slowed to dribbles interspersed with a few last thick, thumping
drops, washing the gravel path to the outhouse. The dust was quelled for a
while. A slight breeze, a small tailwind of the storm passed through. Celeste
sat in the kitchen, relieved that all the power lines still hung from the poles.
When the last of the rain stopped, she went to the front porch and sat in
Mrs. Owens's rocking chair. The darker rain clouds moved out, leaving
snow white dumplings lolling across the sky. She stood at the screen door
to see Dolly Johnson stepping out of her old car wearing jeans, a blouse,
and gym shoes, her hair parted in the middle and pulled behind her ears,
and carrying a small purse.

   "You got time ta visit?" Dolly came up the porch steps and Celeste saw that her overdone make-up and painted fingernails didn't quite fit in with the new Dolly. She had something, a kind of style that made her stand out in Pineyville. The way she presented herself showed courage, bucking the eyes-down mentality of Mississippi.

Celeste unhooked the screen and held the door for her. "Come in. You want a cold drink?"

"Thank you." Dolly didn't move beyond the screened door.

"Sit down, Dolly." Celeste brought her a glass of iced tea and resumed her seat in the rocking chair.

Dolly sat and held on to the arms of the straight-backed chair like it might fly off the porch with her in it. "The rain makes it nice, for a few minutes anyway." Her face was slightly round and nicely shaped.

The heat began to build up, but the late afternoon shower and the small breezes that followed it prevented the day from being a scorcher. Across the road, the sunlight glazed the pile of cinderblocks and wood slats. A wild crepe myrtle grew like a precious gift springing up out of the despair of a vacant lot. The Hudson wasn't parked at the Tucker house down the road. Three children lived in that house, yet it always seemed deserted.

"You hear about them finding the boys?" It had been more than a month since they'd gone missing. Hard to hide three men. But it had been done, and they'd still be under the dirt but for a purchased tip to the FBI.

"Where'd they think they were? On the moon?" Dolly shook her head from side to side.

"Might as well have been. Supposed to be a memorial service over in Meridian." Celeste had already decided she'd go with the Reverend and his wife.

On the narrow blacktop, the meager trickle of cars seemed to be moving too slowly. It was an illusion created by the sunlight.

"Things don't get better around here, I'm sending my children away just as soon as I'm able," Dolly said.

Celeste wondered if that meant she'd leave, taking them with her, or if she'd stay and send them to relatives somewhere. She longed to tell her she would do the same thing, too, though the point wasn't to leave, but rather to pound this place into livability. Even so, Celeste knew as well as she knew her own name that she'd never let a son—especially a son—of her own grow up in a place called Mississippi.

"Did you know Leroy Boyd James?" She hadn't thought about him for some time but now that the bodies of the boys had been unearthed, it brought the earlier death to mind.

"Sure, I did. Wasn't that long ago. Dirty shame the way they treated him." Dolly's eyes searched the air for reasons.

"Does he have family around here?" She wanted to ask Dolly if she thought he'd raped the woman he was accused of raping. Nobody'd said a word about it since she arrived in Pineyville. What did it mean for so many dreadful things to happen and not be discussed? How could you keep doing that, year in and year out, sweeping nightmares under the rug? But those things lived on in hearts and minds whether they ever crossed the lips or not.

"Oh, no. They left town soon after." Dolly sipped her iced tea.

Not only did the Negro people in Mississippi live surrounded by hatred, endlessly fearing all manner of reprisal, they had to do it without a legal drink. Just based on the discovery of the three bodies, every Negro in the state should be having a shot of something a whole lot stronger than iced tea. At Momma Bessie's dining room table, the stories and tales of the dead were interspersed with the splashing of hard liquor drinks over ice cubes. A community of storytelling eased the pain of the church ritual, buoyed the release. Not in Mississippi. Celeste sucked her teeth and wagged her head like an old person.

"How my kids doing in your class? They learning anything new?" Dolly rested her glass on the porch floor.

The subject of their conversation was effectively changed. Was this the reason Dolly had come over? Had her children complained about Celeste? Labyrinth didn't like standing to say her name before she spoke each time. That was baby stuff to her. "Oh, they're doing fine. Reading the newspapers, talking about current events." Georgie stayed quiet but he read well, too.

"Good." Dolly stared through the puckering screen at the orange sand road. The puddles had shriveled to spoonfuls of rainwater on their way to disappearing.

Celeste rocked the chair, grinding the floorboards of the porch. Maybe she and Dolly could just sit there and girl talk, forget Freedom Summer, forget all that still had to be done, all that had already happened. Pretend they were out for lunch with not a care in the world. She wanted to tell Dolly she didn't need to wear so much makeup.

Dolly took a handkerchief out of her purse and gently patted her moist face, blotting the rouge on her cheeks and the oil from her nose. "I don't make no difference between them, you know, and I don't let nobody else make a difference, either." She put the handkerchief back in her purse and fiddled with the clasp.

Dolly rightfully assumed that someone had told Celeste her story. "Surely that's the best thing." Celeste stumbled around to find a calming word to say to Dolly. She hadn't as far as she knew made any difference between them, but Labyrinth was such a stand-out, it was hard not to focus on her. "They're fine children, Dolly. Labyrinth takes good care of Georgie, too. She's protective."

"That's what she's supposed to do. He's the baby." They talked for a while longer about the children, what they were studying, how they got along with the other kids. Dolly seemed to have some other notions in her mind that played across her face, but they didn't come out of her mouth. She was subdued, thoughtful.

"I better be getting on home." Dolly stood. "Thank you for the tea."

There was more she might have said to Dolly, so much she wanted to ask. But Reverend Singleton admonished her to keep a distance between herself and the adults who came to voter education class. She was the teacher first, though all the class members were older. "Come by anytime."

"I'll do that." Dolly got into her car and U-turned on Freshwater Road then turned on the two-lane going toward Pineyville.

In her bedroom, the after-storm evening light slanted through the lacy curtains. The end of Freedom Summer was approaching. The race was on now to see if the work of the summer would net out to something that could change this place forever. A new tension would settle in over the exhausted one that had hovered around the missing civil rights workers. It was time to go see Mr. Heywood. She'd alert the One Man, One Vote office that they were shifting into gear for the final showdown. If they attacked her or any of her little group, she'd need a doctor they could call on. Who? Where? Maybe someone in Hattiesburg. She'd ask Reverend Singleton. She grabbed at straws, trying to gird herself against faceless eventualities.

Celeste opened her dresser drawer and touched Wilamena's unopened letter. It was there. She held, it anticipating distance, afraid she'd never make it through the coolness. She sat on the side of her bed and slowly,

carefully opened it, its two pages folded once. Wilamena had written on
both sides of each sheet.

A landscape in pale colors hinted across the top of the paper. Mountains
and pine trees. *Piñon*. Her mother always liked good stationery, kept boxes
of cards with painted birds, flowers, and landscapes. She'd taught Celeste
from the time she was a child to send formal thank-you notes as gratitude
for the smallest gestures. Wilamena's handwriting etched on the page, the
lines perfectly even like she'd used a ruler.

> *Dear Celeste:*
>
> *I hope you're managing to stay out of harm's way though I don't see
> how that's possible considering where you are. You should be running
> as far and as fast away from that place as possible. I can't imagine a
> reason to even pass through there. Of course, if I hadn't called Shuck
> looking for you, I wouldn't even have known you'd gone to Missis-
> sippi. Imagine that?*
>
> *Now that you're adult enough to run about the world doing what
> you please, putting yourself in harm's way willingly and knowingly,
> there are some things I need to share with you. I'm weary of carrying
> this burden alone.*
>
> *When Shuck and I were married, things grew difficult between us.
> I had your brother, Billy, and a husband who was never home or help-
> ful in the least, and in-laws who never seemed to notice I was there.
> It wasn't easy. I was lonely and isolated. I found work, which gave me
> some relief from the dreariness of my daily life.*
>
> *At any rate, I met a man. We struck up a conversation at Hudson's
> department store, of all places. He asked me to lunch, and I surprised
> myself by going. Before long, it turned into an affair.*

Her next sentences swooped against Celeste like headwinds lifting off
the page, pushing her back on the bed.

> *Perhaps I was looking for someone to assuage my loneliness,
> or maybe it just happened. A bit of serendipity. Hard to think of
> Detroit and the possibility of anything serendipitous, to say nothing
> of romantic. And it was that. Romantic. Secret meetings, lies to cover
> my whereabouts. Imagine that! Windsor was our favorite place. He*

*knew that I was married, and so was he. I got pregnant and broke off
the relationship. I was terrified of the consequences. Shuck and I were
still together during that time, you see.*

*That November, you were born. I don't think Shuck knew about
my affair. I certainly never told him. There was nothing to discuss
really. We were married, if troubled, and I was pregnant. At some
point, much later, he may have had suspicions because you don't really
look like him. But of course that happens in families, especially in
Negro families. His suspicions went away in time. You do, my dear,
have something of this other man's looks, minus that hair of yours
which has a mind of its own.*

*It was long ago. The man never knew I was pregnant, and I never
allowed him to know where I lived. I was the mystery woman. I
don't know if it would be wise to search for him, if that's what you're
thinking. What would be the point? Shuck has been your father, so
why upset the apple cart? Shuck has street smarts. He may well know
the truth. But it's too late now for me to broach the subject with him.
That I'll leave to you, since you're so close.*

Had she opened some stranger's mail? With her mouth dry as ash, she
checked the forwarding address written by someone in the Jackson office of
One Man, One Vote. Yes. Celeste Tyree, c/o Mrs. Geneva Owens, Freshwater
Road, Pineyville.

*After that, I couldn't wait to get out of Detroit. I imagined walking
into him on a street with you and Billy in tow. Imagined a thousand
things. I may never go back to that city for as long as I live.*

*Please take good care of yourself. You'll give and you'll give and
it'll still be crabs in a barrel. I pray you'll be safe. Shuck should never
have allowed this. I always thought him too permissive.*

> *Love from your mother,*
> *Wilamena*

Celeste paced around her room like a caged cat, sat again, her neck in
a painful crick. She reread the words feeling like naked prey in a ghostly
field, her body hairs spiked for danger. *Search for this man?* Her eyes had not
failed her. Had Wilamena gone crazy? She held the pieces of stationery, pine

trees and mountains etched across the top, faint blue sky behind. Calm. She shoved the letter under her pillow, caught an escaping breath in her throat when Mrs. Owens moved about in her room.

It was in the spring, not that long ago, after Easter break from school, that she'd last called her mother. Celeste kidded her about her husband, Cyril, not allowing music in their house, said she couldn't imagine that much quiet. *Shuck couldn't live two minutes without music. I couldn't either.* "Music's not everything," Wilamena'd answered. The air crackled through the phone. She told her she was only joking. In truth, she hadn't been joking. Now she understood her mother's taut response. It had as much to do with her identifying her tastes with Shuck's as anything. A Shuck who was not her father? But she'd said nothing in the letter that could be taken as conclusive proof of anything, except that she'd had an affair and got pregnant at the same time. Had she been sleeping with the both of them? During that phone call, Celeste had asked her what had really happened between her and Shuck all those years ago, why they hadn't made it. Wilamena dodged the question with something about Shuck never being home, always in the streets. Celeste had heard the frantic energy underneath her last words. She hung up with a curt goodbye.

Celeste grabbed the photo of Wilamena and Cyril Atwood from her dresser. He more than likely was passing for white—but if he was, why did Wilamena invite her and Billy to New Mexico to visit? They'd surely gum up the works. Maybe he wasn't. But one thing was for sure. Cyril Atwood had the kind of fair looks Wilamena adored. Even that was a stretch because Wilamena married Shuck, and Shuck was definitely brown. Celeste tore the photo out of the frame and ripped it into pieces. But Mrs. Owens would notice it not being there in its spot. She dug around in her book-bag for the tape she used to put up the children's drawings on the wall of the church. She taped the photograph back together. It looked a sight, the cactus plant not quite on the level of the people standing in front of it. She put it back on the dresser and camouflaged it with her toiletries. She'd have to look at it every time she looked at the photo of Shuck and Billy, every time she brushed her teeth and combed her hair, changed her clothes.

She stood by the dresser, staring at Billy and Shuck like she'd never looked at them before. Billy favored Shuck and she Wilamena. There was no secret in that. She stared at her own face in the mirror. Wilamena's family ran the gamut from dark-skinned to white. It was crazy. Grandma

Pauline told her that whole branches of the family tree had disappeared, gone forever. Nobody seemed particularly interested in seeking them out.

Maybe Wilamena's letter was just a horrid strike, a blow in an ongoing fight. What did she want from her? What if her mother was lying? What if she'd just gotten angry at not being able to find her, at having to always go through Shuck? This was a way to disengage her from Shuck, push Shuck out of the picture. Create a question of paternity, then walk off into the sunset as if it meant nothing at all. Wilamena'd always bristled at the closeness Shuck had with his children, especially with Celeste. Was it possible? She couldn't contain the thoughts in her head. Wilamena had lost her mind out there in New Mexico.

The reek of sweat and mold oozed through the room's air like nitrous oxide. Celeste felt a tickle in her chest, thought she might laugh. She left the letter on her bed and stood at her side window holding the lace curtain. Not a car passed on Freshwater Road or on the two-lane. The quiet roared like rolling thunderclaps in her head. There was no place to run, no person to help her ferret through the morass Wilamena had dumped on her. Did Shuck know anything of this? He hadn't warned her. Not one inkling that this could be true. She searched her mind, went through Shuck's presence in her life, found no holes, no pretense, no warnings. He was there. But in some small alcove of her mind, something sank into place. Some distant memory of a feeling of otherness, of a hidden something that lurked behind doors, in shadowy corners. The unspoken. What would possess Wilamena to do this? What kind of jealousy and loneliness in her own life would encourage her to try to destroy Celeste's closeness to Shuck? The weight of it began scuttling her life as she knew it and finally grounded itself inside her, attached to her like roots. This woman who took herself out of the lives of her children now tried to remove one child's only anchor. It was more than cruel.

She'd never speak to Wilamena again. She'd never say a word about it. Do like the people in Mississippi do. It never happened. She'd throw the letter in the outhouse hole in the morning. For now, she put it back in its envelope and stuffed it into the pocket of her suitcase as if otherwise it might gather strength and run out into the world screaming.

19

Ed Jolivette drove Celeste to New Orleans the day after the memorial service for Goodman, Chaney, and Schwerner in Meridian. She took the chance on going with him, figured they both needed to get out of Mississippi for a break, though Louisiana didn't seem far enough away. Volunteers and local people from all over the state had convened for the service. People had come from New York, Washington, and even California. The speakers brought the truth home, wrapped the congregants' anger and desolation in words that mourned and honored the dead young men. Celeste reunited with Ramona and Margo and they sat under a tree together to share their grief and, like all the volunteers, to compare notes on their projects. The volunteers understood their jobs still had to be completed, that they'd have to carry their sorrow back to their projects and try to find a way to weave it into the work.

Ed's car—another dusty, cigarette-smelling Dodge, a contribution from some car company up north—was quiet but for the heavy breeze whooshing in the opened windows. Celeste eyed him in his mauve and white pullover shirt and denim pants, a burnished prince from some unknown tribe, as they drove south on Highway Eleven. Spanish moss hung from the cypress trees like tangled hair.

Celeste slouched down, head back, arms in a lethargic fold across her chest, seeing through slits as they passed the turn-off to Sophie Lewis's in Carriere. She imagined being alone in the big empty house, the cool of the rooms, the shadows of the potted palms on the walls and floors. Sophie

Lewis toured during most of the summer, Reverend Singleton said. Her voice lifted her up and away from the humdrum of normal life in southern Mississippi, kept her on the move, no settling in here or there to deal with the quagmires of the day to day. She probably never even read her mail, had someone to filter it, to throw the bad mail away. She surely couldn't step out onto a stage to sing a soaring aria if the mire of life weighed on her mind. Protected. Sophie Lewis lived a rarified life.

Celeste didn't read Wilamena's letter again, but she thought about it plenty, debated how much of it was true and how much was just Wilamena's destructive jealousy. In truth, her mother couldn't possibly be sure of Celeste's paternity if she was still living with Shuck when she'd had the affair. If she'd had it at all. Celeste continued to stare into her cracked mirror and into the photographs of Shuck and Billy. Had she imagined the similarity into being? Was that her love speaking and not the facts? And so what if it was?

"Your thoughts so deep, chère, they weighing down the car." Ed glanced over and smiled, with that little-boy space between his front teeth belying the seriousness in his eyes. "Better spread those stones before they take us both under."

She heard him, acknowledged what he'd said with a half smile, then went back to staring out the window.

She hadn't earned this trip, not really. Civil rights workers got rest and relaxation days after big events, arrests, beatings. She, by movement standards, didn't really deserve the R & R in New Orleans. She thought about how, as bad as she'd felt when the cops beat Matt, she'd surely not be able to contain herself if the same happened to Ed. It had been long weeks since her nonviolence training in Jackson.

Celeste counted down the miles to go on the road signs. She thought again of Mary Evans in the train station singing her way out of that bathroom on her way to New Orleans. *It's a good-time place.* They crawled through faceless little Ozona and headed on toward Picayune, passing more tung tree orchards. She steeled her mind against seeing one more Negro person doing backbreaking menial work while a white man sat on a horse or stood around in the shade shouting orders. That was an image that had stood the test of time.

"I got strong shoulders." Ed's quiet voice broke through her reverie.

"They're all right." She imagined them pulling over under the willows and making love in the daylight, but she said nothing. The need for life tried to push all the death out of her mind. Something was dying in the world, in her world, and she had no way to stop it.

"Anytime you want 'em, you can have 'em, sugar." He smiled the slightest bit.

Words might open her cellar doors. No telling what would fly out. Mr. Heywood warned Mrs. Owens about keeping her in her home. The gunshots fired, the warning of worse things to come. The boys were dead. And, Wilamena. What in God's name would be next? "I can drive too, you know." She took the rubber band off her ponytail, unbuttoned her blouse down two buttons, rested her arm on the window opening, the air beating her face and hair, drying the sweat on her scalp.

He ignored that. "At night, we take the back roads, flyin'." He shifted in the seat, moved his dark hands on the steering wheel.

"I thought we weren't supposed to drive at night in Mississippi." Celeste didn't want to be on any back roads, day or night. Fear just from thinking about it charged through her stomach. She closed her eyes, head back, teeth tight, jaw set hearing the voices from the memorial service, thinking of the utter senselessness of the deaths of those three—as if that would stop this movement forward, as if those deaths would end the march of time. But still, they were so young.

"It's better not to, but if you're out there late at night, you better be movin', and you better have a gun."

Celeste glanced over at him. His demeanor had not changed. "You don't have a gun in this car, do you?"

Ed didn't answer her, but his eyes said that if he didn't have one now, he would very soon. Matt had talked that way after that beating on the road down from Jackson, embarrassed that he'd been beaten and not defended himself, hopped up about going to meet with the Deacons for Defense and Justice. A salve that said I am a man, too. It was the memorial service talking through Ed, the three deaths. He needed to affirm that he would defend himself if necessary. Be a man. She put her head back, heart racing, tried to fake a nap.

When she opened her eyes, they were coming into Slidell, Louisiana, heading for a bridge. Neon signs flashed "liquor" like it was being handed out for free. People on the streets walked easy, men in shorts and women in halters strolling in and out of open-air tackle and bait shops. Negro and white people just out lingering. The lake air mingled with a lift from the Gulf, had a bite of coolness in it, but it was funky, too. She sucked it in like it was a healing vapor. She wanted to stop and walk along the dirty beach. She scanned the placid surface of Lake Pontchartrain, the crescent of land on the other side disappearing in a low-slung layer of mist.

Ed maneuvered the car over the old bridge, the tires bumping over the metal ridges and cross planks. Past Ed, out the other way toward Lake Borgne and the Gulf of Mexico, a procession of white boats pointed in toward the shore. She was thinking of a pleasure cruise, of lying on a white deck lounger in a skimpy swimsuit with big sunglasses and a tall cool drink close by. Escape.

"Trawlers. Been out in the Gulf. Probably got shrimp. Sport-fishing boats, too." Ed's voice had the relaxed sound of a man at home.

"I had other thoughts," she said. She couldn't really squeeze a vacation fantasy into her experience of the south. She remembered what Margo had said: *Down to the Gulf, it's still Mississippi, Alabama. Same damned thing.* But New Orleans had to be different. It was already different just seeing people lazing around on the streets, going in and out of stores.

"You ever tasted pompano?" Ed said it like he knew she'd never heard of it.

She played the student well. "What is it?"

"It's a fish." He grinned.

"What kind of fish?" She didn't feel uncomfortable letting him know what she didn't know.

"From the Gulf. They call it Florida pompano. It's good—sweet, even." The fishing boats trailed towards shore like toys on a city park pond. "Makes me hungry just thinking 'bout it."

Pompano. The word had a rhythm just like Ed's way of speaking, and she already knew he was good and he was sweet.

The easy pace of the car, the sun glimmering on the water, and the talk of good eating reminded her of long ago summer Saturday afternoons at Momma Bessie's. Some distant uncle who'd left in the dark to go fishing on Lake St. Claire brought his catch to the old house. Fish scales flew around the kitchen and the blues played on the record player. Everyone talked long and hard about Detroit, about wherever they might've come from in the south, about jobs and houses and relatives. They drank Jack Daniel's and Johnnie Walker Black, and the old ones drank Four Roses. Billy and she and the cousins and the neighbor children tagged around the apple tree in the backyard, ran in and out of the house hearing snatches of conversations that sang like the music. The smell of frying fish devoured all the molecules in the air. Wilamena had already left town by then.

"You gotta see this place when a hurricane blows through. Waves coming off the Gulf, water surges rolling in big as buildings over the land." Ed half-turned to her. He always seemed to be eyeing her for a response, listening, paying attention. He exaggerated to yank her back again from the brink of her tumbling thoughts. She thanked him with her look, then saw the water out the window—it barely lapped against itself, an old dog licking a worn-out shoe.

Cars whizzed by on the bridge—no hateful-eyed stares here, just carloads of people going about their summer lives, children's faces in the windows, looking like they'd jump right out and over the bridge they were so ready for a swim.

They left the bridge and drove through Bayou Sauvage with its houses on stilts in the water, through the mud-slow suburbs and into New Orleans, which simmered in an afternoon swelter so ferocious Pineyville seemed like a cool memory. Hot air rolled in the open windows, a thick funk that smelled like old shrimp shells. She hung out of the car window, her hair a mass of spikes and curls.

The car slowed along with the lethargic traffic on Gentilly, the sun sharp against the windshield on her side. Ed turned onto St. Bernard and they passed blocks of doll-like houses with green shutters and ornate porticos. He told her they were in the area where the black Creoles lived, mixed-race people who traced their heritage back to the French and Spanish. In the days of slavery, the rich young white men had kept beautiful colored women in small houses in the French Quarter, and their children became the free people of color, the Creoles. Many were educated in France and practiced in all the trades and crafts at the time of slavery. Matt called Ed Creole, and his name was certainly French, but his skin color was deep-dark.

He told her of the Negro wrought-iron workers, the musicians, the whole society that grew up separate from African slaves *and* Europeans. She was swallowed up in his talking, filling in the blanks in her mind, angry that none of it was taught in any school she'd ever been in. Those Creoles, he told her, could be as prejudiced as white people. Wilamena would fit right in. He pointed out Congo Square, where the slaves celebrated their free days with festivals of food, music, and dancing and told her until this day, you might find a plate of food under a certain tree put there to appease the gods. Voodoo was practiced there and on the shores of Lake Pontchartrain. His talk took her miles away from the waiting confrontations in Pineyville, the memorial service, Wilamena's letter. A small wedge, a new landscape to build on, and she gobbled it up for fear of the knots and rocks inside her.

Ed parked and led her into a storefront restaurant where people sat on benches at long tables with mounds of red-shelled claw-legged things on newspapers and bottles of beer lined up like bowling pins. The air conditioners slammed out cool air and the front door stood open. Loud pulsing music played over the speakers, men's voices sounding earth-rich and low, their accents so thick she couldn't make out the lyrics. It was neither rhythm and blues nor jazz but it was black, deep black, and it sneaked into her body as she walked behind Ed to a table. He sat her there and went off before returning with a newspaper pouch of crawfish and a waitress behind him carrying two frozen bottles of beer. He taught her how to crack the shells and suck the meat out of the head and the tiny claws. She leaned against the wall, put her feet up on the sitting bench, drank beer, and watched the traffic go by on Claiborne Avenue, Negro people and white people both coming into this place, both eating and drinking. Mississippi wasn't even an hour away.

"God bless New Orleans because one more day in Mississippi, and I might've *volunteered* to throw myself into the Pearl River. Do the Klan and Sheriff Trotter a favor." Celeste swallowed a belch and heaved out a sigh that had comfort all through it. A rich feeling of contentment, like Reverend Singleton's at Mrs. Owens's breakfast table.

"Chère, you can't think like that. Good things going on, too." He'd recovered from his oblique talk of guns and resumed being the nonviolent architect of change. He leaned over his pile of crawfish, liquid drizzling down his chin, hands breaking off the bigger pieces. She wanted to lick the juice right off of his face. The music changed to the rhythm and blues of Otis's jukebox in Hattiesburg.

"Shuck would love this place." She drank her beer and watched Ed rubbing lemon wedges over his hands, then drying them on napkins. People laughed, talked, and swilled beer like it was water, nobody bothering anybody else. "My father." The words bounced in her head, reverberated against her skull. *My father.* Had Ed heard her? Or had she swallowed the words, another expression of her confusion? Tears came to her eyes, and she looked out the window until they returned.

Ed went through the pile of paper napkins she'd assembled from the napkin holder. "Your pa must be a laissez-faire kinda man."

"That's a fine way to put it." She knew he was just that and to the bone, and she worshipped every bit of that quality in him. She knew she could rely on it to get through Wilamena's mess.

For a moment, it seemed there was no one in the restaurant but them. She turned away from his barefaced allure, the strong pull of him making her dizzy, the music spiraling her closer toward him, too. The memory of making love with him in the car on Freshwater Road kept her awake nights. She didn't know if the isolation of Pineyville was magnifying the feeling or if it had a weight of its own that would carry no matter where they were or what they were doing, and for the moment, she didn't care.

Back in the car, full and sleepy in the afternoon heat, rivulets of sweat ran down her chest. The hot car seat branded the backs of her thighs through her slacks. When she put her arm on the window casing, it was hot enough to scorch her skin.

They drove slowly through the French Quarter, where people walked on the streets with drinks in their hands and stood in entryways throwing up in broad daylight. She marveled at the ironwork, the narrow French-named streets, the balconied houses and palms growing like weeds. She'd left America and landed on some island, a throwback place. They drove to the foot of Canal Street to where the ferry docked and she reminded him of being running drunk and laughed. Together, they boarded, the dark currents of the river swirling south, the white riverboats with their bright bunting going north, great barges and cargo ships angling this way and that as they maneuvered into the docks. New Orleans gleamed in the bright sunlight.

She'd imagined they'd be picked up in a hurricane wind and dropped in the sea near North Africa. Instead, they bounced over the muddy currents toward the low roofs and thick trees of another stop in America, in the south, where Negro people talked in song.

Later, after they'd been to Algiers and back again on the ferry, a dark cloud stopped over the French Quarter and it rained. The cloud moved on and the sun reappeared, sheening the city in light. "This time of year, the rain's warm, big drops and soft. Might only pour for three minutes. Maybe rain in the Quarter and be dry as bone 'cross the river," Ed told her.

They drove to St. Charles Avenue and parked. She felt like she was speeding through a world she had to photograph in her mind in order to preserve a few things to dream on. The street looked wet and shiny, rich and old; the traffic noises were like music. They boarded the streetcar and rode all the way to Audubon Park, the grand old houses all along the way stark white against the deep green of the sprawling magnolias and live oaks, the fan palms and philodendrons, the pond cypress and willows, amid splashes of color so vibrant she stared out of the open side of the streetcar, the bell clanging and the car lurching, like a child at Christmas gazing into toy-filled windows. The green cooled everything, held the sun at bay. Ed took her hand when they stepped down from the streetcar and kept holding it when they walked through Audubon Park. He leaned her against the rough bark of a live oak and kissed her in broad daylight. She looked up through the branches, the light of the sky in small patterns coming through the leaves; she reached for him and fell right into his chest, holding onto him for all she was worth. The precious day was coming to an end.

They walked toward Tulane and Loyola under the shade of the giant trees on St. Charles Avenue, then boarded the trolley for the ride back to Ed's car.

"That woman, the opera singer, Sophie Lewis, talked about a place called Storyville. You know it?" The name alone set her adrift. "Said her father owned property."

"Fancy houses of prostitution. Jelly Roll Morton came up through there. Louis Armstrong, too."

"Are the houses still there?" She stalled their departure for Mississippi.

"No, no. It's all gone. He maybe owned cribs, places where black women worked. They had a few black women in the big houses, exotics. They even had one black woman owned one of the fanciest houses in Storyville. I'll drive you by where it used to be."

And he did. Back through the French Quarter, Rampart Street, the Treme, as he called it, St. Bernard Avenue and on to Gentilly, the city glossed by because she couldn't focus on leaving it, on going back to the harsh, sand-grit world of Pineyville.

Most of the ride back, she couldn't remember. She dozed all the way to Mississippi and had no dreams of death.

20

Shuck had become a junkie for Mississippi news. In the low light at the back of the Royal Gardens, he foraged through the *Detroit News,* the *Michigan Chronicle,* and his *Jet* magazine, searching for any mention of Mississippi. He checked his watch for the start of the six o'clock news on television. Seemed like every time he turned it on, somebody else was dead. A president, four little girls in a church, a Negro man walking to his front door, a crazy white man walking down a road alone in Alabama with a sign protesting segregation. Now it was those three boys.

The regulars came in and took their seats, Millicent and Iris at the bar fanning themselves with folded pieces of paper though the air conditioner chugged and the ceiling fans whirled. Shuck nodded to them, his eyes seeing them but his mind unable to focus on them.

Rodney and Chink lumbered in, sweat trickling down their faces, looking more like the tail end of a chain gang than two men with good jobs at the General Motors plant. Posey had their drinks ready before they settled in at their table just beyond the bar; he put in lots of ice, automatically gave every customer ice water, kept the ice machine on all day until the sound of the cubes clunking down into the refrigerator and the new water pouring into the ice-maker became part of the tracks of sound in the Royal Gardens. Shuck grunted towards Chink and Rodney, then his eyes glazed. If the government had any backbone, it would've protected those children from jump street. That was the thought on everyone's mind.

Posey went to the big Wurlitzer and clattered in the coins to play the music Shuck loved, Ellington and Basie, Sinatra and Vaughn, and always Dakota Staton—steering clear of Billie Holiday because her voice revealed too much of what everyone hoped to forget. In the middle of Dakota Staton singing "Broadway," Shuck caught his own distracted face in the bar mirror, mumbled to Posey, "Be back later on," and walked by Chink and Rodney's table, their heads slow-turning to watch him go, behind Iris and Millicent at the bar, who had words ready for him but something in his face caught them, stopped them from speaking. He was gone.

Shuck drove all over the city like an angler looking for a catch on a wide still lake. Quiet. He made his way to the old neighborhood, turned onto Milford, a kind of West Side main street leaning toward decay but still anchored by churches and small family-owned businesses. Milford lived in Shuck, as if he and it were the same thing. He'd been born a few blocks from here, knew this place like he knew all the ways a number could be played, what number attached to every dream in the dream book. He learned the numbers game on Milford at the barbershop and the shoe shine stand. In the afternoons, he'd sit at Momma Bessie's dining room table writing his numbers from memory on the policy slips he refused to carry in the car for fear of being stopped by the police. He stashed the carbon copies in a Florsheim shoebox and secreted them in the cellar behind the jars of canned fruits and vegetables, then paid off the police as insurance. Late in the day, the phone rang off the hook as the numbers fell, coming off the racetrack—first, second, and third race. He covered his bets and played it straight. He moved up from runner to banker.

When he opened his eyes, he was parked on the side street near Manfred's after-hours joint and took a moment to remember that he'd parked there after cruising around the old neighborhood, passing by the homes of people who used to be his clients. Manfred's didn't post any signs. You had to know the entrance was down a short alley between two squat buildings on a small commercial stretch in the old neighborhood. It was dark, homespun, and illegal, a real blind pig that never even opened to the public before ten. Night people ended their days tipping out of Manfred's just before sunrise. It was too early for Manfred's to be busy. Next to the Royal Gardens, Manfred's had the best jukebox in town.

"Hey Shuck, how you been doing?" Ulster "Gravy" Williams, slouching his drunk self at a corner table in the shadows, sat up straight and wobble-walked over to the stool beside Shuck's at the bar. Gravy had a reputation for being slick in an obvious sort of way.

"Gravy. Things are fine, just fine." If anybody else asked him how he'd been doing, he would've asked the same question back. With Gravy, you didn't even need to ask because the answer was coming regardless. Shuck nodded to Manfred, then looked straight ahead at the sparkling glasses and honey-toned liquids in the whiskey bottles lined up in front of the bar mirror. Manfred brought Shuck a shot of Crown Royal with a glass of ice water. He'd been doing the same thing every time Shuck walked in the place for years. Manfred rarely spoke but nodded, kept a black and chrome stool behind the bar for the slow times and a .45 automatic pistol under a towel by the cash register.

"Yeah, man, things good for me, too." Gravy settled on the stool, only the top button on his long sleeved pink shirt open right under his stubbly chin. "Don't see you around here anymore. Yo momma still live up the street?"

"Yeah." Shuck knew better than to feed Gravy with tidbits from his life.

Gravy stared down at his nearly empty glass, a pitiful, hungry-dog look on his face. "Nice, man, nice. Good thang to have yo momma still living and healthy."

In fact, Momma Bessie wasn't that healthy anymore, but Shuck didn't want to share that with him. Easy to see Gravy wanted another drink. Shuck prayed Manfred would cut him off before Gravy fell out on the floor. If he fell out, Shuck would have to take him home because Manfred was there by himself. No way he was going to close down to drive a drunk home. For Gravy, there was no one to call but a taxi.

"Damn sure is." Shuck said it with a finality that would have translated clearly to anyone but a drunk.

Gravy pressed on. "Sorry to hear bout yo daddy passing. He was a upright kinda man."

Old man Tyree had been dead for over a year. Gravy obviously didn't know about the woman who'd turned up at the funeral knowing more about Shuck than he knew about himself, how she'd stayed in the back of the church and then cornered him when Momma Bessie stepped into the first car for the ride to the cemetery. Momma Bessie finally stuck her head through the car window, rolled her eyes good and hard at the woman, and told Shuck to get in the car. All Shuck could do for days after was wonder how in God's name his own father had carried on with another woman for years and never let on to a soul. He never had the heart to ask Momma Bessie how much she knew. But that look said she knew something.

Gravy grinned like the last snake in the Garden of Eden. "How them kids of yours?"

"They're fine, Gravy. Everybody's fine." Shuck emphasized it this time, eyed Manfred, then walked to the jukebox.

Jackie Wilson finished "Lonely Teardrops," too loud without glasses tinkling and rough-voiced men and women talking and laughing. Shuck was in the mood for *his* music. He played "What a Diff'rence a Day Makes" and "While We're Young," by Dinah Washington. He lingered at the glass-fronted jukebox, pretending to study the other selections, hoping Gravy would grow bored and leave. No such luck. He went back to finish his drink, wishing he could move himself down the bar without being too obvious, but Gravy had homed in on him.

"How's your daughter, man? She must be very near growed." Gravy leaned into Shuck, his breath like a breeze from a garbage dump.

Shuck took a swig of Crown Royal that arced down his throat, searing like it was the first drink he'd ever had, then lit a cigarette, blowing the smoke sideways right into Gravy's face.

Gravy didn't even cough but seemed to suck in the smoke and get even higher than he already was. "Man, I got a friend lives up there in Ann Arbor say she saw your daughter, uh, what's her name?"

Shuck took out his handkerchief and blew his nose. He wasn't going to help Gravy with so much as a name. He hummed a phrase, tapped his cigarette lighter on the bar in time to the music.

Gravy slumped, eyed his empty glass, the top of the bar, checked his dull fingernails. "My friend say your daughter was hanging out with a white dude. On the back of a motorcycle. Close. She like them white boys, huh?"

Shuck knew about the white boy. J.D. He'd warned Celeste all about the downside of that kind of freedom. Nothing else he could do. Young people had their own minds. Anyway, the white boy thing in Ann Arbor wasn't going to kill Celeste. Mississippi might. Gravy was behind the times, as usual. "I don't worry much about it, Gravy. She's got to live her own life." He lied. He had worried about it. He prided himself on being a race man, told his children they could find whatever they needed among their own people. But he let it go; he knew times were changing and that was all for the best.

Gravy sat quietly absorbing Shuck's cool response. Shuck figured he was sitting there scheming up on his next attack. He reached for his wallet, ready to get away from Gravy, even though he could sit in Manfred's for hours just listening to the jukebox. Before he got his money out, Gravy caught his eyes in the bar mirror.

"Whole lot of people say that daughter of yours never did *look* like you, man. You know what I mean? Look like something else going on in there." He got the last words tangled and he trailed off as if he'd lost contact with them.

Everything went quiet in the cavern inside Shuck's ears. Heat flashed to his neck and face. His stomach twisted, feeling full of fury like hot rocks. This was all so old, he was stunned by how new it felt. "No, Gravy, I don't know what you mean."

"Nothing, man, nothing." Gravy turned away, tapped his bony fingers on the bar top, slouched over even more.

Shuck took a deep drink then poured the Crown Royal into the water, quickly bringing the glass to his mouth. He held it there when he wasn't taking in any liquid. The diluted drink sailed into his blood like it was hydroplaning down a shimmering highway. His hand began to shake, so he brought the glass down to the bar top with a thud.

Gravy grinned a sheepish little grin, catching Shuck's eyes in the mirror again, pretending to be trying to figure something out. He'd won. Shuck slid some money out of his money clip, slapped it on the bar and stood up. His cigarette hung by a tiny piece of white paper from the corner of his mouth. "Fuck you, Gravy. Check you later, Manfred."

He walked out knowing he'd come close to crashing his glass into Gravy's face. Didn't ever want to hit a drunk. And knew better than to listen to whatever came out of a drunk man's mouth. The street was desolate, warm and still.

Shuck flicked his cigarette to the ground, then sat in the car, watching the tiny round crinkle of fire burn. Maybe it was good Celeste didn't come home for the summer. He'd never be able to talk about that old rumor anyway. Too much time gone by. What difference did it make now? The old rumor had died down in time. Wilamena left the city. That put an end to it, or so he'd thought. More than once, he'd been tempted to ask Alma if she'd ever heard the rumors. She'd never so much as hinted that she had. Best to leave it that way.

Posey knew, or thought he knew. The old-timers who might've heard it had always been cowed, charmed, and cajoled away from the wormy past without a clear word being spoken. It was the way he was with his children. No room for speculation. The regulars at the bar were too young to have even heard about it. Always in the back of his mind, he worried that someone would say something to Celeste, someone would dig up the old bones. In truth, he was never sure what the old bones really were. He'd only guessed some variation of whatever the truth was, but he'd always been a good guesser. He knew he could never rely on Wilamena for a straight, bottom-line answer. Her truth was always her own private blanket, and she didn't share.

He really didn't know what other people imagined when they looked at him and his daughter. He didn't much care. The one who'd wounded him way back was Wilamena. He'd forgiven her long ago, because he knew he'd been no kind of husband in those days. He was in the streets just like she complained. He was a young man without purpose. She left him, left him with their two children, and he grew up. By then, she was gone and Celeste was his. He didn't know the truth but he suspected. It made no difference now.

21

Mrs. Owens must have been standing on the porch because as soon as the dust-roiling Dodge stopped, the screen door swung open, and she was moving down the steps, the path, her apron flipping up from her dress, hands in supplication, moving like a woman half her age through the flush pink and graying light of early evening. "They out trying to find her," she called. Her eyes searched inside the car.

Ed got out first. "Who?"

"Sissy ain't home yet." Mrs. Owens held herself upright like she'd been starched.

Celeste climbed out of the car slowly. In Detroit, children played outside until night during summer. Up and down the sidewalks on roller skates, tearing around on bicycles, playing hide-and-go-seek in the purple-fruited mulberry bushes. "It's not even dark yet." The implacable heat pounded her.

Mrs. Owens stepped back on the dirt path as if shocked the child was not with them, then remembered her manners: "How you doing, Mr. Jolivette?"

Ed held out his hands to Mrs. Owens, engulfing hers, calming her. She wiped her eyes with a corner of her apron. "I was praying y'all picked her up on the road. You know she just worship Celeste." The words "picked her up on the road" sank into Celeste. Highs and lows and dog barks and cicadas, a distant songbird on the wing trying to find home before night. She stood still to hear the quiet melody of sounds rising above the front of the house, merging now, not clear enough to distinguish. *Sissy ain't home yet.*

Celeste ran into the house to her room. On the dresser, Shuck and Billy caught in a calm, ease on their faces, in their sloping arms, Shuck smiling with his eyes, head cocked to the side. Her eyes cut away from the patched-up photo of Wilamena and Cyril Atwood. Poor Mr. Atwood. In the cracked mirror, her face already showed the distortion of another bad dream moving forward, devouring every good thing in its way. Had Sissy come to the back door looking for her? She'd been off in New Orleans having a good time. She'd first left early in the morning to ride to Meridian with Reverend and Etta Singleton, then left Meridian with Ed for the trip to New Orleans the next morning. For almost two full days she'd been unavailable. *Sissy, I left to mourn and then to rest for just a minute, and now you're gone. Don't do this, not today. Get back here.*

Royal blue night coming, cut-out sky with stars that seemed to touch and flicker, like the sky painted into the ceiling of a movie theater in Detroit, she and Billy sitting there staring at the big screen. The fake night of the theater ceiling encouraged illusion. Mississippi was like that: seemed too real to be true, like a dream world, a movie world, yet alive behind a curtain of wet air and monster blossoms, magnolias the size of a child's head. She came back outside.

"How long she been gone?" Ed's contained, sure voice was a balm on the evening air.

"Mrs. Tucker say she ain't been home since early morning." Mrs. Owens pointed to the Tucker house, her voice laying easier now. "Ain't like her."

Celeste didn't move near Mrs. Owens. Guilt curled through her. She wanted to call out that Sissy had been coming to the kitchen to get her freedom school lessons against her father's orders, that Sissy came to the church and hung out by the door. Mrs. Owens knew that already, but no one dared say it to Mr. Tucker. It was their secret. Even Reverend Singleton didn't know. If Mr. Tucker saw Sissy running from the back of the house or running from the church door, he'd punish her. He'd made that clear enough.

"Mr. Tucker and Reverend Singleton out trying to find her. Y'all might as well come on in here cause they know everywhere to look and y'all don't." Mrs. Owens let the screen door thud behind her. It should have been a cracking slam, a sound to break the doomful anxiety into which they treaded.

"She just ran away from home is all." Firecrackers went off in Celeste's head. "Mr. Tucker keeps her on a short rope." She stopped herself from feeding her own frenzy. Thoughts thick as bulrushes at the edge of the Nile. Child gone. *Need some luck here, Shuck. Need a good dream and a better number. Will you still bet on me, Shuck?* "She always stays back by the door looking out for Mr. Tucker the whole time. She loves stories about slaves escaping. Frederick Douglass is her absolute favorite." She waited for a judgment from Ed Jolivette.

Mosquitoes plunged into their skins, making them slap their arms and legs, leaving little spots of blood and black stems. Had Sissy signaled that she was about to flee?

"There you go." Ed didn't say anything else. Did he mean the story of Frederick Douglass inspired a child to flee?

"What're you saying?" Celeste fed the child's wanderlust at every opportunity and now she thought it was too much.

"You came to Mississippi because of stories you heard," Ed said. "A child could dream of leaving for the same reason."

"Dreaming and doing it are two different things." Celeste stared down the road toward the Tucker house. "Shouldn't we check on Mrs. Tucker?" She scratched the new mosquito bites, rubbing the flaking suntanned skin on her arms and ankles.

"Best to wait here like Mrs. Owens said. If Mr. Tucker and Reverend Singleton don't find her, they'll go to the police." Ed slumped across the shoulders as he spoke. "I'm going to sit with y'all for a while, but I got to get back on the road." The chirping wail of crickets started in, like soldiers singing in time to their steps.

"Why don't we go to the police now? If Sissy ran away because of the story, she'll be waiting for night somewhere, then searching for the North Star and trying to follow it."

"They're not our police." Ed sounded like Shuck, one foot in the mainstream and the other running. *God bless the child,* Shuck always said. Who would bless Sissy? *Not our police?* "Don't we have any police?" She mumbled it. Negroes barely had police in Detroit. The old people used to talk about it. If they stumbled onto a suspect or a solution, fine. If someone ratted, informed, they'd proceed. If Negroes didn't have police up there, they sure as hell didn't have any in Mississippi.

"She's a kid. Klan wouldn't want her." But as far as Sissy was concerned, the Klan wasn't the only danger. "If Mr. Tucker saw Sissy anywhere near the freedom school, he might be as bad as the Klan or worse." She put it out there hoping he'd pick it up.

Ed sat down on the porch steps with his legs apart, his elbows resting on his knees. "They don't care how old she is." His tight dark skin creased as if cut by a knife when he spoke. She saw the muscles in his jaws working.

"Doesn't have to be anything like that." Would he even entertain the thought that wherever Sissy was, it might not have anything to do with white people?

"What else would it be?" He took her in with the slightest break in his way of speaking. Something behind the words. He can't let it in. The possibility that Negro people destroyed each other too, even in the face of all the good that was going on. Not now, not during Freedom Summer.

"Negro people are no different from anybody else." She knew it wasn't true, sensed he could launch into epics that revealed how different Negroes were, starting with skin and hair, starting with slavery. Stand-outs, the differences shouted across the sunny landscape, dark skin stealing the light, always in high relief. Shadow people. Melody in the movements. Sorrows in the songs. Slavery changed everything forever. "Mr. Tucker's a dangerous man. Mrs. Owens said she saw the devil in his eyes one time. Like I said, he was real mean about Sissy coming to the freedom school." Celeste walked a few paces on the dry dirt path.

"Somebody's always disappearing in Mississippi." Ed seemed to be disappearing, too. He sounded like he didn't have anything left for this child.

He stood up and she leaned into him. Wasn't it enough that three young men had died? What else needed to happen for this to stop? She felt herself slipping down his body.

"You can't break now." There was still a sliver of light far off toward the west, pulling darkness across the world. She backed away from him for fear someone would see them showing affection in the open air. It was against movement rules to show affection, to fraternize romantically in the open.

"I hope it wasn't that Frederick Douglass story that sent Sissy running." But that's what she felt it was, that and her overbearing father. One way or another, it was the story that sang to Sissy, lulling her to believe that she too could be free by following a star. The freedom sirens opened their arms then pointed their fingers in the direction of her dreams. Messages coming from unseen places.

What felt like the last breath of life sighed out of her. "She must've come looking for me, and I was off in New Orleans having a good time."

"Don't do that." Ed reached for her but didn't pull her in close again.

"She's afraid of her father. Every time she stood in that church door, she knew she was challenging him. I should have been here." Celeste pleaded with him, with herself, with life.

"What were you going to do? Stop her father from being her father?" Ed shook his head.

She inhaled those words. *Shuck pushed his fist gently into her lower spine. Stand up straight before I put a board in your back.* It was always God bless the child, even when it came to something as unknowable as this, even when it came to having the strength to go one more step when you felt the bones in your knees turning to chips. Sissy might've run the long way around and ended up in the trees behind Mrs. Owens's house, waiting for a sign. If the Hudson had turned onto Freshwater Road, she would've taken off through the pines.

Celeste walked into the house, Ed behind her. Mrs. Owens sat in a pyramid of light in the stifling kitchen, stricken and worn-out, with the Bible on the table. *Take it to the Lord.* The back door was open as if some reprieve from the heat would walk up the weather-gray slat board steps, come inside, and sit awhile. Or Sissy, breaking into a run from the line of pines like a dart across the night, a shooting star, calling out, *I don't want to go home.* Celeste knew why she didn't want to go home. She knew why Sissy stayed by the church door, then disappeared, running around the neighborhood hurling herself at people, talking, lingering, laughing, letting everyone know she was any place but at the freedom school. Her alibi. Neighbors told Mrs. Tucker that Sissy stopped by. Mr. Tucker heard it. As long as she was nowhere near that freedom school.

They sat there, the house creaking and settling like it might fall if one more storm hit it. The bony dogs of Freshwater Road suddenly started howling and barking, kicking up dirt, sniffing for food, sending false alarms down the spine as they chased some skinny rat or gopher under the crawl space of another house just like this one.

But weren't they sitting in the kitchen too soon? Mourning begins here. When Grandma Pauline died, they'd gathered in the kitchen to whisper ancient stories, harvest tears, and stare into death's blank face. Even Wilamena had come to town for one day to bury her own mother. Long spaces of quiet as words failed. Sissy was only hiding from her father. *We don't need to be in this kitchen yet.*

Waxed paper covered a plate on the stove. Celeste put the plate into the buzzing refrigerator. Mrs. Owens poured iced tea for her and Ed, then started slowly turning the pages of her Bible. Darkness but for the single lightbulb overhead. They were three poker players in a backroom joint betting on Sissy's return. Ed planted his hands on the table and leaned back away from them in his chair. Steel in his eyes saying *I'm not getting on board the Jesus train.* The service in Meridian had taken its toll.

"I love Thee, O Lord, my strength." Mrs. Owens read from Psalm 18. "The Lord is my rock and my fortress and my deliverer."

Celeste found her lips moving along for a line or two, remembering she'd heard it a million times from Momma Bessie, Grandma Pauline, and every other Negro woman of a certain age she'd ever known. It was when their men died or went wild murdering themselves, or fell into the angry traps set for them every step of the way. They were there on Sunday mornings, fanning and fainting, when life and men became more than they could bear, when they needed the Lord as substitute man, as balm for life's never-ending abrasions.

Geneva Owens closed her eyes. "Lord, Jesus, please spare this child." She slid the Bible to Celeste. "Now, Celeste, you read. Try the 29. That's one we read together." Proud that here she was the teacher.

Celeste turned the thin, crinkling pages. Corners folded here and there. Rainy tear spots, circles of salt eating at the black-ink words and the oily secretions of desperate hands marking use, agreement, supplication. "Ascribe to the Lord, O sons of the mighty, ascribe to the Lord glory and strength." The words moved around in her mouth like sand crabs walking sideways, seeking a tide pool. Shuck didn't give much credence to the Bible. Said it had a way of hamstringing life. Momma Bessie and Grandma Pauline tussled with it, succumbed to it. She didn't have a clue as to where Wilamena was with it. "The voice of the Lord is powerful, the voice of the Lord is majestic." If not this Bible, then what?

Celeste moved the Bible towards Ed. Leaning back in his chair, respectful and disdainful at the same time. Arms folded across his chest. No.

Ed had lost faith. Was life in the south mean enough to wrench a person's faith right from their soul? Celeste thought that it might be, and turned her mind away from the Bible on the table.

Thin streaks of night coolness laced the heavy air. Mrs. Owens turned to the Book of Lamentations and read, "Remember my affliction and my wandering, the wormwood and bitterness. Surely my soul remembers, and is bowed down within me." She closed the book and rose from her chair, breaking the spell of lethargy. In the dim cave of light, Celeste looked into the darkness beyond the window.

Ed drove off into the night, heading for the Hattiesburg project where he'd meet up with Matt. Celeste held her breath as he pulled away, had kept quiet about asking him to stay and sleep again on Mrs. Owens's parlor floor. He and Matt would monitor the Hattiesburg project then continue on to Crystal Springs. She gnashed her teeth when she finally slept, a grinding that she heard in her dreams. Behind her eyes, John Coltrane played a celestial solo on a dark stage in a single circle of light. A white man stood in the middle of the concert hall, raised a gun, and shot him dead. Ed leaped from his seat beside her, his long legs climbing over seat backs, shoulders, people screaming. He tackled the man, took the gun, and shot him. Ed said "goodbye" with his eyes, ran toward an exit, and jumped into an ink-black river. He was gone.

22

The new morning sunlight hammered through the curtains. Thank God her room faced west. Celeste lay on her mattress on the floor, trying to remember what day it was. Just before dawn, she awakened, turned out the light, and napped some more, dreamed. Sissy hadn't knocked on her bedroom window. No hushed child's voice called, "Miss Celeste, I'm out here." The house barely breathed.

Celeste arranged the flat pillows and wrapped her legs around them. She dozed, dreaming of searching for Sissy on the wintry shores of Lake St. Clair wrapped in a blanket of hard-grained sand. The wind flew off the lake in frozen sheets, building the swirling snow into cotton-white dunes. She called to Sissy, her mouth full of snow, then crawled on frozen knees to the last place Sissy could've gone. To the water's edge.

She woke, the heat of the day rising and the sound of a car coming to a graveled finish in front of the house. Good, she thought. A visitor. She smelled baking biscuits and crept to the window. Reverend Singleton, hat in hand, no jacket, white shirt unbuttoned at the neck, tieless, closed his car door. Across the road, bluebirds flitted in deep pink crepe myrtle, and black crows marched in single file along the power lines. Reverend Singleton's hard-bottomed shoes struck the rickety front steps at a slow pace. He knocked on the outside screen door.

Mrs. Owens came from the back of the house. Celeste heard the small flat clank of the hook and eye being released and of Reverend Singleton stepping onto the porch out of the sun. Their voices were submerged in the splash of water as she quickly washed her face in the basin and brushed her teeth. Reverend Singleton and Mrs. Owens sounded as they did on the morning when she'd first heard them speaking together in the kitchen, but more somber.

"Celeste, Reverend Singleton here, want to talk to us." Mrs. Owens voice lifted onto a tight rope, high and breathless, just outside her bedroom curtain.

Celeste repeated her mantra, deep sigh words: *We need some luck here, Shuck.* "Yes, ma'am. I'm up." She did her daily ritual of throwing the mattress back up on the bed.

Reverend Singleton's eye whites were streaked with red lines. Orange and brown dirt smudges pocked his shirtfront. His sleeves were rolled to the elbows. It was crowded with three people, the rocking chair, and the straight-backed chair on the tiny porch, and Celeste wondered if it sank any under the weight. She felt fidgety, her hands searching for anchors, neck locked.

"Sister Owens, might I have a glass of water?" Reverend Singleton's eyes, usually forward-looking, direct, and strong, went sorrowful, sluggish. He seemed too tired to insist on anything.

"I'll get it." Celeste followed the aroma of frying bacon to the kitchen. Mrs. Owens called to her to turn the fire off under the skillet. A tin of fresh baked biscuits sat on the other side of the stove. She got the pitcher of cold water from the refrigerator and poured a glass for Reverend Singleton and drank off a glass herself, looking out the back door. No Sissy in the trees. Her dream flowed into a memory. She stood there holding the pitcher, staring out the kitchen door, not wanting to return to the front of the house.

On the porch, she handed Reverend Singleton the glass and thought of leaving again for something else, anything, to not hear what she knew he was about to say.

"I saw something I thought was orange in the light." Reverend Singleton drank. The water calmed him. "Couldn't tell from a distance. Could've been anything." He stopped to breathe, his eyes picking up life again. "Flowers. Could've been a late-blooming flower from a yellow-poplar tree in there or something. A lilly. Up close, it was pink."

She'd seen them, water lilies, floating on the bayou by the side of the road going down to Sophie Lewis's house.

Their lips went dry. Mrs. Owens backed up a step, stood now in the main doorway—her house behind her, drawing her away from this news. Celeste focused with all her might on Reverend Singleton.

"Don't you want a cup of coffee or something?" Mrs. Owens' hands fluttered as if blocking invisible messages. Her face sank into her head, the creases and furrows in her brow hanging in cliffs and ridges. "I'm makin' some breakfast. You welcome." Mrs. Owens stalled, not ready to hear the rest, trying to pull up the past, the pleasant breakfasts shared with Reverend Singleton when all seemed well. This ruined it all. Breakfast, a last meal before death taps on the door.

"No, ma'am. I been out all night with Mr. Tucker. We been in the woods, been... I got to get home. Thank you, though." Reverend Singleton didn't want to say it anymore than they wanted to hear it.

"What happened?" Celeste knew by now that country people didn't ask a lot of questions, just accepted everything. Like it was fate.

"Sissy was floating in Cataboula Creek southeast of here, her dress caught on some tree roots." His eyes teared. "That's all I know." He finished the water.

Celeste took his glass but couldn't move. Reverend Singleton stood just inside the screen door, while Mrs. Owens blocked the entry to the house. She felt stuck nearly in the middle of the leaning porch.

Shuck, what's the number when death is real? There's no good luck in it. Do we bet on death? Is it the only sure bet going? No phones to pick up, to hear the news from unseen faces. Everything from lips to ears with eyes to see and arms to hold. Sissy floating in the creek. But not the faking, playful deadman's float that kids did in summer lakes and pools back home. What was this? A little brown girl in pink with ribbons in her hair, her dress a water-filled balloon, her lungs new caves for tadpoles and swirling dense water. Not splashing and playing with other children to cool their molting skins in the deepest part of summer.

Celeste's face hardened into a mask so steely the backside of it had to be tears. "What you think?" Now she was talking like a local, even heard Wilamena in her mind telling her not to talk low. Said in her mind, *What do you think?*

Reverend Singleton released his own tears from the corners of his eyes and wiped them away with his hands. "They have to tell us something from over at Morris's. You know." He'd seen her floating. His tears would not be dammed behind any sort of mask. To see is to believe even among the faithful.

"But that's a funeral home. They don't know about investigating a death." Celeste pushed forward with her big-city knowledge even though that was exactly what she wasn't supposed to do. *Let the locals lead.* She cornered herself near her bedroom window, wished she could crawl inside, go back to bed.

"Mr. Tucker's in a shock." Reverend Singleton's eyes said something else to her.

"What's he think?" Celeste couldn't stop herself. It galled her that he was in shock now after trying to quash Sissy by degrees, the girl's child eyes going from great question marks to empty almond shells every time he came near. He had no right to be in shock. "He blames *me*?" The words had crept together into a thought without her even knowing they were on the move.

Reverend Singleton grew nervous and spoke fast. "Now, we know he's not in his right mind today." Poor Reverend Singleton was caught in the middle now, wanting this summer to be about voting rights and elections coming and here they were stuck on the death of a child.

"Wasn't in his right mind before today." Celeste cut her eyes at no one in particular, sat on the window ledge, praying it would hold her weight.

"Shush." Mrs. Owens threw her a look. Celeste lowered her head, a new kind of heat coming out of her body.

"He thinks the idea of freedom school got a hold of her mind, made her do things she wouldn't otherwise do." Reverend Singleton's hands paced the stingy brim of his straw hat. "To him, you and the freedom school, the thoughts about freedom, all the same thing."

"Maybe *he* got a hold of her." Celeste bounced up off the window ledge. Her anger startled them. It was nothing compared to what she felt. She wanted to punch holes in the tacked-on screen, throw the rocking chair out on the road, kick in the ribs of the bony dogs and scream at the trees. She wanted to run down the road and yell obscenities in front of the Tucker house. The older people waited for her to quiet.

Reverend Singleton stepped over to pat Celeste's arm. "Don't you worry. We'll straighten him out soon as the shock wears off."

She knew what that meant. She'd be gone at the end of the summer. That's when the shock would wear off. Whatever breath she had left inside emptied out. Her ears felt hot, full of cotton. Nothing down Freshwater Road looked the same. It narrowed and shrank; the hot sun burned the life out of it.

Mrs. Owens's hands sprang to her heart. "What 'bout them boys took Mr. Tucker's car? They mean as dirt. Maybe they did something?" Reverend Singleton didn't seem to hear Mrs. Owens's question. "They got ways of killing a person. It's not always guns and ropes."

"Sure you right." Reverend Singleton looked at her. "Needs to be checked thoroughly." A nervous little cough. "I sure don't know how she got all the way to that creek down there. It's nearly ten miles."

"Maybe someone drove her down there." Celeste spit it out.

"I'ma walk down and see Mrs. Tucker soon as I get me something to eat. She probably pretty bad off about now," Mrs. Owens said, before turning back inside. Celeste knew the older woman wouldn't want to cry in front of them. Kitchens were the crying rooms for women.

The minister watched Celeste. "Don't you go down there. Never. The word's not out yet so the kids'll probably show up at the church this morning. I'll be back in a few minutes to pick you up."

"What am I supposed to tell them?" Celeste stood, her nose touching the frayed screen, feeling like she didn't even have room to cry for Sissy. She'd make it a short session, send them home with Sojourner Truth and Harriet Tubman.

"Tell them Sissy's gone. Rest'll come later."

Celeste felt somewhere far back a slight relief taking shape that at least this death wasn't another Negro *man* who'd fallen into the region's oldest trap. "That creek's south of here. I just don't see why she'd be going that way. She knows north. Nothing we talked about mentioned going south."

Reverend Singleton's look chiseled her down to the bone. "What're you saying?"

"What I'm saying is, if the police don't investigate..." Her eyes went back and forth from Reverend Singleton to the Tucker house down the road.

"The police don't care about some little black child floating in a stream. The FBI either." Reverend Singleton got in his car. When he took off, a plume of rusty orange dust billowed up and swooned back down.

The flat, horrendous truth of what he said made her tired all over again, made her want to go back on the lumpy bed and hold the pillows between her legs, over her ears. It wasn't that Shuck, Grandma Pauline, and Momma Bessie hadn't said the same thing in one way or another all along. It was different now. This wasn't some unknown person's long-ago story. Not even a crosstown, East Side story she'd read in the daily paper. This was closer even than Goodman, Chaney, and Schwerner. She was a child, like the children in the church in Birmingham, completely innocent, no threat to anyone for any of the well-known reasons. A child who wanted to dream herself out of this place.

"Bodies in creeks and rivers tell their own stories." Mrs. Owens was back at the door, quiet and sad.

"Not unless somebody who knows what they're talking about gets involved." Celeste said it but didn't know if Mrs. Owens heard her.

When Reverend Singleton returned to pick her up, Celeste was standing on the steps, her book-bag locked in her arms. He'd changed his clothes and though his eyes looked weary, he seemed himself again. Nothing moved on all of Freshwater Road except the car heading back for the two-lane. Freedom Summer came first and in the whole scheme of things, Freedom Summer meant more. Deaths had been piling up here for a long, long time. If the movement was successful, that would change. You had to think in terms of priorities, of long-range benefits to the whole community.

As hard as she tried to grapple with this, Sissy's death kept riding over everything else. In her mind, the small deaths made the larger ones possible. Protect Sissy and everything else would fall into place.

Pineyville's town center didn't let on that one of its children had been pulled from a muddy creek. People walked in and out of the stores, pulled newspapers out of the boxes, cruised in trucks, strolled with umbrellas against the sun. The magnolia trees and the live oaks hadn't changed. Mr. Tucker's Hudson wasn't parked behind the gas station.

Tony Mobley sat waiting on the front step. His unusual stillness told her that he already knew what had happened. He got up, opened the church doors, and out came a long-faced Labyrinth, Georgie, and the other children. Now she had to go in there and sit with them, talk with them, help them to cope with the death of one of their own, somehow subtly give them the tools they needed to understand how terrific parents could be but also sometimes how dreadful. She would not be able to name names; Mr. Tucker was respected in Pineyville.

23

Celeste squatted on her haunches beside the spigot as the sun slinked on towards the horizon and the cloudless sky went blue-gray with streaks of orange. String-tied bunches of collards wrapped in newspapers had appeared on the steps of the house last evening and this morning. The water sprinkled and splashed and cooled her legs as she washed each broad-faced leaf front and back. Under the running water, her sun-dark hands shriveled. Her forearms cramped from the repeated motion, and she felt spasmodic aches in her back and thighs from the bending and squatting. Still, the work relieved her, numbed her longing for Ed and her suspicions about what really happened to Sissy. She'd rechecked her map. Cataboula Creek appeared then disappeared south of Pineyville, not far, but far for a child. Sissy was a runner; she could've made it there, but Celeste still didn't understand why she'd even start out running south. She tried to read where the creek flowed from, what river it emptied into. But the map wasn't clear.

When she'd filled the tub with cleaned collards, she carried it around to the back of the house where Mrs. Owens hacked off the coarse stems and rechecked each leaf for bugs and sand. Salt pork and hocks boiled in frothy water, smelling like Momma Bessie's Easter Sunday dinner, then the sweetness of the onions, and finally the greens, the mixing of the three turning into something that made you irrationally hungry, made you want to sit down and devour a plate full of greens with a little vinegar and sliced tomatoes and nothing else.

Celeste sat with a glass of iced tea and untied her red farmer's hand-

kerchief from her hair, folded it into a square, and used it to wipe her
sweat-drenched face. She'd been washing greens all afternoon. She held the
cold glass to her forehead, then her neck. Food was the balm of mourning.
In Detroit, it was food and drink. Death brought the whiskey bottles out
of their handsome cabinets. A mourner might end up drunk in a kitchen
chair, stuffed with food, narcotized against the pain of releasing a loved one.
The eating, drinking, philosophizing, and reminiscing went on for hours,
even days. By the day of the funeral, you were ready to put the deceased in
the ground just so you could rest.

Mrs. Owens drained most of the water off a large pot of cooled greens,
then divided them into bowls that she covered with wax paper and set in the
refrigerator. The last cooking pot steamed up the kitchen, sending vapors
out through the back door and the opened windows. She poured herself a
glass of tea and then sat down with Celeste, the two of them sweat-soaked
and weary. They cooked for Sissy's repast after her funeral tomorrow.

"You oughta open a restaurant in town." Celeste smiled through her
fatigue, felt like she'd been out picking cotton. "White people'd pay for
those greens you cook."

Mrs. Owens's dress front and apron were splotched with greens juice
and water. Her swollen knuckles clutched her iced tea glass, her fingers
beginning to arch out in the wrong directions. "I couldn't do this every
day, girl. Besides, they been getting 'em for free for years. If not mine, then
somebody else's."

Celeste leaned back in her chair, already calling Shuck in her mind,
already asking him to stake the Negro people of Pineyville by helping them
open their own restaurant. The closest Negro restaurant was in Hattiesburg.
Calling Shuck. Only now did she think of what that would mean in light of
Wilamena's letter. She always called Shuck. Before college, she called him at
the club when she got home from school, from dates, from other relatives'
houses. *Calling Shuck.* Now it was changed. Should she tell him? Ask him?
How to form the sentences in her mouth that might separate them in some
unseen way, some subtle letting go of all that had been? Would he still hold
on to her if Wilamena was telling the truth? If Wilamena didn't really know,
what would he want to do? Cast her out into the anonymous world, the
world of miscellaneous unattached people who drifted?

"You all right, child?" Mrs. Owens's hand was on Celeste's arm.

Celeste blinked away the tears that pooled in her eyes. She had to keep herself there at the table with Mrs. Owens, but she wanted to run out the door and down Freshwater Road to cry in solitude. "Yes, ma'am." They had been talking about starting a restaurant in Pineyville, she remembered. "We'll call it Madame Stone's Tea Room and serve whiskey in china teacups, collard greens, red beans with pickled pork and cornbread, shrimp and okra over rice on china plates." Celeste saw the two of them slaving over the collards then serving them on pretty plates. Lace cloths like Momma Bessie used. Teapots of whiskey, homemade in the backwoods and store-bought in New Orleans, poured into delicate cups. No more dry Pearl River County.

"Sounds nice enough. But we be under that jail soon as the sheriff finds out what's in those tea cups. And he will find out. Believe you me." Her eyes sparkled in her grooved brown face. "I don't take to drinking."

Celeste strained to keep up her end of the conversation, had lost interest in the idea. "Who knows? He might like it."

"Soon as we start taking in the money, some jealous no-'count come along and burn it down." Mrs. Owens sounded deep and sorrowful. "I know what they did over in Florida, and I heard what they did out in Oklahoma. People always leaving here and writing back, moving about trying to find some place better. Words travel."

"You mean like that riot in Detroit a long time ago?"

The kitchen grew silent but for the last steaming pot, the humming refrigerator pulling power from the lines in the back, the soft ting of ice cubes on glass. They could've been the early crowd at the Royal Gardens. Work-hard women who stopped by for a gin and tonic and an easy laugh on their way home.

"And more." Mrs. Owens turned toward the back door like a deer in the woods. *Red hats and white sheets coming.* Celeste followed her look, pushing away from the table and ready to drop to the floor.

"You lock that door?" The words stumbled on each other, her body frozen in the chair.

Celeste tried to see into the gray early night outside the door, trying to read the other woman's thoughts. "Yes, ma'am." The sandy earth obscured sound like baffling in a theatre. She waited for Mrs. Owens to move knowing she'd follow her, either to the floor, the front of the house, or to grab a cast-iron skillet to use as a weapon. Not a thought of nonviolence. Then came a faint knocking on the back wall of the house.

"Who's there?" Mrs. Owens went to the door, standing to the side.

Mrs. Tucker came up the steps so that the light of the kitchen revealed her face. "Ain't nobody but me."

Mrs. Owens unlatched the screen and held the door open.

Mrs. Tucker's dress belt hung from one loop and the weight of the open buttons pulled the bodice away from her chest so that the top of her slip showed. She wore no shoes. Her hair stuck out in tufts on one side and lay flat on the other. In the light, Celeste could see what looked like a straightening comb burn blistering on her retreating cheek.

Mrs. Owens sat her down, brought ice from a tray, and held it to the woman's face. "Celeste, pour Zenia some tea."

"You supposed to use butter." The words caught in her throat.

Mrs. Owens continued her first aid. "Not 'less you want to cook it some more."

Celeste put the glass on the table, thinking of Sissy the first time she came running through that back door from among the pines.

Mrs. Owens studied Zenia Tucker. "You scared us to death."

Zenia drank. "Didn't mean to." Her hands shook. Mrs. Owens helped her get the glass to her mouth and back to the table without spilling all the tea in her lap. "I can't stay long." She kept her eyes down. "They went over to Hattiesburg to get Sissy. Him and the Reverend. Take her to the church…" She broke off. Sissy's casket would be small enough to fit in the back seat of the big Hudson. "I can smell them greens all the way down the road. Smell good." Mrs. Tucker's hands rested.

Maybe the aroma of the greens spread through the air all the way into town. A hundred white people drawn to their windows trying to place where the aroma came from, then leaving their houses to follow the scent like hungry ghosts in the night, walking along the two-lane in single file, bringing their glistening faces all the way to Freshwater Road to eat Geneva Owens's greens. Coming to the home they left a long time ago, hands out, hearts out, needy for the love in that pot of greens.

Zenia Tucker sighed so deeply it seemed her heart would have to stop beating. When she inhaled, the words rode out. "If I had a gun, I'd put it to my own head." She dropped her eyes again, searching her lap, her dress, her hands that wrung, one over the other, as if they throbbed with some unrelenting arthritic pain.

Mrs. Owens turned the fire off under the greens. "Well, then, I'm glad you don't have one." She released the lid to rush the cooling. "You've got them boys to raise." From her place at the stove, Mrs. Owens gestured to Celeste to leave the two older women alone.

She excused herself knowing full well she was going to lurk and listen. She crouched on the linoleum floor just behind her curtain door.

Mrs. Tucker's broken voice came in fits and starts through the short hall. "He saying he think them white boys took his car that time killed Sissy. To get back at him for having the car in the first place."

"I've seen them driving real slow by the gas station." Mrs. Owens's voice flattened. "Tryin' to scare somebody. I wouldn't put it past 'em."

If Celeste moved, even breathed too deeply, Mrs. Owens, who knew every sound the little house made at every hour of the day and night, would know she was listening. She leaned her head against the doorless doorframe, feeling the cool linoleum. Ice cubes clinked as their glasses came down on the table after each sip.

"Sure nice your boys give you that refrigerator, Geneva."

It was too big and too modern for the kitchen, but Celeste wondered if she could've made it through the summer without its ice trays and cool little blasts every time she opened it.

"Don't know what I'd do without it." Mrs. Owens stopped. The silence between the two women pounded like muffled drums. A tapping, perhaps a spoon on the tabletop.

Celeste crawled halfway out of her room into the hallway, holding her breath, afraid to lean now for fear the wall would creak. Mrs. Owens only had to peek around a corner to see her sitting there huddled on the floor. The parlor was dark and quiet. She sat there losing the two women for a moment, feeling like crawling into the room where Ed had slept, pressing her body into the floor to find some scent of him.

Zenia's voice relaxed to a smoother flow. "They still sending you something?

"Don't know what I'd do without that either. My hands don't let me do washing and cleaning the way I used to." Celeste imagined Mrs. Owens holding her hands up so that Mrs. Tucker could see the way the fingers were beginning to angle to the right and left. "Course you know that child give me some money for the summer, too. That's been a help."

Celeste liked the way she referred to her as "that child." She was nearly twenty, but it made her feel like some woman's daughter.

"Oh, I didn't know that. Wished my boys was grown and gone from here." Heavy rocks weighted her words. "Maybe I go with them." She sniffled. Celeste imagined her sitting there with her hair, part fresh-washed kinky and part straightened, tears coming down her face, salt stinging the burn on her cheek. Wanted to strain a little farther into the hall so she could see them—but if she could see them, they could see her. She sat still.

"You might not like it. I didn't. Course you younger than me." Mrs. Owens's tone soothed the air as if she were talking to a troubled child who promised to do better the next time.

"If they go, I'm not staying with him." Mrs. Tucker's voice cut like a newly sharpened carving knife when she said "him." "Shoulda taken Sissy and left a long time ago."

"He's a good provider." Mrs. Owens spoke but it was like a crash, like a crane falling from a mountain-high building. She spoke of Mr. Tucker so differently now. This was the man in whose eyes she'd seen the devil. Why was she being so kind? Celeste nearly gave herself away, wanted to stand from her hiding place and scream. Remember the devil in his eyes? Is the devil a "good provider?" She had to remain still.

"Sometimes I think he did it. Chased her to death. I don't know what he was doing with her. He ain't right." Ice cubes clinking, glasses thudding on the table.

Zenia, for the first time, sounded like she had some sense. Celeste felt nothing but confusion.

Silence. Celeste was trapped, couldn't move back into her room or run out the front door into Freshwater Road screaming. She never had gone to see Mrs. Tucker about Sissy. It might have given the woman an opportunity to tell something. It might have given Celeste a chance to say something, too.

"Let me get these greens in the box." Celeste heard Mrs. Owens's chair move away from the table, heard her forking greens into bowls and refrigerating them. "He wouldn't know what to do without you."

The only words flying through Celeste's mind, ready to leap from her mouth were, "Lord, have mercy." She felt as if Mrs. Owens had betrayed Zenia Tucker and her, too. But Mrs. Owens wasn't a betraying kind of person. What did this mean?

"I don't know what to do with him no more." Mrs. Tucker sounded distant.

"You got to think about them boys. They your children, too." Geneva Owens brought her practical reality to the table.

Celeste heard it but somehow it wasn't enough to justify the rest. Mrs. Tucker had to make it through this crisis because of her two other children. Understood. But was staying there with "the devil" the only way to do it? Clarity came so slowly. What else was a poor woman with two other children supposed to do? Run away from home? And do what? Celeste's head pounded.

"I better get on." A chair scuffed the floor. Bare feet softly padding over the linoleum. The back door opened.

"Watch yourself now." Mrs. Owens relatched the screen door, alarms laying quietly in her voice.

"Don't feel I have much to lose one way or the other." She must've been walking away because her voice disappeared.

"It'll be better in a while." Mrs. Owens called it out.

The old pump on the back porch sucked, gurgled, and spewed, the gears grinding in their connection.

Celeste crawled back into her room, sat on the floor leaning against the bed, staring into the lightless room. Sissy had escaped to the only freedom she would ever know. A crank turned in Celeste's stomach. She tried to wrap her racing mind around the possibility that Mr. Tucker molested his daughter, that he killed her. Mrs. Tucker seemed to be saying that and not saying it at the same time. As mean as he was, Celeste wouldn't allow it to take shape in her head. How, in these tiny wood houses where every creak and groan echoed through the rooms? Had Mrs. Tucker covered her head with pillows, put orange dirt in her ears and gone to the outhouse in the middle of the night instead of using her night jar, sat on her screened porch rocking and singing to herself, blotting out the sounds? What about those sons? They wouldn't even know the difference. Zenia Tucker reached for reason in an unreasonable world, but still, Mr. Tucker had a hand in killing Sissy, Celeste believed. If he didn't hold her head under the water, he chased her to the water's edge and damned her to save herself.

The day after Sissy's funeral, Celeste woke to the smells of chicory-laced coffee and frying bacon. A scattered dog bark, a blackbird's cawing. She lay there staring at the ceiling. Late summer felt like a sojourn through hell's basement with no vents and no stairway out. Birds flew short trips from shady tree perches to any nearby water. Dogs slept during the day under houses, cars, rocks. Mississippi's already slow-moving life rhythm became a piteous crawl, the blood flow thickened like molasses.

In Detroit, a thousand cool lakes and pools relieved. When things got too oppressive, the city opened water hydrants to cool the roaming summer children. In Mississippi, you sat and rocked and fanned. You drank iced tea and lemonade until it ran out of your ears, until the sweetness made your teeth ache and your stomach turn.

At the funeral, the Tuckers had sat in the front row near the stained and polished wood casket, which was balanced on two sawhorses with a white drape, the lid half open. The freedom school children placed their strings of flowers across the lid. Other homemade flower arrangements surrounded the casket. Reverend Singleton taught the lesson of II Samuel, Chapter 12, on the death of a child, saying that during the time Sissy could not be found, eyes feasted on tears and hearts cracked, feet trod the forests in the night searching. Now Sissy lived in her new home and it was time to celebrate her placement in God's Kingdom. He spoke of her death without saying what had happened to her, as if she was a sacrifice for the greater good, as if she'd died to pull them together and move them forward. Celeste sat in the church staring at the back of Mr. Tucker's head as she'd done in the car the first day she met Sissy, suppressing the urge to stand and testify against him, to tell all she'd heard Zenia Tucker say in Mrs. Owens's kitchen. The Negro community had closed ranks against the truth.

When it came time to file past the casket, Etta Singleton played "Amazing Grace." Mr. Tucker stood and put his hand out for his wife. She didn't move. It seemed he stood there for the longest time waiting for her to get up. He leaned in trying to pry her from the seat, but she brushed his hands off and lowered her head, her shoulders caving in, sobs coming from her that were so wrenching that soon the entire church body wept openly. Crying and fanning with the desolate music squeezing out the last heartfelt memory of Sissy, and anyone else who'd died in recent memory.

Finally, Mr. Tucker walked alone to Sissy's casket, stood briefly, then took his seat, his head down. Then Mrs. Tucker got up and leaped towards the casket, flinging herself over it, rocking the sawhorses, sobbing. Reverend Singleton, in a white robe that flew out behind him, rushed over to comfort her and to pry her fingers from the edges of the casket. He walked her back to her seat. She stayed well away from Mr. Tucker, on the other side of her two boys, and never once looked at her husband.

When Geneva Owens and Celeste walked past the casket, Celeste set her eyes on the cloth cradling Sissy. She didn't want to see the lifeless brown body that used to be a living, breathing child whose face was all questions. Finally, she looked at the dead child. What marks had been hidden by the mortician's "good" work? Those almond eyes pressed close, set above high cheekbones in a delicate oval face. Dark hair plaited and adorned with white ribbons. Celeste wanted to raise her up out of the coffin and shake the life back into her. Pineyville needed a second line, a better way to release this pain.

When she and Mrs. Owens turned from the casket to resume their seats, Celeste felt the eyes of Mr. Tucker on her like firebrands. He glared with open hostility, seemed ready to come after her right there in the church. The mourners wept and squirmed in their seats, but no one stood to testify, to call out a thought as to what had really happened to Sissy. Someone filled with anger and impatience, some man or woman of the town who'd grown weary of having no police except ones who terrified them, might have stood up for Sissy's life and her death. But they didn't. They mourned her as if by rote, as if mourning children compared to feeding chickens. The Negro community of Pineyville crying, sobbing really, but no one said a word.

They buried Sissy just beyond the sacred ground in the regular cemetery.

On the way back to Freshwater Road, Celeste stopped at the pay phone and dialed the Jackson office, not sure if the words to come would be a begging plea to be relieved of her responsibility or not. She asked to speak to Ed Jolivette and when he came on the line, she didn't know what to say. After a long pause, she got out, "We just buried Sissy." The sun knuckled her under. "I don't think I'm going to make it." Her lips moved, desert winds of heat crossing her mouth, her head leaning against the metal frame that held the phone, knees locked so she wouldn't fall. Reverend Singleton and his wife and Mrs. Owens waited in the car.

24

Celeste dreamed of death like an old person reaching back for life. Sissy, a low-flying angel, swept through her nights. Celeste thought before she awoke that soon she'd be with Sissy, flying free; they'd wave to Mickey Schwerner, James Chaney, Andrew Goodman, Medgar Evers and all the others, and life would be so peaceful and clean, so beautiful, you had to turn your eyes away. Unbearable beauty. That turning away woke her thinking in real time that her days were numbered. She'd been spared when the troopers beat Matt on the highway, untouched when the cops in Jackson picked her up for littering the sidewalk with her fliers. It was about averages. Much like walking on balance beams. You had to fall sometime, and you knew it would hurt. Going to see Mr. Heywood, the registrar of voters, she figured, would be her time for falling.

Reverend Singleton set up a mock registrar's office in the space between the front row and the pulpit steps. He'd seen the registrar's office on more than one occasion and described it for them. A polished dark oak counter divided the large space into a waiting area with hard chairs near the entry door and a typist/secretary area with desks, where three white women sat talking on the telephone and typing. A large Confederate flag was tacked up on one wall of the typist area. The windows on the their side overlooked the main street and the entrance to the building. On the countertop, large ledger books were stacked like squat posts. A small shiny chrome press-bell illuminated the counter. The inner door with "Mr. Heywood" in block gold letters led to the registrar's office. Reverend Singleton said he'd never gotten that far.

Those who had chosen *not* to go on the first try play-acted the roles of the whites, berating the would-be registrants, even pretending to hit them. The first-round volunteers had to fervently embrace nonviolence. The fury unleashed when a Negro person fought back could not be anticipated or measured. *Be prepared to drop to the floor, pray, sing freedom songs, do whatever you can to protect yourself, but do not retaliate.* The moral responsibility for what happened lay then at the feet of the aggressor. Some whites didn't care. Some Negroes wanted to fight, didn't have any more cheeks to turn. Mr. Landau was that kind of man.

Mr. Landau was the only man besides Reverend Singleton to attend all the voter education classes over the summer. But he was still a member in good standing of the Deacons for Defense and Justice in Bogalusa. No way for him to go with the first group to see Mr. Heywood unless he disavowed all violence, self-defensive or not. He'd as soon pull out a shotgun and start blasting if the going got rough—especially against the women. The Deacons would provoke no violence, but they'd let no attack go unanswered. The various church members who'd listed in and out of the class all summer volunteered for the second, third, and fourth groups.

At Sunday church services, Reverend Singleton continued to make reference to the memorial service in Meridian, preached more than one sermon about why the three had been killed, about how that put the torch in the hands of each of them to carry on. He never talked about Sissy. Their children, he said, must know what those young men stood for, that they laid down their lives for freedom. He vigorously underlined the fact that two of the dead boys were white. This freedom was beyond and above race. There was no turning back now. They'd spent the summer in preparation for the days to come and everyone had to be on board the train. If you couldn't ride in the first car, that was fine, ride in the second or the third. It didn't matter if you ended up in the caboose as long as you were on the train. He preached more calmly, laying it out for everyone. Celeste heard Ed Jolivette's quiet, zen-like approach in the reverend's new way of preaching. He fired up the congregation for only the briefest moment. She wondered if the churchgoers were disappointed, if he'd intentionally left them smoldering rather than allowing them to release their pent-up and sometimes furious spiritual passion, a religious passion that had, it seems, as much to do with oppression as with anything else. They were going to need all of that and more to get through what lay ahead.

On a Monday morning, Celeste and Mrs. Owens climbed into the back seat of Reverend Singleton's car dressed in their churchgoing clothes. Mrs. Owens wore her hat, her hair braided and snuggled at the nape of her neck. She brought along her Bible, as if the experience of going to see the registrar of voters had some religious significance. Celeste had washed and ironed her peach cotton dress, but decided not to wear her pumps in case things got out of hand. She wore her tennis shoes—she wanted to be able to dodge any blows without slipping in those pumps, or getting her toes squashed in her sandals. Her hair was pulled back in her usual summer ponytail.

Way down the road, Reverend Singleton stopped for the thread-thin Sister Mobley who stood outside her house in a much-washed summer dress, holding her Bible and a small cotton purse. She climbed in next to Reverend Singleton in the front seat. Celeste wondered if the Bibles were meant to protect them from blows to the head. Or maybe they give solace, a spiritual buttress against the realization that the white people of Pineyville despised them beyond their wildest and worst anticipations, possessing a simmering hatred, an unqualified disdain that could be provoked by a laugh or even a smile, and ratcheted up quickly and irrationally to physical abuse. The local Negroes knew this, but had learned to live in fear of it, had bowed down in the unyielding face of it for too many years to count. The hope was that nonviolence would tamp down the hatred a bit, keep it from erupting like Vesuvius when these awakened Negro people stood up and said, I'm here, I matter. Celeste knew already that this hatred would not be conquered by the summer, or by a winter or any other quantification of time.

"Where you at, Miss Tyree?" Tony stood on the sagging front porch waving, the little man of the broke-down house, left at home to babysit his two shoeless younger sisters while his mother went to register to vote. She'd never heard "where you at?" until Ed Jolivette said it. Now, Tony used it with a smile as if he knew something. It made her blush.

She waved. "All right now, Tony. You take care." She turned her eyes away, pretended to do something on the car seat. At this distance, Tony couldn't read the embarrassment she felt for the poverty the Mobleys lived in. She faced the boy through the open car window again. "See you in school tomorrow morning, Tony." She wanted to tell him what to do in case she wasn't there, in case she was sitting in the Pearl River County jail, but that might scare him.

"I be there." He helped the younger ones wave goodbye.

Sister Mobley leaned in front of Reverend Singleton and called out to him. "Mind the girls, Tony."

"Yes, ma'am." Tony looked like a miniature man, arms around the shoulders of his younger sisters.

The car pulled away. If they got arrested, who in God's name would care for Tony and those little girls? Celeste stared at her hands in her lap, helpless. What if they weren't allowed a phone call? Wilamena waved from the wings, whispering *I told you it was too much to bear.* Shuck stood on the other side, his best-of-Negro-life wallpaper lit up behind him.

"Etta's coming if we get arrested." Reverend Singleton must have seen the forlorn look on Celeste's face in his rearview mirror, spoke as if he'd been inside her head.

She nodded, relieved. "Will she meet the children for freedom school?"

The DeSoto crunched the gravel and sand road. "She'll be there for a bit. Long enough to make sure they're all right."

"Good." Fear cartwheeled inside Celeste—for them, for the children, for every Negro person in Mississippi. She watched the cypress wood shack-houses of Freshwater Road, one in slightly better repair than another, all too small for families, too airy, too rundown to be anything but firewood. It felt like they were going to a funeral.

The Tucker boys sat on their front porch staring with blank faces at the passing car. No sign of Zenia Tucker. Celeste saw them turning into copies of Mr. Tucker already, hoped they'd catch themselves before then. Zenia wasn't much good to them now.

Mrs. Owens fidgeted with her Bible. "What about our bail?" She glanced out at her little house as they rolled by. Everything quiet.

Celeste disconnected her feelings from the house when they passed; she needed to separate herself from everything. Just float. No memories of Ed in the front seat of Matt's car, no day in New Orleans riding on the St. Charles Avenue streetcar and kissing in the shady sunlight of Audubon Park, no need to call Shuck, not even any anger at Wilamena. Just free float. Nothing in her pocket but identification and payphone money. Kleenex. Maybe she should've put in Band-Aids and disinfectant for any wounds. Hard to carry a bottle of mercurochrome, though. They needed a good first-aid kit for Reverend Singleton's car. She'd forgotten.

"What if someone gets hit or something? We might need a doctor." She realized instantly she shouldn't have asked that question in front of Mrs. Owens and Sister Mobley.

"We just have to pray that doesn't happen, and if it does anyway, we'll just have to run over to Hattiesburg. There's a doctor over there who'll treat Negroes." Reverend Singleton put the prayer in it. Mrs. Owens and Sister Mobley kept their eyes hard on the road ahead. Celeste, as embedded as she was in this town and in this moment, shook her head, sinking inside at the neglectful thing Reverend Singleton said. *There's a doctor over there who'll treat Negroes.* How had this insanity lasted for so long? She'd believed her entire life that doctors had a spiritual significance, right up there next to ministers, that they would not traffic in prejudice and bigotry. Healers. They were healers.

"Etta'll come and bail us out, if it comes to that. She's got the money to get started. The Jackson office will send down more with a lawyer," he reminded them. The church body had planned for this day by putting nickels and dimes in a special basket all summer long. Sophie Lewis had also contributed more, just for this. The One Man, One Vote office pitched in money, too. Northern volunteers put in their own bail money. She knew Shuck had followed her instructions. If they were arrested, they'd be in jail for at least a few hours.

"I was sure hoping Mr. Landau would change his mind and come on." Sister Mobley stared out the window.

They neared the town center. Reverend Singleton gripped the steering wheel with both hands. "Well, he's with us in spirit, you know that."

Celeste wished he'd been ready, too, but in truth, she wished he'd come and brought along one of his guns. Be nice to have a man with a gun protecting them when they walked in that building. Maybe someone stationed in the thick foliage of the trees. Maybe he'd bring his whole group of Deacons for Defense and Justice to stand guard. That would change things. All-out war. Celeste chastised herself for dwelling on self-defense with guns. It was a flight of fancy, a protective urge, but it went against everything the movement was about that summer. She'd already heard Matt and Ed speak of the Deacons as if they were black angels, protector spirits. It wasn't just her own terrified thinking. Everyone thought it. And it was natural to do so, to think of protecting oneself, one's community from people who would destroy it. The philosophy of nonviolence wouldn't help against the blows. It might help in rebuilding the character of the south. Later.

The first phone call if they were arrested was to Mrs. Singleton. She'd make the calls to the Jackson office and the FBI. The Jackson office would do the rest. No guarantee they'd be allowed to make any phone calls at all, though. They rode the rest of the way in silence with the breeze planting salty sweat splotches on their faces, their hearts pounding like furious drumming signaling danger.

Then they were in Pineyville, so benign and seemingly unaware, a quaintly painted village with verdant landscape all around. The magnolias stood so still. Early morning walkers and greeters came out of the dollhouse of a coffee shop. No Negroes allowed inside. A man bought a newspaper from the vending machine. Celeste'd done that. A New Orleans *Times-Picayune,* a Jackson *Clarion-Ledger.* Mr. Tucker quietly worked on a car at the gas station, pretending to not see them go by on their way to the Pearl River County Administration Building. Did he know this was their big day? Celeste tried to see in her mind the faces of everyone who'd been at the church on Saturday, their final day of practicing for today. Was there one among them who might have alerted the sheriff they were coming? No way to know. Mrs. Owens stared into her lap, then drifted her eyes out the window. Quiet. Sister Mobley's thin neck might crack if she moved.

Reverend Singleton made a smooth maneuver into a parking space on the far end of the block. Nothing going on in front of the building. Magnolias. Two sheriffs' cars parked, empty. People walking in and out. This was the county seat. People came from miles around to do their business, but Negro people were forbidden to enter through the front door.

They sat in the car. At that moment, Celeste remembered a little detail she'd heard in Jackson: "When we get to the registrar, don't be surprised if they ask us how many bubbles there are in a bar of soap. That's what they're doing up in the Delta." She smiled at them, not sure if they took it as gospel or just thought she was making a joke. It fell flat. Nobody said a word. Reverend Singleton opened his door.

Celeste stepped out of the back seat. This was the reason she'd come to Mississippi. As it was, if every Negro person in Pearl River County voted, they'd be even with the whites nearly head for head. The One Man, One Vote office tallied their canvas of the previous year for every county in the state. Freedom Summer came to Mississippi because of its high population of Negro people. If you broke this bad-dream place down, the rest of the south would be like a cushioned ride in a limousine.

The sidewalk to the building heaved with magnolia roots, and for much of the way there was shade. The air was heavy with a sweet fragrance. Cars were slowing as the drivers realized a small group of Negroes were headed towards the front entrance of the Pearl River County Administration Building.

Reverend Singleton walked side by side with Sister Mobley. Celeste stayed close to Mrs. Owens. Up the entry walk, white faces were shocked beyond words. Heads turning, words trailing off. A woman stumbled while looking one way at them but walking the other. Celeste was going deaf, dumb, and nearly blind with fear. *Keep walking. Remember those freedom songs you've been singing all summer long, remember what Margo said, sing in your mind, hold those words. "Keep on a'walkin', keep on a' talkin', on my way to freedom's land." Mrs. Owens knows these people. They know her. They know Reverend Singleton and Sister Mobley, too. I'm the stranger.* Celeste wanted to hide behind Mrs. Owens's skirts, bring up the rear, get scolded, get some relief from this responsibility of cracking open the stones of the past.

They bunched together in the cool foyer with its gold-framed paintings of the Confederate sons of Mississippi. Celeste focused on the paintings to calm herself, like a dancer spotting during a pirouette. Two-time governor and former U.S. Senator T.G. Bilbo; Confederate President Jefferson Davis; James Vardaman, governor when the Jim Crow laws passed, and night riders galloped on thin-legged horses with kiting white sheets and guns that crackled through rural silences. Pink-faced men in full Confederate regalia. A framed larger-than-life Confederate flag. The foyer was a museum of oppression. No sign of President Lyndon B. Johnson, or even John F. Kennedy, and he'd been dead less than a year. No American flag anywhere to be seen. Were they even in America?

Reverend Singleton ushered them toward the wide stairway leading up to the registrar's office. Polished wood balustrades. Muted sunlight coming in the tall high windows as if they'd entered the nave of a cathedral. People with papers, clicking heels on the hardwood floors, fast-walking, whispering, heading for cover. White men in shirtsleeves, white women in summer dresses, hair up in the heat. The men standing back, folding their arms, fire smoldering in their eyes.

"Y'all ain't supposed to be coming in the front door." Mr. Heywood's clear curt voice echoed off the hard walls and floor, his accent all Mississippi drawl as he descended so fast he seemed to be sliding over the tops of the steps, his flat straight hair rising, his suit jacket catching the breeze, billowing out to the sides under his flapping elbows.

His speed stunned Celeste. He seemed to be flying toward them. He must have been daydreaming out the front windows, seen them coming up the walk, disbelieving his own eyes as they strolled under his calm, thick magnolias, blackening his view of the pearl white flowers. Negroes coming with their Bibles and their reverends and these new-age carpetbaggers.

"Morning, Mr. Heywood. We coming up to see you about registering to vote." Reverend Singleton spoke crisply, all dignified in his gray preacher suit, a pale pink shirt giving him a rakish, big-city air.

Mr. Heywood stood panting in the center of the foyer, using a white handkerchief to wipe the sweat from his forehead. "Is that right?" His tone circled the words with a suppressed, condescending anger.

Celeste inched closer to Mrs. Owens. Sister Mobley clutched her Bible, stiff, erect, lips clenched together. She stepped closer to Celeste and Mrs. Owens, let Reverend Singleton lead. Celeste marveled again at how the white people stayed so white even in the magnified sun of southern Mississippi. It was as if they weren't really there, or really lived someplace else out of the sunshine, some place cool.

"Geneva, I told you to get that gal out of your house. Didn't I tell you that just little more than a week ago?" His anxious sincerity caught Celeste. "That school she's operating is wholly illegal, and she's living in your house while she does it." He pleaded as if talking to a recalcitrant child, as he waved a dismissive hand towards Celeste. *Gal.*

Reverend Singleton stepped back to be closer to the rest of them. Mrs. Owens looked at the floor. Celeste followed her eyes down to her run-over shoes, the leather worn thin, her old-style cotton stockings puckering around the shoe rims and breaking through the leather near the big toe. Mrs. Owens had better. These were her fighting shoes, just as the tennis shoes were Celeste's. She glanced over at Sister Mobley's white, in-service shoes, the shoes she wore to clean houses; they were soft-bottomed, wouldn't slip. Good.

Mrs. Owens lifted her face to Mr. Heywood. They locked eyes. "You did."

From that moment, Celeste knew that they were in for it. She doubted any Negro person had ever looked him so deeply in the eye and lived to tell about it.

Mr. Heywood sneaked glances in all directions. "Do I need to call the sheriff in here?" He scanned the hallways. He didn't need to call very far. Just the sight of them standing there was prompting alarms. Celeste wondered if, in all the years that Pineyville had been a town, had any group of Negro people ever walked into the foyer through the front door? The news was sure to fly all over town.

"We are ready to register to vote." Reverend Singleton persisted. "Now, we've mastered the Mississippi State Constitution, the United States Constitution, and the Bill of Rights."

Mr. Heywood's head jerked in the direction of Reverend Singleton. "I don't care if you mastered the Magna Carta. Niggers don't belong in here. Voting ain't got nothing to do with you."

Celeste heard the words Magna Carta, and niggers, too, as she saw the bloodshot hatred rise in Mr. Heywood's eyes, his face in full flush now. How could he even speak the words Magna Carta in this place? Did he know the Magna Carta? Of course he must. This was a man of poetry, of books, of flowers and trees. She felt Mrs. Owens tremble and put her hand on the woman's arm to steady her. He'd called them niggers.

"We been studying all summer. We ready." Mrs. Owens never said his name. "Ain't no need for name-callin'."

"If y'all don't get the hell out this building, you going be looking at the inside of a jail cell. Now, study that. Go on, now, get out that side door." Mr. Heywood took in a huge amount of air, exhaled. "We forget this ever happened. Now, go on. You hear?"

How generous, Celeste thought. The side door rather than the back door. Progress. Didn't want them contaminating the front of the building again. Something was telling her it was time to go. They'd made their first try. Time to rethink and regroup. Out of the corner of her eye, she saw a man who must be the sheriff fast-walking down the hallway toward them, passing under the white glass shades of the lights that lined the ceiling. A blur of brownish pants and shirt, a silver badge, belt buckle, and shining buttons, a gun handle, a flushed white face, young and hearty. Grandma Pauline would say, "He come from good white stock, strong as dirt." *Nothing to play with.* No movie star cop with a fat cigar. Young enough, she realized, to be with the movement.

Celeste thought it was time to leave, but Sister Mobley spoke. "Mr. Heywood, peoples got a right to registe' and they got a right to vote. We want ta take that test like everybody else. Today. We don't take it today, we gon be back tomorrow, the day after tomorrow, and the day after that. Gonna be more of us next time." She pursed her lips as if fully expecting her words to be the final push to their success.

Celeste hadn't expected thin Sister Mobley, with her hair pressed to stick-straightness, to say anything at all. She turned to look at the woman, not knowing whether to encourage her on or to whisper to her to be quiet, let Reverend Singleton lead. Celeste was proud of her, and confused by her courage.

Mr. Heywood saw it all coming first and backed up a few steps. By the time Celeste caught up with Mr. Heywood's eyes, Sheriff Trotter had spun Reverend Singleton out from the group, picked him up by the lapels of his nice summer gray suit so that his feet dangled above the floor, and thrown him across the foyer. She felt out of step, unable to catch the moment. Reverend Singleton stayed in the air for the longest time, it seemed, his face contorted in surprise, his impeccable clothes bunched up under his chin, the pink of his shirt in a gnarl next to the shock on his brown face. Nothing in their practice sessions at the church had prepared them for this.

Celeste watched not sure of what she was seeing, feeling heat in her ears that muffled the sound until a passing child screamed "mommy," and the child tried to run toward Reverend Singleton as if to catch him. Her mother snatched the girl up, her Shirley Temple curls shaking and shining in the cathedral light. Reverend Singleton's feet came down on the hardwood, and he slalomed backwards unable to regain his balance before finally hitting the far wall and crumpling to the floor. The sound echoed in the cold hard foyer. Celeste wanted to move toward him to help him, not sure if she should drag Mrs. Owens and Sister Mobley with her. *Stay together.* She saw the sheriff to her side, retucking his shirt, and she decided to go for Reverend Singleton, who hadn't budged. His eyes were closed. She moved one foot toward him and before she'd completed the step, she felt the cold metal on her temple, just a circle of coolness, then heard the cocking of a gun.

"Take one more step, nigger, and I'll blow your brains all over this lobby." The sheriff spoke quietly, calmly, with complete authority, his voice thick with accent but somehow smooth, even, not dipping too far, like he might be from someplace else. Celeste doubted one other person in the lobby heard his words—she wasn't even sure she heard those words herself.

The stillness in the foyer deafened thought. Then the sniffle of the child echoed off the polished wood, the beginning of a cry. She remembered her own helpless crying when a blind man had come to the door begging for money, how she'd pulled on Shuck to give the man some money. Reverend Singleton opened his eyes and nodded "no," his body still splayed out like a drunk on a no-name corner. In that flaring moment, Celeste saw black, then lost her breath as it searched around for a way out. *Shuck, I'm dying in Pineyville.* She imagined her face broken into pieces, her eyes hanging by nerve-wires, her nose falling away on the floor. She dried up inside, feeling only the cold metal on her temple. Where was Mrs. Owens? Sister Mobley? Head not turning, breath held, she felt urine on the verge of seeping out and clenched herself tightly closed, her body floating above all need except the need to live. *Please don't kill me in this cold place.*

Sheriff Trotter lowered the gun, the silver barrel whisking through the air at the corner of her eye. "Now, y'all get the hell out of here like Mr. Heywood said." The sheriff spoke again. "Get on." He pushed Celeste forward.

Celeste's spine creaked to life, blood-heat replacing the metallic cold on her temple. She glanced at the sheriff's bright blue eyes and saw that they sank to near-black, saw the badge that read Trotter. She knew his name, had heard it first from Matt and then from Negro people all summer long, had seen him in his car staring hot and mad at her. Eyes as dead as marbles, as hot as a branding iron. Reverend Singleton gathered himself from the floor. Mrs. Owens took Celeste by the arm.

Sister Mobley raised her Bible like a shield. "Depart from evil and do good, so you will abide forever." She waved it at the sheriff, who stood there looking at her. Her bony arm shook. "For the Lord loves justice, and does not forsake His godly ones." Sheriff Trotter ignored her though she spoke directly into his face.

The child across the lobby let out a bawling cry that first caught in her throat and then just kept coming. Celeste turned to see the woman pick up the child, curls bouncing. They raced out the front door, the sobs and whines of the little girl echoing in the lobby.

Mr. Heywood wedged himself between Sister Mobley and Mrs. Owens while Celeste helped Reverend Singleton to his feet. The sheriff shoved them along, the minister's gray suit seams pulling apart under the force of the sheriff's hands. Celeste blessed her tennis shoes, the only things between her and the hard floor. Mr. Heywood tugged the two older women,

Mrs. Owens's hat shifting forward on her head, ushering them energetically down the never-ending hallway toward the side door. The compromise door.

Whites lined the hallway, all hard eyes and gaping mouths. Celeste fully expected them to applaud, but they didn't. She thought about the little girl wanting to help Reverend Singleton when he fell backwards. What would her mother tell her when they got home? Would she say, you are never to help a person whose skin is not white, ever in your life, no matter what? What she told that child would make all the difference in the world, Celeste knew.

"I have seen a violent wicked man, spreading himself like a luxuriant tree in its native soil." Sister Mobley talked to the paintings as if she knew them all. Her voice rang out. "I be back to register. You can't stop me forever."

The somnambulism of Pineyville came to an abrupt end.

When Reverend Singleton stood in the pulpit that evening, the church half-full, his sleeves rolled up, his eyes set in a no-nonsense glare, he told the assembled that no man, white, black, or green, had the right to treat him and the rest as they'd been treated that morning at the Pearl River County Administration Building. He knew, as the word spread through the hinterlands that he'd been assaulted by the sheriff while asking for his constitutional right to vote, that the people would come and they'd be ready. Some people needed more encouragement, more motivation than others. He announced that there would be a pep rally every night until they broke through the wall of resistance at the registrar's office. Negro people would be voting in Pineyville or his name wasn't Reverend Bernard Singleton.

Celeste sat with Mrs. Owens and Sister Mobley in the front row as he'd asked them to do.

"Some of us think the burden for change should fall on just a few. If we don't have more than a few, we might as well have nobody at all." He paced. "You must bring the slow ones along." His anger stewed like the compressed heat in the church.

"That Sheriff Trotter picked me up and threw me, do you hear me? He *threw* me across that lobby. My back may never be the same." He pointed into the air. "He put a gun right to the temple of Sister Celeste. He threatened to shoot this child dead right there in the lobby of the Pearl River County Administration Building. Threatened to kill her right before our very eyes." He reached a hand out towards Celeste. "That registrar of voters,

Mr. Heywood, insulted and embarrassed Sister Mobley and Sister Owens. Do you hear me, now?" He reached both arms out toward them. "Now, let me tell you this. We cannot have this. We did not go there to threaten, we did not go there to hurt. We went there to register to vote. To register to vote. Do you hear me?"

The church moaned. They fanned against the heat and humidity, called on God and rustled around in their seats. The sun faded into dust and there would be the ride home with no protection. From this day forward, Celeste knew, they would be like ducks in a shooting gallery, like renegades, dreadful pariahs to the white community. The whites' hatred of them was no longer beneath the surface but in full bloom, right out there in the light of day and in the darkness of night. They knew that these Negroes had to be stopped or the entire south would change. It was war, and the whites had all the guns. Now their nonviolence would be tested down to its bone marrow, to its core.

Sister Mobley stood up. "I saw it with my own two eyes. It was awful. That Mr. Heywood grabbed aholt of Sister Owens and me, and that sheriff put his gun right to her temple, held it there, then he pushed this child and the reverend out the door. Oh, Lord a mercy." She swooned back into her seat.

Mr. Landau stood and everyone quieted. "I know you don't believe in self-defense. I know. But, if the brothers in the Deacons only drove their cars over there, stayed in their cars with their guns, all this would go a whole lot better."

With no instruction from her brain, Celeste felt her head nod in the affirmative. It sounded reasonable until she remembered that in truth, that kind of confrontation would lead to a bloodbath, and even the Deacons for Defense and Justice didn't have enough guns to win. The whites had all the old laws on their side, too. It just sounded so good when Mr. Landau said it. She had seen the hatred in Sheriff Trotter's eyes, in Mr. Heywood's, too.

Reverend Singleton thanked Mr. Landau and asked him to stay around, to have a word with him at the end of the meeting. Mr. Landau sat down. Celeste would get to hear what Reverend Singleton had to say to Mr. Landau as he and Mrs. Singleton always drove her, Mrs. Owens, and Sister Mobley back to Freshwater Road after the meetings.

Reverend Singleton called for the second group of volunteers to be ready to go with the first group to swell their numbers. They would meet at the church again in the morning and go to the County Administration build-ing again and again and again until someone in this town was registered to vote. He asked them to stand and led them in the singing of freedom songs. The singing felt good to Celeste, released the residual anxiety from the day, from the gun to her temple, but she knew it was only the beginning and only God knew where it would end.

After the singing and the greeting, Dolly Johnson and Mr. Landau stayed behind and volunteered to join the group on the next visit to the county building. Reverend Singleton took Mr. Landau to the side, leaving all the women. Celeste felt she should've been included in that conversation, which she was sure was about nonviolence, and tried to hear what was being said. A few minutes later, Mr. Landau walked from the church without saying another word to anyone. Reverend Singleton gave her a quick nod.

Celeste had hoped against hope that Sissy's death would provoke Mrs. Tucker to stand up and away from her husband as she'd done at the funeral. She had it in her mind that Zenia Tucker would appear at the church door, just as her daughter had done. Celeste prayed that the woman would find the courage to join them as a way of healing her own heart. Her prayer had not been answered and her hands were tied because she could not go to that house and try to convince Mrs. Tucker that this thing they were doing was Sissy's dream, too.

When Reverend Singleton brought the rest of them back to Freshwater Road, Celeste walked to the big mailbox, praying for something, anything that had life outside Pineyville written on it. She reached inside and felt the soft pad of mail. Letters. This place of no phones made letters so much more important, scripted voices from places far away. A storm began to whisper, the clouds gaining girth. She brought the mail out and read her name on an envelope. The return address was the One Man, One Vote office in Jackson, and "E.J" was written above it. The others were for Mrs. Owens. One had a Chicago return address—probably from her sons. She put the letter in her book-bag, grinning right into the dark clouds. She held her face up to catch the fine drizzle that began to fall, seeing Ed Jolivette with the moonlight on his dark skin, catching the whiteness of his teeth. In her mind, he was always dancing.

She placed Mrs. Owens's mail on the kitchen table. In the quiet of her room, the rain pelting the small house, Celeste opened the thick letter and pulled out a small stack of color photos. Cloth on bolts and ribbons in exuberant colors, strings of garlic and red peppers hanging on nails above bins of peaches, grapes, piles of bananas, okra, and tomatoes. Loaves of bread wrapped in paper. And long windowed houses with green shutters and balconies, wrought-iron railings in fleur-de-lis patterns, iron fencing and gates with corn on the cob posts, each kernel in detail. A photo of the St. Charles Avenue streetcar going up the middle of the shady street. For the first time she blessed the fact that she didn't have a telephone in this house. She flattened the letter on her lap like a document, smoothing the fold creases, read "Sugar" at the top of the page. Good. If he was saying something as bitter as goodbye, he wouldn't start with something so sweet. She flopped back on her soft bed. Her eyes stayed on the "Sugar," refused to float on down the page. She heard him saying the word in her ear.

> *I been thinking about you, the way your face made the stars and the moon run for cover, afraid of your glow. You stole my heart and now I'm walking around Mississippi completely heartless. You are too cruel. A woman in the office in Jackson asked me why I looked so sad. I told her I lost my heart and didn't know if I'd ever find it again. Didn't want you to forget the French Quarter, the St. Charles Avenue street car, Audubon Park, and me.*
>
> *Ed*

She closed her eyes, feeling the after-rain stagnation gathering intensity, the ponds festering, rivers slowing, her heart all muddy desolation. This was the kind of viscous humidity that stopped you where you stood, had you staring into space vacantly, not bothering to bathe or change clothes, not able to pass through the weight of the air. She stretched out on the bed, too weary to pull her mattress down to the floor. She held the letter flat on her breasts, clutching the sides of the paper. The letter was her shield, her lifesaver, her hope for a better tomorrow away from this place, a dream of colors and dancing, of sunlight on rooftops. But she knew, too, that this man had a beautiful but dangerous heart. Untouchable in a sense, because she knew that this thing in Mississippi owned him, though they'd never spoken of it. That commitment she trusted, but it was the thing that would preclude all else. She felt drugged, sinking into the mattress, its fine hairy fibers creeping into her nose and stopping the flow of air into her lungs.

25

With one index finger crooked in the steering wheel and his mind on Celeste, Shuck eased the Cadillac to the curb, the sunlight reflecting off the long hood of the glossy car like the stage lights at the Fox Theatre off of Cab Calloway's big white suit. The top was down. Momma Bessie's house sat there like an old memory. It hadn't changed in the slightest since Momma Bessie and his father, Ben, first bought it. They'd gotten in early on the opening of the West Side to Negro people ready to buy the small, well-built, two-story houses. The area grew into a haven for the up and coming, a coveted world, the strivers row of Detroit.

Shuck grew up surrounded by an odd mix of families like his own and resentful whites who were slow to see what was coming and got stuck. Even progressive-minded whites who intended to stay put regardless eventually moved or died out. Now this was old. Other neighborhoods opened. The houses on LaSalle, Boston, and Chicago Boulevards made this one look like a miniature. Even Shuck's house on Outer Drive was no big deal in Detroit anymore. One or two well-off Negroes had bought into Indian Village, even Palmer Woods. Shuck sat in the car thinking that somebody might've already made it into Grosse Pointe—whether the white folks out there knew the buyers were Negroes was another story.

Momma Bessie's deep emerald green lawn, summer-cut high, was well-watered and weed-free. He paid a gardener to do the yards on Outer Drive and here once a week in the summer and to shovel the snow in the winter. Shuck heard his own footsteps on the wood stairs, surveyed the seasoned porch furniture. Momma Bessie took care of things so that they lasted until Shuck had to unhinge her grip from them. She'd used her manual wringer washing machine until Shuck sent her off to Bermuda on a vacation then had the old washer removed and a new electric one installed in the basement. She accepted it, but he knew she would've been just fine with the old one until its L-shaped handle fell off and clanked to the basement floor. It was the same all through the house. Old but shining like new.

Before he crossed the few feet of porch, Momma Bessie had arrived at the front door and swung it open. She rarely gave him time to use his key. She was tall, a subtle mixture of brown and yellow skin, gray hair bunned in at the neck. Shuck had noticed she was beginning that slight tilt forward, heavier now that she didn't work every day, that she was up in age. No one had a clue as to why close people started calling her Momma Bessie, but they did. Mrs. Annie Rose Tyree had been quite a looker in her day. Still wore her housedresses starched and ironed, never went out without a hat on Sundays.

Shuck kissed her on the cheek, saw the delight in her eyes every time he came in the door. He walked through the vestibule to the neat living room with the television angled in the corner, the curtains closed against the sun, the carpet vacuumed with not a footprint in it, the sofa and two upholstered chairs set for conversation or television watching. The coffee table glittered with crystal pieces and mementos of Momma Bessie and Ben's travels in years past. Ashtrays from Bermuda, California, and Las Vegas. In this living room, children had been encouraged to sit on the floor. Celeste and Billy didn't earn chair rights until they entered high school.

He went out the back door to check the yard, the fence and gate, the garage with his father's old Mercury still sitting in there. Momma Bessie never would learn to drive. He should get rid of that car. He walked along the narrow yard pavement, the sun high and hot, marveling at her gardening, the small yard worthy of photographing with its roses and peonies, morning glories and lilac bushes. The ancient apple tree still bore the fruit that she used to make the best apple pies on the West Side of Detroit.

Back inside, Shuck climbed the stairs, hand on the smooth oak railing, checked windows, screens, faucets, drains, the toilet in the one bathroom. Stood in the room that had been his own as a teenager, the room he slept in when he met Wilamena in high school, the room they slept in just before they got married, the room he came back to when she left him. Momma

Bessie hadn't changed one thing. He kept clothes in the closet. Could stay the night here and never bring a thing with him. The past lived in this house, pressed into overcrowded closets, in shoeboxes and hat boxes in the attic. He glanced at the framed photograph on the chest of drawers of Billy, Celeste, and himself standing in front of the Royal Gardens the day it opened. The ghost in the picture was Wilamena. Celeste looked just like her when she was a child. Still did.

Downstairs, he sat at the dining room table where in years past he'd written his policy numbers every day of the week. Shuck could see his reflection in the tabletop. Used to come in with a head full of numbers and bets, a doubled brown paper bag full of cash. Would sit at this table with his small book and rectangles of inky copy paper that he slid in under the top sheet as he wrote down the numbers and the code names for the people who'd made the bets. At each stop on his route, he wrote the numbers and bets for his customers on little papers so each customer had a copy. He never drove through the streets with the numbers slips, knew the police watched for men like him who lived well and never punched a time card. He called in his numbers, put the books in a shoebox in the basement, and took the money to the "bank." Late in the afternoon he'd come back as the numbers fell, coming off the racetrack. In the evenings he'd go pay off his winners.

Shuck played fair and square and people trusted him, and some stood right in front of him and cried when he said he was finished running numbers. He became the bank, let the runners come to him. He'd felt the heat of the police, knew it was time to make some changes. After a good hit, he bought the Royal Gardens and pulled back from the numbers game altogether; luck, he knew, was like the weather, and it was hard to live the good life in jail. Shuck, with his bar and his house on Outer Drive, became a respectable Detroit businessman. His only contact with that other world came through the vendors he needed for the bar. The Mafia controlled the jukebox business and the liquor business, and had a hand in cigarettes. It was all about distribution, and no Negro man had been able to crack that. More than a few, he knew, had died trying.

Momma Bessie poured him iced tea with lemon and a sprig of mint from the backyard and gave him a coaster for his glass. He heard her rummaging in the front hall closet, covering the dress shirts she ironed for him with dry cleaner's plastic, thinking that was why he was there. How many shirts he brought, that's how many she washed and ironed. When he didn't bring them, she acted as if he'd broken her heart. So once a week, he came with a bag of dirty dress shirts and picked up the washed and ironed ones, the starch in the collar and cuffs done exactly the way he liked. She said she turned to her stories on the television, set up the ironing board, and by the time the stories went off, she was finished. Said the ironing was good for her arms, just like working in that yard.

Shuck drank the perfect blend of tea, sugar, mint, and lemon, not a bit sure what he wanted to talk about or if he wanted to talk at all. This house was his touchstone. If he just came in, walked through the rooms, sat for a moment, it convinced him that things held, that everything wasn't just flying off in directions. Sometimes, he knew, he wanted things to fly off, to be forgotten.

Momma Bessie didn't know Celeste was in Mississippi and he wasn't going to tell her. He'd told her, instead, that Celeste had stayed in Ann Arbor for summer school.

"Where's your shirts?" She gently laid the ironed ones across the other end of the dining room table, the clear thin plastic ballooning out then relaxing.

"I'll bring 'em tomorrow." He had the bag ready in his bedroom on Outer Drive, had just walked right by it.

"You hungry?" Momma Bessie headed for the kitchen before he answered. "I got some pound cake in here." She'd cut him a piece and bring it with a fork and a napkin no matter what he said.

"No, no. I'll pick up something tomorrow when I bring the shirts." Shuck knew she felt his distraction.

Momma Bessie put the small plate with a slice of pound cake on a place mat in front of him, then stood in the doorway between the kitchen and the dining room, worry knitting her brow, tautening her sagging jawline. "I saw Alma Weaver down at Hudson's the other day. Said she was teaching summer school. I wondered why I hadn't seen her all summer long."

"Summer's just getting started good." He wanted to push summer along as fast as possible, get it over with, bring Celeste out of that hellhole down south. It was August. He'd lost all track of time. Summer had been whizzing by, but to him it felt as if it was all in slow motion.

"It'll be gone by the time we look up." Momma Bessie's clock ticked on another sphere. Day counting, life counting, needing to group around her those she loved as often as possible. Shuck knew these things.

"Maybe we should start planning something for Labor Day?" He hoped that would calm her down about this summer business. Celeste would be home from Mississippi by then. Something to celebrate, he was thinking, a cookout at the house on Outer Drive.

"Well, we can have a ending to the summer, though we never had a proper beginning, I guess." She turned away into her kitchen.

He ate the cake, the butter and sugar spreading out on his tongue. He washed it down with iced tea, taking in the room where he'd eaten Thanksgiving and Christmas dinners for more years than he could count. Adults at this table, children at the card table set up in the corner. When he bought the house on Outer Drive, the alternations began. Christmas dinner here, Thanksgiving there. But it was never the same. "You ever think about leaving this house?"

"To go where, at my age?" She came back to the doorway.

"To my house." He pushed his placemat away gently.

"What would I do with all my furniture, my things?" Momma Bessie considered his words right there in front of him. He wondered if she'd ever had the same thought.

"We could work it out. Think about it." With Momma Bessie in the new house and Alma, too, with her plants, maybe Celeste would come home, just pack the Outer Drive house with people, make things the way they used to be. Maybe then the new house would feel like this old house used to.

Momma Bessie stared out the back dining room windows to her yard, then turned into the kitchen and rattled around in the sink. "Bring me that saucer and glass when you're done."

Shuck heard the water running, the small clanks of glasses and silverware.

"All right then." He picked up his shirts, took his dirty dishes to her, and went on out the front door calling back, "Be sure to lock up, now."

He saw Momma Bessie standing in the kitchen doorway with her hands on her hips and a stern look on her face. He was leaving too soon, but sitting still had never been easy for him unless he was sitting in a nightspot. She'd think about what he'd said, but he didn't know if she'd ever make the move. Maybe.

He arranged the shirts in the trunk, got in the car, put the top up against the sun, and headed toward Outer Drive. Manfred's After Hours Joint, where Gravy spread his whiskey-soaked rumors, was a mere four blocks away. Too close for comfort. The old neighborhood had run its course.

Decay had long since raced past the possibility of rejuvenation. Too late. The scales tipped in the direction of desertion, departure, letting it go. Time to put the past behind him once and for all. But life rarely granted a once and for all, overlapping instead, under-towing, circling back, linking the inevitable and the unpredictable. If he moved Momma Bessie to Outer Drive, and Alma, too, he'd be as close as he could get to having the home life he wanted. Get this Freedom Summer thing done, Celeste out of Mississippi in one piece and Wilamena out of his head. *Once and for all.*

26

The echoes of shoe heels on hardwood, the rustling of suit pants, the thistle-down of summer dresses swishing on bare legs in the cool lobby as the white citizens of Pineyville went about doing their morning business. Reverend Singleton, as always dressed in a tailored suit like he still lived in Chicago, walked in favoring his bruised back. Stiff-lipped Sister Mobley, the bodice of her print day dress trimmed in white lace, followed clutching her Bible, holding it out from her body like a shield. Geneva Owens, looking ready for church, carried herself as if she'd been coming in the front door of the Pearl River County Administration Building for her entire life. This time they were joined by Mr. Landau in dark summer slacks and a long-sleeved shirt and Dolly Johnson, her cotton skirt and blouse ensemble giving her the look of a clerk typist. The two newcomers stayed close behind the veterans, eyes glued to Reverend Singleton's aching back.

On their first attempt, the whites had dropped their voices to a whisper when the group entered the lobby through the front door. Today, in their self-conscious attempt to ignore them, their voices rose and bounced around the lobby, talking about this and that over the event taking place in front of them. Celeste was mindful of Sheriff Trotter's promise to blow her brains all over the lobby. She wondered why Mr. Heywood hadn't already come tearing down the stairs. Maybe they'd be ambushed at the top of the stairs this time. Inching toward freedom, she thought.

Just as the small group rounded the balustrade to go up the stairs to Mr. Heywood's office, the sure-footed sound of hard police shoes thunking fast through the hall announced Sheriff Trotter and a deputy as young and robust as Trotter himself. Celeste put her hand on Geneva Owens's arm, as much to keep from running as to give support to the older woman.

Trotter and his deputy held handcuffs out and ready. "Y'all back, huh?" Trotter's face pressed toward lightheartedness, his tone a chiding imitation of a benevolent shopkeeper.

Every muscle in Celeste's body pulled tight in preparation for the blows she had every reason to believe would be coming soon. She had a fleeting wish that Mr. Landau hadn't been talked into this nonviolence thing. A few passing whites stopped to watch. When Sheriff Trotter smiled, they smiled with him. He was *their* sheriff.

Reverend Singleton stiffened. "Yes, sir, we are. We've come to see Mr. Heywood about registering to vote." His clear preacher voice lifted above all other voices in the high-ceilinged lobby.

Celeste held her breath. Her jaws clamped, her forehead sank into furrows and frowns in memory of Sheriff Trotter's gun against her temple.

Trotter fumbled for his next words. "Well, he's...he's not here today." His phony jocularity lost heart. "You turn and let me get these cuffs on you. I get y'all situated in a cell, then go see if I can find him. How's that?" His lips turned corners, bent like pipe cleaners. He swiveled Reverend Singleton and brought his wrists together to fasten on the cuffs. Reverend Singleton winced. The deputy did the same with Mr. Landau, who had a face of stone so set and unmoving he might have been a sculpture, a face carved in some forgotten hinterland.

Trotter recognized Mr. Landau. "You one of them working over at Crown Zellerbach?"

"I am." Mr. Landau didn't say "sir."

A silence hung in the air where that "sir" had lived for years. They might hit him, and hard. That "sir" defined the entire relationship between Negro men and white men. Nobody smiling now. Celeste knew that white business owners in town had tried to get Mr. Landau fired from his job when his truck had been identified outside the church during voter education class. So far they hadn't succeeded.

Celeste eased closer to the deputy, hoping he'd be the one to handcuff her. Stay away from Trotter. She scanned the lobby for any Negro people who might be witnesses in case things got out of hand, in case Trotter drew his gun. If any had been there, they'd already scurried out that back door when they saw Reverend Singleton, Celeste, and the others coming in the front. Didn't want to be associated with the protestors, the agitators, hadn't found defiance in themselves yet.

Trotter reached for her arm. His face flushed and his blue eyes hardened into granite the way Shuck's eyes had when he'd met J.D. for the first time in front of the student union on campus. She brought her other arm to the back, making it easy for him.

Unlike the day before, Trotter couldn't have been more polite. He must have been caught off-guard then. It was possible that since the world had its eyes on Mississippi, the state government had decided to at least feign civility towards its Negro citizens. Some national press still swarmed all over the state. No way to know how long it would last. But civility or not, they were headed to jail, and the only thing they'd done so far was come in the front door of the building and ask permission to register to vote.

Dolly Johnson volunteered her wrists in front of her body. The deputy slid her strappy straw bag up onto her shoulder, spun her quickly, and brought her arms around her back with a good yank. A woman from the small crowd of onlookers said, "Oh, my," her voice sounding almost like a fainting moan of sexual pleasure. Perhaps she recognized Dolly Johnson as the Negro woman who had the blonde-haired child and needed to express her joy at seeing Dolly publicly shackled. Celeste gave a look to Dolly, a confirmation that it would be okay.

Dolly's face got pinched and dark. She cut her eyes at the deputy, who cuffed her, then gently pushed her toward the rest of the shackled group, his thin face and diluted blue eyes intent on his work.

Mr. Landau's face masked whatever he felt. Reverend Singleton had spent a good hour convincing him that nonviolence hadn't yet run its course, that there was a power in this he'd never know by using a gun. Now, here he was in handcuffs for trying to do what the Constitution guaranteed. He wasn't a man who could've withstood chains.

The officers handcuffed Sister Mobley and Geneva Owens last, holding their Bibles and purses for them. It was all done in a few short minutes with not a voice raised or a scuffle heard. No need to excite people. The white citizens of Pineyville went back to their business, inured overnight to this new activity in the lobby of the public building. The Negroes had been handled satisfactorily. No guns drawn, no ministers flying across the lobby and crashing to the floor. No aching cry from the lungs of a terrified child. Celeste felt grateful to be alive and maneuvered herself as far away from Trotter as possible. Again, she expected the white people in the lobby to applaud the imminent incarceration of the troublemakers. They didn't.

The deputy hustled Celeste and the other women to the women's jail in an L-shaped lip of the building on the back parking lot, near the Negro entrance. Reverend Singleton and Mr. Landau disappeared, led to the Negro men's section—the jail that Leroy Boyd James had been dragged from before he was shot and thrown into the sludgy Pearl River.

One by one, the deputy removed their handcuffs and pushed them into the cell. When the door clanged shut, the women were standing in a small concrete square with two metal-framed bunk beds, a scummy seatless flush toilet without toilet paper, and a face bowl whose metal finish barely showed through brown filth crusted over it. Not a piece of soap in sight. They hadn't been processed in, no fingerprints taken, no photos snapped. No legal proof that they'd been arrested. The old trick. The other cell across the hallway stood empty. Celeste climbed up to one of the top bunks and figured that Dolly, who was younger than either Sister Mobley or Mrs. Owens, would take the other top bunk. Instead, she sat herself down on the bottom bed, then stretched out on the filthy mattress.

"You might give that bunk to Mrs. Owens or Sister Mobley so they don't have to climb up." Celeste pulled way back on her tone, not wanting to antagonize Dolly.

Dolly looked at Celeste with Labyrinth's expression, all single-minded petulance. "I have a fear of heights," she replied. She sat up, bending over to avoid grazing her head on the upper bunk. Labyrinth's chip-on-the-shoulder attitude came straight from her mother.

Celeste wondered where Dolly got a fear of heights in a low-building town full of, at most, two-story houses. Certainly the houses where Negro people lived were all single story, except the Sophie Lewis mansion, and that was damn near to New Orleans. She doubted Dolly had ever been there.

Sister Mobley threw her Bible and small cotton purse up on the top bunk and made motions to climb up there. "No need for a fuss."

Celeste jumped down to the concrete floor, thankful she'd worn her tennis shoes again. "Sister Mobley, don't climb up there by yourself."

Mrs. Owens lowered her chin, stared at Sister Mobley's ill-fed body. "Sister Mobley, get on that bottom bunk. Now, Dolly, you get your hind parts up on that top one. I'm old, I'm tired, but I'm not too tired to deal with your smart mouth."

Sister Mobley scuffled trying to get herself up on that top bunk fast before the war started. Celeste stood there for support, feeling Sister Mobley's thin fingers digging into her shoulder.

Mrs. Owens came over and took Sister Mobley's bony arm and sat her down on the bottom bed. Sister Mobley popped up like a jill in the box, grabbed her Bible and purse from the top. "I don't mean to be no trouble."

Celeste backed away.

"*You're* not the trouble." Mrs. Owens put her hands on her hips and stared at Dolly Johnson.

Dolly came off the bunk and stood in the middle of the cell. "Who says you get to tell everyone what to do?

The older woman's hand fluttered to her heart and her breath came in tight little fits. "You just like everyone else in here, Dolly. You barely got a pot to pee in and a window to throw it out of." Mrs. Owens paused. "And I'ma tell you something else, you coming down here with us, that Percival Dale ain't gon side with it. No matter what you think, no matter how many times you roll over in that bed with him, when his back's against the wall, he's a white man and to him, you a poor-butt nigger woman with one of his kids to feed. You go on and climb up there to that top bunk. Fear of heights. Whoever heard of such a thing? Ain't no height. It's a bed. And not much of one at that."

Celeste'd never heard Mrs. Owens say so many words in a row, and certainly never heard her express herself with such wrath, the kind she might've wanted to display in the lobby but knew she dared not.

Dolly Johnson's face trembled then folded in on itself and tears listed down her cheeks. "You didn't have to go and say all that, Geneva Owens. That wasn't called for." She took her straw purse from the bottom bunk and threw it on the top. "Mr. Dale don't do nothing for us but help me feed my kids. Ain't nothing else." She sobbed. "Oh I don't want to be in this old place."

"Calm yourself, child. We would all of us rather be at home." Sister Mobley patted her Bible.

"If he does that, he's doing the very least of what he supposed to do. But, I bet he ain't gon come here and see about you in this jail. He's got a wife right around the corner. No point in you coming in here trying to act grand." Mrs. Owens paused, calmed herself, and sat down on her bunk. She took a handkerchief from her purse and wiped her whole face then her hands as if she had water. "Now, Dolly, get up on that bed and take a rest cause we don't know what's coming. Dealing with those children and no husband to help, Sister Mobley more needs a rest than anybody in here." Mrs. Owens shook her head from side to side.

Sister Mobley coughed, and sighed, then opened her Bible, while Dolly Johnson climbed up to the top bunk rolling her eyes at the entire world, bouncing around and causing the springs to grind and squeak. Finally, she settled in, staring at the ceiling. All was quiet except for Sister Mobley turning those crispy-thin Bible pages. A fury of pages turning.

Celeste climbed back up to her bunk, but she didn't want to put her head on a pillow that smelled like rancid sweat and used Kotex. She leaned against the cinderblock wall and threw the pillow off the foot of the bed. It flopped in a dull thud on the floor. She heard the mesh springs under the moldy mattress squeak as Mrs. Owens lay down. She longed for a glass of that too-sweet iced tea, anything cold to drink. She imagined a tall glass of ginger ale loaded with ice, the smell of ginger caught in the froth of carbonation going right up her nose.

More than likely, she thought, the police would allow Reverend Singleton to make one phone call for the whole group. It was Tuesday morning. The One Man, One Vote Jackson office would alert the FBI that six people had been arrested in Pineyville. After the bodies of Goodman, Chaney, and Schwerner had been found, the number of FBI men in the state shrank. *Not enough agents to investigate every complaint.* The Jackson office would send the bail money down and a lawyer if needed. Nothing to do but wait.

"I sure hope they don't beat up on poor Reverend Singleton and Mr. Landau. You think they will, Sister Celeste?" Sister Mobley spoke holding her opened Bible across her chest.

"They may not beat them. Might think arresting us is enough to scare us off." She hoped she was right.

This arrest tactic was yet another way of obstructing them, slowing them down. These tactics had worked for so many years, they probably believed they'd work now. Mr. Heywood and his sheriff knew well that Negro people would eventually be registered to vote in Mississippi. It was a matter of time—but for this year, time meant everything because of the coming national elections. Registration would close. The southern whites would win it by slowing the movement's progress to a crawl. No way they'd win in the long run. Battle lines had been drawn in the red dirt as if the Civil War and Reconstruction had to be relived again and again, an endless replaying of vanquishers and vanquished. Negro people got caught in the middle, the pawns of both, the scorned reward, disparaged and disqualified.

Sister Mobley ran her thin finger down a Bible page, mumbling scriptures.

"It's a good thing those newspaper and television people still shining a light all over the state." Celeste said it to calm the others more than because she had any real belief the press would help them now that the three civil rights workers had been buried. She hadn't seen a television in weeks, had no idea what was being reported to the outside world.

Dolly eyed Celeste. "Haven't seen any of 'em come down here." She rambled around in her purse, pulled out a wristwatch. "I gotta pick up my kids from my sister's."

"It probably won't be much longer." Celeste didn't have a clue as to what might be next or how long it would take.

Sister Mobley kept reading in a whispery voice, so small on that bunk bed Celeste wondered how she'd even brought three children into the world without breaking apart.

"The next group better be ready for tomorrow morning whether we're still in here or not. You can't let up on these white folks. They see it as weakness." Geneva Owens's wise observance quietly relaid the gauntlet. They had to be their own leaders now.

A gray army blanket lay folded across the foot of the bed, as foul as the pillow. The place reeked of urine. This was what she'd missed in Jackson. Now, she'd run out of all of Shuck's city luck. God only knew what else was coming, and it didn't have to happen in this jail. This might be the easy part, just sitting in a foul-smelling place for a few hours. Who knew what the night would bring to Freshwater Road?

"Sheriff Trotter never said *what* we were being arrested for." Celeste rambled through the instructions that had come from the Jackson office. Lists of possible charges, bail amounts, conduct for voter registrants, even words to say in the registrar's office, if they ever got there.

Dolly sat up against her own cinderblock wall, pouting and accusing at the same time. "That freedom school's against the law."

Celeste stared at Dolly. What was this now? Her new appearance and the words coming from her mouth couldn't have been more incongruous. Dolly had been the first to send her children to freedom school. Had she identified herself with the civil rights movement as a matter of style, like a way to dress? Or maybe her fear had taken over, undermining her new persona.

"Darn near everything we do is against one law or another." Celeste kept her eyes on Dolly. Was it possible that feisty Dolly ran back to her sometimes man, Mr. Dale, and talked about everything and everyone who came to the church meetings? Celeste had spent the summer worrying about Mr. Tucker with the devil in his eyes. She searched Dolly's face for an answer, for the truth.

"Who said so?" Mrs. Owens's tone dared Dolly to say that Mr. Dale had warned her about the school.

"It's been in the newspapers."

"You brought your own children first, Dolly." Celeste focused hard on her.

"I didn't know it was illegal." Dolly didn't flinch.

"Because some white folks say it is, doesn't make it so." Mrs. Owens took the space, the very air from Dolly's words. "Besides, we not in here because of freedom school. We in here because of voting."

Celeste nodded "yes" to Dolly, thinking of Shuck's perennial line. *You catch more flies with honey.* She wouldn't let go of Dolly, not with those two children's minds and lives being shaped in the balance. "To them, I'm teaching communism and the overthrow of the government. How they get that from Negro history and art classes is beyond me."

"See, I told you." Dolly spoke gently to Mrs. Owens knowing now that the older woman would not put up with her if she went too far. Celeste's stomach turned. Had she misread Dolly so completely? Or was this jail cell testing Dolly's resolve? How would she find out the truth? And when?

In her materials, Celeste had read of a Negro girl in Tennessee killed by the Klan for teaching freed slaves to read and write. She knew that much about the past. The new laws were descended from the old ones that forbade teaching slaves. Only now it was more about keeping the quality of education so pared down to nearly nothing, so unrelentingly dismal, that it barely prepared a child to be a functioning member of society. But even that failed, because people so desperate for learning glommed on to whatever was available, and some used it to sail to great heights anyway. The freedom schools birthed questions in a place where questioning ranked with impertinence, the reward physical or at least verbal abuse. They did precisely what the whites feared—dug out and discarded the last vestiges of slavery, even those with deep roots in Negro people's minds, holding them down even when the threat had all but disappeared. The movement challenged it all. The old way of life was unraveling again, just as it had begun to do during Reconstruction. That's why she'd come here. That's why she sat in this foul-smelling cell instead of on Shuck's silk sofa in the house on Outer Drive, or even instead of walking down the streets of Paris with J.D. She felt energized.

"Did your house get shot into?" Dolly sounded like she was in a beauty shop, talking about some gossipy thing that happened in the neighborhood. She was just making conversation, Celeste figured, an attempt to make up for her earlier lapse of commitment. A world of things had happened since the night shots were fired into the house.

"Scared me to death." Celeste said. "I slept on the floor for a few nights, still do most of the time. I tried to get under that bed." No need to mention how she'd wet the bed out of fear.

Celeste stared over at Dolly and wondered what she might have been thinking back when she brought Labyrinth and Georgie to the freedom school the first time. Two children she wanted to free from this dungeon of oppression, a married white man as one father and a long-gone black one as the other. She must be terrified. If Percival Dale stopped helping her, he'd be right in a line that descended from slave masters who refused to sign freedom papers for their own flesh and blood. Some things had changed and some others had barely budged. Dolly was surely on that tightrope that Shuck so feared for Celeste.

"They did that back when my husband, Horation, was alive." Mrs. Owens spoke from a reverie.

Celeste heard the quiet in her voice, remembered the old photo of Mrs. Owens and her husband in his World War I uniform hanging above her bed, that oval of fading life, the old woman's memory of him caught and alive in her voice as if he'd only died yesterday.

"White folks something, all right." Dolly's eyes grazed her soiled mattress.

Celeste fully expected Geneva Owens to say, "And you oughta know." But she didn't.

"My Tony wants a gun." Sister Mobley's voice was filled with awe. "He ain't nothing but a child."

Celeste hoped Sister Mobley didn't think she'd filled her son's head with thoughts of guns in freedom school. But she would send Tony to "study" with Mr. Landau in a wink. All summer long, she'd wanted to tip over to Bogalusa to one of those Deacons for Defense and Justice meetings. People needed to be able to protect their homes. *No more cheeks to turn.*

"Mr. Tucker come down and checked on us that night. They sho tore up that car a his," Sister Mobley said. "He had to take it all the way to Jackson to get that glass replaced."

In spite of it all, Mr. Tucker hadn't gotten the point—that it didn't matter that he had not backed the movement. All bets were off. He might as well get on board the train, because he was just as black as everyone sitting in that jail cell, just as vulnerable, just as disenfranchised and disinherited as any other Negro in Pineyville or anywhere else for that matter. He got his car window shot out for nothing. He hadn't helped to build this movement but he paid the price anyway. Sissy had to be tapping him on his shoulder morning, noon, and night. But did he feel an ounce of guilt?

In the small window built high up into the cinderblock wall, Celeste saw nothing but crystal blue southern sky and white cloud clusters floating. Dark clouds hugged the edges. Where was Ed Jolivette right now? He felt like those dark clouds always at the rim of her consciousness, never disappearing, as if he walked with her, touched her arm, or prodded her in some vague way toward the sureness she strove to have. He and Matt must be organizing for the end of the summer project. Voter registration rolls tallied, political work leading to the big changes sure to come in Mississippi. She had to drag Pineyville to the finish line, no matter what, both for herself and because she knew that Ed expected her to do it. And Shuck did too. Not enough that she'd come to Mississippi. She had to move the place along.

Trotter's deputy came through the lock-up door and stood at their cell, his key ring clanking on the bars as he opened it. "You, up top there, you come on with me." He had more Mississippi drawl than Trotter. He beckoned to Celeste with his long muscular arm. His other hand was on his hip, near his gun. "You Celeste Tyree?"

Celeste climbed down from her bunk thinking he knew very well who she was. "Yes." The word "sir" was on a slow passage from her brain, but a fearful quick catch of breath and a missed heartbeat caught it, laid it down.

Good. She didn't want her cellmates to see her fear. She stood up straight, had no purse to grab; there was Kleenex in one pocket of her skirt, her tiny change purse with payphone money in the other along with her Social Security card and student ID. Her number was up. Her luck, Shuck's luck, had run out.

Mrs. Owens stood out of her bed, dread filling the gullies on her face.

Sister Mobley prayed out loud. "Behold, the Lord's hand is not shortened, that it cannot save; neither his ear heavy, that it cannot hear; but your iniquities have separated between you and your God, and your sins have hid his face from you, that he will not hear."

The deputy looked at Sister Mobley with a full face of contempt.

Dolly Johnson scooted to the edge of her bunk, dangling her legs over the side like a child.

Celeste felt like she was being led to the firing squad. The deputy reached for her arm and pulled her through the cell door, his hand like a cold brace on her. He relocked the door.

"Follow me."

He walked, checking her behind him, down the short hall and through a metal door, then down a flight of stairs that she'd forgotten coming up little more than an hour ago. The tan walls were broken by closed dark doors, her tennis-shoed footsteps quietly padding behind his police shoes clomping on the concrete floor. Celeste counted doors, then began humming, "Ain't gon' let nobody turn me 'round, turn me 'round." She didn't remember these doors from their walk into the jail. Maybe it had been the pull of the handcuffs taking her attention. Fear shutting down the mind as it had done in the car with Matt. Her hands were free now. She watched the deputy's holstered gun bouncing gently with the rhythm of his legs.

She couldn't hold the freedom song in her head. When the deputy passed a clean, white porcelain drinking fountain, Celeste saw no *Whites Only* sign. She stopped to drink, delighted to have the cold water in her mouth. It tasted like first snow. As the cold stream flowed down her throat, the deputy shoved her head hard into the fountain. She vomited the water as her mouth slammed into the shining chrome spigot. A quiet crack, then she saw her blood going down the drain as pain shot from her mouth up into her head. Stunned, she moved over to the side, her brown hand slipping from the white porcelain bowl. As she turned to face the deputy, her feet tangled into a knot and she stumbled to the floor, her head and back bumping into the wall. The black of his police shoes was the last thing she saw.

In a tunnel of cottony fog, she heard the words, "That water's not for niggers," then floated off dreaming of following Mary Evans into the *Whites Only* ladies' restroom in the train station on her first night in Jackson. Signs up, signs down. *"Miss'sippi ain't nothing to play with, girl."* Coming back to, her head and mouth throbbing, blood still leaking. Lips were blood-packed things. Her hands were limp, her neck crooked, one leg folded under her at the knee, one straight out. Gym shoes with pocks of orange earth like dried blood from walks to the outhouse, from helping Mrs. Owens in her tiny patch of yard. *Thank God,* she thought. *I wore my gym shoes.* She knew that it was her lip that bled and now felt like an inflated balloon, ran her tongue over her teeth with tears gathering in her eyes.

Celeste heard a second voice and looked up to see Sheriff Trotter standing with his deputy. They grabbed her under her armpits, hoisting her to her feet, her shoes barely toeing along the concrete floor until they reached a door and went into a small room. They sat her in a hard chair, her lip a few paces behind every move she made. The deputy left the room and was back in seconds, it seemed, with a glass of water that he slid toward her on the dark tabletop. She wondered where the water had come from.

"Go ahead. You so thirsty." Trotter stood by a barred window, his arms folded across his chest, his eyes deepened into his head and looking dark. She remembered them as blue, but not today.

Celeste stared at the water, needed to drink, but dared not reach for it. She'd been bullied into self-denial so quickly. Her lip had stopped bleeding, had left blood on the front of her blouse. The lip had disassociated itself from the rest of her mouth. She glanced up at Trotter, whose outline fuzzed in the sunny backlight then cleared.

"Go on." He gazed out the window.

She shook her head "no," words stuck in her chest somewhere. She needed ice more and none was offered. If it had been, she wasn't sure she'd have had the courage to reach for it. Fear of physical pain was too fresh in her mind.

Trotter turned to her. His eyes went yellow in the sunlight. "That lip'll heal."

Celeste's hands lay flopped in her lap, her feet wound around the legs of the chair, her blouse buttoned and blood-splattered and untucked. She felt her change purse in her skirt pocket, hoped her student ID and Social Security card were still in there, too. Throbs like hammer blows along her back, her head, and in her mouth. Didn't know if she'd been hit in the head, too, had been completely out, or just floated in shock on the corridor floor. She was still alive, and she hadn't been raped. Maybe her luck ran still, but thin. She needed to see a real doctor, a dentist, finally took her finger and smoothed it across her front teeth. One tooth was cracked.

"You want a mirror?" Trotter had an overly dramatic look on his face, dismissive of her injury as if it was a fake theatrical moment.

She shook her head again. She'd better wait until she got back to Mrs. Owens's house, then realized that maybe she wouldn't get back there, that they didn't have to let her go. They might do what they did to the three boys, release her in the middle of the night and call the Klan to ambush her. Home never seemed so far away, like a mirage in an ever-receding distance.

"You might well be ruining your future down here meddling in things that have nothing to do with you." Trotter sat on the window ledge, the sun haloing behind him.

Celeste shoved thought to his words, fighting to hold her chin up and level, wanting to hide her swollen lip. "I'm not sure I understand." Then it hit her. This wasn't about being a coed on some plain of trees in a four-seasoned place, or sitting in Shuck's bar pretending to be Dorothy Dandridge playing Carmen Jones with a cigarette hanging from ruby red lips. This was the real deal. She thrust her head up and looked squarely at him, then parted her lips and showed him the crack in her tooth that she hadn't seen herself.

Trotter turned away, eyes drifting around the room, then out the window again. "You're being charged with a felony." Trotter's voice broke into staccato phrases with little beats between. "Endangering the lives of others." He glanced at her. "I can't protect you, and I can't protect those you're dragging into this." He paced in front of the window. "Anything could happen."

She kept her head up, staring at him, her lip flopping around like a too-fat pancake. *No looking down at the dirt. No eyes drifting off to Africa. Just keep looking him in the eye.* Protecting *us* was not what he'd sworn to do. And nothing that happened here would matter in Michigan, and if it did, she'd fight it. True, there were students in southern schools arrested in the movement who lost their places in those schools. She knew better for students coming down from northern schools. His fabricated tactic wasn't going to work.

"*Anything* has already happened. For years." Her voice felt craggy, clogged.

"What if I came to your neighborhood and set about inflaming your neighbors against you?" He glanced out the window again like he was really talking to someone out there instead of right in this room.

Celeste tried to figure which side of the building they were on. The sun wasn't really behind him, but the harshness of the light let her know they were up above the tree line. The jail faced east. It was past noon.

"And when you go back to your life in your big fancy school, what do you suppose is going to happen to these people you've riled up?" He looked directly at her.

She wanted to say she hoped they'd vote people like him out of office. "They'll become full citizens in this state as well as in this country." Her lip moved in slow motion. How did he know that she went to a big university? Ah, the files. There were files on all the volunteers all over the state, files that passed from the White Citizens Councils to the Klan to the local authorities and back again.

"You people seem to think you're the only ones who have rights." He went back to looking out the window.

"I don't think that." She spoke carefully, not wanting her lip to bounce because it hurt, keeping her teeth from touching top to bottom for fear the crack would become a break. "The right to vote, the will to be represented by people who have your interests somewhere in their agenda is all I'm interested in here." She needed to be quiet, rest her panging mouth.

"Have you looked at *your* people?" He had genuine surprise in his voice. "They better off here with us than back in Africa. Wouldn't you say?"

Her anger swelled like tidewater in a storm. "We've been here as long as you. We helped to build this country, too. The only difference is we never got paid for the labor and we can't vote in Mississippi." She needed to calm herself. Be wise. He held all the cards. Let him have his way of thinking. She'd never convert him anyway. Just like she'd never change Wilamena. This cost of being Negro is the very thing Wilamena had warned against. But she wasn't Wilamena and wouldn't be even if she could. "Maybe there'll come a time when all of this seems like a bad dream."

He breathed as if hit, something deep catching him. He turned slightly to the side. She saw his profile, the strength in his body and his forehead. He was a handsome man. When he turned fully back to her, there was something deep in his eyes, as if he wanted to run from everything in his head. Like Ed Jolivette doing a second line at Otis's bar in Hattiesburg. Too much to bear. Ed danced it out. What did Trotter do? The grief stayed in his eyes for a second before the chill returned. The wall slid down like a steel drape.

"We gon let y'all go today. But I'm telling you, you keep this up and nobody will be able to stop the people who'll rise against you. Do you understand?" He walked so close she could smell his sweating body. He turned his face away.

"Yes, I do understand." She followed him with her protruding lip, her eyes so violent, she imagined, Martin Luther King would have expelled her from the movement had he seen her.

The Pineyville Six met again at Reverend Singleton's car, a parking ticket sticking up on the windshield. They climbed in, everyone trying not to stare at Celeste's lip. She sat in the back by the door, behind Reverend Singleton, with Mrs. Owens piled in next to her and Dolly on the other side of Mrs. Owens. The others sat in the front. Celeste leaned the side of her head against the car window, tried to see a reflection of herself in the glass. How bad was it? At this rate, she thought, they'd all be crippled by the time anyone got to register. The back of her head felt as if a wedge of brain had been carved out. Empty. They were being picked off one by one. Reverend Singleton yesterday, her today. It was a plan. Did he understand? They could easily have attacked the whole group physically. They needed to rethink who went to see the registrar. Older people needed to go to the back of the line. Mrs. Owens and Sister Mobley shouldn't go—too old, too frail. But she knew they'd never stand back now. No matter what, they'd keep coming. Dolly and Mr. Landau could take it. She didn't know if Dolly could be trusted. But she needed her to stand with them. Mr. Landau didn't say a word in the car. Celeste figured he was cleaning his gun in his mind.

They drove through town hushed and worn out. Mrs. Owens patted Celeste's arm then sighed into her own exhaustion. Dolly sank into her seat, crossing and uncrossing her legs, impatient to get to her own antique of a car that she'd left at the church early that morning. Reverend Singleton dropped Dolly and Mr. Landau near their vehicles at the church, then proceeded to Freshwater Road.

"Never mind you coming to the meeting this evening. Y'all stay here and rest." Reverend Singleton paused the car long enough to unload Celeste and Mrs. Owens, then took off towards Sister Mobley's house, orange sandy dust swirling behind him.

Mrs. Owens went straight to the kitchen and in seconds Celeste heard the banging sound of ice cubes being crushed, probably by a cast iron skillet. She'd never seen a hammer in this house. She walked to the cracked mirror and stared at her new face, her swollen lip and cracked tooth making her look like she'd been in a car wreck. She didn't know whether to laugh or cry as she sat down on her mattress on the floor. Mrs. Owens brought crushed ice cubes wrapped in a towel for her mouth and two aspirins. Told her to lie down and keep the ice on her lip. Celeste slept and dreamed and sweated. Mrs. Owens tipped in from time to time and changed the ice pack, brought her iced tea and more aspirins.

The house quieted into evening. Celeste felt hunger rumbling around, but didn't want to risk breaking her tooth off completely. She'd have to learn how to take food in on the sides and be careful of biting down with the damaged tooth. How would she not gnash her teeth at night? There were nights in Mississippi when her fear drove her teeth into a gnashing fit, the grinding so loud that it woke her. No dentist in Pineyville would put his hands in her mouth. In truth, she didn't want any Mississippi dentist repairing her tooth.

Sometime in the night, when her ice pack had become a soggy towel and her lip felt closer to its normal size, a reddish-orange flash of light soared into the sky. Celeste stood to see out of her window. The light flamed orange and back to red and then settled into a white light that danced high. There'd been no storm, no trees with burning branches like angry witches running, no wallops of thunder. The flaming light opened a pearly hole in the black sky.

In time, the smell of smoke drifted to Freshwater Road. It had to be the burning of the St. James A.M.E. Church. Nothing else over there. The meeting had broken up hours ago. People were sleeping by now. She remained in the dark by the opened window, her eyes needing to close, to rest, to stop the burning tears coming down her face seeping into her cut lip. The church would burn to the ground taking Mrs. Singleton's organ, the chalkboard, the door that Sissy opened and closed in fear of her father's arrival, the aisle that Ed Jolivette had walked down when he first came toward her, the railing, the wood pews and the folding chairs and Reverend Singleton's precious lavatory with the flush toilet. And the pulpit she'd spoken from on her first Sunday in town. The bell. The platform where Reverend Singleton harangued his congregation to get on board the freedom train. It had all begun in the church. How many songs had Sophie Lewis sung to help Reverend Singleton build his church?

No one came to pound on the door, and there was no sound of clanging bells or sirens, no trucks in motion racing to the scene of the inferno. The flame licks dimmed and died, leaving night in charge of the sky.

27

Celeste had dressed in a yellow cotton skirt, a white sleeveless blouse, and her tennis shoes, and gathered her jail-dirty hair into a slack ponytail by the time Reverend Singleton pulled in front of the house. Before she departed this town someone had to register to vote, no matter what burned to the ground, no matter if all her teeth lay at Sheriff Trotter's feet.

"There's nothing left." Reverend Singleton sat behind the wheel, his suit jacket off, shirt sleeves rolled up. "I drove by there before I came here. Just to see."

She got into the car thinking that she, Celeste Tyree, had to win one small thing. Meanwhile, Wilamena's letter, like a ghost waving at the end of a long dark hall, beckoned her to reread it, to study it as if she'd missed something. Each night she'd put it off, praying for enough ballast to keep Wilamena from toppling her over the edge.

Mrs. Owens came out with her mouth set in a frown. Reverend Singleton took off down Freshwater Road toward Sister Mobley's house. It was their ritual ride now. A deep blue sky the color of Reverend Singleton's preaching robe gleamed above them, calling to mind tropical drinks with tiny umbrellas, not the destruction of the only Negro church in the environs of Pineyville.

Sister Mobley's whole face trembled when she climbed in, barely waving goodbye to Tony who stood on their rickety porch with his two younger sisters, all long-faced. "When I saw that light in the sky, I knew they done burned our church."

"Smell the smoke way over here." Mrs. Owens said. "Still smell it."

"There's little fires around here all the time. From the lightning strikes." Reverend Singleton glued his eyes to the road when they turned onto the two-lane. There was no evidence of what had happened anywhere. The narrow highway was nearly deserted, as usual. The long-needled pines stood tall against the blast of sun. The sandy orange earth lay like a spread of island beach. Here and there were some delinquent bursts of color, usually some long-suffering flower so tired of summer. "But last night was different," he continued. "Buildings burn differently. Longer. Etta and I saw the light in the sky."

Coming up the bumpy road, they all stared at the empty space on the land where the church used to be. They were struck dumb by the absence. To the rear sat the untouched outhouse, shrouded by tree overhang. The space might have been a hand with two missing fingers in the middle. The glorious trees still crowded the space around the clearing. Sister Mobley fell down to her knees in the white-hot gravel, as if the church had been a friend that she'd loved and cared for, and now that friend had died. Mr. Landau had been waiting for them in his truck. He walked over to the blight and stood there, his sculptured head swinging back and forth.

An intermittent crackle broke the quiet as if some hidden bit of fire gasped for breath beneath the ruins. Involuntary prayer mourns erupted, unconsciously and urgently whispered by Reverend Singleton and the others—"Oh, Lord," "What we going to do, now, Lord?"

They walked the nearly rectangular boundary of ash, stopping from time to time to notice some half-burned remnant. Charred pew backs and floorboards sent thin lines of smoke into the cumbrous morning air. There were stick and hinge remains of wooden folding chairs, and one or two metal folding chairs, their brown paint cooked off, standing straight. The iron church bell that had come from New Orleans leaned against a piece of crisp pulpit railing. Reverend Singleton's white flush toilet sat bare to the sun, drizzled in cinders and ash.

Dolly Johnson thundered up the potholed church road in her hand-me-down car and parked off under the trees. She came toward them, her hair swept back in an exact copy of Celeste's ponytail, gym shoes on her feet, no makeup, no nail polish, looking like a veteran of the civil rights movement in her simple skirt and blouse, all clean and pressed. Another sea change, but was it still only a matter of style? Would it carry over after the volunteers went home, after the excitement of Freedom Summer came to an end? Celeste wanted so much for this new Dolly to be real, was willing to forgive her petulance in the jail cell. Maybe Dolly had begun to toss whatever remained of her relationship with Percival Dale on the pyre the day she brought Labyrinth and Georgie to freedom school. She'd propelled herself toward a kind of freedom by going to the voter education classes. The consequences for her might be the loss of her job in Hattiesburg, as well as no more shopping bags of groceries with cash money under the food. Maybe that's why she'd backtracked in the jail cell. She'd had second thoughts about her own ability to make her life work, was probably torn about how she'd manage, if she'd keep her children in this town or leave taking them with her. Dolly had a lot of decisions to make for sure. Dolly said "hey" and Celeste grinned toward her weakly, her cut lip pulling against her smile.

The August sun blanched the gravel stones. Everything but the church seemed lifted up, as if the soft grayness of the ashy shroud and the broken bits of stone were an artfully arranged backdrop. The long-needled pines, live oaks, and stands of poplars all exploded in profusions of green, while the church's remains receded into a black scorch on the earth. Even Reverend Singleton's DeSoto stood out in a shimmer of blue and tan. The corners of his red bumper sticker reading *Register Now—Vote in November* curled away from the chrome fender. Mr. Landau's truck, rust-brown and chrome, sat to the side. Celeste wondered if he had a rifle under the seat, if seeing his burned-down church would be more than he could tolerate.

Celeste started digging through the burned rubble with a long branch of tree searching for some evidence that the freedom school ever existed. One summer of freedom school, then *regular* segregated school all year long, all life long. State schools propped up the status quo, left too many children dull and thirsty or worse, uninterested in learning at all. Children were taught that chattering bruised the air by teachers who told them to shut up. Parents said the same thing for fear their chattering would ignite some simmering hatred. It was the end of the summer project. It was a double-shame, with the church burned, that the children who'd come to freedom school over the summer would no longer be able to see and touch the place where a different idea about learning first took hold. They should be able to walk in there every Sunday morning for church with their portable blackboard off to the side, the Negro history books stacked neat on the shelves, newspapers from other places, their art work on the walls. But it was all burned with the St. James A.M.E. Church.

Celeste poked around with her tree branch and murmured, "Sophie Lewis will not be happy with this."

"She knows Mississippi as well as anyone. But it will break her heart. She has such high hopes." Reverend Singleton, his Kodak camera in hand, took photos of the burned-down church. Then he directed Celeste to smile and to point to her cut lip and cracked tooth. Celeste did as he asked, knowing full well no Kodak photo could show the full damage to her lip and tooth.

"I thought at the end of the summer, I might have divided the books among the children." Celeste held herself to keep from crying, from railing against the south.

"Books or no books, they're not going to forget that freedom school." Reverend Singleton insisted she stand there as he photographed her injuries up closer. "I'ma send these on to Jackson for the FBI and let them decide about what to do with Sheriff Trotter and his deputy."

"FBI ain't going to do nothing. Once they found those three boys, they wasn't going to stay in Mississippi." Mr. Landau walked toward his truck and sat down on the running board, his elbows on his thighs, big hands dangling. "You smell the kerosene?"

"Sure you right, Landau. But I gotta send the photos on anyway." Reverend Singleton sniffed the air for kerosene. "Yeah. I smell it."

"We be all right, Reverend Singleton. Ain't nothing new." Mrs. Owens stood there by him patting his arm. "It's just a building."

Dolly sniffed the air and Sister Mobley walked the perimeter of the church, stopping and staring from time to time, no doubt placing this thing and that in her memory. Celeste headed towards the shadowy cool trees of the sacred ground. The man who gave the church the bell was buried there. Little did he know. Things really did get worse. The smell of burned pine resin and the filigrees of smoke teared her eyes, and then the tears became a steady stream running down her face. Today her mouth was just an irritation rather than a forward-lurching pain. Sissy Tucker's small grave and simple cross lay just at the boundary between the sacred ground and the ordinary cemetery. Zenia Tucker's red geraniums were dulled by their layer of ash.

Celeste rejoined Reverend Singleton and the group in the crystalline light of mid-morning. "Everything's all right in there." She smiled a mini-mal smile to lessen the tug on her lip, knowing her cracked front tooth changed everything on her face. The thought of how she looked in the mirror trying to brush that tooth brought a shiver of giggles. She'd ended up washing the tooth with her finger. She ate a breakfast of eggs and the center of her butter-soft biscuit, taking it in small side bites and chewing gingerly. That tooth had to last until she got back to Jackson, or better, home to Detroit.

"They don't change much." Reverend Singleton relaxed his tie even more, then opened the trunk of his car and pulled out a hammer and a freshly made paint-on-wood sign that he nailed to a tree closest to the rubble of the church. *Help Make Mississippi Part of the USA, Register to Vote Now.* "We can pitch a tent right here if need be." The hammer blows cracked like gunshots through the clearing. He gathered his little group in front of the sign and photographed them. Mr. Landau stood in the back near Celeste, looking like a long lean Sitting Bull. His plum janitor job at Crown-Zellerbach made men jealous, while the women sidled up to him like he had gold in his pockets. She'd seen them at the church picnics over the summer, the younger women batting their eyes and smiling at him, pushing their breasts forward, before sitting primly on the picnic chairs. The men shook his hand quickly and walked away. She figured he must be Reverend Singleton's age—well past the usual age of marriage in the south.

The building had been a symbol. Not just for the movement to help register these backwater Negroes to vote. The church was more than that. It was theirs, their future, a proof of life. Celeste felt a sudden urge now to see where Sissy's body had been found. It would never be all right with her, never rest easy inside her the way Sissy's death had been handled, even by the Negro people of Pineyville. Sissy was a small damage in their minds.

Celeste walked close to Reverend Singleton. "You think you might be able to take me over to the place where you found Sissy?"

"We can do that." He went on about his work, walking around the clearing, taking snapshots.

"Reverend Singleton, are you sure it's all right?"

"Sure, I'm sure. We'll go over there later. I understand." He was digging in the ruins of everything he'd worked for.

Celeste wondered if he, too, had another understanding of Sissy's death that he kept private for fear of cleaving his congregation at a time when he needed them to be united. He'd followed *their* lead on that when he led them in all other respects. There was no hue and cry about Sissy's death—not against the whites of the town and not to question some other possibility. Her funeral had been a personal and private affair, as if she'd died of natural causes.

Mrs. Owens shoved her hands into the pockets of her dark print cotton church dress. "We must go today to see Mr. Heywood." Sister Mobley and Dolly nodded in agreement, their backs turned to the smoking remains. It was the thought on everyone's mind. And coming just after it was the thought of what new violence they'd have to endure before the day ended. Reverend Singleton would have to get the word out that more volunteers were needed, that they'd meet at the burned-down church every evening until they didn't need to meet anymore.

Reverend Singleton grabbed Geneva Owens's hand and put his other hand out for anyone to take. They formed a tight little circle and he led them in a prayer of deliverance from evil, then put the Kodak instant camera in his car, motioned them all in, and off they went. No time to sit around mourning. They bumped over the church road, no one looking back at the scorch, though Celeste could see Reverend Singleton glancing in his rearview mirror at the remains of the church he helped to build, tears squeezing out of the corners of his eyes. She stared out the window; she didn't want him to know she saw him crying.

In town, they drove slowly past the pay phone near the gas station, gazed at Mr. Tucker as he turned his head away. Celeste chastised him in her mind, saying pointedly that it was his church, too, that no matter what else, he needed to mourn that loss. The citizens on the street by now recognized the reason for their ride through town. They glared in hatred or turned their heads away. The woman who sat behind the counter in the small drugstore with the dusty shelves and scant stock stood on the sidewalk. Celeste locked eyes with her as they rolled by, taking all the blame and anger from her look. The woman spat into the air. They rolled on by. Celeste felt them drawing the thread of history through the tidy landscape of this miniature town dressed in magnolia and pine.

Sheriff Trotter's car was parked in its normal spot in front of the Pearl River County Administration Building. Celeste realized in an instant that no one had expected their group to show up again today. You could see it in the jerked-head responses as they parked and walked up that walkway and in that front door. Celeste wanted to protect her mouth; she feared they'd attack the weak ones this time, Mrs. Owens and Sister Mobley. In the foyer, people ducked into offices or hugged the walls.

Celeste listened for the sound of heavy police shoes on the hard floors. They were on the steps going up and still no sheriff came down that hallway. Hands on the smooth banister, as smooth as that porcelain drinking fountain yesterday. Up they walked, afraid to open their mouths, afraid to look in any other direction. They reached the top of the stairs and turned toward Mr. Heywood's office, stunned by their own progress, white people backing away, running in the other direction even. Office doors closing hard. Another drinking fountain—Celeste looked at it, passed it by. Today was not the day for drinking cold water from white porcelain fountains, signs or no signs. Negro people had become so beaten down and broken, they didn't need any *Whites Only* signs. Only outsiders needed that instruction. The press of history and habit did all the work in Pineyville, until this summer.

Mr. Landau took the lead and opened the door marked Registrar of Voters, held it for the rest, Reverend Singleton coming in last. They were in and it was just as he'd described back at the church mock-up. A long dark wooden counter, waxed and old. Windows across the back wall that would look over the entrance to the building. Mr. Heywood must've seen them coming up that walkway on the first day and every day. To the side, another door with Mr. Heywood's name in gold letters. Three white women at desks with small table fans fluttering, acting as if no one had entered the office.

They stood there, the six of them. Celeste waited to hear, "May I help you?" She heard nothing but the slight flip of paper caught in the breezes of the fans. Ledger books on the counter, pens, a small chrome press bell, and hard chairs along the wall for waiting. A large painting of a Confederate soldier full of board-back pride, medals on his chest. And always, a large Confederate flag on full display.

Reverend Singleton and Celeste stepped to the counter just as they'd rehearsed at the church. He coughed. "We're here to register to vote."

Sister Mobley, Geneva Owens, Mr. Landau, and Dolly huddled over to the side out of the way of the door, which might blast open at any moment, full of badges and billy clubs. Celeste's knees turned to rubber; she felt she might drop down, crawl under something to get out of the way of whatever came in that door. She steadied herself by gripping the edge of the counter. It had the polished sheen of Shuck's bar.

Finally, one of the white women walked to the counter, her Peter Pan collared blouse buttoned nearly up to her neck, a gold chain and cross shining at her throat. Her raven hair was combed as neat as Momma Bessie's backyard grass, not a hair out of place, as if it had been roller-set, air-dried, and saved under glass. She didn't say a word, just glared at them as if they were beasts behind the bars of a zoo, then shoved a few stapled papers toward Reverend Singleton, her small wedding diamond and ring glimmering up from her peachy nails. She walked back to her desk, her pump heels clacking on the oak floor. One application. Sister Mobley took it as a victory and breathed out a "Thank you, Jesus."

Reverend Singleton and Celeste stood at the counter studying the voter registration test, which included five pages of multiple-choice questions on the Mississippi State Constitution and a page of requests for personal information about the applicant—specifically, whether you knew if your antecedents had voted before the Civil War, and whether or not they paid taxes. There was no way to tell if the next person would receive entirely different questions or not. The Jackson office had sent copies of the different applications given to Negro and white people. They'd prepared for the worst—that's what the whole summer had been about. Celeste had her best readers, her best test-takers in this first group. If they couldn't get past this application, no one else she'd worked with over the summer would.

Mrs. Owens stepped to the counter, severity and age intermingling on her face, her gray hair bundled back and sweat glistening her forehead. "I would like to registe' to vote, too."

That really launched it. Mr. Landau, Sister Mobley, and Dolly each stepped to the counter and repeated what Mrs. Owens had said. A second white woman, tan and healthy, came forward and delicately slid five more applications across the counter. She wore a jacketed sundress, pearls around her neck, and a slender gold wristwatch. "Y'all go ahead and fill those out. If you can write." Nothing mean in her tone, though. She pursed her lips and went to the desk of the first woman. The two turned their backs to the counter, whispering. The dark-haired woman pushed a button on her phone and spoke quietly. Celeste strained to hear what the woman was saying, but the other woman spoke over her.

"Take turns with those pens. That's all there are. Take your time." She had a curly smile on her lips. "When you done with that, Mr. Heywood might want to ask you some questions."

Celeste wondered if she'd called Sheriff Trotter. Surely he knew they were in the building. Something must be going on, and she needed to figure it out fast. They'd fill out those applications, answer all those questions, and then they'd have to wait and wait to find out the results. No law about that, just history. No games left short of the endgame.

The third white woman, younger, stared openly at them. Celeste caught her eye and saw there was no hatred in her look, only surprise and confusion. Was it surprise that they'd even shown up after the burning of the church, or just surprise that she was a witness to history? She didn't come to the counter, but her eyes went back and forth from Celeste and the group to her desktop, then to the tall windows and the broad blue August sky beyond them.

Time pushed the sun to the afternoon side of the building as they stood at the counter filling out those registration tests. Clouds gathered in surplus then thinned out, and the sun beamed clear and hot again. For all of them to complete their forms took more than three hours. Celeste knew they wouldn't be registered today. Reverend Singleton gathered the tests in a pile, pushing the extra one to the side. "We're done. May I ask how long the wait will be before they're processed?"

"I can't answer that." It was the hostile dark-haired woman who spoke. "Like I said, Mr. Heywood might ask y'all some questions, too."

"Fine. We'll wait here." Reverend Singleton turned to the group. He showed Mrs. Owens and Sister Mobley to the waiting chairs and physically sat them down. They'd finished their applications and gone to hovering around the door, looking anxious to leave. Mr. Landau, Dolly, and Celeste stood with Reverend Singleton.

"Ain't you wanting to register?" The younger woman spoke directly to Celeste.

The world went silent. The two older white women's heads whipped around to her.

Celeste was stunned that she'd even asked her such a sensible and polite question. She fumbled for words.

"No, I'll have to vote at home." Celeste spoke curling her upper lip to cover that cracked tooth, sounding like a crone. In truth, she hadn't yet registered, and wouldn't be able to for another year.

"You sure?" The young woman bit her lip, tried to suck moisture out of her frightened mouth. The dark-haired woman glared at her.

"Thank you. I'm sure. Thank you." Celeste wanted to smile but knew that would only get the girl in more trouble than she was in already.

The other women encircled the younger woman's desk, kept their voices down, but there was no mistaking the anger and hissing in the air.

The Negro people waited.

"I read in the newsletter from Jackson there're some white builders from California going around helping rebuild some of these burned down churches." Reverend Singleton spoke calmly to the group as if they sat in a coffee shop mulling over the morning papers. "They're up in Mileston right now. The community center there got torched."

Celeste had read it. She knew that same little article had also said that the structures being rebuilt were being guarded by Negro men with shotguns night and day. "They're guarding that place now. Twenty-four hours a day. Men with guns sitting out there guarding the workers and the building while it's being built." When Celeste said "men with guns" she lifted her chin and made sure the women behind the counter heard every word.

Dolly looked at her, then at the secretaries. "Well, I heard *that*. It's about damn time." She snapped her head back around to the women behind the counter, looked down her freckly nose at them, then walked closer to Sister Mobley and stood by her like an attendant. Celeste wondered what was going on in that mind: Dolly Johnson coming into herself like a wild person. Trouble ahead.

Mr. Landau grunted. Sister Mobley let out a deep sigh and opened her Bible. Any talk of guns sent her to scripture. Mrs. Owens didn't flinch.

The suntanned woman stood. "We gon have to close now. Y'all have to come back tomorrow. Or whatever."

The three secretaries, the younger one lagging, gathered their purses from desk drawers, freshened their lipsticks, and stood waiting for the group to vacate the office. They walked out not knowing when, or if, their applications would be processed.

Reverend Singleton ferried Dolly and Mr. Landau to their cars at the church clearing, then dropped Sister Mobley and Mrs. Owens on Freshwater Road before taking Celeste to the place where Sissy's body had been found. He drove a mile or so on the two-lane, then turned southeast onto another blacktop bordered by a high ridge of rust-orange dirt with thickets of saplings surrounded by tall stands of long-needled pine. If you didn't know the turn-off, you'd drive right by. Then he turned again onto a sandy dirt and gravel road. Celeste raised her window nearly all the way against the clouds of dust. Reverend Singleton aimed his car into pressed tire tracks that smoothed their passage until they hit a few deep ruts.

"How long do you think they'll make us wait?" Celeste's mind rattled over all the waiting that Negro people had been doing since the end of the Civil War.

"No telling." Reverend Singleton wagged his head in short swipes as if to say only God knew.

They rumbled along, the landscape morphing from pine forest to near desert and back again. A faint pine scent floated on the air. This was indeed a very long way for Sissy to have run, even with her strong young legs.

"You never talk about home." Celeste licked her tongue across her cracked tooth, panting from dust and heat.

He loosened his tie again and unbuttoned the top button of his shirt, keeping his eyes on the sand and gravel road. "I was born right across the Pearl River just outside Bogalusa. My people left the south years ago."

"Why'd you come back?" The car felt like the anteroom to a furnace with the windows closed. Celeste cranked her window down again and let the dust float in. A hand-painted sign nailed to a tree announced Cataboula Creek. Reverend Singleton turned into a car path that had lost most of its gravel and in a few yards pulled up to a mound of dirt and sand the color of old oranges.

"Well, you can't run forever. What goes on here, goes on everywhere. It's a matter of degree. *You* came down here." He grinned, but his eyes had a spark of nostalgia, a longing.

"For a summer, Reverend." She smiled back, her cut lip still tight. "Just for a summer."

"Praise the Lord." He took the key out of the ignition, nodded her out of the car.

Celeste liked him praising the Lord for her sojourn.

The heat lay across southern Mississippi like the grease in a cast-iron skillet over a high flame. A rush of chattering birds lifted up from the thin-boned trees. The place smelled of rotting earth, of dead leaves and worms. It was as if a primeval forest and a sandy plain had overlapped unintentionally and now fought each other for dominance. Rough country.

"Even bamboo grows in here." He walked along, rolling up his shirt sleeves. "There's poplars, black willow, wax myrtle, swamp oak."

Celeste walked at his side until the thickness of the growth narrowed the path, and then she fell in behind him. In a quiet marred only by their padding, crunching footsteps, she heard the gurgling of water. Then Reverend Singleton stopped. It was groundwater swelling out of a rocky pile like a faucet someone forgot to turn off. They stood on the slipping edge of a wide streambed where tree roots grabbed out, naked.

"Where you'd learn so much about trees?" She remembered how he'd also named the trees on the ride to Sophie Lewis's house. She spoke low as if someone else might be there watching them, marking them. She stepped closer to him.

"Always wanted to work with plants. You know. When you get to college, you think you'll have time to study everything. But, of course, you don't. You get about the business of designing a life for yourself. The ministry was always number one. The trees came in second and third." He loped along the creek bank like a guide following a trail. "This is where the creek begins. It runs south to Lake Borgne." Sweat drenched his shirt collar and spotted the cloth across his back. The stream strengthened by degrees, other tiny rivulets joining the original one until a robust flow got going.

"There's no oxygen in here." Celeste stopped to catch her breath, the sweat running down her body as fast as the water in the creek. The density of trees held the sun at a distance, but whatever was gained in coolness got lost in humidity.

"Not much." He walked a few steps from the edge of the creek, which swelled and developed a wavy current, crystal clear with an orange sand bottom. After a while, he stopped. "This is where we found her. I marked the place by this yellow poplar." He pointed to a dark-barked tree with leaves that looked like squares. Celeste followed the straight-arrow trunk up to a break that showed a piece of blue sky. The tree had small cone-like growths on the branches.

"You oughta see the flowers. Like big tulips." He leaned back against the tree and wiped his sweaty face with his handkerchief. "The flowers come in the spring. The leaves will turn yellow in the fall."

"I remember from that ride down to see Sophie Lewis. You pointed it out, but it had started raining." She kneeled down in the soft dirt, eyes searching the area, wondering what message had been rained away, slipped down the current all the way to the Gulf. She sat back on her heels looking at the moving water, the perpetual scale of dried salt on her body feeling like a horror of insects creeping over her skin. She scratched and slapped at bugs that weren't even there.

"When it rains, you know, this stream gets going." Reverend Singleton joined her by the bank. "There's run-off from higher ground."

"I can see that." She pondered it. "But Sissy would've run north. She wouldn't have come this way. We turned south from the two-lane." Celeste stood, brushed the sand and dirt from her knees, stared at the roots and vines gnarling around the mud and sand. "We studied how the slaves figured ways to get to the north, as far as Canada. We never talked about running south."

"She's a child. What'd she know about directions?" He spoke simply.

"We studied it. We talked about the north star, how to find it in the night sky." She held onto her belief like it had come to her in a clairvoyant dream.

"At night." He stood. "She disappeared during daylight. Maybe she got confused." Reverend Singleton stared up at the yellow poplar tree with its napkin-shaped leaves as if he might embrace it.

The water grew more powerful, as if someone turned the spigot up to full. She tried to remember if there'd been a big rain that day. Of course, it rained nearly every day for at least a few minutes. Had it been enough through here to swell this creek? But the creek was swelling by itself. Maybe, in the center, the current was strong enough to grab a child's leg if she was very tired from running, or if she stepped into the water to cool her feet or to drink. She looked up into the trees and couldn't tell where the sun was. She turned in a circle trying to find it until she felt dizzy. Maybe it had been an accident. But with no autopsy, no one would ever know for sure. She shook her head in a renewal of her disbelief at the way the thing had been handled.

"I know what you think. You never liked Mr. Tucker, and he never warmed to what we're doing. I agree with you that he's a hard case. But you can't think he'd kill his own child for standing in the freedom school door." Reverend Singleton tried to quiet her agitation, sounding ministerial. She needed to prick his pat estimation of what had happened to Sissy. Reverend Singleton was a smart, insightful man. He had to believe what she did. How could they be so far apart on this?

"It was more than that. I saw it in his eyes. He wasn't just a man who distrusted the movement, or me because I come from the north. His eyes burned when he looked at me—as if I had done something personal to him. I didn't." The words spilled out of her in a rush.

"It's over now." Reverend Singleton started towards the car. "Let's go."

"Zenia Tucker knows. She's lost her mind. I heard her talking to Mrs. Owens." Celeste followed close, afraid to be more than a few paces from him, eyes going from his back down to where she was stepping, her gym shoes so dirty now they'd forgotten they'd ever been white.

"What are you saying?" Reverend Singleton stopped and turned to her. Anger flashed across his face.

"I don't know. Something's not right. Something wasn't right, the way she was at the funeral." Celeste had lost all sense of protocol; she talked to him like he was a friend, a confidant, not the leader-man, not the minister of the Negro church of Pineyville. Her lip pulled against itself. "She wouldn't let Mr. Tucker anywhere near her. Why? Maybe he was touching his daughter. Maybe she knew it all along and did nothing." Celeste heard her words and was stricken by the power of what she'd said in front of a minister. She began praying in her mind for forgiveness even as the words hung in the thick primordial air.

"You can't say that. It's the most horrendous thing you can say about a parent."

"Sissy was coming to Mrs. Owens's house for lessons. Sneaking in the back door. Maybe he saw her." She finally admitted her own complicity and felt not a whit of relief for doing so.

"Maybe he did. Still, it's no reason to kill a child. Maybe a reason to kill *you,* for interfering with his parenting. You shouldn't have done that, Celeste. We set the rules for freedom school and you broke them by doing something on the side." Reverend Singleton's disappointment in her was profound enough to quiet the birds in the forest trees.

"Sissy needed to come to that kitchen." Celeste's eyes burned. "She had nothing else to hold onto." Another real truth clarified in her mind at that moment—how she'd used Sissy as a pawn in her little power struggle with Mr. Tucker.

Reverend Singleton grabbed her arms and shook her. "What *you* did was wrong. And if you believed he was capable of hurting her, then why would you jeopardize her by teaching her in the kitchen when he forbade it? Why would you do that?" At the moment when she needed Reverend Singleton to pull her into his chest, to give her a forgiving hug, he let her go as if his disappointment had wiped away his duty as a minister to help her handle her own pain. She felt selfish and guilty.

"I heard Zenia Tucker say something. Maybe she didn't mean it, but at least she should've been asked what was going on in that house. And nobody asked her." Celeste shifted the burden back to Mr. Tucker, where she believed it belonged. "She knows something. She can't say much because Mr. Tucker's her bread and butter. Even Mrs. Owens said that to her. I heard it." Her anger began to fade. It was all useless.

"A woman who's lost a child will likely think a thousand different things. It's over now, Celeste. The child's in the ground." He turned his back and walked.

"Negro people hurt each other, too, Reverend. No one will even discuss it." She didn't fight now, just said it quietly as she walked behind him.

"It's over." He walked faster, his footsteps sounding like muffled tom-toms. "Let it go." There was hardness in his voice; a wall of stones had come down between them. "You're a smart girl, Celeste, but you've got plenty yet to learn about life." He resumed his role as chief keeper of the spiritual codes. He offered to lead her out of her confusion and anger, but he knew something about her now that he'd never known before.

His words stung her. Shuck had said the same thing, but it had been playful, not a judgment. What did he mean? That a girl child's death didn't mean as much as the other things pressing on this small town? That this summer was about voting rights and not about Sissy? Bad enough to face the Pearl River County power structure, go to jail, be knocked around. But where was her common sense if not in her suspicion about what had happened? What was the lesson he meant about life? Sissy wouldn't have run south. Sissy wouldn't have run at all if she, Celeste Tyree, had not come to Mississippi. She got into the car feeling deranged, her head pounding from crying, from grabbing at something that kept slipping away. What was it, she thought, that kept so many people from countenancing the possibility that Mr. Tucker might have killed his own daughter?

That night, in the bedroom mirror, her cut frightening as a harelip, the fragile front tooth hanging on by a prayer, Celeste thought again that the people who stayed in Mississippi had a courage she'd never find in herself. Slave ghosts held them tight to this ground, whispering, *don't let that chained horror go unrequited.* They'd been waiting, too. They sang it in the trees in a patois of lost tribes, their dark eyes and lashed backs living in the closets of every house in the south. She wanted to be out of Mississippi, to cross any river that had to be crossed to leave this place. She paced in the small room, stood by the window pining for freedom. She basin-washed the salt and film of dust from her body before changing into her sleep shirt. All the while, Wilamena's letter was glowing like a hot rock in the pocket of her suitcase under the bed.

28

The locals said the quick rains of summer would soon transform into deep storms with masses of dark and thunderous clouds. They spoke of hurricanes that swirled up from the Gulf, rolling across Lakes Pontchartrain and Borgne, pummeling southern Mississippi. Pineyville only tasted what New Orleans, which sat below the level of the sea, ate from a platter.

Celeste had packed and unpacked her suitcase a hundred times in her mind. She first started doing it the night the shots were fired through the houses on Freshwater Road and blasted out the back window of Mr. Tucker's maroon Hudson. Whoever had done it surely believed this would scare the Negro people out of their drive for voting rights and scare her back to where she came from. She fled back to Detroit a hundred times, in her dreams, in her walks to the outhouse, in her daily struggle with the lack of running water, in her loneliness.

The Pineyville Six, as Reverend Singleton continued to refer to them, went back to Mr. Heywood's office every morning. Each time they were told he hadn't yet gotten to their applications. Celeste was walking on a wire, waiting to see if it would hold or sizzle to threads. Registration was closing for the coming elections, but appeals were being filed all over the state because of the extraordinary delays in processing the applications. There was no leaving Pineyville until someone passed that test.

Two and a half weeks after filling out their applications, and then returning to the registrar's office every day to check on their applications, the six went again to see Mr. Heywood. They arrived expecting the same stall they'd experienced on the day before, and the day before that. The three secretaries ignored them, kept their heads focused on their desktops, their little fans decorated with red ribbons kiting in the breeze. The dark-haired woman with the sour face picked up her phone and pushed a button, then replaced the receiver.

"Mr. Heywood be out here in a minute." She waved a look to the six, her eyes never focusing.

The outdoorsy woman with the suntan walked to a file cabinet in the corner by the high windows and opened and closed file drawers as if looking for something she couldn't find. Even the younger woman who'd offered Celeste the opportunity to register to vote stared out the windows, away from them, as the clouds from the Gulf of Mexico rolled through. It might rain, Celeste thought, following the younger secretary's eyes to the window. She wished it would rain hard. She'd stand in the middle of Freshwater Road watching the lightning zag in the sky, feel her bare feet sinking in the sandy mud, feel the pelting drops on her face and in her hair.

Mr. Heywood came out of his office and looked at them with a surprised expression as he wrestled into his brown suit jacket, grabbing papers from the edge of the dark-haired secretary's desk. He stood behind the counter and swiped a handkerchief over his sweaty face. His hair, parted on the side, slid across his receding hairline, revealing an expanse of pale scalp. Celeste noticed again how Mr. Heywood's eyes were darker at the center, surrounded by a blue-gray marbling. They hadn't seen him once since their very first attempt in the lobby, when he'd hustled them out the side door.

"Don't y'all have nothing else to do?" His eyes danced around the countertop, appraised the painting of the Confederate soldier on the wall, the clock, anything and everything but a look at them.

"Not today," Mrs. Owens said, shaking her head no. "How you doing, Mr. Heywood?" A yearning look spread over Mrs. Owens's face, a plea that seemed to beg for his righteousness. He'd told Mrs. Owens to get that "gal" out of her house. He'd said, "Niggers didn't belong in this building." And here they were. No one had called out the Mississippi National Guard to stop them. Mr. Heywood was eating crow because someone more powerful than he had told him that he had to backtrack on his promise of *no Negro voting in his county as long as he had breath in his body.* He had to bend so now he glided above, camouflaging his loss. His lips nearly parted, but the greeting died before it could float into the air. Celeste knew Mrs. Owens had ironed his shirts in years past, had greeted his wife with her baskets of rough-dried clothes. But this was about voting and that had been about ironing.

"Well, we might as well get this over with. It looks to me like Landau, Geneva, and Hazzie Mobley now registered to vote in the State of Mississippi." He didn't look at them for as much as an eye blink, spoke the names without title. In all this time, Celeste never knew Sister Mobley had a first name. Tony called her Ma, everyone else called her Sister Mobley. Hazzie.

Mr. Heywood flipped a stapled page over, wiping his face again with his handkerchief though it was dry, smoothing those errant hairs back across his balding spot. "The other two didn't pass the test." His head wiggled like a kid standing on the other side of a line in a game. Dolly and Reverend Singleton hadn't made it. Reverend Singleton, a graduate of the University of Chicago, didn't pass Pineyville's test. Dolly, one of the best readers in the group, hadn't passed the test. Celeste knew it was a lie.

Mr. Heywood opened the ledger book on the counter. "Come on now and sign this book." He cut his eyes at Dolly. "Need you to print your name and address and then sign your name on the lines." Celeste figured that the eye-cutting had to do with his disdain for Dolly's relationship with Percival Dale. That's what not passing the test was for Dolly. It had nothing to do with what was on the paper. The lie of the south. The second biggest lie of all. The eye-cut was the tip-off. Moments eased by on a breath. Dolly knew the rules.

"You must be out of your mind." Dolly sounded confused, hard, her voice bringing Celeste back into the room.

Mrs. Owens stepped up to sign, proud, her face barely able to contain her personal joy, as mixed as the joy had to be that *everyone* hadn't made it. Mr. Landau and Sister Mobley stepped up right behind her, proud to be signing in that ledger book, finally.

Mr. Heywood leaned on the counter like the keeper of the gate, like the owner of the lock. He'd let them sign in *his* book and then would close it again for God only knew how long before he opened it to another Negro hand. He'd sit on it, bury it in an unmarked grave before he let another Negro hand touch it, unless that hand held a feather duster.

Celeste watched how they printed their names, their addresses, and then, in their unpracticed scrawls, wrote their signatures. She held onto the edge of the counter, euphoric with triumph, wanted to whoop right out loud in the office, to scream that they'd made it. Things would change, and it started right then and there. No more stepping off the sidewalk to let a white person pass. Negroes could laugh, talk, be their Negro selves right there in Pineyville. No running back to the woods. No more looking at the ground instead of dead into the eyes of any white person who came along. This was the beginning, at last, a hundred years after the end of the Civil War, a hundred years after the Constitution gave them the rights of citizenship.

Reverend Singleton braced, erect and proper though she knew his heart had to be breaking. He'd lost his church for this and now he'd lost this, too.

Dolly had stepped aside with a flush on her face to let the others sign the book, but now she spoke again. "What kind of shit is this?" Her voice was barely loud enough for the people behind the counter to hear. She no longer wore a purse to the Pearl River County Administration Building, but rather carried her necessities in her pockets like Celeste. Her tone, her words didn't match her copycat college girl looks. She moved to the counter beside Celeste and stared Mr. Heywood right in his face. "You crazy for sure. I wanna know how come I didn't pass your test?" Her eyes nearly popped out of their sockets, her hands flew to her hips. Her gym-shoed feet paralleled for balance.

Mr. Heywood backed away from the counter. "We don't have that kind of talk in here."

Celeste put her arm on Dolly's arm to calm her. Dolly yanked it away.

Reverend Singleton's dark skin went ashy. "Perhaps there's been some sort of a mistake." He spoke quietly, not a note of anger or threat in his voice. He knew the Mississippi State Constitution as well as he knew that Bible he preached from every Sunday morning. "May I see my test please, too? Show me where I answered incorrectly."

Things were spinning out of control again, going in the wrong direction. Mr. Heywood tugged at the sleeve of his suit jacket. He angled his body to include the secretaries behind him who now stared, eyes wide as if they expected a brawl. Reverend Singleton and Dolly had done the unthinkable—they'd questioned a white man's authority and intelligence in front of other Negro people and white people, too. Panic rippled through Celeste's body.

Dolly banged her fist on the counter. "You got no right or reason to do such a thing." The press bell bounced. Her hand flattened out on the counter top and slapped it. "I know I passed that test. You just trying to punish me for something that doesn't have anything to do with voting."

Celeste grabbed Dolly's arm more forcefully this time, pulled her away from the counter, keeping an eye on the three women in the back. If one of them picked up a phone, it would surely be to call Sheriff Trotter. In her head, she heard one of those women on the phone: *Sheriff, you better come on up here and get these niggers, they gettin' surly again. Mr. Heywood is under attack.*

"Let's go, Dolly. It's a beginning." Celeste hissed the words into Dolly's ear, held her as tightly as Trotter might. She wanted to sock Dolly. "Calm yourself. I'm not going back to that jail cell, and neither are you." They'd gotten a piece of what they came for. That was enough. She bottom-lined it like Shuck would've done. "Let's go, now. Come on. I don't want any more of my teeth cracked in Mississippi."

Mr. Landau, Mrs. Owens, and Sister Mobley finished signing in the big book and stepped back with nervous eyes darting around, nobody knowing quite what to do. Mr. Landau, Celeste knew, had been on his best behavior for the cause of this voter registration drive, but he couldn't be contained forever. They needed to get out of there before something awful happened.

Dolly retreated, tears overlapping the anger on her face. Reverend Singleton moved to Dolly and put his arm around her. "Quiet, now. Just like Sister Celeste said, it's a beginning. We knew going in it wasn't going to be easy. Be happy for the ones who did pass."

Celeste stared at the side of Mr. Heywood's face. "They'll take the test again and again."

Mr. Heywood walked towards his office door. "I guess you may do that. I've done all I'm going to do." He disappeared, closing his inner office door.

Everything went quiet. Just the pearl blue sky and and the roofs of the neighborhood houses peeking through breaks in the trees. Green below, blue above. They were suspended on the second floor of the Pearl River County Administration Building. Celeste longed to get out of the registrar's office, out of the building with its institutionalized disdain for Negro people, out of Mississippi.

The secretaries' voices lifted, chatting about a yard party planned for the weekend. They'd turned their backs on the Pineyville Six. They spoke again as if behind a glass, as if the six were not there. Pineyville's voter registration summer project effectively ended.

Reverend Singleton shook his head in wonderment as he exited the registrar's office, the rest of them filing like wingless ducks behind him. Would there ever be a complete success? Would joy ever ring clear up to heaven? Celeste knew very well that Dolly might never get registered because of Percival Dale. No way to know if Dale's wife had called Mr. Heywood to remind him of the situation. As if anyone in town didn't have an unspoken reference to it on the tips of their tongues at all times. Dolly probably needed to move to New Orleans; she'd fit right in with those black Creoles.

In the cool hallway, Celeste surveyed the people coming and going, searched for any uniforms and clanking handcuffs. She saw none, heard no hard-soled boots hitting floors. She went straight to the drinking fountain and slurped the cool clear water into her mouth, let it sail down her throat cooling her entire body. Reverend Singleton pulled her away, though, telling her the water fountain wasn't included in the package they'd just gotten.

They started down the stairs. Mrs. Owens walked with Reverend Singleton. She had known him longer than anyone else in the group. She would be his comfort as he had been for her. Reverend Singleton, as Pineyville's own civil rights minister, might never sign his name in the ledger book for Pearl River County. They had burned his church, and now they wouldn't let him register. He would pay for being uppity. They wanted him out of Pineyville as much as they wanted Celeste out.

Celeste grabbed the banister and walked down with Dolly, smooth-talking her out of gouging the wall with her car key. Mr. Landau took Sister Mobley's arm as they descended like debutantes floating in the big sunlight of the stairwell windows. Sister Mobley beamed and lifted her head up grandly coming down those stairs from Mr. Heywood's office, clutching her Bible proudly to her heart.

The whites in the lobby barely noticed them. They'd been in this building every day since they took the test, coming in the front door each time. Celeste wondered how long it would take the rest of the Negro people of Pearl River County to come up that front walk, come through the front door, go up those stairs, and demand to take that test to register.

Going back to the car, the sun brazenly hot after the cool of the brick and stone building, Celeste ran it through her mind. Three people made it, two didn't. Only five people even tried. She remembered Ed and Matt stalking around in the St. James A.M.E. Church as if they owned it, questioning her about how many children she had in freedom school and how many adults in voter registration class. Where would her project rank with the others all over the state? She'd find out in Jackson, when the volunteers all met to be debriefed and to say a goodbye that strained against reality. Some of the success of a project had to do with the selling skills of the volunteers and some of it just had to do with how hard and brittle a particular town was. Celeste reminded herself that Negro people all over the south still stepped off the sidewalk to let white people pass. It was entirely possible that some towns didn't register anyone at all. Then again, places like Hattiesburg or even Gulfport or Biloxi might have done a lot better.

Later that night, Mrs. Owens got to pumping water and heating it on the top of the stove and dragged out the portable tin bathtub for Celeste's bath. Said she deserved a victory bath. They pumped, heated, and poured water until she had enough in the big tub for an all-over bath. Celeste closed her curtain-door and sat in that tub like she was in a marble bath in a palace in France. She slid down and rested her head on the thin rim, then folded a towel to use as a headrest. She swooned in it. As the softness of it settled onto her body, she relaxed and then the tears streamed down her face without sobs, without breath or break.

29

In her dreams, Celeste skittered from trumpeting the rights of Negro people as a harried lawyer to being a beret-wearing backroom revolutionary grinding out mimeograph copies until her hands bled. She even turned up as a sad-eyed expatriate languishing in an exotic city sipping muddy coffee in a dark cafe. Ed Jolivette sat opposite her planning their escape.

When the smells of scorched chicory coffee, pork fat, and collards wafted into the room, she woke fully from her dream-drenched sleep. As they had so many times this summer, thoughts of the letter kept her nailed to the mattress. Not just her suitcase but the room itself had become a holding zone for Wilamena's missive. She eyed that glowing Pandora's box peeking from under the bed frame.

"Why did she tell me this now?" Celeste talked to the raw wood ceiling from her mattress on the floor. Grandma Pauline used to say, "Let sleeping dogs lie." Wilamena evidently never listened. Maybe the dog slept for everyone but her.

"Who you talking to in there?" Every grunt and mumble sailed through this house. "Ain't nobody in here but us." Celeste loved being grabbed up in Geneva Owens "us," heard the clanking pots and refrigerator door opening and closing, wondered what could be going on in that kitchen.

"Myself. I'm losing my mind." She called out, still in the habit of speaking as if she had a real door instead of a curtain separating her room from the rest of the house. She got up from her mattress, heaved it onto the bed frame, checked her tooth and her lip scar in the washstand mirror, then stuck her head through the curtain. "Just gonna put on some clothes, Mrs. Owens."

"Take your time, child." The ringing merriment of a freshly registered voter in her voice.

Celeste washed herself, relishing a slight lifting of the morning heat, glorying in the fact that she hadn't sweated away last night's tub bath while she slept. She pulled on slacks, a soiled blouse, and her gym shoes. She grabbed her hair back with a rubber band and stepped into the kitchen carrying her small basin of dirty water, ready to help Mrs. Owens.

Light streamed in through the east-facing back door and the side-window. Mrs. Owens had tied back the white eyelet-embroidered curtains with a black shoestring. Cooking utensils covered the small kitchen table. Every pot and bowl she owned lay around on the stovetop, the shallow counter, on top of the refrigerator. She turned to Celeste and nodded towards the steaming coffee pot, her knotty hands sliding the shell from a hard-boiled egg and adding it to a bowl full of them. "We gon have something around here. A celebration, a something. A hello to votin' and a send off for you. I don't care what else." She'd thrown years off of herself overnight, her apron splotched with dark grease spots and circles of dampness. Joy, Celeste thought, had to be the greatest palliative against age.

Celeste headed for the outhouse with her basin, ready for any relief from her tangled thoughts of leaving, of jail cells and burned down churches, of missing Ed like a lost limb, of Shuck and Wilamena. She poured out the dirty water and used the facility, hating it as much today as the first time she'd used it two months ago. On the back porch, she rinsed her basin with pump water and bleach, and noticed the smooth, hard Mississippi-grown muscles in her arms for the first time. In her room again, she grabbed her pitcher and thudded out the front door to the spigot.

Mrs. Owens was preparing for her goodbye. The thought of it—of leaving—made her stomach tighten unexpectedly.

In the bright morning light, Freshwater Road was so quiet you could hear the clouds whooshing by. She stood by the spigot with the big Mississippi sky unfurled like a vast blue drape. The clouds would come later in the afternoon. Morning birds on the power lines and in the trees chattered in soft whistles. No traffic, no sirens, no students yelling across the Quad, no Detroit Negroes with robust voices calling out of back doors. All summer long she'd ached to be out of this place and now she could barely entertain the thought of leaving.

Time had dragged and flown by simultaneously. She filled the pitcher, the wild spray of good water splashing her pants and arms, deposited the full pitcher in her room, then rejoined Mrs. Owens in the kitchen.

"Who all's coming?"

"Reverend Singleton stopped by this morning, brought these greens from Etta. Already cleaned. Thank the good Lord. And he brought the chickens for frying. I'm making some potato salad, too, and maybe some shrimp and okra. He's gonna tell the others." She paused. "And those children, too. Lord, help me." She chopped onions now and dipped them in ice water, tears running down her plum brown cheeks. "Reverend Singleton puts his best foot forward no matter how hard life gets. We're blessed to have him in this town."

The words sank into Celeste. "Yes, he does." Had she slipped into her room and read her letter? This appraisal of Reverend Singleton rang bells in Celeste's head. Was she telling her to do that, too? Maybe she'd stood staring at the photo of Shuck and Billy and put it all together. Celeste shook the possibilities from her mind. Heartbroken that he wouldn't be voting come November, Reverend Singleton planned a celebration for the ones who would. There was nothing else in it. Mrs. Owens had just been duly noting his generosity of spirit. She had to learn to stop reading her own meaning into everyone else's. She remembered Shuck saying that some blues let you hold on to the belief that no matter how hard life got, sweetness lay like a lost charm in the moonlight.

"Now, I know you want to go to that phone and call your boys up in Chicago. Tell them you're a registered voter." Celeste diced celery, working to pick up the older woman's air of celebration.

Geneva Owens released the lid on her greens, then pulled a pot of cooked potatoes out of the refrigerator. "Well, I do. I will tell them. Do so wish my Horation had lived to see this day."

Horation Owens had fought in the Great War and been injured, came home and never could vote. "He knows." Celeste nearly diced off the tip of one of her fingers thinking about it. The knowing. Who had snuggled Wilamena's lie to their bosom? And, what exactly was the lie? She heard Momma Bessie and Grandpa Ben talking in the kitchen a long time ago.

When Grandpa Ben said they walked the horses from Lexington to Louisville, Celeste asked why. Momma Bessie gave her the question look. "Girl, they didn't have trucks in them days."

"Oh."

Grandpa Ben said he remembered when Jimmy Lee won the Derby. "He won all six races on the card. That was before they stopped letting us ride."

"We used to ride?"

"Girl, the first Derby they ever had was won by a Negro jockey. Oliver Lewis, and his horse was Aristides. Was plenty Negroes riding back then. Riding and winning."

"Where'd the name Tyree come from, Grandpa Ben?"

His mouth tightened and a brick-hard look came into his eyes. "You don't know nothin' about no Tyree."

Momma Bessie's eyes flashed him a warning as Shuck came into the kitchen grinning with Billy right behind him.

"Tyree's a name tapped out rhythms in speakeasys and buckets of blood from Harrodsburg to Detroit. From the bluegrass to the black tar." Grandpa Ben looked right at Celeste. "You got people in the country and people in the town and never been no slaves, either." Shuck came over and kissed her on her forehead and she and Billy ran out the back door to the yard.

When they'd piled fried chicken in a roaster pan, refrigerated the potato salad, rested the greens, and covered the shrimp and okra side dish, Celeste went in to wash herself and dress for the celebration. Mrs. Owens whipped up a batch of cornbread so fast Celeste thought someone had left it on the front steps. They poured tall glasses of iced tea loaded with sugar and sat on the screened porch, Mrs. Owens rocking in her chair, work-sweat pooling at her hair line, puffs of kinky hair poking through her hair net. Celeste, dressed now in clean slacks and a fresh sleeveless blouse, sat on a straight-backed chair and prayed as usual for a cool breeze.

"I didn't want Sister Mobley to feel bad about not having anything to bring." Mrs. Owens stared at the rutty road through the screen. "That's why I went ahead and did the rest. Etta Singleton's bringing a sweet something. Nobody else bringing nothing." She said proudly. "I'm glad to do the cooking, glad you been here to help me."

"I like being a sous-chef." She heard the past tense in Mrs. Owens's words. The thought came to her clearly: why not just stay? Continue the work, rebuild her freedom school. Hide, pretend she never got Wilamena's letter, throw it down the outhouse hole.

"Now, what's that?" Mrs. Owens stopped rocking.

"Cook's helper. I read it in a book."

"Well, cookin' comes from doin', not from readin'." Mrs. Owens rocked her chair, coughed a grunty sound.

"I know." She didn't know, but she understood that she needed to. It had been a summer of doing, of stepping into the fray, not being on any sideline of life. Celeste leaned her chair against the plank wall of the porch, rested her head back, dreaming of her golden day in New Orleans with Ed. The down-shifting light softened and banks of clouds ballooned up from the south. She visualized Wilamena, voluptuous dark wavy hair resting on her shoulders and framing her beautiful face, standing in the rust-orange beach-like soil of Freshwater Road. The image slipped through her mind like a river eel. What was it like for her in New Mexico? No big cities, no black people. She'd spirited herself to a hiding place to be something else, someone else. She'd unhistoried Detroit. And who was Cyril Atwood, anyway? Maybe a border man whose history branched out into a jumbled lineage like Wilamena's. Wilamena might well have been searching for a truer home. Celeste realized she didn't even know where Wilamena'd met him.

"First thing I'm going to do is get this tooth fixed." Running her tongue over the crack in her tooth had already become a quirky habit. She followed it with a lick of her lip to feel the thin scar.

"Yes, indeedy. They got a dentist up there in Jackson who'll do it." Mrs. Owens rested her head on the chair back. "His name is Dr. Fields."

"Negro?" Celeste would be damned if some Southern white dentist would see the inside of her mouth. She sipped the iced tea, feeling the shot of pain as the cold hit that damaged tooth, held the glass in her lap and felt the cool of it at the base of her stomach.

"Yes, he is. Folks travel a good distance to see him." Pride in her voice. "I don't know if there's another one in the state. Must be. I just never heard of him."

They sat there like two codgers, Mrs. Owens slow-rocking her anti-quated chair and Celeste balancing hers on its hind legs and leaning into the wall, the late afternoon heat shushing the birds on the power lines, paralyzing the flies, clamping down everything that moved. The calmness of it slowed her heartbeat. Every day at this time, the place settled its dusty veil. The sky rested. A hot tiny town to live in while the clattering world rushed off. Celeste thought on it. She could run a year-round freedom school for the children, give them what they'd never get in that public school. Have runaway weekends with Ed Jolivette in New Orleans, take drives to see Sophie Lewis. She'd help Reverend Singleton get the rest of the Negro population registered to vote, organize them to fight for a paved road, indoor plumbing. Plenty to do here.

"Can't hardly wait till November, to walk in there and know my name is in that big book." Geneva Owens stared off across the road. "Sure is cause for a celebration."

"It is." Celeste wanted to be there to see Mrs. Owens walk in there and vote, too.

She followed the woman's gaze to the landscape, wondered what she saw beyond the low mounds of sand where wild grasses and weedy flowers stammered to life.

"Used to be a house across there. Hurricane come through and flattened it." Mrs. Owens sat still looking at the few cinderblocks and washed-out cypress planks disarrayed on the ground. Had it been more than a hurricane? By the end of summer, the locals pined for the big cooling storms to cleanse the land and shake Mr. Heywood's magnolias senseless. But they also prayed the Pearl River wouldn't override its banks and that their clapboard houses would stand through another hurricane season and another cold rainy winter.

The older woman put her hands on her knees, then to the chair arms and rose from her chair. "I'ma get myself cleaned up before the others get here."

While Celeste balanced on her tilting chair staring at the rubble pile across the road, Dolly drove up in a swirl of pastel dust with Labyrinth and Georgie and their pink vinyl record player, toting a shopping bag of 45s. They set up the music on the porch and ran a line into the house, Celeste thinking all the while that Dolly wasn't going to register to vote in this town even if she never laid eyes on Percival Dale again. Dolly had taken herself to the place that Shuck warned Celeste against. *A Negro woman with a white man will always be lonely.* Celeste hugged Labyrinth and Georgie, something she'd never done before, and they hugged her back. Freedom Summer was over and in their own small way, they'd won.

"What kinda music you listen to up there in Detroit?" Dolly's skeptical expression made Celeste laugh.

"Same kind you listen to down here in Mississippi." Celeste put her hands on her hips. "Why?"

"Just wanted to know is all." Dolly rummaged through the 45s, arranged a stack on the little record player, and turned it on. Little Richard blasted out, "The Girl Can't Help It," and the crows jumped off the wires, flapping their wings, cawing, and flying around and away. Dolly went in to help Mrs. Owens with the food. Labyrinth danced by herself in the small space, and Georgie sat watching his big sister shake her hips. They'd be lucky if the porch survived. The music rode on the thick air, all the more vibrant because there wasn't anything to interfere with it. The Tucker boys, Darby and Henry, came out of their newly painted house half a city block away.

Celeste walked out in the middle of Freshwater Road in the late afternoon sunlight, beckoning to them to come on over. The now dusty Hudson, parked in a lean towards the gully, stood like a grand maroon and chrome sculpture. Mr. Tucker was in there being his evil self, probably seething because somebody might be having a good time. But Zenia Tucker, who'd barely shown her face since Sissy's funeral, stood half in and half out of their front door.

With Martha and the Vandellas launching into "Quicksand" behind her, Celeste shoved aside all the warnings to stay clear of Mr. Tucker and walked toward the Tucker house under a cornflower blue sky. She kept to the middle of the road, dipping a little in time to the music. The next house down Freshwater Road was Sister Mobley's and well after that other small houses were scattered, built as temporary places for the workers in the lumber mills that used to line the banks of the Pearl River. Pineyville's thin soil didn't support plantations; it had always drawn craggy loners, black and white, who couldn't make it anywhere else. They hid out in the piney woods, floated lumber down the Pearl River until its pristine waters turned black from wasted cargoes and wood oils. A deliriously worn-out river. It was a miracle that a drop of that water ever got to Lake Borgne. Pine forests covered everything right down to the last plain before the Gulf of Mexico, the scent of pine woven into the air. Celeste imagined herself hiding away her life in the piney woods.

"Your house looks pretty." Celeste started talking before she arrived. The white shiny finish arced out against the tangerine soil.

Zenia Tucker seemed caught in the front door just like Sissy had at the church, living in a shadow, hugging a secret that she couldn't even speak herself. "Thank you, Miss Celeste."

"Don't you want to come over to celebrate with us?" She spoke to the boys who stood on the bottom step of their porch eyeing her, pebbles of reticence in their eyes. "We got three people registered to vote."

"That's real nice, Miss Celeste. Wait a minute." Zenia Tucker disappeared, the screen door closing right behind her.

Celeste eased closer, praying Mr. Tucker stayed in his house. Beads of sweat bubbled into streams down her face and body, more from fear than heat. "What you been doing all summer? Haven't seen you around." They'd receded like their parents. She smiled, hoping to break through Mr. Tucker's hateful barricade. "Now, which one's Darby and who's Henry?"

"Nothing. I'm Henry." The Tucker boys had sad eyes, too, but not like Sissy's almond ones, full as they were of questions and reveries of flight. The bigger one, Henry, spoke again. "What happened to your tooth?"

"I ran into a drinking fountain." She gave them a big silly grin.

They didn't believe her, she knew, by the way they glanced at the ground as if embarrassed to be in the presence of a lie. Their father probably told them about the goings on at the county building, fashioning the story to suit his own ends.

"My daddy told me you went to jail." Henry had accusations in his face. "Bad people go to jail."

"I did go to jail. So did Reverend Singleton, Sister Mobley, Dolly Johnson, Mrs. Owens, and Mr. Landau. We all went to jail."

"I Like It Like That" blasted out from Mrs. Owens's porch, sounding so funky her body shimmied a little step to the music right in front of the Tucker house. She hadn't heard a note of music except church music and freedom songs since she was in New Orleans with Ed. Dolly must've cranked the volume up even more. Mrs. Owens wasn't going to have that for very long.

"Oh. Why all y'all go to jail?" Darby spoke up.

"I hope your mother will tell you."

Celeste figured she'd better back off as Zenia Tucker came all the way out into the light, frail, her whole body sinking in on itself, clothes lopsided, hair half-combed, the hot-iron scar on her face healed but ugly. She gave Celeste a large piece of paper. "She'd a wanted you to have this, I'm sure."

Celeste stepped onto their path to reach for the paper, took it, and backed away again just as Mr. Tucker appeared behind Zenia. Zenia Tucker's face stayed as blank as a sheet on a clothesline. Mr. Tucker stepped out onto the porch but said not a word, just stared at Celeste with enough hatred in his eyes to stall an army. Celeste froze where she stood. She turned the paper over slowly, trying to encourage her legs to move away, to go. Sissy had drawn Frederick Douglass with wings in the night sky and the north star up in the corner. The drawing vibrated with color. Douglass's dark skin and beard and huge crinkled hair flowed back in a draft of flight. It was the same picture that had illustrated the front of the Frederick Douglass book. His big brown eyes were bright and full of intent. Sissy must've drawn it at home because she'd never taken a seat in freedom school. Celeste stepped back to the road. "Thank you, Mrs. Tucker." She didn't look again at Mr. Tucker, kept her eyes down. "Well, you welcome to come on over. Mrs. Owens cooked a whole lot of food." No one moved. "Bye, then. Bye Henry, bye Darby. Mrs. Tucker." They said "goodbye" in whispers. Out of the corner of her eye, she saw Mr. Tucker disappear inside his house.

The sun geared west as Celeste walked back toward Mrs. Owens's house, staring at the drawing, tears welling in her eyes, falling down her face. Sissy's self-portrait as Frederick Douglass reminded her that if she hadn't come to Pineyville talking about freedom, north stars, and better places, Sissy would still be alive. She stepped over Labyrinth and Georgie on the front stairs and kept her face away from Dolly, who sat in Mrs. Owens's rocker. She took the drawing into her room, propped it up on her dresser, and stood there crying in silence. In a while, she collected herself and joined Dolly and the children.

When the Chantels whorled "Maybe" through the late-August air, Mr. Landau turned in off the two-lane, parked on the side of the road, and swung his long legs out of that truck dressed in slacks, a brightly colored short-sleeved shirt showing off his muscular arms. He went straight to the kitchen, shaking the little house with his heavy-footed stride. Dolly and Celeste followed him in like big-city pigeons. Sure enough, he had a bottle of gin in one pocket and six bottles of tonic water distributed among all his other pockets, along with two weevily lemons. All from Louisiana. Celeste blessed Louisiana under her breath, then made gin and tonics for Mr. Landau, Dolly, and herself. Reverend and Etta Singleton arrived with more food and all the Mobleys and soon, there was enough to feed the town.

After eating the celebration meal, the never-used parlor became the grown-ups' sit-down place. Dolly and the children stayed on the front porch or bopped to the music on the dirt path. Celeste was glad they danced on the dirt path, because if they kept jumping and bopping around on that porch, it might just fall to the ground. Dolly put on "Duke of Earl" and did her imitation of Gene Chandler with his cape pretending to leave the stage and coming back over and over. With her cracked tooth making her feel like a bucket-of-blood patron, Celeste dropped her jaw at Dolly's smooth antics. The children hollered and clapped for Dolly as the sun dropped to the level of the horizon, the sky slashed with pale orange streaks that matched the color of the earth. The voices of Reverend Singleton, Sister Mobley, Mr. Landau, and Mrs. Owens carried out on the evening air, pulled her inside.

Etta Singleton was down the short hall in the lonely light of the kitchen scraping and stacking dirty dishes. A feast for the bony dogs of Freshwater Road. Across the tiny parlor room, Geneva Owens beckoned to Celeste to come take her seat, then went to the kitchen, too.

Mr. Landau sipped his gin and tonic, large hands engulfing the kitchen glass, as he leaned against the wall near the entrance. "This time, I don't care what y'all say, I'm bringing the Deacons for Defense and Justice over to guard the rebuilding. Ain't no sense in going through this again." Mr. Landau sounded like a man unaccustomed to taking charge with his words; he had his head down so that some of it went into his chest, but the meaning was clear.

"Well, now, Landau, you know we can't put ourselves in a position for a gunfight. We wouldn't win it anyway." Reverend Singleton stood straddle-legged near the front window. Celeste felt his eyes follow her to the parlor chair.

"Won't be no gunfight. All's has to happen is *seeing* those Negroes with shotguns. Ain't nobody gon do nothin'." Landau swigged his drink. "You don't need to do a thing 'sides raise the money to rebuild."

"Lord, have Mercy." Sister Mobley dabbed at her heart with rapid little pats, sitting near Celeste in the only other chair.

"I sure want to be here to see *that*." Celeste heard her voice, scanned their faces in the dimming light, uneasy that she'd intruded in something that the locals were deciding amongst themselves. She reached under the yellowy shade of the one lamp and turned it on, feeling as disenfranchised as they'd been all their lives. Outside.

"We have a small insurance policy. Won't cover much, but every bit helps."

He paused and Celeste wondered if he'd mention going to Sophie Lewis for help in rebuilding the church. He didn't mention her, but caught Celeste's eyes, which surely had questions about why he didn't. Now she was afraid to say the woman's name. Celeste thought over the day they'd visited Sophie and remembered a closeness between them but more importantly, a kind of big pride they had in each other. They were like-minded, only she was free and he wasn't. Clear now. She was the reason he could stay there. He had an exquisite place to run off to, to hide in, to revive himself in, to touch some part of a life he'd left in Chicago, a life of theatre, opera, books, and conversations with people from all walks of life.

The Jackson office of One Man, One Vote would kick in money, too, since they were fund-raising all over the country for the movement. And, the dirt-poor Negro people of Pearl River County would ante up again, constantly repairing and rebuilding; they'd put money up for the church when they needed that money for other things, had already put money up for the church. There ought to be a way to sue the people who burned down that church, make them pay to rebuild it and then some.

Reverend Singleton nodded to her. "We need that freedom school, too. These children getting nothing from that public school. That's what they should've burned down."

Celeste cleared her throat. "I'm thinking I might stay on for a while." She sought agreement, going from one to the other. She wondered if Mrs. Owens and Etta Singleton could hear this conversation out in the kitchen. Mr. Landau nodded, eyes going off somewhere else. Hard to read him. He'd been like that all summer except when it came to self-defense. "If I stay, I'm thinking about maybe setting up a freedom school library in the new church. Even have it so the children can check out books. They can't touch the books in the other library." She curled her lips in, praying they'd condone her staying.

Sister Mobley stared at the white lace curtain then looked up to Reverend Singleton, face placid. "That's true. I don't let my Tony go nowheres near it." She looked sideways at Celeste, rail-thin body nearly swallowed up by the one upholstered chair.

Reverend Singleton's eyes shone in his brown face like the idea of a library was the finest thing he'd ever heard. "I like that." He seemed to see the new church with the freedom school and the library. "I'll need to think some more on that, but right off, it's a fine idea."

Landau grunted. "That would put the salt in the white folks' wound. Not only are we voting, we got our own liberry."

Sister Mobley fidgeted. "Don't want to rile them up too much now."

"Sure you're right." Celeste tried to sound like a local and contain her fledgling joy. Mr. Landau didn't give a damn about riling up the white folks, and with the Deacons for Defense and Justice on board, things would go more smoothly. She saw herself hammering nails into the church beams, the liquid blue sky smiling through slats of newly milled cypress, trucks of Negro men with shotguns parked on the church road night and day. Boxes of books arriving from cities around the country for the children. She had her own business to take care of, too, but just hadn't come up with a way to do it. On the screened porch, Dolly and the children had grown quiet, the music turned off now. In the pale light, the grown-ups huddled in the parlor.

"We better be getting on home. Don't want to be on these roads too late at night." Reverend Singleton gathered himself to leave. "Some folks probably mad enough at us for getting a few registered."

Celeste rose to be the hostess, to walk him to the front porch. The children spoke their goodbyes, their high soft voices subdued by the night. Celeste stared into the dark, the voices still coming from inside the house like an alto chorus.

"I want you to know that how I feel about Mr. Tucker is pretty much the way you do." He spoke quietly and glanced toward the kitchen. They were at the screen door. "But if I'd operated from that belief, the church would've split right down the middle. They don't want to believe Mr. Tucker did anything wrong, so they don't believe he did. You understand?" Reverend Singleton's brow furrowed intently.

"I'm trying to accept it, Reverend Singleton." She felt relieved at learning what he believed, relieved that he confided in her. "It helps that you told me this. I didn't want to feel like I was crazy."

"You're a long way from crazy, young lady." Reverend Singleton took her hands and held them both in his. He called to his wife, and after her goodbyes they drove away.

Mr. Landau finished his drink, took his glass to the kitchen, and came back to the front door, where he lingered as Mrs. Owens said her goodnights, Celeste standing beside her feeling for a feather of a moment like her dutiful daughter. She helped Dolly gather the 45s and unplug the little record player, walked them all to Dolly's old car. Dolly gave Sister Mobley, Tony, and the two girls a ride to their house down Freshwater Road.

Inside, Celeste's mind raced with prospects and excitement. Already, she made lists of things she'd get for the new freedom school and library. She couldn't wait to discuss the possibility of staying on for a while with Mrs. Owens. After finishing the kitchen cleaning, they fell into the hard chairs at the small table, exhausted, enjoying the teasing breezes that trailed in then died too quickly. The country night sank heavily around them, vanquishing any memory traces of music, of talking, laughing people who an hour ago filled the house to its seams.

Mrs. Owens sat with her hands folded on the tabletop. "Horation was in this house tonight. He so enjoyed a gathering." She paused a moment, the night sounds swelling. Cicadas interrupted by the barks of roaming dogs and the creak and groan of trees. A car or truck moving steadily along the two-lane. Pine, rust, thin streaks of sourness and mold scuffled on the air. The shrimp shells would have to be buried.

Deep fatigue and an airy exhilaration mixed inside Celeste. "Want to show you something." She stepped to her room, grabbed Sissy's picture, and laid it before Mrs. Owens.

"Oh, my Lord." Geneva Owens picked it up and held it closer to the light above. "It's beautiful." She rested it on the tabletop.

"Sissy drew it." Celeste said, pride spilling through her words. "Isn't that something? Mrs. Tucker gave it to me. It's Frederick Douglass. Sissy never even sat down in freedom school. She understood everything." She paused, undecided as to whether she should go on, then took the plunge. "I think I need to stay here and keep working with the children. That's what I'd like to do." She stopped, let the words spread out in the kitchen, thought of all that needed to be faced at home, then revved up again. "Reverend Singleton invited me to stay on, wants me to continue the freedom school. My daddy has a friend who teaches in Detroit. I'm sure she'd help me collect books and ship them down here. I can set up a library along with the new freedom school and the children would have their own place, wouldn't have to worry about going to that other library where nobody wants them touching anything. I can just see it." Her words tumbled out, eyes pressed forward, heart beating fast, fingers splayed on the table. "Wouldn't take more than a year to set it up, then I'd go back to school." She lied, feeling like she'd more likely wander the earth like a gypsy. "Lot of people do it. Take a year off like that."

Mrs. Owens watched Celeste, seemed to be reading her like the crinkly pages of her Bible. "Well, you were my child, I'd have you finish your schooling. When you go to Jackson, you'll see what the other summer people are deciding to do. But, *whatever* they do, you need to go on and finish your schooling. No delaying." Mrs. Owens tapped her fingers on the table, a background drumming nearly indiscernible, shoulders sinking a bit, submitting to the tiredness they must surely feel after the day of cooking and cleaning.

"But the freedom school. That public school is set up to keep them back." Celeste pressed her case, desperation flecking the words. "Reverend Singleton said that's what they should've burned down. I can't leave now." Her dream of staying singing through her words, she might have been in the pulpit of Reverend Singleton's St. James A.M.E. Church. She was in a life and death struggle for a place called home, didn't know what else there was in the world that she could count on. *Shuck slipping away.*

Mrs. Owens said nothing for a while, seemed to be considering her words, mulling them over and over. She adjusted herself in the chair, wiped her temples with the corner of her apron. Celeste's head pounded with excitement, the anticipation of working out the details of staying, of rebuilding and teaching Tony and his two little sisters, Labyrinth and Georgie, and maybe even getting the Tucker boys to come. In memory of Sissy, she wanted to stay on, but in the back of her mind she knew that would be a perpetual thorn in Mr. Tucker's side, to wake up in September and find her still there watching him, spreading her freedom songs over the land into the hearts of other young people and old people, too. He'd never be able to tolerate that—he'd punish Mrs. Owens and Sister Mobley, too, by not providing them with the least manly gestures. He wouldn't care then if they all died.

"What about your daddy? I know he would not want you to stay here. You can't let him down like that." Mrs. Owens's forehead creased deeply as if she couldn't imagine Celeste coming up with this idea of staying while a well-providing father sat at home waiting for her to get on with her education, her own life.

Celeste's breathing grew shallow. She knew very well if she stayed here it would break Shuck's heart. She licked her scar-lip, her cracked tooth, nodded her head up and down gently. "He wouldn't like it, but he'd never tell me *not* to do it if I really wanted to." She lied like a pro. She'd lied all summer long, saying she'd write her mother, which she hadn't done and had no intention of doing. Didn't even know what Shuck would feel after he heard what was in Wilamena's letter. Didn't even know if she'd ever tell him.

Mrs. Owens looked askance at her, seemed on the verge of disputing her words, but said nothing for a while. The two of them sat there like boxers in a circle of light, the kitchen table their ring, waiting for the bell.

"It's time for these Negroes to get up and demand better for their *own* children. They live here, they work here, they need to be doing for themselves. You can't spoon-feed people forever, child." Mrs. Owens folded her arms across her chest, blocking any further incursions. "We do the rest on our own."

Celeste sighed so deeply her exhaling breath brought her heart to a near stop. She grabbed at Mrs. Owens's words, moved them around in her head trying to figure a way through. Spoon feed. "But if someone like me is here, some things will go a lot faster." She didn't want to admit the downside—that whites resented the Northerners meddling in the town.

In the quiet that followed, she realized she'd revealed something about herself that even she didn't want to be there.

"There may be truth in that, but they need to do it on their own so they know they done it on their own." Mrs. Owens raised her voice but calmed by the end of the sentence. "You did all you can do to show us to the next point. And it's time for you to prepare for your own self's life. You done plenty for ours. You can't hide here. Reverend Singleton means well, but you got to go home and ready your own life." She slid Sissy's drawing across the table toward Celeste. "This is the time for us that live here. Sissy didn't die so you could stay here. We didn't do all we done so *you* could stay here. That's not what it was about."

The weight of it, and the rejection in it, sent shivers over Celeste's body. Nowhere to hide. The words brought heat to her face and ears. She felt her stomach falling. Mrs. Owens knew precisely what Shuck would say. Celeste looked away, bit her lip, then looked back at Mrs. Owens in fear that she might mumble out the truth. So this was the end of her sojourn in Mississippi, the beginning of letting this woman, this house, and this backwater town go. Now she had to leave—she would never insult Mrs. Owens by staying in town with some other family.

They were quiet. Celeste's head tilted down. She must not cry, she thought. She glanced out the back door, around the little kitchen, the refrigerator humming. Mrs. Owens still as a statue.

"You understand what I'm saying?" Mrs. Owens held her face with her knowing dark eyes.

"Yes, ma'am." Celeste nodded, not understanding all of it, sensed somewhere in what Mrs. Owens said that the Negro people of Pineyville needed the best: no more half-educated teachers, no more zealous "would-be-if-onlys." She'd faked herself out by thinking they needed her as much as she needed them. But everything had changed. This was the end of the first race. The next race would be different.

The house was sleeved in darkness, the one bare light bulb shining on their sweaty tired faces. Celeste looked down at Sissy's drawing, saw the girl in the church door with fear in her eyes, remembered her sitting in the back seat of Mr. Tucker's Hudson with her big sunglasses on staring up at the sky. She'd promised to take her to see a movie on a big screen in the dark. But there'd been no time. Out the back door, the tops of the long-needled pines sketched dark silhouettes against a moonlit sky. Sissy'd found some peace and she needed to find some, too.

"All right then." Mrs. Owens got up from her chair. "Good night, child. Be sure to lock the doors." She passed by her, patted her shoulder, then went into her room and closed the curtain behind her.

Celeste heard the old springs disturb as Mrs. Owens sat on the side of her bed, heard the crisp pages of the Bible. She turned out the kitchen light, locked the rickety back screen and door and the front doors, then went to her bedroom. She propped Sissy's drawing up on the dresser trying to figure a way to pack it. It struck her that Horation and Geneva Owens in the old photo looked as calm and contained in that oval frame as if they'd lived a life of peace, fulfillment, and bounty. How, she wondered, did they subdue so much? With her gone, Mrs. Owens would have her old room again, sleep in the place where she'd loved and cried all of her life. The fatigue of the day overcame her. She went to sleep with the mattress on the bed for the first time since bullets flew through the house; she didn't have the strength to pull it down to the floor.

30

From her window seat on the plane, the opulent green of Detroit's western suburbs reminded Celeste of New Orleans. The highway shot through like a concrete arrow. One frost-cool night in late September or October would usher in autumn and she'd awaken to a celebration of color that was equal parts enchantment and regret. She smelled the burning leaves at curbside on Outer Drive, the feel of air thinning to cold. Ann Arbor was twenty or so miles west, Detroit the same distance east, two worlds that might have been on different planets. She'd come home, though she no longer counted on the meaning of the word, would've stayed in Pineyville for a while longer if Mrs. Owens had agreed to her plan, her maneuver to avoid confrontation with the import of Wilamena's letter. Shuck had always admonished her that she was transparent, too apt to carry her heart on her sleeve. Hard as he'd tried to teach her otherwise, he'd not been successful. Mrs. Owens had read her like a book she'd read before.

That morning in Jackson, Celeste labored to make herself appear like a well-off young woman coming home from a Caribbean cruise. Shuck wouldn't want to see the sweat-drenched, dirty-toed girl she'd become in Mississippi. Her cracked tooth had been replaced with a temporary one by the only Negro dentist in town. The nurse in Dr. Fields's office told her that in the past, Negro people traveled to Memphis to get their teeth fixed, if they got them fixed at all. White dentists in Jackson wouldn't take them as patients. She'd reconnected with Margo and Ramona, all of them staying again in the segregated volunteer apartments for their debriefings.

That morning she'd ironed the best of her cotton dresses, a sleeveless peach sheath with a cropped jacket, for the trip home. She hadn't put on a fully ironed dress in weeks. At Mrs. Owens's house, she'd taken to running the iron over the bodice of a dress and perhaps down the skirt front. It was a thankless and useless task. In minutes, the humidity re-pressed every wrinkle into soft folds of limp fabric. Clothes stayed rough-dried no matter how hard you ironed them, helpless against the humidity.

The smooth look she got from setting her hair on Margo's electric curlers lasted about as long as it took her to walk outside to get into Ed Jolivette's funky movement car for the ride to the airport. She wore her white pumps and carried her bulging green canvas book-bag, its frayed corners and dirt splotches belying all of her primping. A crusty layer of dark suntanned skin obscured the mosquito bite scars up and down her ankles and arms.

Shuck stood back from the gate at the edge of the waiting crowd, dressed in a late-summer brown suit with a creamy shirt open at the collar. His stingy-brimmed hat sat a little back on his head, his forehead the color of dark stained oak with deep red hues. Celeste walked toward him searching his living face for what she'd not found in the small snapshot on her dresser on Freshwater Road. She wasn't there, she feared, not in the shapes or colors. How had she missed it for all those years? Still, she saw herself deep in his eyes, a reflection of him, an extension of the man, a hope lodged in her and her future, her sight and her way of being in the world. Mississippi, she figured, had deepened that. He was begrudgingly proud.

Shuck grinned and frowned at the same time, eyes saying words he'd never speak. "Damn, girl, you black as me." He hugged her and kissed her forehead as he always did.

"It'll fade." She sidestepped that weighty issue and dove into an adolescent litany of how much work it had taken her, Ramona, and Margo to turn her back into someone he'd recognize after living raw in the wilds of Mississippi for two months. She showed him her temporary tooth and told him about the incident at the drinking fountain with Sheriff Trotter's deputy. Anger flashed in the dark brown of Shuck's eyes, and Celeste thought for a moment he might hit the nearest white person. She chastised herself for not waiting until she got into his car to start telling him her Mississippi stories.

He slung her book-bag over his shoulder then slid his arm into hers as he always did when they walked side by side, the way they walked the streets in New York City on a vacation a long time ago. "What you got in here, rocks?" They strolled toward the baggage claim area. "Mississippi dirt. Rocks. Notebooks and stuff." She'd carried that book-bag all summer, back and forth to the St. James A.M.E. Church until it burned to the ground. At the beginning, it held odds and ends, notebooks, maps, chewing gum, a real purse. She really had added dirt and rocks—a small brown bag, now torn, full of tangerine-colored soil from Freshwater Road, and a few white stones from the church clearing, all of which more than likely had tinted and creased Wilamena's letter, which she'd moved to her book-bag, too.

Shuck looked ahead as if searching for an exit to something. "You supposed to be registering people to vote down there, not collecting dirt and rocks."

"Thought I'd have time to study, too. For next semester." She hoped to convince herself that she'd be ready to return to school after Labor Day, suggesting her resolve to him, shaky as it was. Just days ago she was begging to stay in Mississippi, to not come home at all. She might, at that moment, have grabbed the book-bag from Shuck, dug out the letter, and pled for answers right there in the airport. She didn't, and she congratulated herself that maybe this patience meant she'd crossed over into adulthood, left the nebulous field that separated late adolescence from the rest of her life. No demanding answers in inopportune places. Wilamena had hurled her out of childhood, thrown her into deep water.

Passengers zoomed by in both directions, seeming so sure of where they were going and what their lives would be when they got there. She dawdled, her step unsure, no streamline of conversation coming out of her, so unlike her when with Shuck. He'd know something was on her mind if she didn't snap to.

"Momma Bessie okay?" She was relieved to see the baggage claim ahead offering a focus outside of herself.

"Getting old." Shuck tugged a bit as if he had someplace to go beyond the airport. He always had someplace else to go, but it was never very far away.

Celeste pecked around for things to say, the background noise of the airport forcing her to give stature to her voice. "And, how's Alma doing?" She wanted to ask if he was going to marry Alma. She'd wished it in the past but not now. Feeling so on the edge of his world, she fought an urge to hold on tight, to own. But Shuck wasn't *ownable,* and she knew it. Her questions sounded foreign, untied to history, the small talk of an uncomfortable stranger. Wilamena had hit the mark if her intention had been to drive a wedge between her and Shuck, to create a distance, an uninhabited plain. She had to break through, restore the life between them, but she didn't know how. One word in the wrong direction might pitch them over the brink forever. No word at all meant she'd have it on her mind for life, a lonely struggle. Her anger rose again and then she felt Shuck there pulling her into his side.

"She's fine. Going back to work, complaining about how rowdy these kids have gotten." He scanned the luggage for the suitcase he'd bought her two years before. "See it on the streets myself. It ain't pretty."

Sissy's almond-eyed face and the faces of her other freedom school children, reticent and shy, filed through her mind. Tony, with more responsibility than a grown man. Little Georgie, staying in Labyrinth's shadow. And Labyrinth, her little-girl hands on her hips with an expression far more adult than her actual years and with not a shy bone in her body. The Mississippi children were never rowdy—hard to tell when it was country sweetness or just the long grinding effect of being beaten down at every turn. Shuck gave her the book-bag and grabbed the suitcase. They walked out into the thinning humidity, summer geared to lose its swagger soon.

The white Cadillac gleamed in the sunshine of the open parking lot, the convertible top up. After months of no rides at all or rides packed in Reverend Singleton's car or in movement cars that stank of sweat and old cigarette butts, she savored this ride. Even though Shuck smoked, the very first thing you smelled in that car was a gentle memory of Old Spice. She sank into the soft seat with its scent of rich new leather, put her book-bag on the floor, gazed at the dashboard with its sleek space-age look. Shuck quietly smoothed the car out of the parking lot and then east on I-94, well above the speed limit, she noted.

She hammered herself into conversation telling him of getting Mr. Landau, Mrs. Owens, and Hazzie Mobley registered to vote, of spending those hours in the jail cell, of the church being burned to the ground and of the plans to rebuild it. She was careful not to mention her brief interest in staying there to rebuild the freedom school and a library.

"So you went to jail." He floated the Cadillac around the other cars and trucks on the expressway as if they were buoys on a tranquil lake, his tires softly thumping over bumps and ridges. "Now you're my criminal daughter, uh?"

Celeste's laughter was high and thin. "We all did." *Jiggaboo girl, criminal daughter.* She was his fraudulent child. She stared out the window at the landscape as it took on more and more houses, small run-down businesses in lean-to sheds, and weather-beaten garages. The trees saved it from looking like a countryside ghetto. "Well, anyway, it's *better* than it was before." She laid into it, bottom-lining Mississippi Shuck-style.

Shuck exited the expressway at Livernois, going north toward Outer Drive. His silence and his focus on the road ahead told her that he didn't believe Mississippi was better *enough.* It would be a while before she told him about Mrs. Owens's house being shot into.

With the traffic lights and Sunday drivers, they slowed on the surface streets. Celeste scanned the small storefront businesses, auto repair shops, and gas stations lining the blocks of Livernois, everything closed, all owned by mixtures of Negro and white people. No stepping off sidewalks here. Good to be home. She mulled over her last days in Jackson with Ed and the other volunteers as they dissected and summarized the achievements of Freedom Summer. Hard to summarize Pineyville, though. There were so many stories, burned-down churches and houses shot into and injuries and incarcerations, but she accepted the movement's statistical version, its shorthand. Her truest life, she felt, had stretched out over her time on Freshwater Road. Sissy's death. Ed's birth in her life.

Ramona with her bowl of kinky hair and skin so black from the Delta sun that her brown eyes glowed, had registered seven people—Ramona had been in cotton plantation country. You couldn't say *the Delta* without thinking of slavery, without hearing a *cante hondo* blues. Indianola had strong community involvement, a near war going on between the workers on the plantations and the owners. Folks had been riled up before Freedom Summer started. Margo, her blonde hair bleached nearly white and her skin tanned to brown, looking like she'd been a counselor at a sailing camp in Massachusetts, had been in Aberdeen over near the Alabama border. She got four people on the rolls. Celeste kept her chest out anyway because in some towns not one Negro was registered to vote. In her heart of hearts, she wished she'd done better. They reminded each other over and over that it was a beginning, that Mississippi would never be the same. Matt slapped palms and acted hard-edged and street-wise with the other guys; he seemed to look through Celeste when he acknowledged her at all. Some volunteers had decided to take a semester off from school to continue the work through the November elections. She would've done it, too, if Mrs. Owens had let her stay.

In Jackson, they carried the debriefings from the One Man, One Vote office around the corner to Mercer's, the only Negro-owned restaurant large enough to accommodate their group. They hid whiskey bottles secreted in from Louisiana in brown paper bags stuffed into purses and book-bags and took them into the restaurant. They ate collard greens, fried chicken, and cornbread and poured small amounts of liquor into Cokes and orange drinks, then shoved the booze back into their purses. Miss Mercer winked at them when she came out of the kitchen and saw their glazed eyes. Some volunteers had their suitcases stacked in the corner by the door, ready to get out of Mississippi as soon as the eating was over.

When the dinner plates were cleared, they pushed the tables back and danced to the music on the jukebox until sweat ran down their bodies. They were teenagers at an airless basement party, white and black, and after a couple of drinks, they smeared into one thing, a bunch of students from as far away as Stanford University, as close as Tougaloo College right there in Jackson, who'd lived their purpose through to the end of the summer's effort. In a euphoria of hugging and kissing their goodbyes, they prayed for the ones who hadn't made it through, and for the families of Mickey Schwerner, James Chaney, and Andy Goodman, and for Medgar Evers's wife and children and the others. Celeste prayed for Sissy and for Zenia Tucker, too.

Ed waited by the door at Mercer's for her to say her goodbyes. He'd arranged a few hours for them alone in the male volunteers' apartment. They sat with their backs against the wall on the mattress, the apartment a reverse layout but in all other ways the same as the one she'd stayed in her first week and again now with Ramona and Margo, flaunting the rules of segregation during the debriefings. He pulled her into his chest just like he'd done on Freshwater Road and she felt relieved, relaxed in the fold of his arms. They sat like that, the windows open. She saw him dancing his second line at Otis's bar in Hattiesburg, dancing his demons away. She needed to dance her own away. They slid down the wall and faced each other lying on their sides, clung there, pressing their bodies together.

At the airport the next morning, they sat side by side on the black bench seats. He was driving to New Orleans for a week before going on to Boston to finish his last year of graduate school. With people all around them, they grew shy, made elliptical promises to call and write. When her flight was announced, he walked her to the gate, called her "chère," and told her to keep an eye out for him, that he'd never be very far away. She walked onto the plane, struggling against his gravitational pull, didn't want to turn around for fear she'd have missed the flight, missed whatever the rest of her life was supposed to be without him.

Shuck turned onto Outer Drive and it dazzled, drenched in end-of-August sunlight filtering in white dapples through the sheltering trees. Michigan green framed by the rich black earth, back-dropped in blue sky. A northern sky the color of bluebird wings with drifts of graying white clouds riding high. Giant elms glanced over houses, front yards were masterpieces of diligence with hedges and cascading vines, flowers holding on to one last dash of color before tilting over into the soil.

Celeste stood on the porch taking in the scents of newly cut grass, thought of Freshwater Road with its orange sand and gravel chips and bony barking dogs, the outhouses to the back, Mrs. Owens's leaning porch, the screen door that wouldn't slam, and the spigot rising out of the concrete platform. Ed would be in New Orleans by now, even driving under the speed limit.

Shuck carried her suitcase upstairs while she wandered from the silky living room to the wide dining room with bowed windows and cushioned window seats that looked out over the backyard, her favorite place in the house. She ran up the carpeted stairs and stood in her bathroom goggling at the bathtub, the separate shower stall, the tile floor so clean you could eat off of it. Her bedroom with its canopy bed sat like a Hollywood movie set, the matching lamps and bedside tables prim and perfect. Soft light filtered in through the sheers. She pushed the curtains aside, saw the white oak in the back corner on one side of the yard and the towering pine on the other. No piney woods, no limping plants and buzzing power lines, just a spread of green and to the side of the house, a garage that Shuck only used in the dead of winter.

She took Sissy's drawing out of her suitcase and stood it up on the tall white dresser, using a small crystal bowl that held her barrettes to brace the drawing in place. She'd have it framed. She could barely look at it, heard Sissy's little-girl voice in the car, in the kitchen of Mrs. Owens's house, reading. She grabbed the copies of Reverend Singleton's Kodak shots taken at the church clearing, their little group standing in the light in front of the space where the church used to be. She put them with Ed's letter and the pictures of New Orleans on her bedside table to read when she got into bed.

She showered and lingered around the bathroom, amazed that she'd managed to make it through the entire summer without one. She changed into a summer pants suit from her closet, then dumped the big suitcase's contents over onto the carpet. She hoped no Mississippi bugs hid in the corners and compartments—better to take it down to the basement for a good spraying. There on the top of the pile was the blue gabardine jumper she'd worn on the train going south. A totem of the past, the innocent spring blue of hyacinths. She'd never wear it again. She stood before the long mirror inside the closet door, saw how her eyes withdrew into her face now as if they'd become slightly hooded. The cut on her lip was barely visible. Shuck was right. She was darker than she'd ever been in her life. And, she was much older.

She faltered there in the bedroom thinking of Wilamena's letter. Tearing it to shreds would mean nothing at all. The words were imprinted on her brain. Without Shuck, she'd be anonymous, unmoored, as if her only known history had been lived out in Mississippi. The rest had disintegrated into grainy particles, bits and snatches of things that no longer composed a whole. She wondered if, in time, she'd remember anything of her life before this summer, as if the letter wiped her life slate clean. It was time to talk to Shuck. But if Shuck knew nothing, or if he suspected Wilamena's truth a long time ago and had forgotten it over the years or even learned the hard lesson of living with it, the letter would open an old wound and break his heart. Was that something he could've forgotten or forgiven? But if he'd heard rumors, if people had talked in the days when he and Wilamena had their troubles, wouldn't this answer all the questions he'd had in his mind anyway? The truth is supposed to unburden you, free you. Wilamena unburdened herself with no thought to anyone else. No telling what the so-called truth would do to Shuck. He might breathe a sigh of relief for her as much as for himself. And what of those long-ago shadows with Momma Bessie and Ben? Were they real or had she imagined them because boys always came first in that house? That was enough to make any girl feel dismissed at times.

Shuck had put on a jazz record, elegant sounding but enough blues in it to know where it came from. A saxophone wailed. In the kitchen, he heated two plates of food. Celeste set the table recognizing the aromas as Momma Bessie's cooking. They drank cold milk and ate roast beef with creamy gravy over a mound of mashed potatoes and green beans on the side. They listened to the music. Celeste hadn't heard any of Shuck's kind of music since spring break from school.

"I met a Negro man in Hattiesburg who owns a bar only nobody's supposed to drink any alcohol in there. Mississippi's dry, Daddy." She had an urge to say, "daddy" over and over again, just repeat it until all of Wilamena's haint was off of the word.

"If he owns a bar, he must be paying somebody off." Shuck looked at her. "What you doing in some Negro's bar in Hattiesburg?"

"He works with the movement." She left the rest unsaid, the talk about corn liquor, the gun Otis wore all the time, and the fact that he had no whiskey bottles on his bar.

"Oh, yeah?" Shuck had a dubious look on his face.

"I told him my daddy owned a bar. He was impressed." She might've gone on about how she'd sat at that homemade bar bragging of her knowledge of Paradise Valley. Shuck, she knew, wouldn't take to that at all. To say nothing of how many drinks she'd consumed. "He didn't have any of your music on his jukebox."

"Too country, that's why." Shuck drank the last of his milk.

Celeste took their dirty dishes to the sink. Shuck grabbed a dishtowel and stood in the middle of the kitchen waiting for her to wash them. He'd dry them like he used to do, then make a neat stack to take back to Momma Bessie's house with his bag of dirty shirts. "You probably should call your mother and let her know you made it home okay. Don't you think?"

Celeste heard him but decided to ignore what he'd said, thought of all those hard days washing dishes on Mrs. Owens's back porch using the pump. She'd spent the summer arranging water—mineral spigot water, sulfur-smelling pump water, heating tin tub water for a shallow bath, throwing dirty basin water in the outhouse, always running around that little plank board house arranging for water.

"Did you hear me?"

She washed the two plates, the glasses, and the silverware slowly. "I heard you."

"Well?" He leaned a little on the back of a kitchen chair, the dishtowel hanging down.

"I don't want to talk to her right now." The anger in her voice came from somewhere deep that she couldn't have camouflaged if she'd tried. "Not tonight." She caught Shuck out of the corner of her eye looking at her like she'd lost her mind. She was on shaky ground. She pretended to rinse out the sink, kept her head down, then looked up at him. "I'll write her a note in the morning."

"You'll write her now, and we'll take it down to the post office tonight. I need to check on the club anyway." Shuck had put a toothpick in the corner of his mouth, and he wasn't smiling, not his mouth and certainly not his eyes. At that moment he looked like Matt's image of him as a gangster, as a man who might wipe her off the face of the earth if he felt like it. "Get going and while you're at it, tell her you're sorry for worrying the crap out of everybody all summer long."

Without saying a word, knowing she dared not cut her eyes at him, she turned on her heels and slogged up to her room, scrounged around in her book-bag for Wilamena's orange-tinted letter, and sat on the floor near her Mississippi pile. The flat sounds of the television came up through the quiet house. Shuck waited for her, allowing the television to subdue his anger. She looked at the cobbled-together snapshot of Wilamena and her husband. In all the weeks since she'd received the letter, it had never occurred to her to consider if Cyril Atwood might be her biological father. Was he the man Wilamena had the affair with? She stared into the photograph, raced back in her mind to the first meeting. She felt nothing special except that the man didn't appear to be Negro at all. Cyril Atwood, Wilamena protested, was Negro, just not very. Was this some new Wilamena game to be revealed at a later date? Celeste had no intention of going through all this again. She tipped into Shuck's room, took his magnifying glass from his dresser top, and brought it back to her room. She held the glass over Cyril Atwood's image. It enlarged and wavered then settled. She saw nothing of herself in his face, though it was hard to tell from a small photograph. His skin was lighter than her own. So was Wilamena's. No marked similarity of nose, eyes, lips. She put the picture down. She balanced her notebook on her thighs and leaned against the bed frame. Out the windows, the trees swayed against the waning daylight, a gentle sweeping across the sky.

Dear Wilamena:

    Shuck wanted me to write you and tell you I made it out of Mississippi okay. Going back to school in a few days. My regards to your husband.

                                   Celeste

Already, she was going back on her word to never speak to Wilamena again. At least she wasn't responding to that letter. She ripped the page out of the notebook, enveloped it, put a stamp on it. Shuck wouldn't ask to see it. Ed's letter waited for her on the small side table like the golden prize of night, along with the glorious photos of New Orleans. She heard his soft accent in her head telling her to "spread those stones." But, they were her stones, and she didn't know if she could spread them. They were now a part of who she was, the most potent thing that connected her to her mother. Maybe that's what Wilamena intended all along, to enslave her with the past, a past she had nothing to do with. Wilamena had recast herself, too, as weightier, more important in her mind. More burdensome, for sure.

Shuck hustled her into the car, still twirling that toothpick in the corner of his mouth, saying not a word, not needing to. They headed for the main post office all the way downtown, she tapping the corner of the envelope on her pant leg, her tongue licking her new tooth. She barely noticed the city passing by, only that it seemed she'd been gone for a long time. Shuck was too cool for comfort. He waited in the car as she jumped out to mail the note. She could well have dropped it in the public trashcan nearby, but didn't. He'd know. Somehow, he'd know.

"Time for you to start doing better by your own people, and I'm not talking about a bunch of Negroes in Mississippi," he said as she climbed back into the car. Shuck didn't say another thing to her until they got in front of the Royal Gardens.

Celeste pouted out the window, his words a garble in her ears, thinking he was being charitable using words like "your own people."

He relaxed in a slow drive-by of the club, the white Cadillac splashing its reflection in the front windows, Shuck saying he needed to buy a grill gate for the place if he intended to stay in this section of the city. Shuck U-turned in Lafayette Street, then paused by the curb to lower the convertible top. She wanted to go into the empty club, sit at the bar, listen to the jukebox, have a drink. Shuck had other things on his mind. He reminded her of his New York dream of a swankier place down on the riverfront or out in the near suburbs. If they had a place with a restaurant, they'd be open on Sundays for dinner.

They skirted downtown, the Sunday evening city streets nearly deserted, and drove over East Jefferson to Belle Isle, where the picnic crowd was thinning out and the air off the river felt breezy and fresh. The sky took on a lavender hue as they parked and walked, found an empty picnic table facing Canada, and watched the sailboats on the river in the evening light. Even with the river breeze, the residue smells of outdoor grilling laid over the small island.

She didn't know what Shuck wanted to talk about, but this was definitely his place for getting into serious things. They had come here when the school plans were made—the plans she nearly ruined after her freshman year when she got pregnant. Now, she held her breath waiting for him to speak, praying it wasn't about Wilamena.

Shuck started in about her finishing college, about the promises that were made. He said he didn't give a damn if not another Negro voted in the entire United States of America, in the whole world, until the end of time. All he cared about now was her finishing what she'd started. He said she'd never deal with being Negro in America without a college education as well as she would with one. *No ifs, ands, or buts about it.* After that, she could do whatever she damn well pleased, go to the moon for all he cared. Celeste nodded in agreement, Geneva Owens's words in her head. *What's that going to do to your daddy? You not finishing school right now?*

"Anything you want to talk about? Now's the time. When we get back in that car, I don't want to hear another thing except that you're going to keep your promises." Shuck stared off across the river.

Celeste stumbled. "I'm going back to school. I haven't broken any promises. I was only gone for the summer." Still lying. Getting pregnant had taken the prize for broken promises. And, if Mrs. Owens had allowed it, if Wilamena hadn't tried to take so much from her, too, she'd still be down there. Getting good at lying, and why not? According to Wilamena, her whole life was a lie. Except her Mississippi summer. That was all hers.

He turned to her. "You went to Mississippi before you told me a thing about it. I'm getting too old for surprises like that."

"I'm sorry." Quick rehearsals raced through her mind. *Wilamena told me. Is it true? Am I your daughter? Not a soul ever thought we looked alike, not really, but that happens. Is it true? What does it mean? Why did she tell me that?* "You're not old."

He ignored that, his eyes dancing with the anger he'd been holding in all summer long. "You made it hard for me, and you worried your mother. You worried everybody." Shuck quieted. "I didn't even tell Momma Bessie, afraid she'd have a heart attack. What if you'd died down there? Then what?" He released a deep breath like he'd finally gotten the worst of it off his chest.

She didn't know what. She'd been afraid the whole time she was there, but it didn't stop her. And what if she had died down there? What if Sheriff Trotter fired that gun? Would Wilamena track down the man who might be her *real* father and invite him to her funeral?

"I had to go." Mississippi gave her life a higher meaning, shoved it to a different plane, separated her from the past like a soldier who goes to war and always has that as his marker. It would be the same for everyone who'd been there.

"It's not just old people who die, Celeste." Shuck set his dark eyes on her.

"I know that. There were young people who died down there." She avoided his eyes then submitted, terrified that he'd see Wilamena's truth on her face like a neon sign.

"There's a way to do everything. Running off like a thief is not it." Shuck looked back out to the river.

The words dug into her, gouged a space out and sat down. He was talking to Wilamena and to her at the same time, and she knew it.

"I was going anyway." She wilted inside. "I wrote you."

"*After* you'd already gone. Not good enough."

"I had to go." She repeated it, hoping he'd understand what it meant. "Maybe I was just afraid you'd talk me out of it." She figured he did understand, but had to say the hard things.

A pressure built up in her head. She didn't want to do the things that Wilamena had done, couldn't handle being more like her than she ever thought. She was standing in the Pearl River County Administration Building, Sheriff Trotter ready to pull the trigger, the cold barrel of the gun pressed against her temple. Small river waves lapped on the shore. She wished she could walk into the cold water, plunge into the currents, and swirl away on a free ride to nowhere.

In her mind she was saying the dreaded words. *Daddy, I got a letter from Wilamena.* Her mouth couldn't come up with a lick of moisture. The words stuck and clung to the inside, hollowing around, hiding in her throat, jumping into her ears. She held her breath, reaching now for a life vest, water sucking into her lungs against her will.

Shuck sat so still everything else seemed to be moving. She thought the picnic table might just float off down the river, and they were firmly on dry land. Tears coming into her eyes, dropping down her face. Mrs. Owens's voice spoke in her head. *You can't hide here, child.* She wanted to hide somewhere. Crawl under the picnic table, peek out, needed something for herself. If she let go of Shuck, she'd drown.

What does it mean? The voice in her head retreated to a child's place. She wasn't so grown-up. Didn't want to do what Wilamena had already done, drop a load on some unsuspecting person, trip them like an uprooted pavement in the dark.

Shuck sighed, braced his arms on his thighs, his shiny brown shoes on the picnic table seat, the two of them sitting on the tabletop. In the evening light, the red hints in his summer-dark face glowed. He gave her his handkerchief. It smelled of Old Spice, reminding her of the days before these demons scratched at their doors, when everyone was smiling wide. But that was real, too, that Old Spice time. It was all she had of a past. She thought she heard his heart thundering.

He put his arm around her shoulder. "You have to start thinking about how it's going to feel to the other person. It's not just you in the world by yourself."

"I know." The Wilamena truth retreated. Something in the way he spoke, the way he chastised her for being so thoughtless. He was banking on her not being totally in Wilamena's image.

Shuck's eyes stayed on the water, the currents in the river moving the surface water fast, the last reflection of light laying flat on the river, or was it now the moon? This sideways glance of faded light. "You know you're going to have to go out to New Mexico, spend some time."

Not another tear fell from her eyes. It was the lie she'd told Mrs. Owens. *Going to New Mexico for Christmas to see my mother.* She got caught every time she lied. Now here she was stuck again.

"She's angry at me." She knotted her mind around the known reasons for Wilamena's anger. Her refusals to go to New Mexico, her comradeship with Shuck. They sat there, night bearing down, the twilight noises rising, car horns honking on the evening air behind them, single waves slapping the rocks nearby. Windsor's lights dancing.

"I think she's angry at *me*. She called here trying to find you. She shouldn't have to do that. You gotta do better, Celeste." Shuck's head wagged from side to side as if to say she'd better do better to get the pressure off him. He needed that, too.

She wanted to ask why Wilamena was angry at *him* after all these years, but she was afraid to open another box, let another tribe of demons fly free. It was the answers to the simple questions that stumped you. "You're right. You're right." Thinking she'd rather break a leg than go out to New Mexico. "I guess I can go for Christmas."

"Is that a promise?" He was the lawyer and she was testifying with her hand on the Bible.

"Yeah, I promise." How could she spend two weeks with her mother when they had not a thing to talk about, not a common interest in anything? How could she be in that house with her after the letter? She'd do it for Shuck. And what if Wilamena brought up the letter? Her note? Would they have a knock-down, drag-out about it? More than likely. They'd be like erupting volcanoes, burning lava sliding over everything and years of black rock before green ever showed its face again. She'd never bring up that letter to Wilamena. Would refuse to discuss it. Just let it sit there like a rocky shore, no invitation to dock. It was going to be some Christmas.

"She's lonely out there." Shuck had "I told you so" in his voice.

"Why is *she* so lonely?" Celeste had never thought of her that way.

"Hard to talk to those people. Engineers. Don't know what's going on." Shuck looked back at his gleaming white Cadillac parked at the curb yards behind them.

She thought he might just get up, go to the car and drive away. Be a memory. That her whole life had been a dream. "She married him."

"Yep." A certain get-up-and-go in his voice.

"She oughta be happy. She likes it out there." The words came out soft, but in her mind, the sarcasm floated. She remembered how Wilamena over the years had described the aspen trees glowing golden in autumn, the snow on the piñon trees, how her stationery had a rendering of the New Mexico mountains and sky.

"I don't think she's been happy a day in her life." Shuck's head moved back and forth like he was grinding the meaning of it all into something he could carry in his pockets.

Celeste heard him loud and clear. Maybe that was why Billy left home and didn't seem to want to come back. The waters were too muddy for swimming, too much work to keep everyone on an even keel, somebody always falling overboard. Kept clear of it all. Billy was older, wiser. Some day she'd have to talk to Billy about all this.

"I feel like an old person." She clasped her hands onto her knees like Mrs. Owens did when she was ready to get up from her rocking chair.

"You got nothing but future." Shuck squeezed her into him then let her go, lit a cigarette, the sharp quick clank of his cigarette lighter a percussion behind the lapping water. "You wanna smoke?"

She took a cigarette and he lit it, holding his hand against the breeze coming off the river. She drew in the smoke, let it curl down her throat into her lungs, coughed. "Haven't smoked since I left Ann Arbor."

"Good. Don't start up again." He blew the smoke out in white puffy ringlets, and she could feel his body relaxing next to her.

"I won't, Daddy." The word echoed just the slightest bit in her head, then settled down. She'd smoke this one, feel the deep stirring the tobacco gave to her stomach and lungs, the flutter in her heart, float out the smoke evenly, hold the cigarette like one of Shuck's polished women in his best-of-Negro-life wallpaper, then never smoke again. "Daddy" wasn't some miscellaneous, bone-dry word, some throwaway to be tossed to a tired dog. It meant everything. Wilamena lost her father when she was very young and maybe she just didn't want anybody to have what she'd never had, especially not her own daughter. Some people were like that. Celeste didn't know how she'd ever talk to her mother when the time came or what she'd say. She knew that she, Celeste Tyree, would never tell Shuck about that letter, and she knew Wilamena wouldn't either. Shuck would never allow her to. That was good. It would end right here. Somehow, she had to get herself to New Mexico and celebrate Christmas without tearing into Wilamena. Christmas with no music.

During the hottest days of her Mississippi summer, she'd longed for autumn, the cool at the edge of the wind, the flamboyant leaves sketched against a boyish blue sky. It was as if you were on a viewing stand celebrating the end of a glorious parade that too quickly disappeared down the street.

THE END

Acknowledgments

∾

Janet Fitch, Journeyman Fiction Workshop, William Reiss, James Ragan, Professional Writing Program, University of Southern California, Lee Chamberlin, The Squaw Valley Community of Writers, James D. Houston, Shelby Stone, Naomi Harris Rosenblatt, Bill Galvez, Gail Berendzen, W.O.M.E.N Inc., Beverly Todd and Friends Three, Nancy O'Connor (Mrs. Carroll), Dennis and Denia Hightower, Asaad Kelada, Shirlee Taylor Haizlip, Emmett Nicholas, Otto and Kay Nicholas, Louise Burgen, Rudy Lombard, the Ebell of Los Angeles, Kynderly Haskins, Kenneth Reynolds, and Douglas Seibold.

In writing this book, I referred mostly to my own first-hand knowledge of both Mississippi and 1964, but I also read many of the books published about that era. A few I kept close at hand were, *The Origins of the Civil Rights Movement* by Aldon D. Morris; *In Struggle* by Clayborne Carson; *Walking with the Wind* by John Lewis; and *Free at Last?* by Fred Powledge. A major character in this book is a reader and collector of *Jet* magazine, and I am grateful for the important work done by Johnson Publishing. Also, in Chapter 2, a character makes reference to a fictional *Detroit News* article about Mississippi during the run up to Freedom Summer. While the article is fictional, the statistics mentioned are real, drawn from *Eyes on the Prize* by Juan Williams. I also found *The Detroit Almanac,* edited by Peter Gavrilovich and Bill McGraw, to be a goldmine of tidbits about my old hometown.

ABOUT THE AUTHOR

Denise Nicholas is an actor and writer who has starred in numerous films and TV shows, including *Room 222,* for which she earned three Golden Globe nominations, and *In the Heat of the Night,* for which she also wrote several episodes. She lives in Southern California and is currently at work on a memoir.

Suggested Book Group Discussion Questions for *Freshwater Road*

Reading *Freshwater Road* with your book group? Use these recommended questions to help further your discussion.

1. What did you know about the events of Freedom Summer before you began reading *Freshwater Road*?

2. Celeste's decision to go to Mississippi is shaped by many different factors. What do you feel motivated her the most, and why?

3. The sense of violence, and vulnerability to violence, plays a major role in *Freshwater Road*. Is there anything about this sense of violence that surprised you in the book?

4. Nonviolence and nonviolent resistance, even in the face of hostile, violent aggression, was a hallmark of the civil rights movement. What do you think of the way different characters in the book discuss the principles of nonviolence?

5. There were both men and women among the volunteers. What is most distinct about the different experiences they had in Mississippi?

6. How does Celeste's relationship with Ed Jolivette shape the meaning of her experience in Pineyville? How does it shape her experience with the civil rights movement in general?

7. The older black people living in Pineyville have conflicted feelings about the young volunteers coming to Mississippi, and Celeste's father has conflicted feelings about Celeste's decision to become a volunteer. What do you make of those conflicted feelings?

8. Celeste's interactions with the young sheriff of Pineyville are among the most singular in the book. What do you make of those scenes where she encounters him in person?

9. The novel's story progresses largely in a straight line over the course of the summer. How did that storytelling style affect your reading experience?

10. While she's in Mississippi, Celeste learns something about her parents that has a major impact on her understanding of her own past. What do you think of her decision about how to handle that information?

11. How did the book change your understanding of Freedom Summer and the people—both the young people who came to Mississippi and those who already lived there—most affected by it?